THE
HIDING
SEASON

ALSO BY A.C. GLASS

As Ava Glass

The Chase

The Traitor

The Trap

THE HIDING SEASON

A.C. GLASS

CENTURY

CENTURY

UK | USA | Canada | Ireland | Australia
India | New Zealand | South Africa

Century is part of the Penguin Random House group of companies whose addresses can be found at global.penguinrandomhouse.com

Penguin Random House UK,
One Embassy Gardens, 8 Viaduct Gardens, London SW11 7BW

penguin.co.uk
global.penguinrandomhouse.com

First published 2026

001

Copyright © Moonflower Books Ltd, 2026

The moral right of the author has been asserted

Penguin Random House values and supports copyright. Copyright fuels creativity, encourages diverse voices, promotes freedom of expression and supports a vibrant culture. Thank you for purchasing an authorised edition of this book and for respecting intellectual property laws by not reproducing, scanning or distributing any part of it by any means without permission. You are supporting authors and enabling Penguin Random House to continue to publish books for everyone. No part of this book may be used or reproduced in any manner for the purpose of training artificial intelligence technologies or systems. In accordance with Article 4(3) of the DSM Directive 2019/790, Penguin Random House expressly reserves this work from the text and data mining exception.

Set in 14.2/17pt Fournier MT Pro
Typeset by Six Red Marbles UK, Thetford, Norfolk

Printed and bound in Great Britain by Clays Ltd, Elcograf S.p.A.

The authorised representative in the EEA is Penguin Random House Ireland, Morrison Chambers, 32 Nassau Street, Dublin D02 YH68

A CIP catalogue record for this book is available from the British Library

ISBN: 978–1–529–97200–9

Penguin Random House is committed to a sustainable future for our business, our readers and our planet. This book is made from Forest Stewardship Council® certified paper.

For Anna McCormack
Who told me about the houses on the mountain

PART ONE

Montana

ONE

There are moments in your life that change everything. One step left, and the bus doesn't hit you. One step right, and it's game over. I stepped right the day I took the job in Montana.

If I'd just stood up during the interview and told Gina, 'Thanks, but no thanks. This isn't for me,' my life would have been so different. But back then I was shattered, flat broke and running out of options, and Gina was offering a lifeline. Or at least that's what I thought she was offering. So I grabbed the line with both hands. And it dragged me under.

Maybe I should have seen it coming, but I'd been lucky until then. I stopped being lucky six weeks before I met Gina. Six weeks before I took the job. In those days, I was a different person — married, and living in Lansing, Michigan. No pets, no kids. Brandon and I had talked about babies many times, but he always thought later would be better. And then suddenly I was thirty-eight and it *was* later, but still he found reasons. And me? I let it go. I always let things go.

Of course, not having kids meant we could afford a cute three-bedroom house on a twenty-five-year mortgage. And after a while I was able to quit my job teaching high school and try to make it as a freelance writer. That had been my dream since college.

And we were happy. Or at least, *I* was happy.

I found out Brandon wasn't happy early on April the fourth, when he walked into the kitchen and told me he was leaving.

I remember it all so clearly – we always remember the worst days best. I was drinking a cup of coffee and writing two hundred words about a new sushi restaurant for a local blog. The early spring sun poured through the window. I was standing at the counter because I worried I sat too much, and I'd read an article somewhere about how we should all stand more. So I was standing when Brandon walked in, his eyes filled with resentment, as if I were the one bringing bad news.

'There's something we need to talk about,' he said, and his voice was oddly cold and stiff.

I wonder how I looked to him, my smile fading as I realised what he was telling me. The bafflement and hurt in my face. It was the worst thing that had ever happened to me. The most shocking, horrible thing. My luck abandoned me then – in an instant.

Like a gunshot in a quiet room, that moment split the silence of my life. And the reverberations are with me still.

A month later, a 'For Sale' sign went up in front of our house. I didn't want to sell – I didn't want any of this – but the house was in Brandon's name, so he could do what he wanted, and what he wanted was to sell it and spend more time with his assistant, Hannah.

It's the oldest story in the world. It's almost embarrassing how blindsided I was. But none of my friends were surprised. It turned out they'd seen the signs I'd completely missed.

'I knew Hannah was trouble,' my friend Sarah said ominously when I told her what had happened. 'Always clinging to Brandon, and blinking up at him with those big eyes.'

I said nothing, because I'd never noticed Hannah clinging or blinking at Brandon. I'd trusted both of them completely.

Somehow that made it worse, knowing it had been obvious to everyone and I'd simply been a fool.

The humiliation and heartbreak were so crushing, my whole life in Lansing felt tainted. It was impossible to stay. Every place I went — every corner I turned — reminded me of all I'd lost.

So I did the only thing I could think of: I ran away.

I didn't tell anyone what I was doing — not Sarah, not even my parents. This was my breakdown, and I was going to do it my way. I packed most of my belongings into a storage unit, put everything else in my car, and headed west. I didn't stop until I reached Montana.

I suppose I wasn't the first person to try and disappear in the Rocky Mountains, nor the last. There is something about the wilderness that calls to a broken spirit. Frankly, there wasn't a lot of planning involved. I simply wanted to be as far from the smoking wreckage of my marriage as I could get.

I thought about driving until the land ended somewhere in Washington or Oregon. But I'd gone to college in Bozeman, and it seemed like a safe place to start again, and to heal. That was the plan, anyway.

Bozeman is a lively college town planted right in the middle of the state. Founded by a failed gold prospector, it still has a Wild West scruffiness about it. Low-slung and unpretentious, the town looks as if it's been scattered carelessly across a valley surrounded by towering mountains. But that didn't mean it was cheap and almost immediately I was in trouble. I'd hoped to live on my savings for a few months while I found my feet, but everything cost more than I'd expected. The tiny one-bedroom apartment I found to rent cost three times what I'd have paid in Michigan.

Even in the haze of my misery, I couldn't ignore the fact that I needed money. I wasn't going to last if I didn't find work.

It was late May by then and schools were out, so I couldn't get work as a teacher. I made a few phone calls to local magazines, but no one was looking for new writers, and I wasn't qualified to do anything else.

This shouldn't have been a surprise. In all of human history, nobody has ever looked around at a job that needed doing and thought, 'I know. I'll hire a poet.'

And I'd never been a serious writer. Most of what I'd written back in Lansing had been listicles. Magazines love them. They're just short, pithy lists of facts about random things. They're terrible but addictive.

Here's a listicle of jobs I applied for in Montana that I didn't get:

1. Bartender at the Come as You Are
2. Waiter at a café on East Main Street
3. English tutor for a wealthy Russian family
4. Writer at the Montana Live Blog
5. Cleaner at five different hotels

I applied for everything. As the rejections accumulated, I hit rock bottom. Somehow, at thirty-eight years old I had ended up with nothing. No husband, no children and no talents that were of any use to anyone.

That was my state of mind when I saw this ad on a local jobs website:

> Well-paid post overseeing exclusive development near Bozeman. Flexible working hours. Must own reliable vehicle, be self-motivated, and be able to handle isolation.

I didn't have much, but I had a decent car, and isolation was just what I wanted. I applied before I could think about how vague the ad was, and how dangerous vague ads can be.

Less than twenty-four hours later, my phone rang and a husky voice said my name.

'Maya Landry? This is Gina Kushman from Big Sky Land Management. I've got your application here, and I wondered if you could come in tomorrow morning for an interview.'

I had to force my voice to stay steady as I said yes, yes, I could fit that interview into my busy schedule. I scrabbled around for a pen while she gave me the address.

After I hung up, I danced around my living room, hopeful for the first time in months. And then abruptly, I sat down on the floor and cried like a baby.

I hadn't cried since Brandon left me. For weeks, I'd felt too empty to cry. Hollowed out. Now, suddenly, out of the blue, everything hurt and I couldn't breathe. I heard myself gasping, a guttural, wounded sound that frightened me, but I couldn't stop. I ached for the future I would never have.

For the plans Brandon and I had made. For my perfect little house. For the babies I'd wanted to have.

I don't know how long I sat there, poleaxed by grief, tears tumbling from my face onto the grey sweatshirt I'd been wearing for three days straight, until at last my sobs became tiny gasps, and finally just . . . breathing.

It was then, I think, that I made the decision. I was going to sort my life out. I was going to that interview tomorrow, and I was going to get that job.

May is still winter in the Rocky Mountains, and it snowed three inches that night. I woke before dawn to find the city had disappeared, hidden behind a hushed veil of white. There was no sound from the streets. I looked out of the window of my tiny apartment with a kind of awe. Everything was pure and new – as if the past had been wiped away. Maybe, I told myself, this was a sign. Maybe I really could start over.

I took a long, hot shower, letting the water remove any traces of my tears. Afterwards, wrapped in a towel and shivering, I ferreted through the stacks of untouched cardboard boxes until I located the iron and smoothed the creases out of my only blazer.

I dried my hair and put on make-up for the first time in a month. When I was finished, I stood in front of the mirror in the narrow hallway. My cheekbones were sharper than they'd been six weeks ago, and my trousers were a bit loose, but I looked presentable. Nobody would guess I'd spent the day before sobbing on the floor.

I wasn't sure I liked that fact; that much pain should leave marks.

I arrived at the downtown office building ten minutes early. The marble-floored lobby was warm and eerily empty as I stamped the snow off my boots.

'Can I help you?'

The male voice echoed, and I turned to see a security guard at the front desk motioning for my attention. He had small, suspicious eyes and an ill-advised dark moustache that hid his entire mouth, making it hard to tell whether he was smiling or frowning.

'I'm here to see Gina Kushman. I'm Maya Landry.' My voice was nervous and uncertain.

'Wait here,' the guard said brusquely, and picked up the phone.

His call was brief. When he hung up, he directed me to the elevators.

'Top floor,' he said.

Gina Kushman was waiting for me when the lift doors opened. She wasn't at all what I expected. From the call, I'd thought she'd be motherly and fiftyish, but instead she was my age, tall and so fearsomely slim I could see her pelvic bones through the smooth grey fabric of her dress. Gina was new Montana money, styled and impeccable. Her dark hair gleamed as she thrust out a slim hand.

'Maya?' Her grip was firm, and she had a flawless, professional smile. 'I'm Gina. Thanks for coming in. This way.'

Clutching my damp overcoat and surreptitiously straightening the hem of my blazer, I followed as she led me at a brisk pace past the reception desk with its sign reading 'Big Sky

Land Management'. The M in Management had been styled like jagged mountain peaks.

I'd only been in the state a few weeks, but it seemed to me that every M in every sign in Montana is styled like mountain peaks.

The clicking of Gina's high heels on the hard floor echoed as we walked past a row of empty glass-walled offices, and I was suddenly very conscious of my scuffed rubber-soled boots. I'd never cared much about clothes. I always said that if I couldn't go somewhere in jeans, I wasn't going. But next to Gina I felt childish and rumpled.

Aside from our footsteps, the only sound was a phone ringing, unanswered, somewhere on the floor. Gina gestured expressively at the shadowy rooms we could see through glass walls. 'The snow. Lots of people working from home today.' She gave me an approving glance. 'Great that you weren't put off by the weather.'

'I'm not afraid of snow,' I said.

'You used to live in Michigan, right? Bet you got your share of weather there.' Gina ushered me inside a spacious meeting room where black leather chairs gathered around a dark wood table like a conclave of priests.

'You'd think people would be less precious about snow in a town like Bozeman,' Gina continued as she set down her tablet on the table. 'After all, the Bridger Hotel lights a blue beacon on the roof when there's powder on the slopes. But everyone took their snow tyres off in April, and now they're as cautious as southerners.'

Her tone was light, but I sensed steel lay beneath that

and I wasn't wrong. As soon as we were seated, she fixed me with a direct look. 'If you'll forgive me for starting with this, Maya, you seem a little overqualified for the work we're looking for.'

Instantly my fantasy of the past being washed away faded. I was going to have to explain myself, somehow, and I had nothing to offer but the truth.

'I'm looking for a big change in my life,' I said, choosing my words carefully. 'I love the countryside, so I'm searching for something that will allow me to spend time in the mountains. I don't mind being alone all day – I'm comfortable with that. When I saw your ad, I thought it sounded perfect.'

Gina tilted her head, her dark eyes sharp. 'You say you're looking for change. Why is that? Did something happen where you were before?'

'Not at work,' I assured her hastily. 'I've been a freelance writer for more than a year. It's just . . . something in my personal life. That, um . . .' I searched for words. 'Anyway, I'm looking for a fresh start.'

I hoped she'd let it go. But Gina's gaze didn't waver.

'Look,' she said after a second, 'if we're going to work together, we have to trust each other. That's the only way. My bosses will want to know everything about you. I simply can't hire someone who doesn't trust me enough to tell me the truth. So, I'm afraid this just isn't going to work.'

Her tone was cool and final. It was over.

It all happened so fast, there wasn't time to think about why the people she worked for needed to know about my personal life. In that moment, all I knew was I'd lost this job.

I was so angry with myself. Why hadn't I just told her the truth?

Tears burned my eyes as Gina started to rise from her seat.

'*Wait*. I'm sorry, it's just that my marriage recently ended.' I spoke abruptly, desperation colouring my voice. 'That's why I need a fresh start. It's the only reason I moved here.'

Gina watched me silently as I continued to explain in broken sentences. 'My husband . . . he . . . he walked out on me. He'd been cheating with someone he worked with. Someone I knew. And I had no idea. So I left Michigan and came here, but I haven't been able to find a job and I haven't got any money. I don't know what I'll do if I can't find work soon.'

As I spoke, my face flamed. Saying this to a stranger didn't feel empowering; it felt like taking off my clothes and walking into a crowded room.

I don't know what I expected Gina to say, but in the end she said nothing. Instead, she held up her left hand.

'I get it.' She tapped the empty ring finger with a manicured nail. 'I know that exact feeling.' She paused, her lips pursing, and then angled closer, lowering her voice. 'Can I confide in you, Maya?'

It took me a second to find my voice. 'Uh . . . yes.'

'My husband cheated too.' She lowered her voice. 'The nanny. Twenty-three. Blonde. All the clichés. Humiliating.'

We stared at each other, unexpected compatriots emerging from the trenches of marriage.

'While we're telling the truth,' Gina continued, 'you should know I picked your application because you're my age. Most of the applicants have been too young. I don't think they'd be able to handle the isolation or the responsibility. And because of security issues, we don't want this to be a temporary thing. We're looking for someone with a bit of life experience.' She paused. 'The problem, Maya, is that you're a journalist. And to be perfectly frank, that makes my company nervous. Our residents expect *total* privacy. They don't want anyone to know that they even have homes here, much less what is contained in those properties. We're dealing with high-income people. Famous people. They are very particular.'

'Look,' I said. 'I really wasn't that kind of journalist. Not Woodward or Bernstein. More like, "You should try the amazing new steakhouse on Broad Street." I won't write about my work or anything I do here, I promise.'

My words tumbled out. I was nearly breathless with desperation to convince her.

Gina regarded me steadily. 'I know what kind of writing you did – I've researched you. We're careful. I want to hire you. I simply need to be sure I can trust you.'

Trust. That word kept coming up. But in the moment, I almost didn't notice. Nor did I wonder why the company might be so paranoid. I just kept trying to say the right things.

'You can trust me, Gina. I swear it.' I pressed my hand against my heart, and felt it flutter beneath my fingertips. 'I won't let you down.'

Gina held my gaze for a long while and then leaned back

in her chair. 'Do you know what a non-disclosure agreement is? I'd need you to sign one.'

'I will,' I said immediately. 'No problem.'

But Gina wasn't finished yet. 'You should know, if anything you see on the job ever makes it into the press, the company won't hesitate to come after you. You need to understand that at the very start. Just so we're clear.'

Looking back, *that* was the moment when I should have walked away. If I'd just said, 'Thanks but no thanks, I won't give up my right to speak about my own life,' I wouldn't be where I am now, telling this story.

But that's not what I said.

'That's fine,' I told her. 'I won't ever write about it.'

And I meant it. I think I'd have done anything to get that job, and I suspect Gina knew that because, unexpectedly, she smiled.

'Maya, you're in. I think you'll be ideal.'

I let out a long, shaky breath, but Gina didn't seem to notice as she slid her tablet closer to me. 'Take a look at this place. I want you to know where you'll be working.' She tapped the screen and I watched as a camera soared above a high mountain range, zooming towards a sturdy, three-level house with huge windows and a wide front veranda, before sailing through a series of exquisitely decorated interiors. Room after room flew by, each more luxurious than the last. Stone floors, high ceilings, huge fireplaces, beds piled lavishly with cushions – each image rushing into the next in a stream of elegant excess. And then the camera was outside again, swooping above the house and following the long, curved driveway through manicured grounds and thick forest before suddenly leaping higher to show many more of these grand houses dotted among the rocky slopes of the mountain.

'This is The Gateway,' Gina explained, with a hint of pride. 'It's an exclusive private ski community about forty minutes from here.' She gestured at the window and its snow-covered view. 'The weather today might fool you, but ski season is over and almost all the lodges are empty now. They'll stay empty until next winter. Most of our people only come in for the height of the season. Your job will be to take care of the empty lodges.'

'Take care of?' I looked at her as the images continued to rush by on the screen.

'Each owner has an individual set of requirements,' Gina explained. 'Some will want you to water the plants, feed the fish, open the windows to air out the rooms, dust, vacuum . . .' She swirled her hand to indicate that whatever they asked, I was to do. 'There are forty-five lodges in total. You must visit each empty lodge at least every two weeks. They are a considerable distance apart, but a mileage stipend will be included in your wage packet. And I think you'll agree the salary is generous for the work involved.' She paused, angling back in her chair to meet my eyes. 'Well, does this sound like something you want to do?'

It wasn't at all what I wanted to do. I wanted to be a writer married to the man I loved, with a cute house and a future together, but that dream was gone. And I needed to begin again. This was the first step.

When I spoke, my voice was clear. 'When do I start?'

TWO

Time flew. I was learning constantly: learning the town, learning the job, learning how to be alone. At first, each day I got through felt like a triumph. And then one morning, I didn't think about my life back in Michigan, and what might have been. Instead, I thought about how blue the mountains looked, or how good the coffee tasted. I still had no idea if I'd made the right decision coming here. But does anyone ever truly know where they belong? We all throw a dart at a map and hope it finds home.

By then, it was July. If you've never experienced it, I need to tell you that summer in central Montana is glorious. It almost never rains. The deer come down to the foothills to eat the tender grass. Wildflowers blanket the hillsides, and the breeze rolls in cool and fresh off the Bridger Mountains to sweep the valleys clean.

I remember very clearly one Wednesday in July when I stepped out of my apartment into the clear morning light and found myself thinking, This is nice.

Part of it, of course, was that The Gateway had turned out to be a good job. I had a lot of freedom, and that gave me time to heal. Nobody told me which houses to do on which days, and I didn't clock in or out, but Gina always seemed to know when I'd been up on the property, so I liked to be on time. And on this particular day, I left for work at eight o'clock on the dot.

As the city fell behind me and the vast wilderness opened up ahead, some of the tension in my chest eased. The drive up the mountain took nearly an hour and it was often the best part of my day. It's hard to feel anxious when the waters of the Gallatin River sparkle in the sun like God herself just threw a handful of diamonds on it.

Fields of wheat and soybean and sorghum stretched out around me in lush waves of green and amber, giving way to pastures of long, shaggy grass dotted with the vivid gold and blue of arrowleaf and larkspur flowers nodding in the sun.

Out of nowhere, I had a flash memory of my honeymoon, twelve years earlier. Brandon and I had gone to a four-star hotel in Utah – it was way too expensive, but his parents had given us some money, and we used part of it to book four days of bliss. It had been summer then, too, and the flowers scattered confetti on the roadside. On the drive, Brandon held my hand and sang along with Coldplay on the radio. He had dark blond hair and narrow blue eyes, and just looking at him made my stomach flip. He was mine then.

'Forever?' he liked to say, as if looking for reassurance.

'Forever,' I promised. And I, at least, had meant it.

'*No*,' I said aloud, shaking the memory away. I reached forward to snap on the radio. The soothing voices of *Morning Edition* flowed over me, with talk of war and peace and baseball. I let it wrap around me like a blanket and focused on my driving.

As it climbed into the mountains, the highway twisted and turned, following the bends of the river. I liked that the road was so loyal to the water. Hundreds of miles from here, that small, glittering river would join up with the Jefferson and Madison rivers to form the Missouri – one of the world's mightiest waterways.

There was probably a lesson in there about starting small and having faith, but I was too jaded for that. I just liked it.

I was almost sorry when I reached the low black sign with its artful logo of three white pines and two words: 'The Gateway'. I signalled and turned off the highway, at once entering a quieter, more refined world. Smaller, and much steeper than the highway, this curving lane was smooth and perfectly manicured. The people who owned houses up here wouldn't put up with anything less than perfection.

Soon, more inky-black signs began to appear, warning that this was private land. 'Gateway Members Only'. The road bent and twisted, writhing up the mountainside. Almost immediately, the radio signal began to fragment, the NPR voices cracking and breaking, until I reached forward and switched it off.

Nothing worked up here. The lowest section of The Gateway was at seventy-five hundred feet. The highest was over nine thousand. I knew from experience that well before I left the highway my phone lost all signal, and the radio usually followed. I didn't pass a single car as I drove uphill. No one trailed behind me.

At The Gateway, I was cut off from the world.

But that was fine with me. I wanted to be alone. It was what I was meant to be, after all. An ex-wife. Table for one.

I suppose I was still wallowing in it. The grief. The self-pity. I hadn't made a single friend in Montana. How could I? I wouldn't talk to anyone.

In Michigan, I'd had an active social life. I'd gone to yoga every Wednesday; I went out with friends at least every couple of weeks. But all that had died with my marriage. I worried sometimes that the split with Brandon had made me mistrust everyone. And if it had, I wondered if that would last forever.

A few friends back home tried to keep in touch, but I didn't make it easy for them, and I'm sorry about that now. I was too lost in my own sadness to realise I was hurting other people.

The only person I spoke to regularly was Gina. She'd accompanied me on my first couple of days working at The Gateway, showing me the ropes. I'd found her likable but distant. As polished as a gemstone. I couldn't imagine us becoming soulmates.

At last, a black metal gate appeared ahead. Like Gina, it managed to be both elegant and forbidding – eight feet tall, each dark rail topped with a sharp spike. Through it, I could see green trees and jagged rocks.

The little guardhouse next to the gate stood empty, the windows shadowed. That wasn't unusual. Ed Anderson was the guard on duty, but The Gateway covered thousands of acres of mountainside, so our paths only crossed once or twice a week. Ed was in his early sixties, a large, gruff man.

It seemed to me that both he and Gina were oddly protective of The Gateway. Ed was the most obvious about it. On my first day, he'd ignored me when I'd said hello.

Turning to Gina, he'd said coldly, 'Can I speak to you privately for a moment?'

I'd stood by the car as the two of them walked towards the gatehouse, but sound carries on the mountain and I'd heard their voices clearly.

'What happened to Justin?' Ed demanded.

'He quit.' Gina's voice was even. 'I told you that.'

'And I told you to find a way to keep him,' Ed snapped. 'Why didn't you offer him more money?'

'It wasn't my call,' Gina said. 'I don't get to make those decisions.'

'Well, I don't like it,' Ed groused. 'Who is she?'

'I've vetted her thoroughly.' Gina sounded as if she was trying to be patient. 'Don't worry about her – she's my responsibility. All you need to do is your job.'

'Yeah, well, my job's supposed to be security, but nobody ran her by me.' I could imagine Ed thrusting a thumb towards where I stood, trying not to look as if I was eavesdropping.

'Thanks for your input, Ed,' Gina told him icily. 'I'll pass it on to the board.'

'You do that.'

When Gina emerged from the shed, for a split second I'd seen the tight lines of irritation on her face, but by the time she reached me, the marks had all been smoothed away. She flashed one of those professional smiles.

'We're good to go,' she'd said, and got into the driver's seat.

I'd wondered then why Ed was so paranoid. What kind of threat could he possibly think I might pose? But I had a feeling questions like that wouldn't be welcome.

Even weeks later, Ed never seemed thrilled to see me, so I wasn't sorry to find the gatehouse empty as I stopped the car and leaned out of the window to punch a code into the backlit metal keypad. Gina messaged me a new code every Monday morning, along with key codes for each lodge. These were unique to me, and they were wiped on Friday evening, with new codes released the following Monday. It was a fairly secure system. I only received codes for empty houses. If any owners were planning to be on site, Gina let me know, but so far that had only happened a handful of times. This week, The Gateway was supposed to be completely empty, aside from Ed and me.

When I punched in the last digit, the gates shivered and began to slide open. While I waited, I leaned out of the window, breathing in the pine-scented breeze. At this elevation, the air was as thin as Venetian glass and seemed to contain virtually no oxygen. It had taken me two months to get to where I could walk up here without growing breathless. Even my car engine had needed to be adjusted so it could run with less oxygen.

It was much cooler at this altitude than it had been down in Bozeman; the wind had a real chill to it. Looking up, I could see the long stretches of cables for the ski lifts and brightly painted gondolas above the treetops. All the lifts were closed for the summer, but there were ski slopes for every level of ability, from easy to death-defying. I'd seen the maps in Gina's office, the mountain traced in lines of blue and red and yellow, showing the different ways to hurl yourself down it. Gina said there were private ski patrols on the mountain at all times in the season. There was even a café at the top of the highest peak, as well as trails for snowshoe hiking and snowmobiling across The Gateway's twenty thousand acres.

It was for all the world like the kind of ski resort you or I might go to, except for this one you first needed to buy a lodge for ten million dollars, give or take.

When the gates had opened, I drove through onto a lane surrounded by trees and high hedges. Everything here was designed for absolute privacy. From the main road through the resort you could not see a single rooftop. If you didn't know better, you'd think this was a road to nowhere, lacing up in a series of switchbacks before curling back down again. The lodges were all neatly hidden down long drives that sliced off into the mountain's generously shielding forests and folds.

Each house sat on at least six acres of land, although some had much more than that. No house had a view of anyone else's lodge, and none of the buildings were signposted, although each had a name beautifully set out on a slate sign near the front door: Eagle's Lodge, Hawk's View, Mountain House . . . You get the picture.

Each lodge was unique, and made to the owner's specifications. Some were built of stone, others of oak — but all were lavishly decorated with mounted elk horns and stacks of firewood arranged by size. There was something pleasantly false about it all. The houses were cartoon versions of ski lodges, with everything except elves and pixies dancing around the kitchen island.

At first, Gina hadn't given me the names of any of the owners, although she'd said coyly, 'Trust me, you've heard of them.' But when she was training me, she opened up a little and told me about the social media billionaires, the Hollywood producers, the bankers and the politicians, including one former vice president. No wonder they didn't like strangers here.

But none of them were around right now. As far as I could tell, Ed and I were the only people who came here every day at this time of year. Most of the time I didn't see a soul until I made it back to the highway and joined normal life again.

Today I decided to start up on the ridge, so I drove uphill, making my way along a winding road steep enough to make the car's engine struggle, until finally I turned a sharp bend and a three-storey stone building loomed ahead of me. It had a high, peaked roof and enormous windows across the top two floors. Behind it, there was nothing but mountain, towering blue, green and grey. An endless wall of stone and pines.

The drive looped around a large marble fountain to the grand front door. The slate sign near the porch read 'Pine Ridge Cottage'.

Cottage. That was laughable. Only if a cottage held six king-sized bedrooms, with a cedar sauna and a steam room downstairs.

When I stepped out, the cool breeze blew my hair off

my brow, and I tucked a strand absently behind my ear as I checked the list of codes on my phone.

It was so quiet, my own breathing sounded deafening.

With no town nearby or any busy roads, there were none of the familiar sounds. No lawnmowers or leaf blowers, no trucks rumbling in the distance or kids shouting as they chased each other around. But it wasn't really silent. It just took a while for my ears to adjust to the noise of the mountain: the low, wave-like roar of wind through the pine trees, and the cheerful chittering of chipmunks as they dashed along branches, sending twigs scattering down in a clattering rush.

I pulled my earbuds out of my pocket and scrolled to a podcast about an unsolved crime in Mississippi. It was the story of a woman who'd walked out of her house one day and never come back. They'd found her car parked by a river and everyone thought it was suicide, but the presenters, who had no legal experience whatsoever, were quite certain it was murder and were spending hours slowly revealing their reasoning. Their smugness irritated me, but the story was too compelling for me to stop listening.

I often listened to true crime podcasts; I found them comforting, in a strange way. The terrible things that happened to people were so much worse than my own situation, it put my problems into perspective.

The woman in this podcast – April McKay – had been my age when she disappeared without a trace. She had two little kids, and she was devoted to them. I couldn't get those kids out of my mind. They'd be teenagers now, and still wondering where their mother was.

I typed the numerical code into a small, black device on the front porch. The lock released, and the door swung open as the confident voice of the podcast presenters launched into their dubious evidence.

'Living just a few miles away, Ethan Frayne was out on probation, after being convicted of multiple violent attacks five years earlier . . .'

Inside, the house was cool – the stone walls and triple-glazed windows created a natural air conditioning – but it smelled stale. I slipped off my shoes and left them by the door, then hurried around opening windows, my socked feet padding against the dark walnut floors.

The living room was spacious, with three sofas and chunky armchairs arranged around a fireplace that took up the better part of one wall.

Double doors led into the kitchen, which was so big that a long oak table surrounded by ten chairs fit comfortably. Beyond that room, a second seating area held deep leather sofas and a wall-mounted television.

The place was at least seven thousand square feet, including the heated pool and cinema downstairs. I opened the cupboard in the utility room and took out a cloth and some cleaning spray and began hunting for dust. I swiped the windowsills and tables and the heavy picture frames on the walls before running up to check the bedrooms. Everything on that floor looked spotless and untouched, so I headed up to the top level.

I was moving fast; I had a good system by now.

Back in the living room again, I took a key from a wooden

box on a shelf and unlocked the French doors. A few leaves and a light layer of fragrant pine needles had blown onto the stone terrace, and we couldn't have that. Grabbing the broom I'd left out on my last visit, I brushed the invading evidence of the wilderness off the tiles and teak chairs.

My gaze wandered from the house to the thick forest looming at the edge of the manicured lawn. Whoever built this place had carved a square of space from the woods and planted a modern suburban lawn, but it seemed to me that the trees had never given up on their land. The towering pines leaned in possessively. As I stood there, a shadow shifted in the trees, and I thought I saw a flash of colour: drab brown, like a hunting jacket. With the broom still in my hand, I stared across the landscape to where the mountains were arrayed like lumpen giants, and fumbled with my phone to turn off the podcast. The air was fresh and cool, and when I pulled out my earbuds, I could hear nothing but the rush of wind.

You notice weird things when you're alone all day: movements out of the corner of your eye, shadows that shift oddly. You imagine stuff. It's as if being entirely alone is unnatural to humans, and we constantly search for each other. Wishing people up out of the emptiness.

I leaned back and gazed up at the sky; for a second, I thought I heard the faint sound of a car engine. But it had to be the wind.

Overhead, a wide-winged raptor soared in lazy, silent circles against the cloudless blue. In the clear sunlight, I could see every detail of its dark, gleaming feathers and long, narrow head with its fierce five-inch beak, as sharp as a rapier.

It was a golden eagle. A breathtaking beast of a bird. As I watched it, my work forgotten, its huge wings arched, catching an updraught. I knew eagles nested up here, but I'd never seen one this close before, and I shielded my eyes to get a better look.

It was so near, I could see the glint of its dark eyes and the red tongue inside the open beak, tasting the air, until, at last, it flapped its wings once and soared away towards the treetops in the distance.

I exhaled slowly, awestruck. I longed to stay right here and watch the light move across the hills, but I was already behind. I had three more lodges to do today.

Reluctantly, I put the broom away and headed inside, locking the French doors carefully.

I ran back up the stairs to shut the windows on the top floor, latching everything into place before dropping the dusting cloths into a bucket in the cupboard. After giving the living room one more glance to make sure everything was neat, I walked out and closed the door, listening for the mechanical click as the lock engaged.

The mountain was hushed and still. Even the chipmunks had fallen silent.

In that moment, I thought I must be the only person up on the mountain that day, and I relished the peace and perfect solitude. But I wasn't alone.

Someone else was up there with me. Someone was watching.

THREE

It was after six when I made it back into town that evening. The sun was still high – sending long shadows stretching across the pavements in neat military formations – but the air was much cooler now, and I shivered when I got out of the car.

It had been a long time since Barns Street held any barns. Instead it contained a series of modest two-storey buildings clad in grey render. The design was so featureless and angular, it could be mistaken for Scandi if you squinted.

Each building held four apartments, two upstairs and two down. I ran up the windowless staircase of number fourteen and unlocked the door marked C.

I remember that apartment so well. In the end, I didn't even live there three months, but if I close my eyes now, I can still see the long, dark hallway, with a tiny bathroom on the left and a little living room on the right. Beyond these lay the kitchen and a bedroom, and that was that. Small and imperfectly formed. It was the first place where I'd ever lived alone.

My life until then had always been shared. I'd gone straight from living with my family to shared dorm rooms, and from dorm rooms to shared houses, and from shared houses to living with Brandon. Now, at last, aged thirty-eight, I had my own place.

I tried to see it as a positive. Here I was, making my own way in the world. But it still didn't feel like home. I didn't feel like I was on my way; I felt adrift.

I'd barely set my bag down when my phone dinged, and I pulled it out of my pocket. It was a message from Sarah back in Michigan. The phone dinged again as I held it – another message.

We hadn't spoken in a few weeks, and I frowned as I opened them.

The message read: *I'm so sorry, Maya. He's such a bastard.*

My stomach dropped. Somehow I knew, without reading anything else, what she had to tell me. But I made myself keep going.

Her next message told me I was right: *Brandon told Miles today that he's moving in with Hannah. I don't know how to tell you this, honey, but she's pregnant.*

The phone clattered to the floor. I closed my eyes.

Miles was Sarah's husband. He and Brandon had been golf buddies for years.

I sat for a moment, staring at the wall across from me, seeing nothing except Brandon's face that day in the kitchen as he explained how he couldn't love me because he was 'in love with someone else'.

I'd thought of them thousands of times over the last fifteen weeks, in terrible made-for-TV-movie images: Hannah, blonde, young and pretty, laughing up into Brandon's adoring face as they cooked dinner in a stylish kitchen, played with someone's puppy, had sex in my bed . . . My mind had tormented me with thousands of excruciating scenarios.

The worst part about it was that I'd liked Hannah. She was funny and smart. When she'd first been hired, I told Brandon he'd finally found a keeper. She knew her way around every piece of software, had sorted out his schedule in days, and sent me a card and a box of chocolates on my birthday.

On the day she moved into a new apartment, I'd gone over to bring her a houseplant and a casserole too, in case she didn't have the chance to cook. She'd shown me around proudly, laughing at the chaos. I'd stayed for hours to help organise the kitchen.

I thought we were friends.

When Brandon and I had thrown an anniversary party last year, Hannah came in a short black dress and high heels, looking stunning. Was she already sleeping with my husband then?

Looking back, I felt so stupid. I hadn't known then that I should be jealous of her.

'I don't get a chance to dress up very often,' she'd confided with a self-deprecating laugh. 'I've had this dress hanging in the closet since New Year's, and I just felt like wearing it.'

Foolishly, I'd believed her.

I'd worn blue jeans and a sweater to that same party. Why had I not tried harder? At some point, I'd stopped thinking of myself as young and attractive and started seeing myself as old and insignificant. Insignificant people don't dress up for parties. I wonder if I even brushed my hair that night. I can't remember.

No wonder Brandon looked at Hannah, with her red lipstick and her slim legs, and decided he'd made a mistake.

I'd hated the two of them for the last three months. I'd wanted them to have a terrible, tawdry affair and then get what they deserved – a bitter, acrimonious break-up. But that wasn't going to happen. They were going to buy a house and raise a child together.

A baby.

I could imagine the two of them leaning over a bassinet, cooing at a tiny infant. The perfect picture of a perfect family.

Tears flooded my eyes.

Brandon said he didn't want one. He'd said it over and over. But the truth was, he didn't want one with me.

'Stop it.' I stood abruptly. I couldn't stay here thinking about this or I'd end up weeping on the floor. And I wasn't going to do that again.

With grim determination, I stripped off my work clothes and changed hurriedly into a pair of jeans and an oversized white shirt. The jeans fit loosely enough that I needed a belt. When I glanced in the mirror, my hair – auburn in good light; brown with copper strands right now – was a mess, so I smoothed it back into a ponytail, and tucked in the shirt to stop it billowing around me, snatched my bag off the floor and raced out, slamming the door behind me.

Other people. That was what I needed. I had to surround myself with distractions.

I told myself it was too beautiful an evening to waste on self-pity. And it was. The evening summer sun sent a golden haze across the low buildings, like a wave of honey. The air shimmered with it. All around me people were walking, riding bikes, going about their lives, and as I watched them, I felt the iron band around my chest release its grip just a little.

In those days, I sometimes went to a place called Cooper's, a few blocks away. It was nothing fancy, just a basic bar with neon Budweiser signs and Springsteen on heavy rotation. I'd never spoken to anyone there except to give my order to the bartender; Cooper's was the kind of place that let you be alone. Tonight, though, for the first time since I'd left Michigan, I genuinely wanted to be with other human beings.

I found an empty stool at the bar and sat down.

The bartender was called Jay, although he spelled it just 'J'. Like the letter J. He had tattoos in random patterns up his arms, and wore his dark hair in unfortunate dreadlocks, but he was OK. Always polite.

'What can I get you?' he asked, tossing his head to get the coils of hair out of his eyes.

He had nice eyes, I realised. Dark blue, with long lashes. If eyes are the windows of the soul, he had a nice soul, but I wasn't convinced any more that eyes were windows to anything.

'I'll have a whisky,' I said, but then corrected myself. 'No, strike that.'

Before I opened Sarah's text, I'd been hungry. That sensation was long gone, but I ordered a microbrew and a chicken burger with something like defiance.

J gave me a puzzled look but said, 'Sure thing. You got it.'

I wasn't going to starve to death for Brandon and Hannah. I would eat, and drink one beer, and then I'd go home and never think about them again.

But I did think about them. In particular, I remembered the time I stopped by Brandon's office without warning to drop off his phone, which he'd forgotten at home. As I approached, I could see the two of them through the glass door of Brandon's office. Hannah stood next to him, and they were laughing about something. They were close together, her hand resting on the back of his leather chair, and he was looking up at her with something like adoration.

When I walked in, they'd both stopped laughing. Hannah had stepped back quickly and picked up a notebook from Brandon's desk.

'What'd I miss?' I said, smiling like an idiot.

Everything, as it turned out. I'd missed everything.

J set a glass of beer in front of me, jerking me out of my reverie.

'Enjoy,' he said.

I took a long drink. I had to stop living in the past. It was done, and there had to be a way to start over.

Cooper's was full of the after-work and after-class crowd, gathered in clusters and pairs to dissect the day. I let their conversations flow over me in soothing, wave-like snippets.

'I start the new job on Tuesday, which is good because I've already spent the salary.'

'I've thought about changing my major to history, but you can't get a job in history, can you? I mean, it's not a *career*, it's a *time*.'

'Did you see him on television last night? What a moron. How do people vote for that jackass?'

My burger arrived, and I made myself eat. At first, I approached each bite like a hill I had to conquer, but gradually I realised the food was good, and my body needed it.

As I took a sip of beer, my gaze fell on a man on the other side of the U-shaped bar. The only man in Cooper's in a suit, he stood out. He wasn't wearing a tie, and the top two buttons of his pale blue shirt were open, exposing a triangle of smooth skin.

He was just my type. Late thirties, his dark hair slightly wavy, a shadow of stubble on his defined jawline. He was drinking whisky, his gaze off in the distance, but I had the strangest feeling he'd been watching me while I ate.

I pegged him as a business traveller, maybe arrived in town today. He could have worn that suit on the plane; it was a bit creased. But how he had ended up at Cooper's, I couldn't imagine. It wasn't exactly in the touristy end of town.

He glanced back and our eyes met, but we both quickly looked away.

You should talk to him, I told myself. Just go over and say hello. Try it.

Could I do that? Could I talk to a random, attractive man in a bar? I didn't think I could. The last time I'd dated, I was twenty-five years old. How did dating even work at my age? Did I have to use an app? Was it required?

'You through with that?' J appeared in front of me, gesturing at my empty plate.

I jumped, flushing slightly.

'Yeah, thanks.'

He scooped up my plate. 'Cool. Get you anything else?'

I glanced at the guy across the bar again, but his place was empty. The half-finished glass of amber liquid the only indication he'd ever been there.

I was too late.

'No, thanks,' I said. 'I have to go.'

I told myself it was just as well the stranger was gone. I wasn't ready yet. And after Brandon and Hannah, I didn't think I could ever trust anyone again.

FOUR

Thursday dawned bright, the sun melting across the craggy reaches of the hilltops and peaks.

Up on the mountain, a steady breeze rushed through the forest, and by noon I'd already completed my first two lodges. One of them was my dream house. Stillwater Cabin was a glorious five-bedroom, stone-fronted building. I loved everything about it: the bookcases filled with volumes I longed to read, the charming windows with their little curled black latches, the kitchen – just the right size – with traditional glass cabinets and an oak farmhouse table.

I could see myself in that living room on a snowy day, by the fire with the perfect book. A curious warmth and welcoming feel pervaded the whole place. The light slanted silkily across the oak floors, and the views were the most spectacular I've ever seen, taking in the deep, green valley and long, curving ski slopes. I loved working in that house. Stillwater days were the best days.

So, I left it reluctantly, closing the door gently behind me, regretting the click of the lock.

Inevitably, the following house would be a comedown, so I decided to break my usual routine and do my least favourite house next.

White Pine Lodge was the most ostentatious of all the houses in The Gateway. Eight bedrooms, plus a 'bunkhouse' that was really a two-bedroom guest house with its own living and dining space. It was decorated garishly, with white tiled floors that showed every smudge, and shiny chrome fixtures that looked cheap but had probably cost a fortune.

In White Pine Lodge, there were no books at all. In fact, there was nothing that showed personality. It was a big, flashy house for big, flashy people. A lawyer, I thought, owned this place. Not the good kind of lawyer but the slick kind you can't trust. With empty eyes and a huge bank account.

It was one of the lower houses, and I usually did those on Fridays, but it felt right getting it over with now.

The driveway stretched for nearly a mile through thick forest that shadowed the narrow lane so completely, I was momentarily blinded when I emerged back into the light. I had to squint to see the hulking oak-framed structure in front of me.

As I blinked, I thought for a second I saw a curtain in the front window move. But when my vision cleared, everything was in place.

A trick of the light.

There were three steps to the front door, and I climbed them with my head down, searching my phone for the right code. On that day, the code was 1098. I will never forget it.

The door opened smoothly. For a second, I stood in the open doorway, sliding my earbuds into place, restarting the podcast before I stepped inside. The latest clues the podcasters had found included a wedding announcement for a woman in California who looked strikingly similar to the missing mother.

'*On this episode of* Back in Black,' the podcaster intoned, '*we're going deeper into the story of April McKay. Did she escape her life, rebrand herself as Mary Kenna, and move to California? We start by looking into Mary Kenna, to find out whether everything about her was invented . . .*'

Focusing on the voices in my ears, I walked into the wide entrance hall and closed the door behind me.

Instantly I had the sense that something wasn't right.

This house should have been warm inside, but the air felt cool against my skin and smelled of the outdoors, as if a door or window had been left open. But that wasn't possible. Nobody had been here since my last visit two weeks ago, and I was zealous about closing everything before I left. Surely I wouldn't make a mistake like that.

I hurried my pace, dread rising in my chest. The temperature didn't make sense. What if I *had* left the back door open? Coyotes could have got in, or raccoons. They could have trashed the place.

I'd get fired.

The podcasters were still talking as I raced down that long hallway, but I couldn't hear them any more as I reached the living room and skidded to a stop.

Instantly I could see the French doors were closed tight. A small sigh of relief escaped me. But there was a smell that shouldn't have been there. A *human* smell of sweat and something else.

I yanked the earbuds from my ears, and the silence roared in.

Light pouring through the glass gave the pale room, with its white tiled floor and ivory rugs, an unearthly glow.

'Hello?' My voice trembled. 'Is someone here?' The words echoed in the quiet.

I hadn't paused the podcast, and tinny voices kept talking through the earbuds in my hand, but I made no move to reach for my phone to switch them off. Something was wrong. I could feel it like electricity on my skin. Every nerve in my body tingled and my stomach clenched as I took one tentative step forward and then another, expanding my view of the room until it encompassed the white sofas, the rectangular glass coffee table, the fireplace built of soft-grey stone.

Empty. All empty.

I took three further steps. And froze.

A man lay on the white rug. His face was the most horrible thing I'd ever seen, purple and contorted, the tongue protruding grotesquely.

But it was his eyes that stopped me in my tracks. Ice blue and wide open, staring at the ceiling. Those empty eyes. I'd never seen a dead body before, but I knew, without question, that this man was dead.

I don't know why I didn't scream, but I did not. Instead, I stood very still. I could no longer hear the tinny voices. In fact, all sound had ceased, as if the world itself had receded. No birdsong, no breeze through the trees outside, no electrical hum.

Then, as quickly as they had gone, the sounds of the world returned in a flood: the podcast hosts still talking, the terrified rasp of my breath, the *thud thud thud* of my heart.

My gaze darted around the space, but there was no one else in the room. Just the man lying on the rug.

I didn't understand how he could be there. The house should be empty.

Who was he? Where had he come from? Gina always alerted me if one of the owners was going to be there. She'd said nothing in her messages yesterday or this morning. Nothing at all.

By then, I was standing above him. I didn't want to touch him, but I felt I had to check if he was alive.

As I crouched slowly beside him, the man's vacant blue eyes seemed to watch me, aware of my fear. My hand trembled visibly as I reached out to touch his wrist.

His skin was smooth and cool but not cold. His chest did not rise or fall. The eyes fixed on the ceiling were glazed. And up close, I could see what I had not noticed from across the room – a thin, clear plastic line laced around his neck like a delicate noose, pulled tight, the skin around it florid and raw.

I stared at that translucent noose for what felt like minutes but must have been no more than a split second, and then I was in motion, leaping to my feet, racing across the room, hurling myself out the front door. I slammed it shut behind me, fumbling for my phone, but the device slipped from my numb fingers, thudding to the ground. Swearing, I snatched it up again, only then remembering that there was no phone signal up here. None whatsoever.

Slowly, I turned and looked back at the house. There was Wi-Fi in there, but it was password-protected. It was the same in all the lodges. There were no landlines. There was no way for me to reach anyone.

I needed help. Somebody had killed that man. And they could still be here.

Ed Anderson. I needed to find him. As usual, he hadn't been at the guardhouse when I arrived, but he must be on the property somewhere. There was a landline inside the guardhouse.

All at once, I felt light-headed. I couldn't seem to get a breath of that thin mountain air as I raced down the front steps to the car, yanking open the door and hurling myself into the driver's seat, punching the button to lock the doors.

At some point I must have begun to weep, because when I looked through the windscreen, the trees blurred in a wash of deep green.

Swiping my cheeks with the back of my hand, I started the engine and floored the accelerator. In seconds, I was heading back down that long, shadowy drive through the trees. Although I checked the rear-view mirror constantly, there was never anyone behind me. All the same, my hands were so tight on the wheel that my fingers ached long before I reached the black iron gate.

The guardhouse was dark and quiet. There was no sign of Ed. All the same, I ran to the door and tried the handle – locked tight. I pounded on the wood in futile frustration, peering through the glass at the computer and phone on the desk.

'Ed!' I shouted. My voice faded instantly, absorbed by the branches of the impassive pines. 'Ed!'

There was no one else up here. I didn't know where Ed was and I couldn't wait here. The killer could be on the grounds. I had to find help.

Shivering now, I leapt back into my car and started the engine, heading for the gate. My eyes fixed on the rear-view mirror, I waited impatiently until the gap was wide enough to squeeze the car through.

At last, I was out and racing downhill towards the main highway. Whatever had happened in that house, I needed help.

FIVE

The nearest place I'd ever got a phone signal was a gas station and diner called The Halfway, about fifteen minutes down the mountain. I drove like a lunatic, hitting ninety miles per hour, passing anyone going slower on the curving two-lane road. Semi-trucks blew their horns disapprovingly as I flew past them.

For the first time in my life, I wanted to get pulled over. I broke about fifty traffic laws until, finally, I pulled into the parking lot in front of The Halfway and slammed on my brakes. I had two bars of signal.

With a sigh of relief, I dialled 911. A calm female voice asked what my emergency was.

At last able to tell someone, I found my words emerging in short, jerky phrases. 'I found a body. On the floor. Of a house. At The Gateway.'

'A body? Are you saying there's a dead body?' The voice sounded more interested now.

'Yes. A man. He's . . . I think he's been strangled.' I remembered that purple face, the protruding tongue.

If this was a surprise to her, her voice didn't show it. 'Ma'am, we're going to help you. Are you somewhere safe right now?'

I looked around me at the parking lot, the rustic wooden structure of the café.

'Yes, I'm fine. I'm not at the house.'

'You left the body?'

'I had to. There's no signal up there.'

'Can you give me the address where the body is?'

'It's at The Gateway. The house . . . it doesn't really have an address that I know of. It's called White Pine Lodge.'

There was a pause. 'I'm sorry, is White Pine Lodge the street?'

'No, it's confusing. It's the house name. It's in a private development called The Gateway, off the Gallatin Highway. It must be in your database somewhere.'

'The Gateway? Private development?' The woman sounded increasingly baffled, and I couldn't blame her.

'It's a ski resort,' I explained. 'But private. I work there.'

There was a pause, and then the woman said, 'Is that the one with the black signs?'

'That's it.' Relief flooded my voice. 'I don't know what that address is or even how to tell the officers where to go. I couldn't find the guard, and there's a locked gate.'

I could hear the sound of furious typing.

'Can I have your name please?'

'I'm Maya Landry,' I said. 'L-a-n-d-r-y.'

'Are you're talking on your own phone, Ms Landry?'

'Yes,' I said.

She asked for my home address, and I gave it to her woodenly, wondering why she would need it. Finally, she said, 'You said there's no one manning the gates at the facility?'

'That's correct.'

'Do you have keys or a code to open the gates at the facility?'

'Y-yes...'

My voice grew uncertain as I realised what she was about to ask.

'The deputies are on their way. Would it be possible for you to meet them outside the gates and let them in?'

My eyes fluttered shut and I held the phone away from my ear. There were no words to describe how much I did not want to go back up that mountain. But there was a dead man waiting.

'Sure. I'll head there now.' My voice was tight, but I felt I had no choice. I'd found the body, so I owned the body.

Still, I didn't hurry back up the mountain. Instead, windows rattling as big trucks roared by, I sat in The Halfway parking lot at the edge of the highway, thinking about the body on the floor, the smell in that house, the sense that I was being watched. And Gina. At some point, I had to let her know what was happening. She'd want to be up there, defending her clients' privacy rights like a pit bull protecting a piece of meat.

However this all turned out, I knew I would be blamed for the disruption to the perfect peace of her beloved Gateway.

Through the open car window, I heard a faint wail of sirens in the distance, and with a sigh, I started the engine and shifted into gear, dropping my phone into my pocket.

I'd call Gina later, once I had all the facts.

When I reached the tall iron gates, I found two male deputies in forest green uniforms, six-pointed stars glinting on their chests, waiting for me.

Police terrify me. Police sirens make my heart race. Getting pulled over for a speeding ticket would leave me nauseous with anxiety.

I've never been in trouble, and yet even as a child I lived in fear of going to prison. I suppose I had a good imagination, which can be an awful thing when you're young. If anything is possible, then anything *bad* is possible.

Maybe that's why I was so into true crime podcasts. All those awful crimes, all those police investigations. Each one of them a tiny needle jabbing my subconscious fears.

The taller, heavy-set deputy stepped towards me. 'Are you the person who reported a body?'

My mouth went dry. 'Yes. I'm the one who . . . It was me.'

The shorter deputy jutted a thumb at the gates. 'You live in there?'

He was wiry, with thinning dark hair and narrow, suspicious eyes. I didn't like the look of him. His left hand hovered too near the pistol in his side holster.

I was shaking again, and I saw him notice that with interest.

'No. I work here. I . . .' I searched for the words to describe my job before settling on, 'I'm a caretaker.'

The two of them exchanged quick, unreadable glances. The shorter one said, 'Right. Tell us what we're going to find in there.'

I took a deep breath. 'In . . . in one of the h-houses – it's called White Pine Lodge . . . I went in to check the house today and air it out, and there was a b-body on the floor, in the living room.' The words poured out of me in a rush. 'It's a man. There was fishing wire around his neck. His face was horrible. I think he'd been strangled.'

'Did you recognise him?' he asked.

I shook my head.

'Did you see anyone else up there? Anyone at all?' the larger deputy pressed. He was so tall, my eyes were even with his square shoulders, and I noticed he wore a narrow brass name tag that read 'Jennings'.

Before I replied, I thought again of that curious sense I'd had of being observed, but I shook it off. I'd been freaked out. It was my imagination.

'Nobody.' My voice was firm.

'Well, then.' The taller one motioned at the keypad near the gate. 'You better open that for us.'

I walked stiffly to the gate and punched the numbers into the cold metal keypad.

'Where're we goin'?' the shorter one asked when the gates began to slide open.

'It's hard to describe,' I told him. 'There aren't any street names in there. You better follow me.'

As I walked to my car, I heard Jennings comment, 'Always wanted to see this place. Never had cause.'

'Guess it's your lucky day,' the shorter one observed, and Jennings snorted a laugh.

They got into the car, with Jennings behind the wheel. He

backed up with an expert's speed to allow me to drive through the gates first.

As I retraced my journey up the steep road, I drove carefully, conscious of the two officers behind me and the things they might be saying. Even though it was just their car and mine, I signalled before turning onto the road up to White Pine Lodge.

Immediately, the heavy shadows of the pine trees blacked out the sun. My hands had begun to tremble again and I ordered myself to stay calm.

You're not in any trouble, I reminded myself. You haven't done anything except report a crime.

All the same, when White Pine Lodge appeared ahead, my lungs tightened.

Everything looked just as it had when I'd fled thirty minutes ago. The door was closed tight. The curtains hung straight and true in the windows.

The sheriff's car stopped next to mine. As they got out, the two deputies peered up at the ostentatious timber-framed house with its huge windows and stone steps.

'Stay here,' Jennings told me.

He walked to the right to look around the side of the building while the shorter one moved in the opposite direction. Neither of them spoke, but each seemed to know precisely what the other would be doing, their steps in near sync.

The shorter one glanced at me, and I saw that his name tag read 'Ross'.

'Where's the body?' His voice was low.

I gestured at the front door. 'Inside.'

He gave a terse nod. 'You got a key?'

'No, it's a . . . a code,' I stammered. 'Like the gate.' I held up my phone, as if this explained everything.

'The same code?' Ross pressed.

'The number is different for each lodge, and all the codes change every week.'

'OK. Tell us *exactly* where to find the body inside.' Ross's tone was tense.

I described the long hallway and the living room. 'He's there. On the floor.'

Jennings motioned sharply at the front porch and spoke in a low voice. 'Open the door and then stand by your car until we give you the all-clear.'

I walked up the front steps to the keypad, and the two deputies flanked me. I heard the snapping sounds as they released the straps holding their pistols in their holsters.

Once again, I punched in the numbers: 1098. The door unlocked.

'Get back,' Ross ordered, and I stumbled down the steps as both officers pulled their pistols and pointed the barrels into the shadows.

'Sheriff's department!' Jennings shouted, kicking the door the rest of the way open and angling the gun down the hallway. 'We're coming in. If you have a weapon, put it down *now*.'

The two men exchanged glances. Jennings nodded as if Ross had said something. Ross entered first, his steps quick and confident. Jennings followed immediately. Each man pressed his back against a wall.

Holding my breath, I watched as Ross elbowed open the door to his left, which I knew held a small bathroom, and pointed the gun inside.

'Clear!'

Jennings strode ahead with his gun in his hand, announcing, 'Sheriff's department!' in that authoritative tone that sent a chill through me.

Time passed. I heard the word 'Clear!' over and over, then the sound of footsteps on the polished wood stairs as they walked up to search the bedrooms, the bathrooms, the spacious walk-in closets.

After a few minutes, Ross called, 'Ms Landry, come in here, please.' His voice was cool.

I swallowed hard. I didn't want to see the body again; that face, purple and contorted. But I could hardly refuse.

Slowly, I climbed the steps into the house. The air was warmer than it had been earlier and the smell of sweat was no longer detectable as I moved cautiously through the hallway to the living room. Before I reached it, I could hear the detectives talking in low voices, their feet shuffling on the white floor.

I'll have to mop, I found myself thinking, absurdly. Those tiles show everything.

When I stepped cautiously into the long room, the two deputies stood watching me. Their expressions were a curious mix of baffled and angry.

'What's this about?' Ross demanded. 'Is it some sort of joke?'

'What do you . . . ?' I began, but as I looked past him, my heart stuttered.

The white rug lay in front of the fireplace, precisely where it had been earlier. But it was empty.

The body was gone.

SIX

'I don't understand.' As I spoke, my gaze remained fixed on that pristine white rug. It was perfect, every line straight and smooth. There wasn't so much as a speck of dust. I couldn't understand what I was seeing.

'Is this some sort of prank?' Ross rounded on me. 'It's a crime to file a false report with the police. We could take you in for this.'

Faced with his fury, I felt terrified.

'I swear to you, I'm not making this up.' I pointed at the rug beneath his feet. 'Half an hour ago, he was right there.'

'We have searched this house from top to bottom.' Ross pointed at the vaulted ceiling. 'Every room, every closet. The back door is locked, and there is no key in evidence. No sign anyone came in or out. Not only is there no body, there's no sign of a struggle. No evidence of disturbance. In fact, we can find no indication that anyone has been here today at all.'

Jennings stepped forward. 'There's an alarm here, right?'

I nodded mutely. Every house was equipped with an alarm connected to the doors and windows. My code switched it off automatically.

'So if someone was killed here today, why didn't that go off?' he asked.

He was right. How had anyone entered this house without triggering the alarm? How had they even got through the gates if they didn't live here?

When I didn't speak, Jennings gave a brisk nod.

'So you see,' he said reasonably, 'we have to conclude that you have invented a crime and brought us here under false pretences.'

I thought of the man I'd found lying on the floor. The bulge of skin around the wire that had killed him.

'But he was here,' I whispered helplessly. 'I saw him.'

'Well, if he really was here, he wasn't as dead as you thought,' Jennings said dryly.

'That could be it.' Ross flashed a grin at him. 'Maybe he was napping and you woke him up.'

'And then he walked out into the woods, which is why we didn't see him on the way here.' Jennings chuckled. 'But he cleaned up and locked the doors before going. That's a real thoughtful corpse, when you think about it.'

Their ridicule sent heat rushing to my face. 'He *was* here,' I insisted. 'He'd been strangled. And you're standing there, laughing. My God. What is wrong with you?'

The smiles faded. 'You're not helping yourself, lady.' Ross's face hardened. 'We could charge you with obstruction. You'd have a permanent criminal record. In fact, I think we should do that. I'm pissed off about coming all the way up here for nothing on a busy day.'

Fear rose in my throat like bile, but Jennings made an

impatient gesture. 'Come on, I don't need the paperwork. It'd waste even more time.' He gave me a cold look. 'But I want you to know something. You kept us up here when other people with real problems needed us. You ought to think about that. Whatever your issue is, you could cost someone's life, pulling shit like this.' Glancing at his partner he said, 'Let's go.'

They walked towards the door, their utility belts jangling. I heard Ross speak into his radio. 'Dispatch, Unit 381 leaving the scene. Note it as a false report.'

A voice spoke back. 'Copy that, Unit 381.'

I stood in that white living room, listening to them talk in low voices. One of them – probably Ross – sniggered. Then the doors of the patrol car slammed, and with a rumble of engine, they drove away. Leaving me alone in a house without a corpse.

It was after seven o'clock when I pulled up on Barns Street and climbed the stairs to my apartment. My movements were leaden and I felt utterly drained.

The day had left me with no good options. On the one hand, I knew I should have called Gina to tell her what had happened, but I simply didn't know what to say. If the police thought I was deluded, what would she think? After all, I'd seen that pristine carpet with my own eyes.

I'd felt at times over the last few months that I wasn't really myself. Now I began to wonder in earnest if something might truly be wrong with me. What if I'd imagined it all? Was this what it was like to have a complete breakdown?

The idea that I might have somehow dreamed the body was horrifying.

The experience had been so disturbing that after the police left, I'd simply gone back to work, visiting two more lodges. But I'd been anxious the entire time. Frightened that there had been a dead body, and just as frightened that there might not have been.

Nothing else happened, and I didn't see anybody on the property. But Ed had been back in his guardhouse when I left for the day, his grey head visible through the windows, so I decided to stop.

When I tapped on the door, he looked up.

'How's it going?' he'd asked, reaching for the thermos of coffee he always kept with him, whatever the time of day.

'I was just wondering if anyone else was on the property today,' I said.

Ed frowned as he poured hot liquid into his cup. 'Nobody but you and me. Why?'

He didn't know about the police, then. He hadn't checked the CCTV or seen their car. It was almost a relief.

'I thought I saw someone up by White Pine Lodge,' I told him.

His set the thermos down and screwed the cap back on before replying.

'Did you check the house?'

'Yes,' I said. 'It's secure.'

'Well, I haven't seen anybody, and I was over on that side a couple of hours ago, but we should make of a note of this for the record.' He reached for a pen and notepad. 'Can you be specific about what you saw?'

My heart fell. I was getting in deeper and deeper. I'd have to lie now about what I'd seen. I couldn't tell him about the police – that would just lead to more trouble. I had to get out of this.

'Oh, it was probably just my imagination,' I said quickly. 'I didn't really see anything worth recording. I thought I heard someone in the woods, and I just wondered if maybe the landscapers had come up or something . . .' My voice trailed off.

From beneath his thick eyebrows, Ed gave me a doubtful look and put down the pen.

'Well, if you didn't see anything, it's not worth putting it down. Was it just a noise?'

'Yeah,' I said. 'I heard a car. But it could have been the wind.'

He rocked back in his chair and picked up his cup. 'The mountain plays strange tricks. I was once walking over by Silver Sage Lodge and could have sworn I saw a mountain lion on the path right in front of me. Scared the bejesus out of me. But there wasn't a thing there.' He took a sip of coffee and nodded. 'The light, the wind . . . It all confuses the eyes and ears. You get used to it.'

He wasn't wrong – I had also seen things out of the corner of my eye up at The Gateway. Things that hadn't been there when I turned to look. But that body had been right in front of me.

Now, sitting in my living room, I kept going over it all in

my mind. I couldn't have imagined the corpse. I'd touched his skin. I'd smelled his sweat.

Only one thing made sense. Someone must have taken the body away and cleaned up the room. But if someone had removed the body during the thirty minutes it took for the police to get there . . .

They must have been nearby when I was in the house.

They would have seen me walking in. And then rushing out to my car a few minutes later.

As the light faded, my thoughts wheeled and turned like a flock of crows until I felt a sharp pain in my hand. I looked down to find I'd been picking unconsciously at my cuticles. Blood was oozing from my fingertip.

Swearing softly, I ran to the kitchen and poured water over the wound.

By the time my hands were dry, I'd made up my mind. I had to tell someone.

I picked up my phone and called Gina.

When she answered, I could hear the noise of a crowded room. She raised her voice to be heard. 'Maya, what's going on? Any problems?'

'No. I . . . I was just wondering if there was somebody else on the property today,' I stammered. 'It's just, I thought I heard cars, and maybe . . . voices.'

'Oh, really?' Gina sounded puzzled. 'Well, the maintenance crew weren't up there today. The family that owns Snowy Ridge are due in this month, though. I know you don't usually do that house anyway, but it could have been them you heard.'

Snowy Ridge was one of the highest houses, far from White Pine Lodge.

I hesitated before asking cautiously, 'Nobody's staying at White Pine Lodge right now, are they?'

It seemed to me there was a pause before Gina replied, but it was noisy where she was and she might just have been trying to understand me.

'No. That owner hasn't been here in over a year. I think he's selling the place,' Gina said. Somebody spoke to her and she covered the phone, muffling her reply. When she returned to our conversation, she sounded impatient. 'Look, Maya, I'm at a dinner party and I can't really talk. Is there something else you need?'

I bit my lip hard, wishing there was any way to tell her the truth and not sound completely insane. But there wasn't.

'No, I just wanted to let you know that I'd heard something, in case it was significant.'

'Thanks for letting me know, but I wouldn't worry. Sound travels strangely up there,' Gina said, much as Ed had done earlier. 'Those noises could have come from miles away.'

I hung up and stared at my phone. Ed's and Gina's explanations for what I might have heard had been nearly identical. It was almost as if they'd known I might ask. But that didn't make sense.

Nothing made sense.

I couldn't stay here alone with my thoughts. I walked to the bathroom and washed my face. As I reached for the towel, I looked out at the overgrown garden. I didn't have access to it – it belonged to the ground-floor apartment – but I longed to get my hands on it and pull up those weeds. I missed my roses back in Michigan. I'd nurtured them like the children I didn't have.

A few minutes later, I headed out on foot to Cooper's.

It was about a ten-minute walk to the bar, but if I'd hoped the journey would settle my thoughts, it didn't. My worries were still teeming when I walked in.

The place was much more crowded than it had been the night before, and I stood near the bar, waiting until two men finished their Bud Lights and stood unsteadily.

'Gotta take a piss,' one of them slurred to the other. 'Meet you outside.'

He'd barely taken two steps before I pounced on his bar stool.

The padded seat was unpleasantly warm, and I tried not to think about exchanging electrons with a drunk who'd just wandered to the men's room.

The jukebox shifted from Van Morrison to Veruca Salt, and a guy wearing an expensive-looking T-shirt that said 'BROOKLYN' on the front played air guitar with his beer bottle.

J was in the weeds, with people stacked three-deep at the bar and only one barback helping, so it was a few minutes before he made it over to me and picked up the empty bottles, his lip curling with distaste as he dropped them in the bin.

'Why do people drink this shit? Don't answer that. What can I get you?'

Despite everything that had happened that day, it occurred to me that I was starting to like J.

I ordered a microbrew, adding spontaneously, 'And a shot of tequila.'

J gave me a quick, interested look, but said only, 'You got it.'

I watched as he poured the beer into my glass and set two empty shot glasses on the bar. He upended a tequila bottle, letting a stream of clear liquid fill each small glass. When he'd finished, he slid a shot across to me and picked up the other, waiting until I raised mine.

'To better times,' he said.

'I'll drink to that.' I downed the shot.

The tequila burned a line from my oesophagus to my stomach, but it felt good. Like fire burning away the day's confusion and fear.

J scooped up both our glasses and dropped them in the sink with a clatter. I pulled a twenty-dollar bill from my wallet, but he shook his head. 'That one's on the house.'

'Why?'

It was impolite, but I was caught off guard. It was the first time he'd ever given me anything for free.

J shrugged, his dreadlocks shivering. 'You never order shots. Let's just say I like to encourage bad behaviour.' He flashed a quick, mischievous grin, and then turned back to the crowds, holding up his hands. 'Who's next? Be honest. God knows if you lie.'

God knows if you lie.

For some reason, those words needled me. I'd lied to Gina,

yes. But I'd had no choice. I was in the middle of something I didn't understand.

Just like that the thoughts were back, demanding answers. Who was the dead man? *Where* was the dead man? Who'd killed him? What was I going to do?

'It seems to me,' a voice said at my elbow, 'that you're in trouble.'

I looked up, startled. A man had taken the empty bar stool next to me. He was familiar-looking, clean-shaven, with a strong jaw, wavy hair and sharp eyes. He wore a button-down shirt and dark slacks that looked slightly out of place in Cooper's. It took me a second to recognise him without his rumpled suit and five o'clock shadow. When I did, I spoke without thinking.

'You've shaved.'

His left eyebrow rose.

'I mean . . . I saw you here last night,' I explained, flustered. 'Your suit was . . . Well, I thought perhaps you'd just got off a plane. You . . . hadn't shaved.'

His eyes were so piercing it unnerved me.

'You're observant. That can be dangerous.' He gestured at my untouched beer. 'Do you want another?'

I shook my head.

He lifted his hand with such authority that J, who was ringing up a bill, slammed the register drawer and stepped closer, despite the crowds calling for his attention.

'A double J & B,' the man said. 'On the rocks.'

J nodded and turned away.

The man didn't look at me while J poured his drink and set

it on a coaster. His silence seemed to draw in the air between us, constricting it and leaving me with the sense that I should fill the gap. But somehow I knew I shouldn't do that; I shouldn't talk to him at all.

I angled my body so that I couldn't see him and focused on my beer. I didn't know how long had passed when he spoke again.

'You work up at The Gateway, don't you?'

My breath caught. How could he know that? Who was he?

I darted a look at his face, but his eyes were fixed on some point in the distance.

He took a long sip of whisky, and set the glass down carefully on the cardboard coaster. When he spoke again, his voice was low and calm.

'You saw something today you shouldn't have seen. You're in danger. I've come here to warn you to get out as fast as you can. And don't look back.'

SEVEN

All the air seemed to leave the room so completely, I was sure everyone must have noticed. But nobody looked at us.

When I finally found my voice, my words came out in a whispered rush. 'What are you talking about? How do you know what happened? Were you there?'

'Stop.' His eyes met mine with a flash of impatience. 'You don't have time for this, Maya. You should be packing.'

'I don't—' I began, and then paused, frozen by a sudden realisation. 'How do you know my name?'

'That doesn't matter,' he said. 'What matters is that you're in trouble.'

But I was too afraid to listen. 'Who are you?' I demanded. 'Why are you telling me this?'

'I'm telling you this because I don't think it's fair what they're going to do to you.' The man picked up his drink and took a baleful sip. 'And because it's supposed to be my job.'

He wasn't making sense. I looked around for help, but J was chatting to a brunette on the other side of the bar with his back to me. And I didn't know anyone else.

The man next to me spoke wearily. 'The bartender can't help you. The police can't help you. Nobody will believe you. Only *you* can help you.' For the first time, he turned to face me directly, those steady eyes holding mine. There was no madness in them, only something like regret. 'Listen to me, Maya. Go home, pack a bag, get on a plane, get out of this town, and never, ever look back. Do anything else and you're dead. That's all there is.'

Do anything else and you're dead. My heart contracted. I didn't want to believe him, but I'd seen death today. And somehow this man knew that.

I pressed my fingertips against my forehead. 'I don't understand why you're saying this. Who are—'

The man thumped his fist on the bar, and I got the impression it took effort to restrain himself enough not to punch right through the brass and wood, but in the noise and crowds, nobody noticed as he leaned towards me with frustration.

'You're not *listening*. The people who did what you saw up there want you gone. They know who you are. They know everything about you. Why were you there, Maya? You don't go to that house on Thursdays. You shouldn't have been there at all, but you were, and now you have to pay for that. It's not fair, but the world isn't fair, and you know that as well as anyone.'

The thing is, as I write this down, it's all so clear and straightforward, but in that moment, it was as if the man was speaking another language. Because how could he possibly know I wasn't supposed to be at the house today?

I remembered the sounds I'd heard over the last few days while I was at The Gateway. The car engine that shouldn't have been there, the faint sound of voices I couldn't place.

The sense that someone was in the woods. And the pieces fell into place.

Someone had been up at The Gateway this week – watching, planning.

But no. Why would anyone do that? *How* would they do it? The Gateway was secure.

'I don't believe you,' I said flatly, and reached for my beer. 'Besides, I saw nothing today. I went to work, and then I went home. And I don't know you, and I want you to leave me alone.'

Under the bar, out of sight, his hand shot out and took my left wrist, holding it tightly, sending beer spilling over the top of my glass.

'Listen to me.' His voice was intense. 'You're Maya Watson Landry. You're from Grand Rapids, Michigan, but you've been living in Lansing for the last fifteen years. Your mother's a teacher, you're not close. You married Brandon Landry – a mistake – when you were twenty-six. You lived together for twelve years until he walked out with a younger woman. That was when you came here and took a job at The Gateway. You have no friends, no boyfriend, and having a drink here alone twice a week is your entire social life.'

Hot tears burned my eyes and I twisted my arm, trying to escape, but he wouldn't let go. I felt stripped bare. Stripped and exposed as a failure.

'Who are you?' I demanded, my voice quivering.

'I'm your only friend,' he said. 'And I want you to believe me. If you don't, you're going to be as dead as the man you saw earlier today.' He shook my arm. 'You remember his face? Everyone looks like that when the wire tightens. You'll look like that if they get to you. Everyone dies ugly.'

I saw no lies in his face, only desperation. I couldn't seem to breathe.

At that moment, the crowd standing around the bar moved and someone bumped into him. Instantly, the man released my wrist and jumped to his feet, one hand reaching for the back of his waistband as he spun around. For a split second, I saw a glint of metal there.

A drunk kid in an MSU sweatshirt gave him a startled look and held up his hands.

'Sorry, dude. My bad,' the kid slurred, and sloped away.

The man watched him go, breathing heavily.

I felt the fight leave me. Whoever this man was, he was armed. And he knew my whole life.

My wrist ached and I rubbed it gingerly. I could see the red marks of his fingers on my skin. If I'd wanted to think this was all a bad dream, those marks said otherwise.

When the man sat down again, I turned to him, forcing myself to stay calm.

'Who was the dead man?' I asked quietly. 'Why did they kill him?'

'Come on, Maya. You keep asking the wrong questions. You're smarter than this.' His voice was tight, but he seemed rattled.

'What's the right question?' I asked.

He didn't miss a beat. 'How much time do I have? Where should I go? That's what you should be asking me.'

I swallowed hard. 'How much time do I have?'

The answer was short. 'Hours. Not many of them.'

'Hours.' I repeated the word in a whisper. The room was stifling, but goosebumps rose on my skin all the same. 'Are you telling me the people who killed that man are going to kill me tonight?'

'Now you understand.' He emptied his drink, the ice rattling as he set the glass down again. 'They're going to do it and I can't stop them. I wish to God I could.'

In that moment, he sounded so bitterly unhappy I believed him completely. And that's when I really, finally got what was happening. I was going to die. I'd seen that body and now it was all over. Just like that. All my plans, all my hopes, gone. Thank you for playing. Better luck next time.

My stomach twisted with such force, I doubled over.

He gave me a puzzled look. 'What's wrong?'

I couldn't reply — the tequila I'd drunk earlier seemed to be fighting its way out of me. I jumped to my feet and ran across the bar, shoving through the crowd. The song on the jukebox had changed again and Bruce Springsteen was growling something about showing faith.

The music followed me as I crashed through the door and into the street, where I threw up on the sidewalk, leaning against a lamp post, the metal cold beneath my hands. I felt wretched. Utterly confused, and completely alone.

When I finished, someone thrust a cotton handkerchief in front of me.

'Take it,' the man from the bar said. He must have followed me out.

The cool breeze chilled the beads of sweat on my forehead

as I accepted the white cloth without looking up and wiped my mouth.

Finally, I turned to face him, my shoulders hunching, braced for the next blow. But what came wasn't what I expected.

'I'm sorry,' he said. And I got the odd sense that he meant it.

'Me too,' I replied.

'What are you going to do?' he asked.

I made a helpless gesture with the white handkerchief. 'I don't have anywhere to go.' My voice broke and I fought to keep control. 'Why would anyone want to kill me? I don't know anything. And nobody believed me about the body anyway.'

For a moment, he didn't reply. He looked down the road, a muscle working in his jaw. I heard someone talking loudly across the street and the crashing chords of 'Thunder Road' escaping from inside Cooper's Bar.

When he spoke, the man's voice was measured. 'They want to kill you because you're the only person who knows what happened up there today who doesn't work for them. You're a problem. In their minds, the obvious answer is to eliminate you. Get rid of you, get rid of the problem.'

'How do you know all this?' I asked, blinking back tears. 'Who are these people?'

He shook his head hard. 'I can't tell you that. I'm sorry.'

'Oh, come on.' I held up my hands. 'If you know so much, surely you know who they are? Anyway, how do I know you're not one of them?'

'If I was one of them, I'd hardly be telling you to go right now, would I? I'm trying to save your life, Maya. That's all.' He held my gaze unflinchingly. In the glow of the street light, his eyes were a sharp, cool blue. And there was no deception in them.

My body sagged. 'But I can't run away. I've got a job. An apartment. Car payments.'

'Your job and your apartment aren't worth your life.'

'That's easy for you to say.' I looked away, my lower lip trembling. 'They're all I've got.'

Unexpectedly, he reached out and touched my hand, his touch gentle. He stepped closer.

'Please listen to me, Maya. You can start over. This isn't the only place for you.'

He made it sound so simple, giving up my job, and my home. But I'd worked hard to get here – to find a new life. And no, it wasn't perfect and I didn't love it, but I was just getting settled, and now I'd have to do it all again, from scratch. This time with a gun at my back.

The last few months had taken everything I had to give. My home, my husband, my money, my career . . . And now the few things I'd managed to scrounge together would go as well. Leaving me with nothing.

I felt utterly defeated.

'Look,' I told him with a sad smile, 'I know you mean well and please don't think I'm not grateful, but I can't do this. If these people come to kill me, well, it was nice knowing you. Give my car to charity. I don't have anything else.'

And with that, I turned on my heel and walked away.

'Maya,' he called after me. 'Please listen to me. You're making a mistake.'

But I didn't look back, and this time he didn't follow.

All the way home, my footsteps felt untethered from gravity as I searched for some way out of this situation. Maybe the man was a compulsive liar? Or he might be a psycho who enjoyed terrifying women. Both of those were possible.

The only problem was, I believed him. The way he'd looked at me before I walked away – the pleading look – that had been real. He'd meant everything he'd said.

But what could I do? It was one week from payday, and my bank account held three hundred dollars. The car had needed two new tyres a few weeks ago and that had wiped me out. I wouldn't get far on three hundred bucks. I didn't have a credit card any more. Brandon had shut down all our shared accounts when he left, and I hadn't set up a new card in my own name yet.

I imagined calling my mother to ask for help. 'Hi, Mom. Do you have a thousand dollars I can borrow to flee a murderous gang? No, I don't know who they are. Oh, and I need the money tonight.'

Ridiculous. The whole thing was insane. Of course I couldn't run away.

Suddenly I was furious with Brandon, of all people. It seemed to me that this was all his fault. If he hadn't dumped me out of the blue so he could screw someone younger and feel younger himself, none of this would have happened.

Everyone had let me down. Every man, anyway.

By the time I reached Barns Street, I was choking back

tears. I ran up the stairs and locked myself in my apartment, turning on all the lights and yanking the curtains shut.

The first thing I did – and this seems insane, looking back – was brush my teeth to get rid of the acid taste of vomit. You never know what you're going to do when you think you're going to die, but it turns out for me dental hygiene came first.

When I'd finished, I rinsed the toothbrush methodically and splashed water on my face. After that, I just stood there, resting my hands on the sink and staring at the mirror.

In the glass, my eyes were wide and frightened and my skin was as pale as milk.

'What am I going to do?' I asked myself. But no answer came.

The next few hours were a blur. I paced from kitchen to living room to bedroom and back again until my feet hurt, but I could find no way out. I couldn't call the police – after what had happened earlier they already thought I was a fantasist, so there was no way they'd believe this story. I might even get myself arrested; Jennings had made that abundantly clear.

Really, I had only two options – I could hope the man was lying and sit tight, or I could run.

At about one in the morning, I decided to run.

I didn't know where I would go or what I would do; I just knew I had to get out. Moving quickly, I started throwing things into a bag, grabbing items of clothing, bathroom stuff . . . anything that came to hand. I wasn't thinking clearly. All my senses were acutely tuned to the street outside. Every car that drove past made me jump.

Now that I'd made up my mind, I wanted *out*.

I was just finishing when I heard a noise outside my door. Still holding the packed bag, I stopped moving to listen.

The apartment walls were thin, and through them I heard footsteps and the hushed hiss of whispers.

I'd waited too long. They were here.

For a split second, I stood frozen, staring at the door, then I threw the bag onto my shoulder and swung around, looking for a way to escape. But my apartment was upstairs, and there was no back door. In fact, only one window didn't overlook the street in front — the bathroom window. But it was too small and too high — a narrow, metal-framed aperture. Surely I couldn't get out that way?

I heard a rattle outside the door, followed by an ominous scratching sound.

I held my breath, backing slowly down the corridor.

The sound came again — metal against metal, louder this time — and I understood. They were trying to break the lock.

Instantly I was in motion. I ran to the bathroom and looked at the window with despair — it was far too small. Only a child could get through.

But I had to try.

Through the glass, I could see only darkness. I threw the bag out and heard it land on the grass one storey below with a soft thud. Then I climbed on top of the toilet and began squeezing through the small open window. I tried not to think about how I could find myself trapped in that window, waiting to be killed.

Somehow I got my head and shoulders through, scraping

skin off in the process, and then it grew much tighter. I squirmed around until I was looking up at the dark sky, then pushed my heels into the toilet seat, trying to squeeze my hips through.

The air outside was cold and crisp, and the sharp edge of the window frame dug into my flesh. A rough piece of metal caught my jeans and I heard the fabric rip, but I kept going, swearing under my breath as I twisted my hips left and right.

And then, to my astonishment, I was through. My back wrenched as I kicked my feet loose of the window frame and dangled by my numb hands for a second. It took all my strength to hold on. In the dark night, it was like hanging in space.

How far away was the ground? I couldn't remember.

Exhaling, I closed my eyes and let go.

I hit the ground hard, tumbling over onto one side. My left ankle burned, and my breath hissed between my teeth.

In the late-night stillness, I heard a loud *crash* from above as they broke down my front door.

I forced myself up. My ankle ached, but it held my weight. Scooping my bag off the ground, I limped across the overgrown yard to the broken fence I'd always wanted someone to fix. As I ducked through it into the alleyway behind the house, I was glad they hadn't.

The narrow alley was pitch-dark, but at the end of it, street lights glimmered and I raced towards that glow, my bag thumping against my shoulder, my ankle burning with every step, my heart hammering in my chest.

Just as I reached the road, I heard the roar of an engine,

and a black car shot into view. There was no time to run or to hide. Its brakes screeched as it came to a stop directly in front of me.

The passenger door swung open and I flung up my hands to shield myself. From between my fingers, I saw the face of the man from the bar, peering out at me.

'Get in,' he ordered. '*Now.*'

For the duration of one breath, I hesitated. I didn't know anything about him. He was definitely connected to whoever had killed that man. He had to be part of their group, whatever he'd said.

But I had no one else to help me. And they were coming.

I jumped inside the car and slammed the door.

As soon as I hit the seat, he floored it, the force of the speed pressing me back against the leather.

In seconds, we were gone.

EIGHT

'Hold on,' the man told me tersely, and spun the wheel, turning into a side street.

I was thrown against the door with bruising force, and I clung to the safety handle above the window, trying not to cry out.

'Put on your seatbelt,' the driver growled, his eyes fixed on the road ahead.

'I'm trying.'

Clinging to the handle with one hand, I used the other to stretch the seatbelt across my waist, but he turned again and the belt escaped my grip and skidded away. I grabbed it once more and this time snapped it into place.

I twisted in my seat to see out the rear window. In the distance, a pickup truck turned a corner behind us and sped onto the otherwise empty street.

'Who is it?' I asked.

'I don't know,' he said, and turned again without warning, the rear tyres skidding out before he wrestled the car under control. 'I've never seen that truck before. But I don't like it.'

For a second, the street behind us was empty. Quickly, the

man spun the wheel, pulled into a dark alleyway and cut the lights.

We both sat silently, looking out of the rear window. Four seconds passed, and then the truck raced past our hiding space, its engine revving.

When it was gone, the street fell quiet. No other cars passed. There was no noise aside from the rustle of my clothes against the leather seat and the ticking of the engine.

'Did they see us?' I whispered.

The man kept his eyes on the street, his expression intense.

'I don't think so.' He started the engine, reversed fast into the empty road and drove in the opposite direction.

My heart, unaware the danger had momentarily passed, pounded until finally I sank back in my seat.

'I think we lost them,' I said. And then couldn't believe I'd said something like that.

'Maybe.' The man held out his hand. 'Give me your phone.'

I didn't move. 'Why?'

He turned to look at me. For the first time, I noticed that his hair was chaotic, as if he'd also had to run. The colour was high in his face.

'Maya, I'm on your side.' He softened his tone. 'Please give me your phone. I'm trying to help you.'

Still, I hesitated. I cannot tell you how much I longed to trust him, but all I knew for certain in that moment was that I was in a strange car with a strange man, pursued by killers

I'd never seen. My ankle was throbbing, and my phone was my only lifeline. I didn't want to give it up. And yet, when I thought about it, who was I going to call? The police, who thought I was a lunatic? My ex-husband, who had moved on? My boss, who didn't really know me? In the end, there was only him.

My bag was still in my lap. Reluctantly, I found my phone and held it out. He took it, rolled down his window and threw it out into the street.

I watched it go with regret but no surprise.

'Phones can be tracked,' he explained, before I could speak. 'I don't want anyone to know which way we're headed.'

I watched him sceptically. 'I thought only the police could do that.'

He didn't look at me. 'There's a lot these people can do that they shouldn't be able to. They're very well connected, and right now they're paranoid. That's a problem for both of us.'

City lights flashed by us, and I tried to catch a glimpse of the street signs as we flew by them.

'Where are we going?' I asked.

'The airport.'

'You're heading the wrong way.' I pointed back. 'It's north of town. You're going south.'

'Not the local airport. They'll be watching it. We have to get further away. Someplace they won't expect.'

I can't explain why this chilled me more than losing my phone.

'Who *are* these guys? You make them sound as powerful as the government.'

When he didn't reply, I turned to look at him. Beneath his dark jacket, the lines of his shoulders were taut, his attention flicking from the road ahead to the mirror to see the road behind.

He was afraid. And that made me feel better. Because if he was one of the killers, he wouldn't be afraid right now.

'Who are you?' I asked.

There was a long pause before he responded.

'My name is Riley Maguire. I'm a federal agent.'

I stared at him in frank astonishment. 'A federal . . . Are you telling me you're a *cop*?'

'That's what I'm telling you.'

I couldn't believe it.

'Why on earth didn't you say that earlier?' I demanded. 'Why'd you have to be so freaking mysterious?'

'I couldn't tell you before now because I couldn't be certain I wasn't being followed.' He shot me a glance. 'Talking to you at that bar was dangerous enough without telling you the one thing that could get us both killed.'

'I don't understand. If you're a cop and you know about the murder, why don't you arrest the people who did it?' I asked.

Riley kept his eyes on the road. 'It's not that simple.'

'Of course it's *simple*.' My voice rose. 'They're murderers. It's your job to put them in prison. Why are you running away?'

Riley's hands tightened on the wheel. 'There's a lot you don't understand, Maya.'

'Then *educate* me.' I glared at his profile.

The light ahead of us turned red, and the car rolled to a stop. Riley took his hands from the wheel and met my gaze. In the amber glow of the street lights, his face looked infinitely weary.

'I've been undercover inside a criminal group for more than two years, gathering evidence to bring down the organisation. They're a large crime syndicate with huge resources. They think I'm one of them.' He paused, his expression darkening. 'Or they did until today. I'm not sure what they think now.'

'I really don't get it,' I said. 'Surely you could tell someone. I told the local police and they didn't believe me. But they would believe you.'

'I can't tell them.' Riley's voice was even. 'It would blow my cover.'

'Oh, come on, that's ridiculous,' I said. 'A man is dead. Surely that's more important than your cover?'

'I'm not disagreeing with you, but it's not my choice.' I could hear the frustration in his voice. 'The FBI thinks stepping in at this time would ruin a multi-year operation. If we don't bring this group down, there will be many more murders. They want to leave this crime for the local cops to figure out.'

'How can they figure it out?' I asked. 'They don't have any information.'

Riley shrugged. 'It's their job to solve murders.'

I threw up my hands. 'But there's no body. There's no crime scene. There's no proof a murder even happened.'

'That was the whole idea.' Riley looked at me. 'And then you showed up.'

The light turned green, and we started moving again.

'You know, you really do *not* ask the right questions,' Riley said, as he signalled to pull onto the highway. 'Here's what you need to know. There will be a news story out by tomorrow saying that US Senator Robert Castleton of North Carolina has been reported missing. He was in Montana on a fishing trip with friends. He went for a hike this morning, and he hasn't returned.' He paused. 'He won't ever return. There will be a search. Many people will volunteer to look for him, but nobody knew precisely where he was going, so it won't be a focused search. His body will never be located.' He lifted his fingers from the steering wheel. 'Now do you understand what we're dealing with?'

I tried to speak, but my throat was so tight the words emerged in a shocked whisper.

'He was a *senator*?'

I remembered the body lying on the floor. The smell of sweat and death. The thin wire around his neck.

'Can't you tell the police?' I pleaded. 'You could do it anonymously.'

Riley didn't answer for so long I thought he wasn't going to. He stared straight ahead, his brow furrowed.

'To understand, you need to know the whole story,' he said at last. 'Senator Castleton was a greedy man. He's one of the people I've been investigating. I'd hoped to produce enough evidence to put him in jail for a very long time, but it's too late for that now.'

The last sentence seemed to be directed at himself, a criticism.

I watched his face. 'They killed him because he was greedy?'

A slight tilt of his head, a flick of the fingers of his left hand. 'Essentially. The head of this organisation had been *donating* to the senator for many years in return for certain . . . actions. The senator complied quite cheerfully at first. But when he wasn't needed any more, he missed the money. He made demands. Threats.'

A long-haul truck roared by us, making the car shudder. Riley waited until it had passed before picking up the story.

'At a certain point, a calculation was made that it would be best if the senator could not put any of his threats into action. And that was taken care of today.' He glanced at the clock on the dashboard, which showed that it was nearly two in the morning, and corrected himself. 'Or yesterday.'

'You couldn't stop them?' I pressed.

'I was not informed of the details of the plan.' Riley's voice was tight. 'They suspect they're being watched and the inner circle is getting smaller. This time I wasn't in it.'

The world outside the car had grown very dark. We'd left the lights of Bozeman behind and were winding through the mountains. Small towns and gas stations flashed by, each a star-like blink of light in the thick of the night.

'Why do you think they're suspicious of you?' I asked.

Another vague tilt of his hand. 'It might be paranoia on my part. Things have been different lately. Strung tighter. Killing Castleton . . . that was extreme, even for them. Then they sent me to follow you immediately afterwards. I think they wanted me out of the way while they got rid of the body. Now I don't know where they've put it, so I can't even help the police find it, and the odds are those bastards will get away with this like they get away with everything else. And because I was there when it happened, now I'm—'

He stopped himself with visible effort.

'Anyway,' he said, after a second, 'it's fucked. All of it. And I don't know how to unfuck it. But I'm not going to let them kill you too.' His hands tightened on the wheel. 'I've got to get one thing right, at least.'

For a while after that, both of us sank into our own dark thoughts.

I kept thinking about his words. *I'm not going to let them kill you too.*

It had all felt like a bad dream until that moment. Now though, it was real. The bitterness and worry in his voice had been unmistakeable.

Ahead, Highway 90 was a long stretch of black and white in the cold glow of the car's headlights. The further we got from Bozeman, the quieter things became, until it was just us on an empty two-lane road, weaving between the giant hulks of the mountains, their peaks lost in the shadows. I knew that in a while – a hundred miles, perhaps – we'd end up in the prairie, everything as flat as the business end of an iron.

Unexpectedly, I yawned. The dotted line in the road had begun to blur. My arms felt heavy.

'You should rest,' Riley said. 'We've got a long drive ahead of us.'

But I didn't want to sleep. I rubbed my eyes with my hands. 'Which airport are we going to?'

'Denver,' he said.

I straightened. *'Denver?'*

Colorado was hundreds of miles away.

He nodded. 'It's busy, and they won't be able to watch it even if they want to. It's the safest option.'

I leaned back into my seat, my mind working. Denver. It had to be nine, maybe ten hours' drive. But I was too exhausted to fully absorb it.

For a moment, my eyes drifted shut, and then I thought of Gina and they flew open again. My job. My apartment, with its newly broken door. My *car*. Was it all really gone forever? Could that be possible?

What would I tell my parents? Or Sarah? What would Brandon think when he wanted to tell me he was having a baby with his pretty, young girlfriend, but couldn't find me?

I can't deny that there was something quite pleasing about that idea. At least one good thing was coming out of all of this.

I knew my thoughts weren't making sense. I was so tired I'd begun to shiver, and my bones ached.

Riley cast a quick glance at me, and then, driving with one hand, removed his jacket and handed it to me.

'Wear this,' he said.

'I'm fine,' I insisted, although my teeth were chattering.

'It's the adrenaline.' He turned his attention to the road. 'It drains away and it feels like you've run a hundred miles in the pouring rain. Being warm helps.'

The jacket was soft and smelled of leather and fresh air. I slid my arms into the sleeves and some of the ice left me. In a little while, I stopped shivering.

My body longed for sleep, but I resisted the pull. There was so much I wanted to know, but my thoughts were growing muddy. When Riley spoke, he sounded far away.

'I don't understand why you went to that particular house when you did. You usually put it off.'

I thought about that spontaneous decision to go to White Pine Lodge. Why had I done it? I'd so enjoyed that morning, spending time in my dream house, and then I'd gone to my least favourite.

'I don't know,' I said tiredly. 'I was having a good day, and I guess I thought I shouldn't be. So I made myself go do it.'

He frowned. 'You thought you shouldn't have a good day?'

A puff of air escaped my lips. How could I explain? It would sound insane: *I don't deserve to be happy.*

'It wasn't a conscious decision,' I said, finally. 'I hate that house. I decided to get it over with, that's all.'

He seemed to accept this.

I thought about the emptiness up on the mountain. 'I don't understand where Ed was,' I said, thinking aloud. 'The security guard. Did he not see you? Or ask what you were doing up there?'

Riley gave me a sideways glance. 'Ed Anderson wants to

retire next year,' he said flatly. 'The people I was with made that easier for him.'

'They *paid* him?' I was suddenly wide awake.

I thought of gruff, grey-haired Ed. So protective of The Gateway. Accepting a bribe so a murder could happen.

I'd asked him about White Pine Lodge yesterday afternoon, and he'd lied without a hint of a qualm.

'What do you think of Gina?' Riley asked unexpectedly.

Again, I felt thrown off balance. He seemed to know everything about me and my life, and the people at The Gateway.

'I don't know . . . she's OK,' I said cautiously.

'Did she tell you not to go to White Pine Lodge yesterday?'

Riley's tone was casual, but there was something behind it that I couldn't identify.

'No,' I said. 'She didn't tell me anything. Why?'

There was a pause before he replied. 'Just something I was thinking about.'

I sank back into my exhausted thoughts. Riley made it sound like everyone at The Gateway was somehow involved in this crime, but it didn't make sense. Gina? Involved in a murder?

I thought of her expensive dresses and high heels. Her hand sliding a legal form across the table for me to sign.

Had I truly misunderstood every single thing happening around me?

What about Riley? Could I trust him?

I turned to watch his face, pale in the glow from the dashboard. His fine forehead creased with thought.

'Why didn't you let them kill me? You didn't stop them from killing the senator.'

Riley's eyes remained fixed on some point in the jet-black night.

'I guess,' he said, after a long silence, 'I'd had enough killing for one day.'

'That's not an answer.'

He lifted both hands off the wheel. 'Look, what do you want me to say? If I could have stopped Castleton being killed, I'd have done it in an instant, even though he was a terrible human being. But it's worse with you. You're just a normal person living your life, and you walked into the wrong house. You don't deserve to die for that. I couldn't . . .' He stopped, as if searching for the words. 'I couldn't let that happen. You were right earlier when you said it's my job to help people, and I've been failing at that lately. Maybe I've been failing for a long time.'

There was a bleakness in his voice that I could feel in my chest. I couldn't see his eyes in the darkness, and I wondered what I'd find there if I could.

'I can't keep failing,' he said. 'I didn't get into this job to fail.'

'Will you get in trouble for helping me?' I asked.

'Not if I'm careful.'

'But this group — won't they notice you're gone?'

'Not necessarily. They sent me back to Chicago tonight.' He glanced at me, his eyes glittering. 'All I have to do is get you on a plane. If I play this right, they'll never know I helped you at all.'

This gave me a strangely empty sensation. Like I'd stepped off the edge of something.

Wherever I was going next, I was going on my own.

As if he'd had the same thought, Riley said, 'I suppose we do need to talk about this. Do you know where you want to go? It can't be to immediate family. These guys will watch your parents. I wouldn't go to Michigan at all.'

I shook my head, my lips tight. America felt huge and limitless, but I'd spent my whole life in one small part of it. The places I'd heard the most about were all intimidating. I'd never been to California – it didn't seem real. Florida was sunny, but my dad was there. New York seemed overwhelming.

Suddenly I just wanted to go home. But I didn't know where that was.

'I can't believe this is happening,' I whispered, and buried my head in my hands.

I'm not a child – I know this sort of thing happens all the time. People step out of their houses one morning and their lives are fine. They've got a job, two kids, a car they're paying off, a mortgage . . . And then something happens – a car accident, a terrorist attack, a tornado – and that's that. Their house is gone, their life changes. Everything's different.

If you think about it, it's actually not that unusual for a life to be upended without warning. We should be more prepared. But we're not. None of us are ready.

We're all in such denial that when it does happen, it feels like you're the only one. You are alone, a pioneer in a world of complete loss.

Riley cleared his throat. 'It won't be forever.'

'How long do you think?' I asked. 'Weeks? Months?'

There was a pause before he replied. 'A year. Maybe longer.'

The uncharacteristic hint of dissembling in his voice told me longer was more like it.

Years, then. An unfathomable length of time. I'd be forty. Probably older.

My heart was a stone in my chest. It was as if I was staring down a prison sentence.

Everything was moving so fast. This car. This day. My life.

'There must be somewhere you want to go?' Riley said.

I shook my head. I wanted to stay in the place I was leaving. I wanted to go back.

For a long time, neither of us spoke. And then he said, 'How about Texas? It's big. And I don't think they'd look for you there.'

I'd never been to Texas. I tried to imagine it – wide open spaces, vast deserts, long freeways . . . And oilfields? Did they still have those?

I answered cautiously. 'I don't know much about Texas, except cowboys and pickup trucks.'

Riley smiled. 'Sort of like Montana, right?'

It sort of was, when he put it like that. If I couldn't go home, I could go to a place that felt a little like home.

I had to live somewhere. At least Texas was a place I'd heard of.

'What do you think?' he said, turning to look at me. In the

darkness, his expression was unreadable, lost to the night. 'If you go there, I know some people who could help.'

Outside the car windows, Montana was a dark blur. Most of it was behind us now, anyway. We'd be in Wyoming soon. Already my connection to it was beginning to fade. Montana was the past, whether I liked it or not. What was the future?

'Sure,' I said. 'Texas sounds fine. I'll go there.'

PART TWO

One Year Later

NINE

July turns Austin, Texas, into an oven. It's already too hot when the sun begins to rise, yet the heat increases steadily until, by noon, the streets shimmer like boiling oil. The glittering office towers and apartment blocks that in recent decades replaced the trees and grass reflect the heat back down on the people below, and the mercury climbs and climbs. On Sixth Street, or 'Dirty Sixth' as the locals call it, the bars are peaceful during the day and the restaurants are quiet. Like Bourbon Street in New Orleans, Sixth Street's action happens at night, so I always took the day shift when I could. I liked the emptiness — the sense that the street was waiting for the crowds to return. And I was relishing it as I walked to work — the faint, yeasty smell of spilled beer, the glitter of someone's fallen sequins on the sidewalk, air conditioning blowing an icy wave from an open bar door, carrying with it the smoky sound of blues guitar.

I'd learned to walk slowly in the heat — at two thirty in the afternoon, it was a hundred and thirteen degrees. You might think that was too hot for walking, but poverty is the mother of desperation and parking was insanely expensive. For months now, I'd left my car in a cheap lot at the edge of downtown and taken the last half-mile on foot. It only bothered me if it was raining, and today the sun was high in that pale summer sky and the air brushed my skin like warm silk.

'Hey, Lara!' The voice came from across the busy street.

I looked over to see a tall, curly-haired young man in a black apron waving at me from the doorway of the Pecan Café.

I smiled and lifted my hand. 'Hey, Gabe!'

'You want a coffee?' he shouted over the tops of the cars passing between us.

I gave him a thumbs up and he disappeared inside while I waited for the light to change so I could cross.

Gabe was a sweetheart. I worked around the corner from the Pecan and always went in on my breaks. We'd struck up a friendship early on that had survived him asking me out on a date and me telling him I was coming out of a bad marriage and I wasn't ready.

In truth, at twenty-seven, he was far too young for me, but I didn't want to tell him that. How could I explain that although I'd turned thirty-nine a few months ago, I felt seventy in my bones. The last twelve months had aged me.

Besides, Gabe knew nothing about me. He thought I was a former teacher from Kansas, and I intended to keep it that way.

What he needed was a sweet grad student from Dallas. Not me.

Of course, logic like this meant I hadn't gone on a single date since I'd arrived in Austin. I could talk myself out of dinner with any man in three minutes flat. Love is about honesty, and I was a liar now.

Maybe this was why I thought about Riley Maguire so often. I'd not heard from him since that night a year ago, but he lived in my mind rent-free. I knew very little about him, except that he'd swept into my world, ruined it and then saved me, all in one night.

When you don't know much about someone, you can fill in the blanks with everything you want them to be.

So I thought about Riley a lot, and didn't go on dates with anyone.

With my mind teasing the tangled knots of my past, I stood on the corner, barely glancing at the cars rumbling by.

When I'd first moved to Austin, I'd stared at every face, jumped at every shadow, slept with every light on. But after months of nothing – nobody following me, nobody asking questions – I'd stopped worrying quite so much and accepted that I was safe.

I still didn't sleep well, though. The nightmares hadn't gone away.

When the light turned green, I crossed the wide boulevard towards the door where Gabe had disappeared.

The Pecan Café was a cute, old-fashioned place with big windows and a bicycle parked permanently out front, its basket full of flowers. Inside, it was all polished wood floors and whitewashed walls, and the air smelled deliciously of baking cookies. At the counter, Gabe was waiting for me, holding a large iced latte with a single pump of mocha.

'My hero,' I said, reaching for my wallet.

'Don't you dare.' Gabe held up an admonishing hand, his smile sending dimples deep into his cheeks. He looked about twelve. Far too young for me.

'Gabe, come on.' I waved a ten-dollar bill at him. 'Take my money.'

He shook his head, dark curls tumbling into brown eyes. 'Wednesday is Free Coffee Day. Ask anyone in this room.'

I glanced around. A grey-haired man sitting at a table nearby with a copy of the newspaper spread out in front of him gave me an amused look.

'It's Free Coffee Day, all right,' he assured me, in a thick drawl. 'Didn't you see the sign on the door?'

'Oh, for heaven's sake.' I held the cold cup to my heart. 'You're a saint, Gabriel Rodriguez. Come in on my shift later — I owe you a drink.'

'Count on it,' he said, with a wink.

Waiters and bartenders in Austin look out for each other like family. I loved being part of that community. Contrast that with my own mother, who had not forgiven me for losing Brandon, and who believed that I currently lived in Seattle.

I was still early for my shift, so Gabe and I stepped outside and chatted for a bit, leaning against the sun-baked wall. Spotting us, a tall, skinny bartender from Ida May's stopped to join us. I'd met him before but couldn't remember his name for the life of me and it would be awkward to ask now, so I just smiled.

Gabe said, 'Hey, man,' and I wondered if he couldn't remember the guy's name either.

'I need one of your coffees or I'm going to die,' the

nameless bartender told Gabe. 'I have never been this hungover in my life.'

Gabe gave him an assessing glance. 'This looks like a three pumps of mocha problem.'

'Three at least,' the guy agreed, and changed the subject. 'Hey, did you hear one of our busboys was mugged last night right off Sixth?'

'Seriously?' I said.

'About five blocks that way.' He pointed in the direction I'd just walked. 'Took his tips and his phone. This place is getting wild. Be careful out there.'

Gabe glanced at me, suddenly serious. 'You working the three-to-eleven today?'

I took a sip of the creamy coffee and nodded. 'Jamie has class tonight, so I'm covering for her.'

'You'll be walking back?' He sounded worried. 'Should you take a cab?'

'It'll be busy by then,' I reminded him. 'I'll have a thousand tourists and summer-school kids to walk me to my car.' I glanced at my watch and straightened. 'Speaking of work, I better get on.'

Gabe went back inside with the bartender, and I headed around the corner onto Trinity Street, which shimmered in the afternoon heat. Treeless, it held a sprawling modern office building on one side and a small row of older shopfronts and restaurants on the other – new and old Austin staring each other down across a strip of tarmac.

The Speakeasy Bar and Grill was three doors down. If the Pecan Café looked straight out of a small-town square, the

Speakeasy appeared to have dropped into central Austin from Washington, DC. An awning in hunter green shaded the long row of windows. When I stepped inside from the bright sun, I had to pause while my vision adjusted.

The restaurant was done in sophisticated matt shades, the tables were walnut and the banquettes and chairs were leather, arranged to create an illusion of privacy. The deep green walls held paintings in dark wood frames. The air was a perfect sixty-eight degrees and smelled of grilling steak. Jazz swirled from hidden speakers. The overall effect was of an exclusive private club. As you might imagine, it was very popular with politicians and staff from the state capitol, who could walk here from their offices.

The governor came here fairly often, sometimes with his family but usually with an entourage that included a very attractive communications advisor thirty years his junior who always sat right next to him.

Everyone who was anyone in Austin knew the Speakeasy was a safe place to let their hair down. All the staff were warned when hired that gossiping about the customers was a firing offence, and I was fine with that. Gossip was a luxury for other people. I had too much to hide to find it entertaining.

'Hey, Lara.' Elaine Neil, the manager, intercepted me on my way to the staffroom. She was in her forties, small and curvy, with dark skin and a puff of hair that defied gravity. 'I'm giving you section three. Is that cool with you?'

I was pleased. Section three was in the bar; people there were easy to handle and tipped well.

'Sounds good.' I draped my arm across her shoulders and

tried to look at the table list on the tablet in her hand. 'How are bookings?'

She tilted the device so I could see the long list on it. 'Full to the brim. It's going to be a busy one. And I am so far behind, as usual.' With that, she hurried off towards the stockroom, clutching the tablet like a sword.

Elaine was a dream boss who clucked around us all like a worried mother hen. She had an uncanny awareness of who really needed her attention and who could muddle along just fine on their own.

I turned down a short, dark hallway, past the restrooms. The door near the end had a sign reading 'Private'. I pushed it open.

Unlike the dining room, the staffroom could best be described as having a modern prison ambience, with scuffed walls, rejected dining-room chairs, and the remnants of the waitstaff's lunches scattered around.

The uniform at the Speakeasy was all black with a white apron. I finished my coffee while I got ready, stowing my bag in a locker before grabbing a pristine apron from the neat stack in the closet and cinching it around my waist.

I dropped my empty cup in a waste bin and stood in front of the mirror to fix my face. I looked so different than I had back in Lansing that I barely recognised myself. My hair was short and blonde now, and I was about fifteen pounds lighter, although my face no longer had the pinched, hollow look it had acquired in Montana. The Texas sun had literally put colour in my cheeks.

The tag pinned to my chest read 'Lara'.

My Austin friends thought my name was Lara Gibson. They believed I was a thirty-six-year-old former teacher from Kansas City who'd moved here to try and make it as a writer.

This was close enough to true that I never felt like a fake. It was one of the things Riley had taught me during that long car journey to Denver.

I could still hear his voice in my head. 'Write yourself a story that you can believe.'

I believed in Lara Gibson. In fact, sometimes I believed in her more than I'd ever believed in Maya Landry. Maya had worried about everything until all her bad dreams came true. Lara simply did not give a damn. She worked double shifts at the bar, and took self-defence lessons three times a week. She was confident.

The door swung open and Nick, the lead bartender, burst in, talking on his phone.

'Well, just put her down and leave her for half an hour. Let her cry, she'll be fine.' Giving me an apologetic wave, he listened for a while and then said, 'I know. But you're no good to her if you're wearing yourself out, sweetie.'

Well over six feet tall and with an athlete's build, Nick was a guitarist from New York who did a lot of session work that didn't begin to pay the healthcare bills he and his girlfriend had acquired when their baby was born six months ago, which was why he'd come to work here. He had an infectious smile and a pleasingly strong accent, like someone playing a New Yorker in a film. Everyone lined up to buy drinks from him and tip over the odds.

'Well, you gotta learn to let her cry,' he said gently. 'The doc said she's healthy. You keep picking her up and it sets her off . . .'

I finished putting on my lipstick and closed the locker.

Nick ended the call and opened his own locker to take out a vape.

'Sorry about that. The baby's teething. It's awful to see her like that.' Glancing over his shoulder to make sure the door was shut, he drew on the vape. A curious chemical scent filled the air. We weren't allowed to vape in here, but everyone did when Elaine was busy elsewhere. The restaurant smells tended to mask the telltale scent. 'I think Abi's having a nervous breakdown. I feel guilty as hell 'cause I'm always working and she's alone.'

'You're supportive, though,' I told him. 'That matters a lot. She knows you're there for her.'

I felt like a fraud, talking about relationships and parenting. What did I know? My marriage had crumbled, and I didn't even have a cat.

'Yeah, it's hard, though, bein' stuck at home like that.' He drew on the vape, which clicked and rasped. As he exhaled scented steam, he gave me a bright look. 'You're section three tonight. The drunk tank. Nice one.'

'I love it.' I tucked my locker key in the pocket of my apron. 'Everyone gets really generous with tips after the third martini.'

'You got that right.' He laughed a puff of steam into the air as I headed to the bar, where I prepped my section with Chet Baker's velvet voice crooning 'Let's get lost' from the speakers.

The leather armchairs were mostly empty now, but it was Thursday and the afternoon drinkers would start arriving by around four o'clock. We usually got the business meetings first. The whole 'Let's discuss this over a drink and see if we can come to an arrangement' crowd. They were on expense accounts and so it was top shelf all the way. Later, we'd get pre-dinner drinkers, then post-dinner drinkers, along with those who hadn't been able to get a table in the restaurant and were settling for dinner in the bar.

In the calm before the storm, I wiped down the tables and put out fresh candles, and thought about Riley again, and that night driving cross-country. It was a year ago this week that we'd raced through the darkness across the Continental Divide.

Without any effort, I could remember every minute of that night. My sprained ankle, the cold air. The crash of my door breaking open. The way my fear had turned to relief and then exhaustion.

And everything that had happened later.

But it made no sense to dwell on it. Montana was long ago. Maya Landry had disappeared. Lara Gibson was happy and safe. Her life was good. The end.

'Hey, Lara,' Nick called from the bar, and tilted his head to where four people were waiting to be seated.

I straightened my shoulders and smiled.

Time to get to work.

TEN

As Elaine had predicted, the Speakeasy was packed that night. I was constantly on the move, racing from table to bar to kitchen, carrying trays of drinks and food, cleaning up, collecting money, and then starting again. It was relentless. Even Nick sweated at times, and he was a machine.

My section was interesting, though. Lots of political aides came and went, and four journalists relocated to the bar after dinner and worked through our supply of tequila as they celebrated someone's promotion. Nobody gossips like a reporter, and the people in this group were top of the game, sharing scandalous stories about this political aide and that senator and something that had happened in the bathroom at a party his wife hadn't come to. I didn't catch it all, but I gathered enough. In fact, I showed too much interest; at one point, the tall, thin one I recognised from the local CBS station pulled out a chair and patted it.

'Have a seat,' he told me, to roars of laughter from the others. 'You can hear better from here.'

All of them were regulars. One of the things I liked about the Speakeasy was that we kept people coming back. There were a few in my section, though, whom I'd never seen before. A group of women with expensive shoes and what sounded like Mississippi accents drank wine spritzers for a few hours. And later, two men sat in a corner, talking quietly and drinking more slowly than most of my tables. Their conversation looked intense but private; they always fell silent when I neared. They had northern accents, or at least no hint of a southern twang. And their suits looked expensive. I pegged them as businessmen, in town for a conference.

Nothing about any of the strangers set off warning signals. Even the quiet men were polite enough, and when they left, I saw that they'd tipped well. Can't ask for more than that.

Eleven o'clock rolled around fast. We were still busy, so I offered to stay late, and Elaine gave me one of those beaming smiles that seemed to bathe me in a warm glow of approval.

'You're an angel, Lara,' she said, straightening the tie of my apron and patting my shoulder in that way of hers that made me feel like her favourite daughter.

It was after midnight when I finally dropped my apron in the laundry bin, collected my bag and headed for the door.

After hours in the air conditioning, stepping outside was like walking into a sauna. The day's heat hadn't eased at all.

Around the corner, Sixth Street was partying hard. The famous neon lights atop the bars and restaurants lit up the sky in acid green, hot pink and mustard yellow, music poured from every door and window and a river of people flowed in a watercolour of baseball caps, miniskirts and burnt-orange University of Texas T-shirts, swirling around the barricades and parked bicycles before re-forming again and streaming on to the next bar or late-night restaurant. An invisible fug of greasy food, alcohol and marijuana smoke hung in the air.

I paused on the corner, my shoulders rising to my ears. I wasn't paranoid any more, or so I told myself, but I liked to be careful. You can't see danger in an ocean of faces. You can't watch your back with a thousand people behind you. But this was the fastest way to my car.

Stifling a sigh, I stepped into the crowd.

Right on cue, a man stopped in front of me. By my guess, he was about my age, but his edges were very worn. His baseball cap had a sweat line, and thin strands of brown hair straggled underneath it. His face was puffy and an unpleasant smile twitched his mouth.

'Hey, sweetheart. You all alone? Lookin' for a friend?'

'No,' I told him shortly, and walked away.

His friends howled with laughter. I heard him call after me, 'Well, that wasn't very friendly at all.'

They didn't follow me, but the encounter bothered me. Now and then on a night like tonight, a single moment could set my nerves on edge and suddenly I was timid, defeated Maya again.

Trying to shake off the tension, I chose a blank space in the crowd and dived into it, finding myself at the edge of a cluster of young women who paid no attention to me as they laughed and chattered, tapping down the street on high heels.

I stayed near them, skirting a recent pool of vomit with the skill of an expert.

'That is so disgusting!' the woman nearest me exclaimed, crashing into a friend as she tried to avoid the mess.

It was all normal, but I still felt uncomfortable, so as soon as I got the chance I veered into a side street and made my way to Seventh Street, which was much less busy.

In the relative quiet, I should have felt better. And yet, when a police car shot by me, blue lights swirling, siren wailing, I jumped.

It was as if my instincts had got the wrong message and were warning me, suddenly, that I was in danger. My heart raced and my palms had begun to sweat.

As I hurried through the shadows under the interstate, cars thundered above me, briefly drowning out all other sounds. After that, I left shining modern Austin behind me and walked into a faded fringe of scruffy old Austin.

A dog barked somewhere in the distance, and I heard a voice shouting in Spanish. The beating of my heart seemed loud now, and the thud of my black Nikes on the pavement echoed.

And there was something else.

I slowed, cocking my head to listen. Were there other footsteps?

I spun around, my bag swinging, fists raised, all my self-defence lessons ringing in my ears. ('Stay low. Go for the knees or the balls. Keep your head down.')

But the long street behind me was dark and empty. So why didn't it *feel* empty?

Beneath my black T-shirt, sweat trickled down my spine.

I knew perfectly well that I was being irrational. There wasn't anyone following me. I was fine. But my body thought I was in trouble. My body wouldn't listen to my mind. My breathing grew shallow and frightened, my heart fluttered painfully.

It's just panic, I told myself. Breathe. Stay calm.

But I wasn't calm, and as I neared the long, narrow parking lot where I'd left my car, I broke into a run, gripping my keys in my right fist like a handgun as I hurtled past a faded sign reading: 'Cheapest Parking in Austin. Save a BUNDLE.'

Gabe had been right. I'd been crazy to walk on my own tonight. I should have asked Elaine for a lift. Why hadn't I done that?

By the time I reached my silver Honda, my hands were shaking and I fumbled with the key fob, nearly dropping it before I found the right button and heard the click of the locks releasing. With a stifled gasp of relief, I yanked the door open and jumped inside, slamming it shut and punching the lock button.

I spun around to check the back seat, as I did every time I got in the car.

It was empty. Of course it was empty. It was always empty.

All the same, my hands shook as I clicked the seatbelt into place and started the car. The bright, cold glare of my headlights showed the rows of dusty cars and nothing else. Nobody hiding and watching. Nobody following. No danger.

I took in a deep breath and exhaled slowly through pursed lips, the way I'd learned. And then another breath.

Gradually, my hands steadied and my heart rate slowed to something like normal.

It had been over a month since I'd had a panic attack like this. When I'd first moved here it had happened all the time.

On one memorable day, I'd had three panic attacks and ended lying on the floor in the staffroom at the Speakeasy, sobbing while Elaine held my hand and said softly, 'You're going to be OK, honey. There are no monsters in this room. I'd never allow it.'

Elaine had been a critical part of making me feel safe. I'd never fully understood why she took me under her wing the way she did, but from day one she seemed to see through my façade to the broken woman who hid behind it, and she had just reached out her arm and pulled me in. She and Jamie – they had saved me as much as Riley had. I really believed that.

I shook my head, trying to shake my thoughts into place. Why was I so emotional tonight? It must be because this week was the anniversary of my escape from Montana. A full year of safety. A year of freedom. A fresh start.

I'd never dared to see a real therapist after everything that happened – what was the point when there was so much I could never tell? Instead, I'd checked out books on trauma and grief from the library, and I'd found things that really helped. I deployed some of them now, breathing in for a count of four and out for a count of six as I navigated Austin's street grid on autopilot. According to the books, that kind of breathing tells your body you're safe.

But you also have to say stupid things.

'You are safe here,' I told myself aloud, signalling left at the turning onto the interstate and waiting for the light to turn green. I repeated it four times, like a mantra. 'You are safe here. You are safe here.'

By the time I parked under the sprawling branches of the live oak tree on Dove Lane, I was calm again. It was nearly twelve thirty and the neat 1950s houses were all still. I walked up to the grey bungalow at number 47, unlocking the door quietly in case Jamie was asleep, but as soon as my keys clattered in the wooden dish by the door, she called out, 'Is that you, Lara?'

'It's me,' I said, and followed her voice. 'What are you doing up?'

The living area was open-plan, with a large lounge arranged around a limestone fireplace, and a small dining area backing onto the kitchen. Surrounded by piles of legal books, Jamie was stretched out on the sofa in her pyjamas and a long cardigan, her laptop open, glasses perched crookedly on her nose. Her dark, wavy hair was tousled and she pushed it out of her face as she yawned.

She had the bar exam in three weeks, and she was sleeping even worse than I was.

'Sorry,' she said. 'I can't believe how late it is. Did Elaine make you stay?'

'I offered.' I dropped down onto the armchair, kicking off my shoes with a sigh. 'It was busy, and I didn't want to leave them without help.'

'It's my fault. I shouldn't have made you switch with me.' Jamie sounded contrite. 'I know how much you hate working late.'

She had a slight Texas accent and the kindest heart I think I'd ever known. In the time I'd been in Austin, Jamie had become my closest friend. She looked so tired, I decided not to tell her about the panic attack on my way home. She had enough on her mind.

Reaching out, I tapped her foot lightly. 'Don't be silly. You had a class, and I got two hundred and fifty dollars in tips, so I can pay my rent this month. Which should make the landlady happy.'

Jamie smiled, but her eyes lingered worriedly on my flushed face before she replied. 'Well,' she said. 'Have you eaten? I made a veggie lasagne. It's on the stove.'

'I'm starving.' I jumped to my feet.

Aside from a few snatched French fries in the kitchen, I hadn't had anything since the iced coffee that afternoon. I was sure the lasagne wasn't a coincidence; Jamie knew I never ate when I worked.

The pan was on the oven in the small kitchen, covered in foil. The dishes had all been done and everything put neatly away. Jamie was like that. Living with her had made me neater.

I splashed some water on my face before spooning a generous portion of the still slightly warm lasagne onto a plate. After pouring a glass of red wine from the open bottle on the counter, I returned to the living room.

While I ate, we caught up on each other's news. She told me about her class, and I told her about the drunk reporters and Nick's teething baby, making her laugh when I did his New York accent.

But after a while, her eyelids began to drift and she yawned and stood up, stacking her law books into geometric piles. 'I've got to get some sleep. You going to stay up?'

'Just for a little while.'

After a late shift, I always felt wired. I knew it would be at least two hours before I felt sleepy at all.

Jamie stood and stretched. She was taller than me, with long, muscular legs. She jogged three miles every morning, and was constantly telling me I should go to the gym. I was always helpfully explaining that I'd rather eat my own hair.

'I've got class in the morning, so I'll be out of here early.' She yawned again, covering her mouth with the back of her hand. 'You probably won't be up yet, so I'll see you at work.'

I held up my hand as she passed by, and she slapped her palm against mine without slowing.

'Sleep tight,' I called after her.

I washed my plate and put it away before topping up my wine. Then I picked up the throw she'd folded and took her spot on the sofa, curling up in the warmth she'd left behind. It took me a second to locate the remote control on the coffee table, hidden behind a book with the scintillating title *Deconstructing Legal Analysis: A Primer*.

I switched on the television and cycled through the late-night talk shows, the movies, the endless reality shows, before landing on the news. There were floods in Missouri, there'd been a mass shooting in Miami, and the King of England was visiting India. I watched him walk down narrow roads, hands clasped behind his back, leaning forward to listen as a small group surrounded him.

After a while, I turned the sound down, picked up my wine and thought about my panic attack earlier. It still puzzled me, and I went back over the way I'd reacted, the sudden, crippling fear that had nearly immobilised me.

I wondered what Riley would say if he were here.

I took my phone from my pocket and scrolled to the R's in my contacts. Riley's name was the only one there. For a moment, my thumb hovered above it, and on impulse I clicked on it. His name and number appeared instantly with the green call button below. So tantalisingly near. I could dial it any time I wanted. I could do it right now.

It might seem odd that I could feel so close to someone I scarcely knew, but I genuinely believe when someone saves your life, you're connected forever. It creates a new line on your family tree, and their name goes above yours on the branch, right beside your parents.

My parents had created me, but Riley kept me alive.

He alone would understand how I felt tonight. He alone knew everything I'd been through. There wasn't one other person in the world who would get it. Even Jamie, my best friend, couldn't ever know. And Elaine, my surrogate mother. Nobody knew the truth.

Oh, this is stupid. It's been a long day and I'm tired and getting drunk.

Grumbling to myself, I drained my glass and walked to the kitchen, where I stood at the sink, peering through the window at the verdant little garden behind our house.

Dove Lane was very quiet – it was why Jamie had chosen this neighbourhood. Close to the countryside, where she liked to go hiking at the weekends, but still in the city.

'I'm a country girl at heart, but if I'm ever more than ten

minutes from a Starbucks I break out in hives,' she'd told me once.

I smiled at the thought. It was so her.

But as I stood at the counter, staring at the delicate branches of the plum tree backlit by the moon, it wasn't Jamie I was thinking about. It was that long drive through the night. And everything that had happened to bring me here.

ELEVEN

Each second of the journey to Denver is seared on my memory. It took more than ten hours – thirty-six thousand seconds – and I remember them all. I still don't know how Riley did it. He barely took breaks, stopping only for gas and molten, industrial truck-stop coffee. I was no help – exhausted and limping on a swollen ankle, dazed from finding myself on the run.

As I thought about it, standing in my Austin kitchen, it seemed a thousand years ago. And yesterday.

The first time we stopped was at a giant gas station somewhere near the Montana–Wyoming state line. In the thick of the night, with its huge array of lights, the place glowed like a spaceship. It was July but still cold enough that I could see my breath as I walked to the door. There must have been two dozen semi-trucks parked outside, and yet inside it was dead quiet and very warm. The smell of fried food made my stomach roil, and I ran to the bathroom and leaned over the sink, retching. But there was nothing left inside me to come out. In the mirror, my hair was wild and my skin looked blotchy.

'What am I doing here?' I whispered, and my voice echoed softly off the white tiles and the long row of empty cubicles.

I was going to Texas. Where I knew nobody. To start over with nothing.

The eyes in the mirror looked back at me with confusion and fear.

Something whirred to life behind me, and I started. But it was only an automatic air freshener sending a stream of chemical, floral scent into the air.

My nerves were wrecked, and I exhaled slowly, lowering my head over the white basin. I had to make a decision. Did I trust Riley or not?

If I wanted to run away from him, this was my chance – the truck stop was huge and anonymous. He'd made no effort to stop me from leaving his side. I could slip out a door and disappear into the cold countryside, and Riley would never find me. But where would I go?

No. Riley was the best chance I had. All I could do was hope to God he was telling me the truth.

I splashed water on my face, scrubbed my hands with the thick pink soap from a wall-mounted jar, smoothed the tangles from my hair with damp fingers.

When I'd finished, I found Riley standing in front of a display of sandwiches. For a moment, I stood just out of his view, watching him. In jeans and a dark jacket, he looked like any other weary late-night traveller. I observed distantly that he needed a shave, but the shadow on his jaw suited him. His brow was creased with thought, as if he were considering the problems of the world instead of ham or tuna. He seemed as tired and worried as I was.

When I walked up to him, he turned to me, his eyes

scanning my face, and I thought he looked relieved. Had he known I was thinking of running away?

'You OK?' he asked, and the concern in his voice took me by surprise.

'Yeah.' I stood next to him, gazing at the rows of plastic-wrapped triangles. It seemed surreal to be choosing food right now. But I was shivering even though it wasn't cold, and if my body was too empty to vomit I needed to eat.

'I'll have the turkey.' I picked one off the shelf.

Riley took a roast beef sandwich and headed to the coffee bar. I followed, watching as he grabbed two of the largest cups and filled them from the machine, adding milk and sugar to both without asking.

'I don't take sugar,' I told him.

Riley just handed me the cup. 'It'll help with the shaking.'

On our way to the cash registers, he snatched two baseball caps from a rack and added them to his growing collection.

At the counter, a weary-looking woman with tattoos completely covering her forearms rang up the purchases without glancing at us. While she worked, Riley added chocolate bars, bags of nuts and bottles of water to the pile, and she ran them through doggedly.

Finally, she handed us a plastic bag and said, 'With the gas, that's ninety-four dollars and twenty-six cents.'

Riley pulled a roll of bills from his pocket and handed her five twenties.

Cash, I observed. Untraceable.

The wallet in my bag held about two dollars and a debit

card I was beginning to suspect I might not be able to use. With each passing minute, it became more apparent how completely unprepared I was for what was happening to me. In some ways, I simply couldn't accept that this was all real. It was as if someone else was doing all of this. And I was just watching.

That changed when we walked out and I saw the way Riley's eyes scanned the forecourt; how he turned to look around the corner, missing nothing.

The cold fear returned to my stomach, but I waited until we were inside the car to say anything.

'Are we safe now?' I asked him, as we pulled back onto the highway.

Riley, who had been unwrapping a sandwich with one hand and steering with the other, paused.

'Nobody knows you're with me,' he said, after a second. 'They have every reason to think you're still in Bozeman. By the time they realise you're not, it should be too late.'

But I could hear all the things he wasn't telling me. The empty spaces between his words loomed.

I set my sandwich down. 'But they must have seen your car at my apartment. That truck followed us. They'll know you're helping me.'

Riley shot me a sideways glance.

'I told you earlier, they've never seen this car before,' he said. 'I bought it yesterday.'

'You bought it *yesterday*?'

He took a bite of his sandwich and chewed it before replying. 'I've been doing this a long time. I've got good instincts. Let's just say I had a feeling I might need a fast car. Let's leave it at that.'

I looked around at the leather upholstery, the flashy dashboard. 'But it looks expensive. Where'd you get the money?'

'Where my money comes from is not your problem. You're still asking the wrong questions, Maya.' Riley's voice was cold.

My cheeks burning, I turned to face the dark road ahead, holding my coffee cup close to my chest. I felt so helpless and frustrated. Every step I took led to a precipice. The only direction was down, over and over again.

'I'm sorry.' My voice was small. 'I just want to understand what's happening.'

A silence fell. And then Riley made a sudden gesture.

'I'm sorry too,' he said. 'I didn't mean to snap at you. I know you have questions, and you have every right to ask them. But if you're doubting me, or who I say I am, don't. I am on your side. If you believe nothing else, believe that. I needed this car. I had ways of paying for it, so I did. Let's leave it there.' He glanced at my untouched sandwich. 'And I wish you'd eat that thing. I don't want you passing out on me.'

There was no deception in his voice. No careful choosing of words.

Whoever he was, wherever his money came from, Riley had just driven me a hundred miles and bought the sandwich in my hand. I needed to have some faith.

I peeled back the plastic wrap and pulled out the sandwich. It was mass-produced, probably filled with chemicals, but when I took that first bite, it tasted delicious. I think I could have eaten cardboard right then. I didn't even mind the sweet coffee. For some reason, that tasted good too. The sugar seemed to warm my bones.

The miles rolled by in the shielding darkness. Riley finished his sandwich and rolled up the packaging, throwing it onto the back seat. I did the same.

The silence between us felt more companionable now, less threatening, and I uncurled a little in my seat, studying him over the top of the giant cup of coffee that sent heat through my hands.

'Can I ask about what happens next?' I asked. 'Because . . . I haven't got money to pay for anything.'

Riley's shrug said that was the least of our worries. 'We'll work it out. There are ways. You'll need a new identity, but we'll handle it. There's time.'

'I don't understand how I can just start over with another name,' I said. 'I'm not in a witness protection programme or anything like that. Won't I need documents? Proof?'

We went round a bend and Riley braked slightly as he replied. 'Do you have any idea how many people go missing in this country every year?'

I shook my head.

'Six hundred thousand.' He gestured at the tiny glimmers of light in the distance – evidence of small rural towns. 'That's more than the entire population of the state of Wyoming. Imagine that. The entire population of a state disappears in this country every year. And what happens to them?'

He glanced at me.

'Are they murdered?' I suggested cautiously.

'A few,' he conceded. 'But most simply run away. The FBI spends a lot of time looking for people who don't want to be found. And most of the time, we don't find them, even with our experience and our resources. The thing is, people run away every day. They're hiding from bills, or ex-husbands, from the law, from trouble. There are plenty of reasons to disappear.' He glanced at me, his eyes a glint of blue in the dashboard lights. 'If it were really hard to do, that many people wouldn't do it.'

After that, I lapsed into silence. I was going to join those people. Number six hundred thousand and one. Slipping into the corners of this country and leaving all my history in a furnished apartment in Montana, never to be collected.

Someone else would pack it up, give it to charity.

There was, I had to admit, something appealing about the idea. After all, what was I leaving behind that I'd really miss? Not Brandon. Not a thriving career – what a joke. Not a family who adored me.

When I looked at it that way, I didn't have much to lose.

Maybe, I thought, staring at the white line on the edge of the road, I can find a way to do things differently this time. I could create a life that *mattered*. I could learn from my mistakes and make better choices.

Soon my mind became lost in the possibilities of this odd future, and I must have fallen asleep, my head in the crook of my arm resting against the cold glass of the car window, the engines rumbling. I don't know how long I was out. I remember little of my dreams, save for fear and running, long fingers grabbing at my shoulders, voices shouting.

I woke with a cry and sat up, staring around wildly, trying to figure out where I was.

From the shadows beside me, I heard a voice, steady and calm.

'It's OK, Maya. You're safe.'

It all came back in a rush. Riley. The car. The senator. Murder.

Safe. What even was that?

And yet there was something remarkably steadying about Riley's presence. He seemed to fear nothing, and fearlessness is as contagious as fear. His calmness calmed me.

Still, I didn't sleep again that night. I stayed awake, my feet on the dashboard, clutching the remnants of my cold, sugary coffee until we pulled in at another truck stop.

This time, before we walked in, Riley gave me the baseball cap to wear. 'Just to cover your hair,' he explained. 'Help you fit in.'

He handed me one of the T-shirts he'd bought at the last place. 'And put this on while you're in there. Just in case.'

When I pulled the T-shirt on over my shirt, it hung down to my thighs, but I didn't ask any questions. As we crossed the forecourt, Riley looked around carefully. I should have thought more about it – if he wanted to change my appearance, he was still worried about being found – but it must have been nearly five in the morning by then, and I felt drugged with exhaustion.

This truck stop was smaller than the last one, but it

wasn't empty. Two sleepy-eyed men stood by the soft drinks machine, talking in low voices. They glanced at Riley and me as we walked in and then returned to their conversation.

Riley paid them no attention and headed straight over to the coffee machines.

'You want another sandwich?' he asked. I shook my head.

He betrayed no nervousness, but when he paid in cash, I noticed he kept casting quick, surreptitious glances at the two men. They'd moved to the food section now, and had their backs to us.

They were large men. One wore an old, stained baseball cap. The other had thin dark hair and his shirt had seen better days.

Riley never looked at them again, but as we walked out, he seemed tense.

'What's wrong?' I asked.

He unlocked the car and stood waiting while I got in. When he shut his own door he said, 'It's nothing. They look like truck drivers, but there are no trucks here.'

He was right. The fuelling area was empty except for us and a glossy black SUV. That must be theirs. There hadn't been anyone else.

I could see what Riley was thinking: they didn't look like the kind of men who would drive that expensive car.

'Do you think they're . . .' My voice trailed off.

Riley started the car and backed away from the pump, his eyes sweeping the forecourt, peering into every dark corner.

'I don't think anything,' he said. 'I'm just getting out of here. Right now.'

TWELVE

We pulled out of the gas station without haste, Riley keeping our speed steady. His eyes were fixed on the rear-view mirror, watching the dark road behind us. I sat staring straight ahead, my hands clenched in my lap.

It was the first time I'd really seen him rattled, and it scared me.

'Are they following us?'

'I don't see them,' he said. 'But I'm not taking any chances. Hold on.'

He slammed on the brakes, throwing us both forward, and then turned the steering wheel, taking a sharp left off the highway. For a split second, I thought he was driving into a field, but then I spotted the farm road half-hidden in the high grass ahead of us. I don't know how Riley noticed it in the dark.

The car fishtailed, and Riley wrestled it back under control. Before I could get a picture of where we were, he turned off the headlights and we juddered down the uneven dirt road in absolute darkness.

My heart rose to my throat. I couldn't see a thing.

'Riley,' I heard myself whisper, clinging to the door handle.

'Don't worry,' he said.

Finally, he stopped and turned the car around until we faced the highway. He kept the engine running but all the lights off.

Cars and trucks were nothing more than bright stars shooting by with a roar.

'What are we doing?' I could hear the fear in my voice.

'Let's just give it a minute,' he said.

I held my breath, listening to the rumble of cars in the predawn darkness, watching the flashes from the headlights as they passed.

I started to ask again what we were doing, but bit back the words. I was beginning to understand how Riley worked. The point wasn't to see the SUV go by, but to make sure the men didn't see us. He didn't know if they were looking for us, but if they were, he wanted us to disappear for long enough that they couldn't figure out where we'd gone.

I don't know how long we sat there – it was hard to track time in the dark – before Riley let out a small sigh and started the engine.

'I don't think it was them,' he announced, and began driving slowly across the rutted road to the highway. 'But whoever it was, they're long gone.'

We never saw that SUV again. But the tension from that moment stayed with me.

We talked less after that, each of us lost in our tired thoughts. So it was in near silence that we watched the sun rise over the flat, featureless prairies of Wyoming. I will never forget that view: vivid streaks of gold, amber and fuchsia stretching slowly across that endless black sky until the blinding rays of the sun climbed up over the horizon and chased the darkness away, leaving only blue and gold.

Neither of us spoke about the beauty of it, but I was so grateful for the light, I almost wept. There had been moments when I'd thought that night would last forever.

If Riley felt the same way, he didn't say. He just pulled a pair of sunglasses out of his pocket and kept driving.

It was early afternoon when we finally reached the crowded Denver suburbs.

Riley drove directly to a hotel near the airport, paying cash, to the surprise of the receptionist, who stared at the stack of fifty-dollar bills as if she'd never seen anything like it.

Riley smiled pleasantly and leaned against the check-in counter.

'I just sold my car,' he explained. 'Haven't had a chance to go to the bank. Might as well put the cash to good use.'

If I'd been her, I'd have believed him. There was no evidence that he'd just driven all night. He'd thrown on a blazer as we walked in the door, hiding his rumpled shirt, and the whiskers shadowing his cheeks looked artful. When he smiled, his eyes lit up.

The receptionist smiled back and handed him two room keys. 'Enjoy your stay.'

Conscious of the truck-stop T-shirt and the mud on the knees of my jeans, I'd hung back behind Riley while he handled the arrangements. When he handed me a room key, I felt the receptionist's curious gaze on my back.

The number written in her neat script on the key card's holder was 707.

Lucky number seven. That had to mean something, right?

At the elevator, Riley pushed the up button but didn't get in when the doors opened.

'Go get some rest,' he told me. 'I have some things to do. I won't be too long.'

'You're going out?' I couldn't hide my dismay.

His eyes held mine steadily. 'You'll be fine. I'll be back in a few hours.'

There was no point in arguing, and I told myself it didn't matter that he was leaving me, but as I walked down the long corridor to my room alone, I was filled with an odd, tense energy, as if I'd never done any of this before. I had to stop myself from running. When I reached room 707, I slid the key card against the reader and when the light turned green, I threw the door open and dashed inside, pressing the door shut behind me.

The bedroom was large and bright, with an oddly utilitarian floor of the sort you often find in hospitals. After the long hours in the car, it felt strange not to be in motion. If I stood very still, I could feel the tyres against the road beneath me.

I wouldn't let myself think about what I'd do if Riley didn't come back. He had to come back. Even behind closed doors, I felt exposed and vulnerable, as if the men who'd tried to kill me could see me here. I double-locked the door. But that wasn't enough to get rid of the feeling, so I dragged the chair from the desk and propped it against the door handle.

Then, at last, I really assessed myself. I stank of sweat, and my clothes were filthy.

The first thing I needed was a shower. I stripped off the garish T-shirt, which had an image of a big rig in pink and turquoise on the front, and dropped it on the floor with my muddy jeans. In the bathroom, I made liberal use of all the tiny free soaps and shampoos, and when I emerged, I felt almost human. Even my ankle felt better. When I opened the bag I'd brought from Montana, I discovered that I'd packed reasonably – including a toothbrush, underwear and jeans.

But seeing those familiar belongings sucked the oxygen from my lungs. I swayed on my feet, so tired and bewildered I almost couldn't stand.

I stumbled across the room to close the curtains, and wearing nothing except a damp hotel towel, climbed between the cool sheets.

Lying in that unfamiliar bed, I thought about my little apartment in Bozeman. I thought about the dead body on the floor. And I thought about Riley. I thought about that moment I woke in the middle of the night, and his calm voice telling me I was safe.

In one night, I'd become completely reliant on him. How was I going to travel the rest of the way alone?

That was my last thought before nothingness overtook me and I finally slept.

Sometime later, I was jolted awake by a knock on the door.

I woke in total darkness, and went from unconscious to standing erect beside the bed with my hands clenched before I could get my bearings.

Hotel room, I reminded myself. Denver.

Then the knock came again.

Tap tap tap.

Subtle but clear.

Hesitantly, I took a step closer to the door, the tiles ice beneath my feet, air conditioning freezing my bare skin. I'd lost the towel in the bed and stood naked in front of the door, with goosebumps crawling across my skin.

'Maya, it's me.' It was Riley's voice.

My heart jumped, and I glanced down at my body, skin pale in the dark room.

'One minute,' I called, my voice still hoarse from sleep.

I dashed across the room to the desk where I'd piled my clothes and grabbed a pair of clean jeans, yanking them on before pulling a T-shirt over my head. I was still tugging it into place as I raced back to drag the chair away from the handle.

The door opened with an odd whoosh of air.

Standing in the harsh glow of the hall lights, Riley still wore the same clothes he'd had on all night. The shadows under his eyes had begun to resemble bruises.

His gaze skated over my hurriedly donned clothing and sleep-tangled hair, and something flickered in his expression but was suppressed as quickly as it appeared.

'Good. You slept.' He stepped inside, closed the door and switched on the lights. 'I was afraid you'd just be pacing and worrying.'

We stood in the narrow entranceway, forced close together. He must have at least showered, because I could smell the clean scent of soap on his skin. His attention moved from me to the rest of the room and I followed his gaze to the bed – the covers mussed where I'd flung them back. The towel that had been my only night clothing lay tangled in the sheets, and my dirty jeans were heaped on the floor where they'd fallen when I'd discarded them hours earlier.

Suddenly it felt like we were too close to each other. I took a hurried step back, stumbling against the stupid chair.

'Sorry.' I rushed over to collect my dirty clothes, bundling them into a ball. 'It's a mess.'

He gave a faint smile. 'It's fine, Maya. Don't worry.'

Of course he was right, and it didn't matter. All the same, I snatched the towel off the bed and threw it all in the bathroom, closing the door and pressing my back against it as Riley walked across the room to throw open the curtains. Outside, the sun was low in the sky, already slipping behind the warehouses that filled this unlovely part of Denver.

'What time is it?' I asked.

'Just after five,' he said.

I blinked at him. 'You were gone hours. What have you been doing?'

'Settling some business. I had to get rid of the car, among other things.' He pulled a folded piece of paper from his pocket and handed it to me. 'Here. I've booked you on a flight to Houston. It leaves in two hours.'

'Houston.' I said it slowly, as if coming to grips with a foreign language. In a way I was. Houston felt as far away as Paris or Berlin. And I was going there without Riley. How was that going to work when I could barely spend a few hours in a hotel alone?

As if he knew what I was thinking, Riley took a step towards me but stopped, his hands at his sides.

'Look,' he said gently, 'you're going to be fine. I've got a plan. A friend of mine will meet you at the airport when you arrive. I've spoken to her, and it's all arranged. I'll explain it all on the way.'

She, he'd said. A girlfriend? Or just a colleague? And how could she help me set up a fake life? How could anyone?

'But what will I do there?' I asked plaintively, willing him to change his mind and come with me. Not daring to ask.

'Don't worry about that right now.' Riley picked up my bag, which lay open on the desk, and placed it in my hands. 'You need to pack. And then I'm going to take you to the airport and get you checked in.'

Still, I didn't move. I thought about our conversation in the car, about disappearing like thousands of people do every year. 'What about my name? Will I be Maya Landry? On the plane, I mean?'

'There's no way to get you on a plane at such short notice without using your real name,' he said. 'But I don't think that's a problem.'

'Why isn't it a problem?'

'The people looking for you won't look here,' he said patiently. 'They have influence and reach, but they don't have access to everything a government does.' He glanced at his watch. 'All you have to worry about right now is packing a bag, brushing your hair and coming to the airport with me.'

I touched my hair and felt the wild, sleep-tangled mess of it.

He was right. It was too late to argue about this. We'd talked it all through in the car. Besides, when you have few options, and almost all of them are terrible, you choose the one that scares you the least.

'OK. I only need a minute.' Carrying the bag, I went into the bathroom and shut the door.

The light was brutally bright, highlighting everything wrong with me. I tried to brush my hair, but it had dried wildly, so I pulled it back into a ponytail. I put on a bra and tucked in my T-shirt. When I finished, I was surprised to find I looked almost . . . fine. No evidence of the last twenty-four hours marked my skin. To any stranger, I'd be just another woman, tired at the end of a day, about to get on a plane.

'Are you ready?' Riley called from the bedroom. 'We need to get moving.'

And I was ready, I realised. I *could* do this. I'd made it this far, after all.

I opened the door and walked out to join him.

'Let's go,' I said.

There was a shuttle bus from the hotel to the airport, and we got on it with all the other travellers, sitting awkwardly on vinyl seats, neither of us speaking. Riley had taken my bag and his, setting them both in his lap. The ride took nearly half an hour, the bus stopping at other hotels before finally rattling up to the departures lounge.

Why do they call it a 'lounge'? It's more like a warehouse, if you ask me, huge and echoing, with screens flashing panic at you in bright red and yellow. It makes your blood pressure shoot up the second you walk in.

Riley, who still carried both our bags, was giving me a dizzying stream of information as we walked towards the check-in desk. 'If anyone asks, you're going to visit friends. You've got a round-trip ticket, so you shouldn't attract any attention. Do you have any liquids in your bag?'

'What? No.' I felt dazed, trying to keep up with him, trying to remember what I had in there. 'Just toothpaste, I think.'

'Good. Don't get stopped and searched. Here, this is for you.' He handed me a cell phone and charger. I stared at it blankly as he continued to talk. 'It's a burner. It's got a SIM card inside, but you should throw it away once you're in Houston and buy a new one. Let's stop here.' We paused under the departures board while I examined the phone. It had a fifty per cent charge. 'If you can charge it on the plane, do.'

He handed me my bag and I started to put the phone inside, but he stopped me, touching my hand lightly.

I looked up at him, and found a sudden intensity in his expression that made my heart stutter.

'There's only one number programmed into that phone.' He held my gaze. 'You can reach me on it any time. It never changes. If I'm working, it might take me a while to get back to you, but I will call as soon as I can.'

For some reason, this knowledge sent a flood of hope and warmth through me. It must have shown on my face, because he pressed my fingers with his and continued.

'Maya, it won't be safe for us to talk. For a lot of reasons. Please only call in an emergency. I need you to agree to that, for both our sakes.'

So, this really was goodbye.

'Of course, that makes sense.' My voice was even. I pulled my hand back from his and slipped the phone inside my bag, zipping it carefully before looking up at him.

Again, that flicker of something in his face. But it was there so fleetingly, I couldn't read it.

'I don't think,' he said carefully, 'we should walk to the desk together. It would be best if you go alone. I'm catching another flight.'

'Where are you going?' I asked before I could stop myself.

I was surprised when he answered without hesitation. 'Chicago.'

'That's home for you,' I said, thinking how far it was from Texas. 'I'm glad.'

'It's not my real home,' he said, and that small bit of truth felt like a parting gift, somehow.

He glanced at the board. 'Your flight is on time. It leaves in an hour. We have to go.'

I searched his face. 'I can't thank you enough for everything you've done. You saved my life. I hope . . .' I faltered, and then found the words. 'I hope I'll see you again someday.'

I held out my hand. He looked at it for a second, and then took it. His fingers were warm.

'What happened doesn't have to be the end for you,' he told me. 'I mean that. Make it the beginning. Go to Texas and make yourself happy there.'

My throat suddenly felt tight. I didn't trust myself to say anything else. I didn't want him remembering me as a weeping woman. So, I lifted my hand in farewell and walked away. I wouldn't let myself look back.

I checked in without incident – I wasn't even nervous. After all, what was there to worry about? I had a ticket in my own name. I was just getting on a plane like everyone else. In the end, there wasn't time for nervousness anyway. I had to rush through security to the gate, where the plane was already boarding.

Riley had booked me a window seat. When I'd settled in, I turned my face to the glass, a mixture of emotions churning in my chest – excitement, trepidation, anticipation. I can honestly say it was the first time in a long time that I wasn't sad. I wasn't thinking about dead bodies, or Brandon and my crappy marriage, or all the things that could never be. I was just wondering what would come next.

The plane taxied, gaining speed, the airport warehouses blurring outside the window in the gathering shadows. It was almost night again, I realised. One had barely ended and the next had already begun. And then the ground dropped away and we were airborne, unfathomably light for a moment, as buoyant as a balloon. Below us, Denver glittered, surrounded by jagged mountain peaks.

And then it all disappeared behind the clouds.

I let out a breath and leaned back, bumping my knee against the power plug in front of me.

The phone, I remembered. I needed to charge it.

I still held my bag in my lap. Opening it, I reached for the charging cable and noticed an envelope I couldn't remember seeing before tucked in beside it. Curious, I pulled it out. It was thick and quite heavy, as if it held legal documents.

It definitely hadn't been there when I packed back at the hotel. It was unsealed.

When I lifted the flap and peeked inside, I drew in a sharp breath.

It was filled with hundred-dollar bills.

Snapping the envelope shut, I glanced around furtively, but the woman next to me was staring at something on her phone and paying no attention to me at all. Nobody else could see.

Huddled over my bag, I opened the envelope again and touched the bills, flipping through them with wonder. Ben Franklin's dispassionate face stared at me over and over and over. I'm not sure I'd ever seen that much cash before. I didn't dare count it, but there had to be at least ten thousand dollars in there.

When he'd taken the bag from me on the shuttle bus, Riley must have slipped it inside.

Turning the envelope over, I noticed a few words written on the back in neat, square writing.

Start again. Make better mistakes this time. Call me if they find you.

THIRTEEN

My first glimpse of Houston was from five thousand feet above it. A sliver of moon hung bright and sharp in the distance, and all I could see below was a carpet of lights that seemed to stretch on forever. It was late by then, but I don't think I'd ever been more awake. I remember precisely how I felt in that moment because the sensation was so rare to me – I was filled with hope. It was as if the fears that had weighed me down since Brandon walked into the kitchen that cold spring afternoon had finally begun to lift. The key to it all was in the bag at my feet: I had money, and with it, the chance to change my life.

It was Riley I credited for that. In the hours I'd spent on the plane, still reeling from what had happened, he'd already begun to take on a kind of mythical status in my mind – Achilles striding to the rescue. I suppose I needed a hero, and he was the closest to one I'd ever seen.

I'd forgotten in that moment *why* I had the money, and why I was flying to Texas. I'd blocked all of that out, and I was simply letting myself feel lucky.

Walking from the plane into the airport, I clutched my bag to my chest as if it were filled with gold. I would have protected it with my life. It was all I had.

With no luggage to collect, I followed a crowd of weary business travellers straight to the exit, where my confidence quickly faltered. The arrivals space was industrial and mostly empty; the shops and rental-car desks were shuttered. A shambolic row of tired men in cheap suits held up signs with names scrawled on them. 'Davenport', 'Garcia', 'Epstein'. Their eyes flickered across our faces with a mixture of wan curiosity and disinterest. Behind them, a few people waited, glancing up from their phones to watch us emerge.

I hesitated at the edge of the group, uncertain of what to do. Riley had said *she* will meet you, but very few women were in the small crowd.

A dark-skinned woman in a T-shirt and jeans gave a cry as I walked out, but she ran straight past me to hug a lanky youth who had to be her son, so similar were their eyes and cheekbones.

Near a closed coffee shop, two other women stood together – one well dressed and in her sixties, with a puff of dyed blonde hair, the other a younger version of her in leggings – but they both looked right through me.

The air conditioning formed a chilly sheen on my skin as I slowly circled the echoing space, wishing I'd asked Riley for more details.

A steady stream of people made their way towards the exit, where signs promised shuttle buses, taxis, and parking. After a few minutes, I joined them, heading out through the automatic doors.

The second I stepped out of the building, a wave of heat

and humidity draped across me like a hot, damp towel; within seconds, I was sweating from every pore.

The collection area was dark and chaotic, with multiple lanes of traffic where shuttle buses queued in long rows to take people to hotels and distant parking lots. Taxis rumbled through constantly, offering their services to groups of travellers who stood amid mountains of luggage. The air smelled of hot tarmac and diesel fumes.

Spotting my confusion, a taxi driver in a stained shirt ambled over to me. 'You need a lift? Where you goin'? Downtown?' A cigarette smouldered in his left hand, and tiny clouds of smoke wafted at me with every word.

I took a quick step back. 'Oh, I—'

'Maya! There you are.' A slim woman in fitted black trousers and a snug dark top appeared at my side out of nowhere, beaming like an old friend. 'I've been looking for you *everywhere*.'

She had a perfectly oval face, dark hair and tawny skin. Her make-up was perfect, her eyes were acutely alert, and her grip on my arm was much tighter than it looked.

'I . . . I . . . was looking for you, too,' I said cautiously as she pulled me into a warm hug.

The taxi driver shrugged and ambled away in search of other prey. As soon as he was gone, the woman let me go.

'Sorry I'm late. Riley told me the wrong flight number.' The woman talked fast, her smile never fading. 'He likes to keep me on my toes. Come on, let's get out of here. I hate airports.'

Without waiting for a reply, she strode towards the parking garage. I hurried after her, the bag still clutched to my chest.

'Thanks for coming to get me,' I said inadequately.

'Not a problem.' She gave me a quick, interested look. 'I do have some questions for you, of course, but we'll get to that.'

She stopped at a machine and pulled out a card to pay for parking, and I felt instantly guilty that she had to pay money to collect a stranger. This entire situation was unbearably strange.

'I'm sorry, I don't even know your name,' I said. 'Riley wouldn't tell me.'

She gave a brief laugh. 'Yeah, he's Mr Security. Too many years undercover.' She held out one hand, meeting my eyes. 'I'm Amber. Nice to meet you.'

Her skin was cool against mine, her grip solid.

Releasing my hand, she turned to punch a code into the machine, and waited as it churned and spat out a ticket.

'Have you spoken to Riley?' I asked hesitantly. 'Is he OK?'

'Not in the last couple of hours. He called me before his flight left and told me it was all go.' She gave me a second curious look. 'He said he'd made sure you got on the flight. He was afraid until the last minute you'd bolt. He nearly missed his own flight, waiting for yours to take off.'

'He waited?' My fingers tightened on the bag. 'I never saw him.'

Amber observed my reaction with interest but said

nothing, tucking the ticket in the back pocket of her fitted black jeans and heading off again with a casual, 'This way.'

We headed straight to an elevator. Inside, Amber pushed the button for the fourth floor and tilted her head down to look at her phone, giving me the chance to study her properly. In the harsh fluorescent light, she looked younger than Riley, I thought – mid-thirties maybe – but her enigmatic expression reminded me of him. It betrayed no signs at all of what she might be thinking.

I should have been tired, but my body thrummed with nerves and energy until it was hard to stand still. Now that I was here, I wanted to get started and begin this new phase of my life. I wasn't scared any more – quite the opposite. Nobody could have followed me this far. The dead senator, whose name I'd already forgotten, was up near the Canadian border. I was a few hundred miles from Mexico. I'd done it – I'd lost myself in America.

As long as I stayed quiet about what I'd seen, I'd be fine. I had to be.

On the fourth floor, Amber walked confidently down a long row of cars, stopping beside a silver SUV.

'This is us.' She gestured at my bag. 'You want to put that in the trunk?'

'No.' I said it too quickly, clutching the bag. 'I'll keep it.'

'Up to you.' She shrugged. 'Hop in.'

The car was spotlessly clean and smelled of warm plastic and leather. When she started the engine, the icy breeze from the air conditioner chilled the sweat on my face. I tilted all the vents to point directly at me. Houston was a sauna.

Amber didn't sweat. Her skin was poreless, and despite the hour, her eyes were clear.

She wasn't acting like this situation was odd to her. If anything, she seemed intrigued by it all.

'Can you tell me how this is going to work?' I asked as she backed out of the parking space. 'Where are we going?'

'That's sort of up to you. How much did Riley tell you?' she asked, piloting the car onto the down ramp towards the exit.

'Not much.'

Amber retrieved the receipt from her pocket and fed it into the barricade at the exit. The light turned green and we pulled out onto a wide, brightly lit boulevard lined with chain hotels and vast airport buildings.

'Look,' she said, 'there's a lot to talk about and I think it's better done on a full stomach. I didn't get a chance to have dinner. Do you like burgers?'

Twenty minutes later, we were seated in the cheapest-looking diner I'd ever seen. The tables were well-scrubbed Formica, the floor was ancient linoleum, and the walls were rough 1970s wood panelling. A sign on the wall was mounted with what looked like a real steel revolver and the words: 'Protected by Smith & Wesson'. Country music poured from the speakers.

We ordered at the counter before hunting for a place to sit. Clearly this place had a reputation, because even after eleven o'clock at night nearly every table was full, but we found a spot in the corner.

Amber watched me as I looked doubtfully at the mixed

crowd, which seemed to include a sizeable number who'd come straight from a bar, alongside hospital workers still wearing their ID tags, and college students.

'I see your face, but trust me, this is the best burger place I know.' Amber tapped the table with her knuckles. 'In Houston, it's not the decor people care about, it's the food. We'd eat sitting on a rock surrounded by rattlesnakes if the cooks really knew what they were doing.'

I didn't have long to wait to find out if she was right about the place. A girl in an apron, her long black hair braided into a rope that hung down to her waist, arrived in minutes with a tray stacked with food.

'Two single beef and cheese?' Without waiting for an answer, she set the food in front of us.

The burgers were served in plastic baskets and wrapped in greaseproof paper. They were gigantic and came with heaping portions of home-made fries.

Suddenly I became aware that the last meal I'd eaten had been many hours earlier. I wolfed down half of my burger without breathing.

As she watched me devour the food, Amber's eyebrows rose. 'Didn't Riley feed you?'

I answered with my mouth full. 'We were busy.'

Amber took a delicate bite of her burger and wiped her mouth with a napkin. 'Look, Maya, before we go any further, you're going to need to tell me exactly what's going on. Riley's obviously made you a project, and I would like to know why.'

'What do you mean?' I took another giant bite. I was

barely listening to her. I had never eaten a more delicious burger in my life. And no matter what we were going to talk about, I had no intention of not finishing it.

'Fine. I'll share, and then maybe you'll share.' Amber took a sip of iced tea from a large plastic glass. 'Here's my story. Riley and I used to work together. I've known him seventeen years. We met when we were both rookie cops here in Houston.'

I stared at her, a French fry halfway to my mouth. Riley didn't have a southern accent at all.

'Riley's from *Houston*? Really?'

'He didn't live here his whole life. I think his parents moved here when he was a teenager. So he's sort of local. He went to college at UT, and then joined the police.'

It was impossible to imagine Riley as a floppy-haired college student at some gung-ho Texas university. Impossible.

'And that's where you met?'

She nodded. 'We started with the police at the same time, climbed the ranks together until, five years ago, he joined the FBI and I joined another agency. We stayed in touch, but lately I've rarely heard from him.' She leaned forward. 'My point is, I know him well, and in all that time, he's never asked me for help.' She searched my face. 'What's going on?'

I pushed my basket aside and wiped my fingers with a napkin, deciding how much to say.

'How much did he tell you?'

'He said you were in trouble and it was his fault, and that you needed a new identity and a place to lie low for a while.' Amber recited the facts almost clinically. 'That's it. If you want to know his exact words, he said, "I've done favours for you over the years, now I'm calling in my cards. You have to help her."'

I could imagine Riley saying it. I was touched and a little puzzled that he was calling in his cards for me.

'What's going on? What kind of trouble are you in, exactly?' Amber pressed. 'This isn't idle curiosity. I need to know this in order to find the right place for you.'

I cleared my throat. 'I . . . I found a body. In Montana. Yesterday. Someone important.'

'Somebody important . . .' Amber's eyes widened. She leaned forward and whispered the words, 'Senator Castleton? But his body hasn't been found.'

'The body disappeared while I went to get the police. The cops thought I'd made it all up, they didn't even make a report, but the murderer saw me. Riley says the killers are the people he's been undercover with. And now they want to kill me.' I drew in a deep breath. 'So we decided I should come here.'

It felt odd saying these things in a room surrounded by people, but nobody was even looking at us.

Amber reached into her pocket and pulled out her phone. She typed something and held it out to me.

The phone was open to the *New York Times*. The headline read: 'North Carolina Senator Missing in Montana'. It had a picture of the man whose body I had found. But here he was alive, his cheeks ruddy with health, his blue eyes smiling at the camera.

I took the phone from her and scrolled down.

Senator Robert Castleton went missing on Thursday, authorities said. He'd gone to Montana for a fishing vacation with friends — an annual trip, according to those who know him.

But on Thursday, he left his rooms early, leaving a note saying he'd gone for a hike in the mountains near their lodge. He never returned.

Senator Mike Thurgood said, 'Bob knows the area well, and is familiar with the mountains. He wouldn't take any risks. But it's wild country and anyone could have a fall. So we're worried.'

Gallatin County Sheriff Greg Walterson said forest rangers and deputies had searched the immediate area without any luck. Tomorrow the search will be widened to take in trails further afield. He's asked for volunteers to join the police.

'We know the senator is a capable hunter and hiker, but some of these paths are dangerous, especially after recent rockfalls. Anyone can have an accident. So we're calling on experienced trackers to help. If he's been injured, we need to find him before it's too late.'

The search will commence at sunrise tomorrow.

I read the rest of the details quickly. It was exactly what Riley had expected.

'They'll never find him,' I said, handing the phone back. 'But he *is* dead.'

My voice was flat, but reading those words had made it all very immediate again.

'You saw the body.' Still doubtful, Amber tapped the picture on the screen. '*This* man?'

I nodded. 'He'd been strangled.'

'Oh, fuck me.' Amber lowered her phone quickly, setting it face down on the table. 'This is big. Jesus, why didn't Riley tell me this?'

'Riley said he told the FBI, but they wouldn't intervene because it would damage his investigation. I don't think he trusts his own people any more. He's angry at them.' I met her eyes. 'They went too far, the FBI. They let a man die.'

Amber dropped her head into her hands. She stayed like that for a long time. When she looked up again, she said, 'Let me get this straight. As far as the organisation that killed the senator knows, you're the only person who knows what they did.'

'Yes.'

'And it's the people Riley's been undercover with who did this?'

'Yes.'

Amber said, 'We're going to need to bury you deep. I don't think Houston is right for you. Not right now. We need some place with a lot of movement – where people come and go. Have you ever been to Austin?'

I shook my head.

'It's a good town. Lots of students, politicians, tourists. You can disappear there. And there are plenty of places to live.' She nodded to herself. 'Yes, Austin for now. And then we'll see.'

To be honest, I didn't really know enough to have an opinion about where I should live, but Austin sounded fine.

'Next thing,' Amber continued. 'You can't be Maya Landry, not for a very long time.' She typed something into her phone. 'We're going to need new first and last names, social security number, driver's licence, and a fake work history.' She glanced at me. 'What do you do for a living?'

How could I answer that question? A housewife? A caretaker? A betrayed woman?

'I'm sort of a writer?' I said, doubtfully.

'Of course you are.' Her tone was tart. 'I can't help with that – it's too hard to fake. Do you have any useful skills? Can you wait tables? Tend bar?'

In that moment, it occurred to me that I had never been a useful person. From the start, life had sort of taken me into its current and I had bobbed along, a piece of flotsam. I became a teacher because it was easy, a wife because Brandon had asked, a writer because it was my hobby. But I'd never had any ambition at all. No drive. No control over what happened to me.

That's a horrible thing to discover about yourself at thirty-eight.

'I was a waitress in college,' I told her numbly.

'Perfect. You can easily find a job waiting tables, and then start writing under a new name. If you're talented, you can build a new career.'

I flinched at this blithe statement, and Amber gave me a steady look across the white Formica and empty food baskets.

'Don't get me wrong, Maya, I know this is going to be the fight of your life. Riley wants to save you, and I owe Riley more than I can explain, so by God, you're going to be safe, but much of this depends on you. All I can do is put a sword in your hand and a shield on your chest. It's up to you if you win or lose. Do you understand?'

For some weird reason, this made me feel better.

'I understand.' I met her gaze. 'I'm ready to fight.'

'Good.' Amber gave me a tight smile. 'Let's get started.'

FOURTEEN

The government can create a complete identity for the people they wish to hide, but if you want to hide yourself it's much harder. Luckily, I had Amber.

'First, we need a new name for you,' she said, after our table had been cleared and we'd ordered cups of coffee. 'Something you'll remember easily and learn to answer to. If someone says that name, your head will need to pop up, just like it does now when I say *Maya*.'

She said it loudly, and I jumped.

'That's it.' She pointed at me. 'That's the reaction I need when I say your new name.'

I thought for a while as I stirred the cream into my cup.

'I always liked the name Emily,' I said.

Amber gave a slight headshake. 'You need something closer to your own name. Two syllables, lots of vowels. What's your middle name?'

'Denise.'

'Not that.' Amber said it decisively. 'Any family names we could use?'

I thought about my aunt Juanita, my cousin Michelle, my ex-mother-in-law, Paula, and all the female relatives I'd known growing up.

'My grandmother was Lara,' I ventured. 'Her maiden name was Gibson. I always thought that was a pretty name, Lara Gibson.'

Amber thought for a second and then nodded. 'That would work. Two A's, soft consonants. Could you live with it?'

'Yes . . .' I thought it through. 'I like it.'

'Well, hello, Lara Gibson.' For the first time, Amber smiled. 'Say it to yourself. Repeat it. Get used to it. From now on, never think of yourself as Maya. Even when nobody's around. Whenever you do something, think, "Lara is taking a step. Lara is drinking coffee." It's weird, but after a while it becomes comfortable, and then you'll surprise yourself by forgetting it's not your real name.'

She spoke like someone who knew all about it. Someone who'd done it herself.

I studied her with interest. She was so intriguing. Like Riley in some ways, but at the same time very different. Self-assured, opaque, strong.

What had she said at the start? *He joined the FBI and I joined . . . what?*

'How do you know all this? Who do you work for?' I asked.

'Later.' Amber, who had been typing into her phone, glanced up at me. 'I'm going to put Lara Gibson in a safe house for a couple of weeks while I get the paperwork together. Have you got enough money to get by? It has to be cash. You can't draw from your old accounts for any reason. Not ever. You need to shred those cards.'

'Yes, I'll be fine.' The bag I'd thrown from my bedroom window lay at my feet, the envelope of cash safely inside.

'Good,' she said. 'I'll get everything together as quickly as I can, but it's a little tricky so it might take some time.' She paused. 'What about your past? Your bank account, your apartment, your job back in Montana?'

'Riley said he'd take care of it. I think he's going to tell them my father died and I had to go home.'

She considered this. 'That could work if he handles it right.'

At that moment, the bell above the glass door jangled. Every time it happened, I glanced up instinctively.

This time, I froze. It was two police officers, guns on their hips, bulletproof vests like ships' prows on their chests. They surveyed the room intently, as if hunting for someone.

I dropped my gaze before their eyes reached us.

'Amber,' I whispered. But she couldn't hear me above the blasting Nashville music and the chattering voices around us.

'Now,' she murmured, 'what's—'

'*Amber.*' I tried again, desperately not looking at the police officers.

Out of the corner of my eye, I saw two pairs of legs clad in dark polyester walking to our table. I gripped the Formica with my fingertips.

'I'll be damned,' a voice drawled. 'Bailey was right. That is Amber Karr right in front of me. Get the handcuffs.'

I gasped. Amber's head jerked up, and I saw one hand reach for her bag. But as she took in the two police officers, the hand dropped and a slow smile spread across her face. 'Mark Wilson, you've got to be kidding me.'

She stood up and punched the dark-skinned cop on the arm. 'What are the chances? Why aren't you in prison?'

Wilson's boyish grin took ten years off him. 'Because they ain't caught me yet. Can't arrest a man if he's too smart for you. What the hell are you up to, girl? I heard you're working for the spooks. But that can't be true. They've got an entrance exam.'

They all laughed. I stared at Amber, but she kept her back to me, leaning her hips against the table.

'Don't believe everything you hear.' She turned to the second cop, who was the same age as the first, I guessed, but balder and thinner. 'Bailey, surely you can do better than hanging out with this troublemaker. You're a good cop.'

They talked and laughed for a few minutes. Amber seemed perfectly relaxed, but I'd noticed that when she stood up she'd slipped her phone into her bag, out of sight.

I kept my head down, but after a while, Wilson glanced over Amber's shoulder at me. 'Who's your friend?'

Amber angled her body to include me. 'This is my cousin Lara, who just flew in from California. Lara, this is Bailey and Mark. I used to work with them when I was young and foolish.'

Forcing a smile, I said hello politely.

'I didn't know you had family in California.' Bailey studied me with interest.

Thinking fast, I said, 'Oh, I've only lived out there a couple of years. I got a job there.'

Bailey made a joke I can't remember now, and soon their attention slid away. It was Amber who held their interest. After a few minutes, she glanced at her watch.

'Well, boys, I hate to love you and leave you, but it's getting late and my cousin here is going to pass out on us.' She smiled at them. 'God, it was good running into you two. It's been too long.'

Following her hint, I stood up.

'Damn straight it's been too long,' Wilson agreed, still blocking our way. 'Hey, whatever happened to Riley? I ain't seen him in a dog's year.'

'Yeah.' Bailey turned back to her. 'The two of you were an item for a while, weren't you? What happened there?'

My gaze shot to Amber, but she didn't blink.

'Oh, come on, we were no more an item than you two are.' Her tone was dismissive. 'Anyway, he's in Chicago, I think, or DC. Working with the Feds. I never hear from him.'

'Can't believe both of you ended up in the big league.' Wilson shook his head. 'What happened to standards?'

It took more teasing and laughing, but we finally made it to the door, leaving the two police officers inside.

We walked to the car in silence. Only when the doors were locked, did Amber let out a breath and say, 'Jesus Christ. Why the hell did I run into them tonight?'

Without waiting for an answer, she started the car and backed out onto the street. Her brow was knitted, and I could see her thinking, calculating risks and dangers.

'They didn't seem to notice me,' I said. 'It was you they were focused on.'

'It's not now I'm thinking about.' She kept her attention on the street ahead. 'It's later.'

She didn't explain further, and I decided not to push it.

One thing was clear, whatever Amber said about everything being fine and my new identity being tricky but doable – she was more worried than she let on. Just like Riley.

Neither of them was telling me the full truth. They didn't want to scare me.

The following hours – even days – are a blur. I spent that night in a large modern hotel in far-west Houston. I stayed in the car while Amber got the key, and then she let me in through a side door. You might think I'd have a sleepless night, but as soon as she was gone, fatigue hit me hard and I fell into bed.

She picked me up at nine the next morning. By then, the concerns she'd felt at the burger place seemed to have evaporated, and she appeared perfectly cheerful.

When I got into the car, she handed me a giant coffee and a bag of doughnuts still warm from the fryer.

'Road food is calorie-free,' she announced.

That day – was it a Saturday? Who knew any more – we drove to a neighbourhood near the University of Texas campus in Austin, and parked in a nondescript complex of furnished apartments. One was to be mine.

Her explanation for how she'd arranged this so quickly was vague.

'We have a list,' was all she said.

She told me the lease was not in either of our names, and

that I could only stay there for two months. That gave me eight weeks to find a job and a place of my own.

At first that seemed too fast – how would I do all that in so little time? But when we stepped into the furnished apartment, I decided eight weeks would be fine, actually. Even Amber seemed dismayed as we surveyed the small, featureless rooms, which smelled of cheap disinfectant.

'Home sweet prison,' she pronounced, wrinkling her nose. 'I had to find something fast, but I didn't know it was this bad. Well, at least it's temporary.'

I didn't really mind. As long as I was safe, it didn't matter what it looked like. But it bothered Amber. She searched the house, opening every cabinet, muttering, 'If I find one damn bug . . .' But there were no bugs. Just a grim, dark apartment.

When it was time for her to go, she hesitated, standing in the doorway, looking from me to the scuffed walls and sagging furniture. 'Are you sure you'll be all right here?'

'I'll be fine,' I assured her. 'I'm going to explore the town, see if I can spot any help-wanted ads.'

'You'd be better off looking online,' she said.

'I haven't got a computer,' I reminded her. 'Or Wi-Fi.'

'Good point.' She studied me, her lips pursing, then pulled out her keys. 'I'm going to send you those documents we discussed, and those will help. No one can find you here, I'm certain of that. And nobody is looking for Lara Gibson, so you should be safe.'

'I am very grateful to you for helping me. I can't thank you enough.' I meant every word. 'And thanks for those doughnuts. They were amazing.'

'Well,' she said as she opened the door. 'Be safe, Lara Gibson. Good luck.'

I watched through the small bedroom window as she got back in the silver SUV and drove away. Only then did it occur to me that she never had told me who she worked for. She also hadn't offered me her telephone number, or any way to reach her.

I suppose in her mind she'd done what Riley had wanted, and now it was up to me.

I should have felt lonely, but I didn't. I was scared, but I was also excited. I had that curious adrenaline rush that made it hard to sit still.

Unpacking took all of five minutes. I only had three tops and two pairs of jeans, so right away, I was faced with the kind of practical problems that brought me down to earth. I needed to do laundry, for instance. And I needed more clothes. And food.

I hid Riley's money in the freezer – it was unoriginal, but it was my only option. After that, I set out to explore the little apartment complex and find the laundry room. It was around noon by then, and the sun was baking the streets.

The place was eerily empty – only a few people seemed to live there in the summer. Someone had left a half-empty bottle of detergent on a shelf in the laundry room and I borrowed from it before leaving the machine to wash the Montana dirt out of my jeans.

Back in the apartment, I took a few hundred dollars from the freezer and put it in my pocket, which made me feel like a drug dealer, and then headed out in search of supplies.

I liked Austin straight away. There were charming old houses near downtown, and the breeze held the green smell of cut grass and some sweet flowers — maybe jasmine or honeysuckle. I kept taking deep breaths of that soft, warm air.

I know this sounds crazy, but it already felt like home. I hadn't even been in the city an hour, but I knew I'd be happy there. It's weird how that works sometimes with places. It's like falling in love.

The shops around the campus were extremely useful. I got kitchen essentials, a few books at a used bookshop, and some bright summer clothes at a funky store where everything was discounted twenty-five per cent.

By the time I headed home, I was weighed down with my purchases. When I passed a hair salon, I stopped so abruptly the bags swung. I peered through the window at the bright rows of shampoos arranged like candies on a shelf.

Right now I still looked like Maya Landry. What would Lara Gibson look like?

Amber's only guidance about this on the ride to Austin had been, 'Do something different.' The clothes I'd bought that day *were* different — no jeans, for one thing. Instead, ankle-length trousers in blue and black, and no T-shirts. Lara was going to dress like a grown-up.

On impulse, I stepped inside the salon. A young woman with perfect blonde hair greeted me. When I asked for an appointment, she scrolled around her computer, and then looked up and said brightly, 'I've got a cancellation Monday at noon, if you can do that time?'

I said I certainly could. My calendar was free.

She considered my lank, dark hair with some concern. 'What are you looking for?'

I thought for only a second before replying, 'A whole new me.'

She clapped delightedly. 'Those words are music to my ears. I can't wait to get my hands on your hair, honey,' she said. 'What's your name?'

'Lara Gibson.' I said it without hesitation. Lara Gibson was going to have a haircut. Lara was going to cut it all off.

She entered it in the computer and I gave her the burner number before heading back to the apartment. I found my way without a problem, remembering the blue house on the corner and the magnolia tree with its long, arched branches. My steps were quick, despite the heavy bags. The heat didn't bother me; the traffic was fine. I felt different. I felt *light*.

I put my clothes in the drawers of the battered chest in the bedroom and the food in the fridge, like a normal person would. I opened the windows to air out the smell of cleaner and let in the scent of flowers.

For the first time, I believed I could do this. I could start from scratch and be happy.

I was going to make this work.

FIFTEEN

Those first weeks passed quickly. I didn't miss Montana and I certainly didn't miss Brandon. I'd changed, somehow. You know how when a computer starts glitching, the thing you're supposed to do is turn it off and on again? Well, it was as if everything that had happened had reset me. I'd come close to death – close enough to feel the ice on its wings – and I wasn't about to waste the time I had left. I saw Austin as a gift. A second chance.

And that wasn't all that had changed. In those first days, I altered everything about myself. I cut my hair short and dyed it blonde. For the first time in my life, I wore make-up. Sometimes when I looked in the mirror, I didn't recognise myself. I even walked differently, with new confidence. Lara wasn't timid. She didn't sleepwalk through her days. She didn't let the current carry her. She chose her destination.

Of course, I followed the news of the search for Senator Castleton avidly. As Riley had predicted, volunteers and police scoured the mountains but found nothing. Nobody seemed to remember Maya Landry reporting seeing a dead body the day he disappeared. Anyway, White Pine Lodge was nearly fifty miles from where Castleton had been staying with friends.

After a week, the images of police with their search dogs and the senator's broad, smiling face moved from the front page to page three, and from there to page six. After that, it went quiet.

As the days passed with no news, I began to believe it was over. Wherever the killers had taken the body, it wouldn't be found. And therefore the killers had no reason to search for me.

This comforted me until, three weeks after I moved in, someone knocked on my door. It was nine in the morning. I'd just poured a cup of coffee and I nearly dropped it.

My heart leapt to my throat. Nobody knew where I was except Amber. And that had been a man's knock.

I tiptoed cautiously to a window and tilted the curtain aside to look out. The apartment building was a 1980s construction — two-storey brick. I was on the ground floor, and my door opened into a charming courtyard — or at least, a courtyard that would have been charming if someone took better care of the plants. As it was, it was slightly overgrown, and the shrubs were singed from the summer sun.

A man stood in front of my door with a look of exasperation on his face, an envelope in one hand, a motorcycle helmet tucked under his arm.

He certainly didn't look like an assassin.

I reminded myself that I was safe here. And that nobody would send a motorcycle courier to kill me.

Clearing my throat, I called, 'Who is it?'

'Delivery for . . .' I watched as he turned the envelope

over, a slight frown creasing his forehead. 'Lara something. Can't read it.'

He pronounced it 'Laura'. He was young. No more than twenty-five. His sleeves were rolled up, and I noticed tattoos on his right arm of cartoon characters: Tweetie Pie and Daffy Duck.

Surely nobody with Tweetie Pie on his arm ever killed anyone?

Cautiously, I unlocked the door. I was barefoot, in my sleeping shorts, my hair still unbrushed.

The man gave no indication he was likely to attack. He just seemed relieved someone was there.

'Are you Laura?' he asked.

I lifted one hand, realising belatedly that I still held a cup of coffee in it. I'd completely forgotten it was there.

'That's me.'

'Good. I didn't want to take this all the way back to Houston. She said to make sure I put it in your hands.' He held out the envelope.

She said. It had to be from Amber.

'Thanks,' I said, taking it from him. 'Drive safe.'

'Yeah.' He said it doubtfully and walked away.

The envelope was so light it might have been empty. As soon as he was gone, I ripped it open. It held three cards and a sheet of paper. The first card was a Kansas driving licence in the name of Lara Gibson that looked too good to be fake – its holograms were perfect. The photo was the same image used for my Michigan driving licence, which I had cut into tiny pieces and thrown in the trash bin. The other cards were a blue-and-white social security card and a Visa credit card. The sheet of paper held a list of dates, employer names and phone numbers in Kansas. It was a complete work history. A note scrawled on the paper said, *Here's your starter kit. The rest is up to you. — A*

I stared at the cards in astonishment. How could I have a credit card in a name that wasn't real? How had she done this?

Amber, I decided, had to be some sort of spy. Not FBI, she'd made it clear that wasn't it. But she was something. CIA, NSA . . . some ominous trio of letters.

I sat down with my coffee and studied the work history. According to the list of references, Lara Gibson had worked in a steakhouse in Kansas City, a pizza place and a coffee shop, and most recently had been manager of a small family-owned restaurant in the suburbs. I had a feeling that every phone number would provide a glowing reference.

With this I could get hired, I realised. I really was free.

Later that morning, I bought a refurbished laptop, using a worryingly large chunk of the money from the freezer, and headed to a coffee shop with good Wi-Fi. That afternoon, I sent out ten job applications. As I walked back to the apartment later, I practised what I'd say in answer to interview questions.

'Why did you move to Austin?'

After my recent divorce, I was looking for a fresh start. I have a cousin in Houston, and I know Austin well. It's a city I've always longed to live in.

'How have you been supporting yourself in Austin?'

I have a small divorce settlement, which has given me the freedom to set myself up here. But I long to get down to work again. I can start tomorrow, if you want?

In my mind, I sounded confident. I was Lara, with her degree in English from Kansas University and her struggles to have a writing career. Her life was similar enough to mine that I forgot which of us was real sometimes. What is real, anyway? I could prove I was her.

The only problem was, I didn't get any of those jobs. Nobody replied to my applications at all. Nobody said yes, and nobody said no. They simply didn't bother to respond.

It turned out restaurants and bars in Austin weren't holding their breath waiting for a thirty-something divorcee new to the city to join them.

I filled out more applications, and I started pounding the pavement, popping into restaurants I liked the look of and asking if they needed help. Over and over again, the answer was no, thanks.

As weeks ticked by and the end date on the tiny apartment loomed, my worries rose.

The freezer stash of Riley's cash was getting smaller. Each time I took out another bill, I felt like I was draining my own life's blood. I didn't dare count how much was left.

I couldn't call anyone for help; I'd already been given the best head start. I had to find work.

Besides, my own parents believed I was living in Seattle, working for a website. My mother was thrilled that I finally had 'a real job'. Every time I spoke to her, she asked how Brandon was doing, so you can imagine how often I called.

No, there was nobody who could help me get through this. I simply had to head out again and find places where I hadn't yet applied. Which was why, late one afternoon, I walked into the Speakeasy.

I'd been exploring the side streets off Sixth, stopping in every restaurant. A few minutes earlier, I'd met Gabe, the manager at the Pecan Café, for the first time. With real regret, he told me they didn't need help right now, but he'd keep my details. He told me that sometimes they needed part-time help after the students and legislators returned to the city in September. He gave me an iced latte for free as consolation – the first of many.

It was when I walked out of the Pecan into the late-afternoon sun that I spotted the neatly striped green awning in front of a restaurant around the corner. I was tired by then, and feeling defeated, and all I wanted was to go home. But the Speakeasy looked promising.

When I stepped inside the restaurant, the air felt cool and dry against my skin, and jazz streamed jauntily through the speakers. It was late afternoon, in the lull between lunch and dinner, and the dining room was empty, but in the bar, a group of tourists in shorts and T-shirts sat drinking longneck beers, while at another table two men in suits were examining something on an electronic tablet and talking quietly.

I seated myself on a high leather bar stool with relief. My feet ached from walking and my soul hurt from rejection.

Giving up wasn't an option, but in that moment it was pretty tempting.

I rested my chin on my hand as I stared at the rows of gleaming bottles. They were so clean, not a speck of dust on them. It was as if they were polished daily.

I could do that job, I thought wistfully.

'Good Lord, what happened?' a female voice asked.

I looked up to see a tall, athletic woman with dark curly hair and warm brown eyes standing behind the bar, looking at me with bemused concern.

I straightened. 'What do you mean?'

'You are the picture of dejection.' She had a musical Texas accent and the most sympathetic voice I think I've ever heard. It was the kind of voice you pour out your worries to. A perfect bartender's voice.

'It's nothing.' I tried to look more positive. 'I've just been job hunting.'

'I see.' She reached for a silver cocktail shaker and held it up. 'You need a drink. What's your poison? Do you like margaritas?'

'I do,' I said slowly, thinking about my tired feet. 'But I shouldn't. I need to try a few more places today.'

'Oh, hell no.' She spoke decisively. 'You're done for the day. What your face says to me is, "I need a margarita or I'm going to throw my next application through a window tied to a brick." And that won't get you far.'

Even as she spoke, she'd begun to pull out bottles of top-shelf tequila and triple sec and set them in front of me.

'What is it with people making me drink things?' I asked. 'The guy at the Pecan made me drink iced coffee.'

'Gabe?' She smiled, pouring tequila into the shaker. 'Gabe is pure gold. An angel from heaven. That wasn't coffee, that was manna. He was feeding your soul.'

She shook the shaker with a professional's strength and speed, flipping it in the air and catching it right side up. She gave me a cheeky smile. 'People tip extra for that move, but you get it for free.'

She poured two salt-rimmed glasses full to the brim and set one on a jaunty green-and-white coaster in front of me. Lifting her glass, she held it up until I raised mine.

'Here's to getting that job,' she said. Our glasses clinked.

I took a sip. Ice-cold, smooth lime and tequila – if there's anything more refreshing than that on a hot day, I've never heard of it.

I sighed. 'Damn, that's good.'

She grinned. 'The bartender here is *amazing*.'

Despite everything, despite my day, I found myself laughing. 'She really is.'

She leaned an elbow on the bar, her eyes studying me contemplatively. 'What kind of job are you looking for?'

'Anything,' I said. 'Waiting tables, cleaning. I managed a place back home in Kansas, but I'm happy to start on the bottom rung here.'

'You're new in town?'

'I've been here five weeks. I'm in a temporary rental and that expires soon, and I need a job to get a permanent place. You know the drill.'

'We've all been there.' Her eyes studied me thoughtfully. 'Are you a student?'

'No. Just a worker bee.'

'I doubt that.' She took a sip of her drink. 'What's your passion? Nobody moves here just to wait tables. Everyone in Austin is a musician or an actor, a screenwriter . . . Everyone's looking for a little magic.'

I flushed. 'I'm a writer,' I confessed. 'Or at least put "aspiring" before that.'

She clapped her hands. 'I was going to guess writer. You didn't strike me as a guitar player. You're too friendly.'

'What about you?' I took a sip of my drink. 'What's your passion?'

'Oh, I'm the worst.' She feigned seriousness. 'I'm a law student. I'm going to make the world terrible. You know the old joke: What do you call ten lawyers chained at the bottom of the ocean?'

I shook my head. 'I don't know.'

'A start.'

I laughed. 'That's horrible.'

'And yet so funny.'

'If it's awful, why do you want to do it?' I asked. 'Why be a lawyer?'

She picked up a cloth and began polishing the already clean bar. 'I just love it. Law books, courtrooms, the arcane rules, judges – the whole thing. All rise, hear ye, hear ye . . . I love it all.'

There was truth in her voice, and I wondered what it would feel like to love what I did for a living that much. I wanted to experience that someday – to be so certain I was doing the right thing with my life.

She tilted her head, considering me. 'Are you a good waitress?'

I hesitated, just for a second. For some reason I didn't want to lie to her. She had a kind of gentle honesty that you could see from the first moment. She wore it on her skin. She glowed with kindness.

But I *really* needed a job.

'Well, I was a manager for a while, so I might be a bit rusty. But I was good before I got lazy.'

She didn't reply right away. Instead, she watched me, as if making up her mind. Then she straightened, sweeping up both our empty glasses and setting them in the sink.

'What's your name?'

'Lara Gibson.'

'My name's Jamie. Wait here a second. There's someone you need to talk to.'

Before I could ask what she meant, she disappeared through a door.

As she left, I didn't dare to hope. I don't know how many places had rejected me in the last couple of weeks, so many that I'd sort of forgotten that acceptance was possible.

Hastily, I grabbed my small bag off the back of the seat, pulled out a compact and powdered the shine off my nose, smoothing my hair with quick motions. In the mirror, my eyes looked bright.

I'd just set the bag down when the door swung open and a

small, curvy woman with dark skin and a watchful expression emerged, holding a laptop in one hand, which she set on the bar as she stood next to me. Her posture was as straight as a dancer's, and she examined me with the attention of a psychologist before speaking.

'You're Lara?'

I swallowed hard. 'Yes.'

'I'm Elaine Neil, I manage the Speakeasy.' She had a strong voice – one that was used to being listened to. Something in her cautious demeanour told me she wasn't thrilled that Jamie had dropped this in her lap. All the same, she was here talking to me, and that was a good sign.

'It's nice to meet you.' I sat up straighter. 'I'm sorry for showing up without an appointment, but I was passing.'

'I get it,' she said. 'It's hard out there right now. So many students work locally, and a lot of places prefer to hire them because they're cheap.' She tapped the bar with her fingertip. Three gentle thumps. 'We don't do that. We like our staff to be permanent. Our customers are mostly regulars, and they want to see the same faces every time they come. We're a family here – that's how we want it. Are you looking for a permanent place?'

'I am.' This, at least, was true.

Still she watched me. 'Jamie says you're a writer?'

'Well.' I flushed. 'I want to write. I don't have any published work yet. And I would do it on my own time, I want to make that clear. When I'm at work, my attention is on the job I'm doing. Nothing else.'

'That's what I like to hear.'

'I like this place – I want to work here,' I told her quickly. 'I'll clean. I'll wait tables. I'll tend bar. Anything you need.'

Elaine held up a hand. 'Hold on. I've got a few questions.' But she sounded amused. 'Jamie says you managed a place in . . .' Her brow furrowed. 'Where are you from again?'

'Kansas.'

'Right.' Her expression told me she had no particular thoughts about Kansas. 'Well, we don't need a manager, that's my job.'

'*God no.* That's not what I . . . I'm just looking for . . . I'll do whatever . . .' I fumbled my words.

'Don't panic.' Elaine held up a hand. 'I'm not offended. Just giving you the lay of the land. I don't want any confusion.'

We both fell silent.

I could sense that she was making up her mind. It only took seconds, but it was excruciating.

Instead of speaking, she turned the computer around to face me. The screen held a blank electronic application form. She tapped it with a short, neatly manicured nail.

'Fill this in,' she said. 'Then we'll talk.'

I filled in the form with my well-rehearsed pack of lies, and in the interview that followed, I finally got to say all the things I'd been practising for weeks.

I started my first shift that night, working as a barback for Jamie. The next day, they tried me waiting tables, and everybody agreed that was a better place for me.

After the first week, they put me in the permanent rotation and the freezer money stash stopped shrinking. With only days until the sublease on the terrible apartment ran out, I began looking for a new place to live. When I mentioned this to Elaine, she told me casually, 'You should talk to Jamie. She's looking for a housemate to help pay the bills.'

And with that, the last piece fell into place. Maya Landry was gone forever. Lara Gibson was happy at last.

SIXTEEN

And so I settled into being Lara. I loved my job, and I loved Austin. In the early days, I still had occasional panic attacks that knocked me flat, but those went away with time. Eventually, life as Lara felt wonderfully normal. And after a while, I didn't think about Maya any more.

In what little spare time I had, I wrote short pieces for *Time Out Austin*, an arts and entertainment website. I'd started doing it for free at first, but then I got a tiny fee for each piece they accepted. Mostly I wrote observations about moving to Austin, along with advice for newcomers – the best art, the best theatres, the best music clubs, that sort of thing.

This was why, one Saturday, midway through a double shift, I was spending my dinner break in the staffroom writing a last-minute article.

When Elaine bustled in with her tablet in her hand, she waved her reading glasses at me accusingly. 'Is this how you take breaks now?'

I looked up at her desperately. 'Help. I've got to write seven hundred words about Mexican food in Austin. Right now, even two hundred words seems like too many.'

Elaine trained a glare at me. 'You want my help? Do I get a percentage?'

'You want a percentage of twenty-five bucks?' I asked. 'How about five dollars?'

'Tell them enchiladas are underrated,' Elaine said, as if I hadn't spoken. 'Also, there's a place called Polvos on First Street that's wonderful. A friend of mine runs it. And tell me this, why is everyone so obsessed with burritos? They all taste the same, no matter where you buy them.' She pointed at the steak sandwich sitting at my elbow. 'Now, you can pay me back by eating that. You need vitamins.'

'Yes, Mom.' I laughed.

'Hmph.' Elaine's disapproving expression spoke for her. For a while, she fussed around, straightening the room, making sure I ate, before she hurried out again, tablet in hand, muttering to herself.

I would never have admitted it to her, but I loved how much she worried about me. She was more of a mother to me than the one God gave me.

My own mother didn't seem to miss me, so I hadn't felt it necessary to inform her that I'd used a thousand pounds of the freezer cash and a significant amount of my tips to hire a divorce attorney back in Michigan to get me out of that marriage.

The process had been complicated by the fact that Maya Landry didn't really exist any more, but I was getting better at this. First, I'd got a post office box in Seattle – you can rent them online, it's surprisingly easy. The contents of that box were forwarded to a PO box in Austin once a month. I picked it all up in person.

And so it was that ten months after I moved to Austin,

and two months before Elaine chided me about eating my sandwich in the staffroom, I'd received my divorce documents.

When I held the papers in my hands — proof that I was free of my marriage and free of the past — I thought I'd feel happy, but that wasn't the emotion at all.

It was all over. Brandon and I had met in our twenties and got married too soon. I had been hurt for so long by the way he'd left me, it was hard to believe I had ever loved him. But I had.

I could remember every moment of the day I met him, at a party. He'd been sitting on the sofa, laughing at a joke, fair-haired and blue-eyed, and he'd looked up as I walked in. And the way he looked at me — I'd felt noticed.

Later we'd talked in the crowded kitchen as people milled around us. We'd kissed for the first time at two in the morning on the back porch, the moon shining on us like a beacon.

I was shy and cautious, and he was brash and determined — we didn't make sense as a couple. When our friends found out we were dating, they were bemused. My friend Sarah, who had known me since college, said, 'But he's an accountant.' Like someone else might say, 'But he's a criminal.'

'I like him even though he's good with numbers,' I'd told her.

And it had worked, that relationship. Brandon was always encouraging me to be braver. It had been his idea that I should quit my job teaching and try writing for a while.

'I just got a promotion,' he'd said. 'If you're ever going to do it, now's the time.'

And then he'd hired Hannah to be his assistant – confident, pretty, young Hannah. And everything had changed irrevocably and completely. Forever.

The night I picked up the divorce decree from the mailbox centre, Jamie and I had got very drunk.

'You're a divorcee!' she kept exclaiming while mixing margaritas in our kitchen.

She was more than ten years younger than me, and to her both marriage and divorce seemed exotic and far away.

It took real effort to prevent her from reading the divorce papers, where she would have seen my true name.

'I don't want anyone to read them,' I insisted, holding them out of her reach. 'They're toxic. I want to burn them.'

At this, her brown eyes had lit up. 'We *should* burn them,' she'd announced, slurring her words slightly. 'You need a cere—' She hiccupped, holding up one hand. 'Ceremony. Like an unmarriage. Getting divorced is a beautiful thing and we should respect that. Let's do it.'

To me, that seemed like a very good way to get rid of the last evidence of Maya Landry.

Which was why, at one in the morning, we had traipsed out into the backyard of our little house in west Austin with a bottle of tequila and a barbecue lighter to set my divorce decree on fire.

It was a cool, clear night in early May, and we were both giggling and shivering as Jamie pulled out the long, skinny lighter and I held the papers above it. Her hand wavered as she laughed.

'You have to say some words,' she instructed.

The houses around us were quiet and still, and we were whispering like schoolchildren.

'What words?' I lowered the papers, still giggling.

'I don't know. Something about how this is the start of the rest of your life.' Jamie waved the lighter vaguely. 'You're letting go of the past . . . yada yada.'

'Gotcha.' I'd lifted the document again so that the paper with its legal writing was poised above the lighter. 'Well, I guess I want to say . . . Fuck you, Brandon.'

'No, no, no.' Frowning, Jamie shook her finger at me. 'You can't say anything negative or you'll get bad luck. It has to be positive.'

Given that she was inventing this ceremony, the rules were hers to make. We paused to drink more tequila and laugh some more, and then tried again.

Jamie held up the lighter. 'Now, don't think, just talk. *Go.*'

I cleared my throat. 'Right. Well. I guess I want to say . . .'

My voice trailed off. Jamie gave me a nod of encouragement. As I looked at her trusting face, for the hundredth time I wished I could tell her the truth.

I swallowed hard and tried to find the right words through a haze of alcohol. When I did speak, I started slowly at first, picking up speed as my thoughts formed.

'It was so hard getting here, but I'm very grateful that I ended up in this place with friends like you, Jamie. My old life wasn't good for me at all. Brandon wasn't good for me. Now I feel like I've got a family of my own choosing. I think I'm becoming the person I always wanted to be. And I feel so incredibly lucky to be free of the past. I'm ready for what comes next.' I paused. 'Yada yada.'

'Amen.' Jamie clicked the lighter and the flame leapt to life.

I tilted the document so a corner could catch, folding the top a little so Jamie couldn't see the name *Maya Denise Landry* written at the top.

The flames climbed over the paper slowly at first, and then quickly and voraciously, until the words themselves seemed to glow in the night: *It is therefore ordered, adjudged and decreed by the court that a Decree of Divorce is hereby . . .*

I held the document at arm's length until it grew too hot and I dropped it onto the damp grass. As we watched the last golden embers of my marriage fly up into the night sky, sparkling like fireflies, Jamie draped an arm across my shoulders.

'You're free,' she whispered.

To my surprise, there were tears on my cheeks.

'I'm free,' I repeated, and my heart swelled.

It felt true. As if our invented ceremony had worked, and the past had been lifted from me and I was finally free of Brandon, and Hannah, and the family that hadn't loved me as much as they should have done.

But it was an illusion. You can never leave the past behind; it follows you always. As immutable and persistent as a shadow.

I don't know why I found myself thinking about that ceremony as I ate my steak sandwich in the staffroom two months later and borrowed what Elaine had said about burritos for my article. (They really are the same wherever you buy them.) By the time I'd finished and sent it through to my editor, it was after six o'clock and I needed to get out onto the floor for the dinner shift.

As soon as I emerged from the back, Jamie motioned me over. Her bar exam was now less than a week away and she looked permanently exhausted.

She tilted her head to a table in the corner. 'Do you know those guys? They were asking for you.'

Still tying my apron around my waist, I shot a glance at where she indicated. Two middle-aged men sat across from each other. Both wore blazers and button-down shirts and had short, neat haircuts. Nothing about them was particularly familiar.

'I don't think so. What'd they say?'

'They just asked if Lara was working tonight. They said they wanted to be in your section.' Jamie picked up a bottle of Grey Goose vodka and began mixing a dry martini. 'You must have waited on them before. Anyway, I thought you might want to go shmooze a bit. Get a good tip.'

They didn't seem familiar at all, but that wasn't a surprise. I waited on so many people, only the most interesting ones stayed with me.

When Jamie finished making the martini, she pierced three olives on a skewer, set the drink next to an old-fashioned on a tray and pushed it towards me. 'This is their order. Get over there and make yourself some money.'

I picked up the tray and made my way to the corner table.

'Good evening,' I said brightly. 'I'm Lara. I've got your drinks. Who's having the martini?'

They both turned to stare at me. One was stocky and muscular, with tanned skin and dark hair. The other was thinner, with grey hair. They both examined my face so intently it was unnerving.

Too long passed before the man with grey hair said, 'I'm having the martini.'

'Great.' I set the drink on a coaster in front of him and turned to the other man. 'And you must be drinking the old-fashioned. Good choice.'

They watched my every move as I set the drink down along with a bowl of nuts.

'So,' I said, to break the silence, 'the bartender said you asked for me. Have I waited on you before?'

Again, that uncomfortable pause.

'Yeah, that's it.' The dark-haired guy glanced at the other. 'A few months ago, when we were in town for a conference.'

Neither had a southern accent; they both sounded New York to me. The younger one had the kind of hard face that made a smile look like it had lost its way and ended up there by mistake.

The greying guy had a softer face, more fatherly, but his eyes were cold.

'Yeah,' he agreed, 'we're back again. And we remembered this place made great cocktails.'

I flashed a professional grin at them. 'We're the best in town. Well, I'll be taking care of you again tonight, so if you want food or any drinks, don't hesitate to flag me down. We're glad you came back.'

When I walked back to the bar, I felt oddly relieved to be done with them. There wasn't anything wrong about them, they seemed nice enough, and we got a lot of travelling business types in there. But it was weird the way they stared at me, like they were going to have to draw me as soon as I walked away.

'Hey, Lara.' Maddy, the waitress whose section I was taking over, walked up to give me a rundown on the tables. As I listened, my gaze wandered back to the corner table. The two men were leaning towards each other, talking. They weren't paying any attention to me at all.

'And,' Maddy concluded, 'table nine just ordered two margaritas on the rocks, no salt. They'd like an order of fried zucchini with that.'

'Got it. Two margaritas, zucchini.' I hurried to the computer by the bar to type in the order, and put the men out of my mind.

It was a busy night. There must have been some sort of class reunion at the university because we had a big crowd of people who were all exactly the same age, looked a little self-conscious, and got very drunk.

I tried to keep an eye on the men in the corner, but they didn't ask for much. They ordered food, and nursed a couple of drinks, but their early attention on me had waned.

It wasn't until later, when things calmed down a little

and some of the reunion crowd had stumbled off down Sixth Street, that one of them motioned me over to the table again.

It was nearly eleven o'clock by then. Jamie was in the back, restocking, and the bar was quiet.

'What can I do for you?' I asked. Their glasses were mostly full and the dinner plates had already been cleared away.

'We'd like the bill,' the dark-haired one said. 'And if you have a second, we wondered if you might settle a bet.'

His tone was light, but for some reason a warning chill ran through me. I forced a smile. 'Oh yeah? What's the bet?'

He pointed at his companion. 'He thinks he's met you before. In Montana. Bozeman, to be precise. Have you ever been there?'

Everything stopped. The room fell silent; the floor sank away beneath my feet. I tried to breathe, to reply, but for a second, I couldn't make my lungs inhale.

'Me?' My voice sounded thin. 'I'm afraid not. Have you ever been to . . .' For a split second, I couldn't remember which cover story I used here. Kansas? Seattle? Then it came to me. 'Kansas? That's where I'm from. I've never been as far north as Montana, although I'd love to go.'

The two men exchanged glances.

'No,' the silver-haired man said after a pause. 'Never been to Kansas. I'm surprised. I was sure it was you I met in Montana.'

'I must have a doppelgänger.' It hurt my face to smile. 'Anyway, I'll go get you that bill. Give me two seconds.'

Aware that they were watching me, I made myself walk steadily to the computer at the bar and put my hands on the keyboard, but when I tried to type, my fingers wouldn't cooperate; my hands were ice-cold.

I could hear nothing but a hum of fear in my head.

I thought of how Riley had described the crime syndicate he was investigating, and I was certain it was them – the ones who'd killed Senator Castleton. I'd never seen them in Montana. I'd never seen them in my life. They were strangers. They recognised me because someone had shown them my picture.

My vision blurred with unshed tears. All I'd done to start over here – the little house on Dove Lane, Elaine, and Jamie. *Jamie.* The sister I'd always wanted, who cared about me, and I'd lied and lied to her, and now . . .

A rush of emotions was coming for me like a cold wind, but I shook my head, forcing them all back.

Later I would deal with this, but I couldn't fall apart right now. I might as well confess to them that I was Maya Landry, the only witness to a murder nobody knew had happened.

I swallowed my pain, straightened my shoulders and got on with printing the bill, slipping it into the narrow leatherette folder with *The Speakeasy* embossed in angular gold on the cover.

I took a deep breath and made myself walk back to the corner table.

'Here you go,' I said cheerfully. 'Will that be cash or card?'

With effort, I met the grey-haired man's eyes directly, filling my expression with innocence.

'Cash.' He reached into his pocket and drew out three hundred-dollar bills, dropping them on the table. As he did so, I noticed something about his hand. The third finger on his right hand was too short. There was no fingernail. It looked almost as if the fingertip had been neatly cut off.

He kept his eyes fixed on my face as I stepped forward to collect the money. 'Keep the change.'

I made myself smile as I scooped the cash into the folder.

'Thank you very much. It's been a pleasure serving you. I hope I'll see you here again.' I said it crisply, as if I didn't have a care in the world. Tucking the folder into the pocket of my apron, I walked at a measured pace back to the bar. Jamie, busy restocking the fridge, didn't glance up as I strolled through the swing door into the back hallway.

The second I was out of view, I stopped and fell back against the wall, covering my face with my hands. My legs felt weak.

'Oh God,' I whispered. 'Oh God. Oh God.'

I was in so much trouble.

I reached into my pocket and pulled out my phone.

For a single second, I hesitated. I had no proof of my suspicions, but I knew what was happening here. This was real. And there was only one person who might be able to help.

I scrolled down to R, and opening a new message, typed three words.

They found me.

I hit send.

SEVENTEEN

I don't know what I expected. Maybe sirens and spinning lights, or Batman swooping out of the sky. What actually happened was . . . nothing.

There was no reply. My phone didn't ring. I don't know how long I stood in the corridor with my back against the wall, staring at the phone like it would somehow explain what I should do. Eventually, Jamie walked through the door, her arms filled with a towering stack of empty boxes for the recycling bin, and caught me there, still as a statue.

'What's going on?' she asked, frowning. 'You look strange.'

My mouth had gone dry, and I swallowed before I could reply. 'Strange how?'

'I don't know.' She studied me, the boxes in her hands forgotten. 'Like you've seen a ghost.'

Straightening, I shoved the phone into my pocket. 'I've got a bit of a headache. It's been a hell of a week.'

'Which is my fault,' she said, guilt in her voice, the stack of boxes wavering a little. 'This stupid exam. You've had to fill in for me so many times.'

'Don't be an idiot. Come on, let me help you with those.' I

reached for the top box. 'Why do you carry so many of these at once?'

'Laziness,' she smiled, and let me help.

We dumped the boxes out back and I said I'd come help her close up in a minute, and then headed straight to the bathroom. I stood at the sink, staring at myself in the mirror; my face was pale, my pupils were huge. Jamie was right – I did look strange.

I had to calm the hell down. Whoever those men were, they didn't know anything for certain yet, I reasoned. They merely had suspicions. They were here collecting information, and I hadn't given them anything.

I dashed cold water on my face and forced my mouth into a smile.

Once again, I checked my phone, but my message just sat there.

They found me.

What had Riley told me a year ago? Something about not keeping his phone with him when he was working, but that he checked it often. What did that mean? I'd never really thought about it before. What if it was days before he saw my message? By then, it might be too late.

The door swung open, and my head jerked. A woman walked in – a customer in a snug black dress with high heels. Her long blonde hair hung in waves. She barely glanced at me, heading straight to the cubicles.

My movements felt heavy and awkward as I made my way back into the bar, a pantomime of walking normally. Despite my efforts not to look, my gaze was drawn to the table in the corner.

They were gone. Two half-empty glasses were all that remained.

Somehow that didn't make me feel safer. Woodenly, I went through the paces of cleaning tables, helping Jamie restock – all the normal end-of-shift work – but I kept hearing the dark-haired man's voice in my head: *He thinks he's met you before. In Montana.*

I checked my phone a hundred times, but Riley did not reply.

When the restaurant closed for the night, Jamie and I caught a lift from Alec, one of the waiters, to where my car was parked. All the way there, the two of them teased me about parking in 'the ghetto', as they called it.

'It's not a ghetto, and it's cheaper,' I kept insisting, although my heart wasn't in it. 'I'm saving a fortune.'

'You don't need money if you're dead,' Alec said.

They both laughed, but it didn't seem funny to me. Death's only amusing when you think there's no chance of it happening any time soon.

Later, in my own car, I had the strongest sense that we were being followed. I stared into the shadowy glass of the rear-view mirror, my hands gripping the wheel, but in the dark on the freeway it was impossible to tell what car was behind us or how long it had been there.

Nobody followed when we turned off, but by the time I pulled up in front of the little house on Dove Lane, my head really was pounding.

Even when we were safely inside I was a bundle of nerves. I triple-locked the door and peered through the front window. The street was empty. No strange cars; no men in suits.

'You expecting trouble?' Jamie sounded amused.

I gave an unconvincing chuckle and let the curtain fall. 'Just not planning to go out again tonight.'

My voice sounded stiff to me, but she was already walking down the hall and didn't notice. While she was in her bedroom, changing out of her work clothes, I checked the back door and the windows – all locked solid. But what did that matter? At any moment of the day or night, I could summon the memory of the *crack* my apartment door in Montana had made as it gave way.

At least, I figured, I must be slightly hard to find out here – the rent was in Jamie's name only, and all the bills as well. For all intents and purposes, I wasn't here.

Still, a soft voice in my head said, *if they found me at work, they can find me here.*

'Are you hungry?' Jamie called from the kitchen. I heard the sound of cabinets opening and closing. Before I could answer, the phone in my pocket vibrated, and I pulled it out. It was a text message from Riley.

Sit tight. I'm on it.

Relief flooded over me, warm as a blanket. He was on it. Everything was going to be fine. I'd be safe again.

'Lara?' Jamie stood in the living-room doorway, a knife in her hand. 'Did you hear me?'

'I'm sorry. What did you say?' I spoke slowly, my eyes straying back to Riley's message, hoping for more.

Her brow creased. 'Are you hungry? I'm making a sandwich.'

'No, thank you. I ate at work.'

She didn't leave the doorway. 'Everything OK?'

'It's good. Just a message from someone I used to know.'

'Back in Kansas?' She looked intrigued. 'Is it a guy?'

'Yes,' I said.

'An old flame, back for more,' she guessed. And headed to the kitchen again, talking loudly so I could hear her. 'I don't know how you're not hungry. You worked like a stevedore tonight. What was with those two men, by the way? The ones who asked for you. Did they tip?'

'Yes,' I said. 'Pretty well.'

She emerged a few minutes later with a sandwich and a glass of wine and dropped onto the sofa where a few of her law books were still stacked.

'God, I'm wiped, but I need to do at least an hour of study before bed.' She opened the textbook to a point she'd marked, sighed and took a bite of the ham sandwich. 'I can't wait for this test to be over.'

'You're going to ace it.' I spoke automatically. It was my constant reply to her.

'From your lips to God's ears,' she said, and settled in to read.

'I'm going to crash,' I said. 'See you in the morning.' My tone was abrupt, but she didn't notice.

'Sleep tight,' she told me absently, already absorbed in her notes.

Jamie's ability to concentrate on a dime had always

astounded me. Hand the girl a book and in two seconds she's no longer with you; she's lost in the words.

My room was a sizeable space, big enough for a double bed, a dresser and a desk. A ceiling fan whirred overhead, creating a pleasant breeze. My window overlooked the backyard, and I pushed the curtain aside to look out. It was dark and quiet.

And yet I could feel panic like a lump in my throat.

I'm safe, I told myself. I'm safe. I'm safe. I'm safe.

But psychological tricks only work when there's truth to the things you tell yourself. And I didn't believe I was safe. Not for one second.

Twenty minutes passed before my phone rang. When it did, I snatched it off the bed next to me. 'Hello.'

'Maya.'

My breath caught in my throat and I squeezed the phone hard. It had been so long since anyone called me Maya. It was like catching a glimpse of home.

'Riley? Thank God,' I whispered.

'I'm sorry it took so long to get back to you. Tell me what happened. Don't leave anything out.'

He sounded just as I remembered – calm and measured, as if we were talking about a baseball game or a vacation we might take. As if no time at all had passed.

I told him about two men, and what they'd said. When I finished, Riley said only, 'I know it sounds unlikely, but it could be a coincidence, or maybe they actually did know you back then, somehow. Don't panic yet.'

'I'm not panicking,' I lied, even as my stomach churned.

'Good,' he said. 'Now tell me about the two men. Describe them in as much detail as you can.'

I told him all I could recall about their features. 'I think the dark-haired one was about a hundred and ninety pounds, muscular, maybe five foot eight – not tall. His nose was crooked, liked it had been broken at some point. The grey-haired one was taller and thinner, over six feet.' I thought about his hand pulling money from an expensive-looking wallet. 'He had a fatherly face, but one of his fingers was damaged. The third finger on his right hand – it looked like the fingertip had been cut off.'

There was a long silence.

'Dammit,' Riley said softly. 'How did they find you?'

And with that, all my hopes collapsed.

I looked around the bedroom – so comfortable and safe – and my eyes filled with tears.

'It is them, then.'

'It is. I know them.' For the first time, I heard frustration in his voice. 'I honestly don't see how they tracked you down. You followed the rules – it should have worked.'

I pressed my fist against the middle of my forehead.

'I've been sitting here thinking about it,' I told him. 'I got divorced two months ago. I think it must have been that. I was careful – none of the paperwork came to me, it all went to a post office box in Seattle. But the timing . . . It can't be a coincidence.'

I heard his sigh from across the country. 'Divorce records are public, Maya. If they were watching for your name in all legal records, they'd have seen that you'd filed. From there they could start to piece it together.'

I couldn't think of anything to say. I held the phone away from my ear and fought back a sob.

Stupid. I'd been so stupid. Why hadn't I thought of that?

Riley spoke quietly. 'You've actually done really well to avoid them as long as you have. None of this is your fault. But we are here now, and we're going to need a plan. Whatever you said, and however much you denied being Maya Landry, they'll have seen through it. They're going to come back for you. So I need you not to go to work tomorrow.'

I opened my mouth to argue – I couldn't do that to Elaine, we were so busy. But then I changed my mind. Riley wouldn't ask if it wasn't necessary. He'd been right about everything.

'OK,' I agreed reluctantly.

'In fact,' he continued, 'don't do anything you normally do. Don't go to any place you would ordinarily go to. Stay home if at all possible. I've got to figure this out. It's going to take a day for me to get a plan together, so I need you to lie low.'

As he spoke, I reached out with one hand and gripped the cushion next to me, as if trying to hold on to this house, this home, this life I'd made.

'Am I going to have to leave Austin?' I asked.

'Maya, I don't want to make you do anything. But it won't be safe for you there now.'

I closed my eyes and a tear slipped down my cheek.

'I understand,' I whispered.

'Look, I've got to make a phone call,' he said. 'Are you going to be OK?'

Was I? I was living like a fugitive. My life had been destroyed once and it was about to happen again. Everything I'd worked for . . .

'I'll be fine.' My voice was dull.

'Good. I better go,' he said. 'Hang tight. I'll be in touch.'

After the phone went dead, I stared at the small, blank screen without seeing it, trying to understand the strange note I'd heard in his voice at the end.

Riley was scared.

And if he was afraid, then I was in real danger. We both were.

EIGHTEEN

The next morning at nine o'clock, for the first time since I'd started working at the Speakeasy, I called in sick. A migraine had come over me during the night.

'I'm so sorry to do this,' I told Elaine, hating myself more with every word. 'I know how understaffed we are right now.'

Her sympathetic response only made me feel worse. 'Don't worry about it, sweetheart, we'll figure something out. You just focus on getting better.'

After I hung up the phone, I sat on the couch, staring at the walls. I was so exhausted, I could barely see straight. I'd been up all night, tormented by grief and doubt. For hours I'd conducted a debate with myself. What if Riley was wrong? I couldn't leave my life here based on a couple of guys asking questions in a bar. Even if they were who he thought they were, what if I just stayed anyway? What was the worst they could do to me?

But then I kept remembering how he had sounded – the sudden intake of breath when I described the man with the missing fingertip. The change in his tone.

I dropped my head into my hands.

With every breath, I could feel my new life slipping away. It was ironic that the day was so beautiful. Bright sunlight poured through the windows, filling the room with a warm glow. Through the glass, I could see the vivid green lawn and Jamie's pink and white roses. They were getting weedy — we'd been so busy, and now everything needed attention.

At this thought, my eyes filled with tears again. Would I be here to help in the garden? Or would I just disappear and leave her to handle everything alone? How would she react to coming home and finding me gone?

When I'd left Montana, I'd never looked back. My apartment and everything in it — Riley had handled that. Or at least, he'd promised he'd handle it. I never knew what he'd told my landlord or Gina, or how he'd had my things removed, or where they had ended up. But I'd spent so little time there, it wasn't too painful to abandon it all.

Leaving Austin would be very different. This was my home. Jamie and Elaine were my family. Leaving would break my heart.

Thinking about it hurt so much it was hard to breathe. It felt as if someone I loved was dying. My heart raced, and my lungs compressed. Perspiration dotted my forehead and my hands and feet tingled. I knew this feeling all too well, but knowing didn't help. It felt like the world was crushing me.

I pressed my fist against my chest, feeling the panicked-bird fluttering of my heart, and blew out a shaky breath through pursed lips.

There's a technique called 'box breathing' that I'd used before, where you imagine with each breath in and out that you're building one side of a box. When you have a complete box, you start again, building a new box. It works. And it worked then. My breathing eased, and the tingling stopped, but the pain in my chest stayed. Maybe it always would.

I needed to shower and get myself together, and yet I just sat there, unable to convince myself to move.

That's where I was when Jamie walked out of her bedroom ten minutes later, dressed in running clothes, her earbuds in one hand. I must have looked odd, because she gave me a puzzled look.

'What's up?'

'Migraine,' I told her. 'Excruciating. I don't think I can work today.'

Frowning, she sat down on the sofa next to me, studying my face. She pressed the back of her hand against my forehead, her fingers cool and soothing.

'I have to say you're really pale. Are you nauseous?'

'A bit.' I avoided her eyes. 'I just think I need to rest.'

I couldn't stop thinking: What if this is the last time I talk to her? What if this lie is the final conversation we have?

Clearly concerned, Jamie looked down at the earpieces in her hand. 'I was about to go to the gym. I was going to head straight to the library from there, but I can come back instead and bring you painkillers and soup.'

I shook my head hard. 'Don't change your plans. Honestly, I'm going straight back to bed.'

There was a slight sharpness to my voice. Whatever happened next, I needed her not to be here for it.

Jamie watched me doubtfully. 'You sure? I hate leaving you alone when you're sick.'

'It's just a headache, and you've got studying to do. Don't worry about me, I'll be fine. Go on with your day.'

'Well, if you're certain.' Reluctantly, Jamie gathered her things, one bag with a change of clothes, and another, heavier bag holding her laptop and books. When she was ready, she lingered in the doorway.

'Call me if you need anything. I'll keep my phone on in the library.'

'I promise.' I forced my voice to sound normal, but my insides were being shredded with knives. 'Now, get out of here and go learn how to be a lawyer.'

She flashed that sunny smile and headed out.

I listened to the familiar thud of her footsteps, and then the door opening and closing behind her.

'Oh God.' Gasping, I doubled over. I felt the loss of her so keenly and I wasn't even gone yet.

I was fighting back sobs when a key turned in the lock and I heard Jamie storm back in. I sat up quickly.

'My stupid car won't start again.'

I wiped away my tears with the hem of my pyjama top before she made it to the living room.

'I keep telling you to sell that thing and get something reliable,' I said.

Jamie drove a ten-year-old Ford that was constantly breaking down.

'I know, I know, but I wanted to wait until after my exam.' Too distracted to notice that I'd been crying, she dropped her gym bag and gave it a frustrated kick. 'Now I'll have to get it towed, and by then the whole day will be lost.'

No, she couldn't be here. I couldn't let that happen.

'Listen. Take my car.' Standing up, I walked past her to the bowl by the door and pulled out my keys. 'I'm not working today, you might as well use it. Call the repair place when you get to the gym – have them come tow yours.'

Jamie's face lit up, but with her hand outstretched, she hesitated. 'Are you sure? What if you need to go somewhere?'

'Delivery companies exist. If I need anything, I'll use them. In a crisis, I'll call you. Leave your car keys with me, and I'll give them to the tow truck driver when he gets here.'

'You lifesaver.' Jamie gave me a happy hug, and I leaned in to her warmth, inhaling the clean, floral scent of her perfume. How much longer did I have to be her friend? Hours? A day? And then Lara Gibson would disappear the way Maya Landry had. And I would lose everything.

'You're a hero,' Jamie said. 'I'll call the repair place from the gym.'

'But you shouldn't fix it this time,' I made myself say. 'You should scrap the damn thing.'

'It just needs to survive a few more weeks,' she said, and the determination in her voice almost made me smile.

Grabbing her bag from the floor, she headed out again, calling, 'See you later!' over her shoulder. But I couldn't let her go this time.

'Jamie,' I called.

She glanced back, the door already half-closed.

'You're going to be an amazing lawyer.'

She crossed her fingers. 'All I have to do is pass the test.'

I wanted to tell her that I knew she was going to pass. She

could make the earth rotate backwards through sheer will if she wished. But I didn't trust my voice, and it would have sounded weird anyway, so I just lifted my hand in farewell.

After she'd gone, a heavy silence fell over the house. Outside, suburbia went about its normal day. Our neighbour's landscapers arrived, and the nagging insect buzz of lawnmowers and leaf blowers drowned out the hum of cicadas and the constant, quiet rumble of the air conditioner.

It was cool inside, but I could feel the heat of the July day radiating through the window glass.

I have to get up, I thought again, and didn't move.

The awful thing was doing nothing and waiting. Briefly, I considered surprising Jamie by cutting the grass, just to be doing something. But the idea of dragging the lawnmower out of the overstuffed shed seemed far too difficult. Everything seemed difficult. All I was able to do was sit and stare at my phone, wondering when Riley would contact me again and ruin my life.

Finally, I glanced at my watch and realised it was ten thirty. An hour and a half had passed since Jamie had gone to the gym, and I was still sitting on the sofa.

'This can't go on,' I announced, my voice echoing in the emptiness.

Resolutely I got to my feet and went to take a shower. This process seemed to kick-start some survival instinct, and once I'd dressed and combed the damp tendrils of my hair into shape, I actually felt hungry.

I made a slice of toast and ate it without enjoyment, standing at the French doors in the living room, looking out over the little backyard. By the time I'd finished, I'd made a few decisions.

Whoever the man with no third fingertip was, I wasn't going to let him kill me. There were things I wanted to do in this life, and due to a series of unfortunate events, I hadn't got around to them yet. I needed time. And I intended to fight for it.

I didn't really have to wait to hear from Riley. I had a pretty good idea what he was going to say, and I needed to get ready.

This time, I didn't intend to be at home when my door was kicked in.

Fired with purpose, I marched to my bedroom and packed an escape bag. I hadn't done a bad job last time under the circumstances, but this time I knew what I needed – three days' worth of clothes, something to sleep in, toothpaste and toothbrush, shampoo. Everything I'd want for a few days in transit.

When that was done, I moved the bedside table eight inches to the left and knelt beside it. Using a butter knife, I lifted a loose piece of skirting board out of the way and reached behind it, pulling out a fat envelope.

Sitting back on my heels, I opened it. Inside was a grey-green stack of cash.

Have you ever noticed money has a smell? Anyone who's ever worked in a bank or run a cash register will know that. It's a sweet, vaguely cloying scent. Not unlike an incense made of leather and old books. To me it smelled like safety.

This envelope held what was left of Riley's ten thousand dollars, along with as much of my tips as I'd been able to set aside over the last year. I didn't know how much was in there – I'd never counted it. The amount didn't make any difference; it was having it that had mattered. And only now did it occur to me to wonder why that was. Had I always known that this day would come? In my heart, had I always carried the knowledge that you cannot escape your past? That whatever you do, however hard you run, eventually the truth comes for you?

I counted out two thousand dollars and set it aside. The rest I returned to the envelope and placed it inside the packed bag, zipping it tight.

After that, I made my bed and straightened my room, putting everything neatly away. By the time I finished, it looked as featureless and blank as a guest room. Waiting for the next occupant to come along.

I'd kept precious few documents, and few personal things, so I didn't have much to get rid of. Again, fodder for future conversations with therapists, but for now, an easy clean-up.

In the kitchen, I found a piece of paper and a pen and stood at the counter, thinking for a moment before writing quickly, the pen slashing a short message. When I finished, I signed it *Lara*. I couldn't sign anything else. It was the only name she'd ever known for me.

My heart still ached, but I wasn't crying any more, and I was grateful for that. A cool curtain had fallen between me and my emotions. My brain stepping in to say, 'Well, this is terrible. I'd best protect you from that level of hurt.' It wouldn't last forever, but it would get me through this day.

I put the note and twenty hundred-dollar bills in an envelope, and placed it against the pillows on Jamie's bed.

I was just closing her bedroom door when I heard the angry vibration of my phone ringing from the kitchen.

Riley, at last.

I ran to the kitchen and grabbed the phone from the counter.

'Hello?' I said breathlessly.

'Is this Lara Gibson?' The voice was male, Texan, unfamiliar.

I tensed.

'Who's asking?' I replied cautiously.

'Ma'am, this is Sergeant Arthur Rogers with the Austin Police Department. I'm looking for a Lara Gibson. Is that you?'

My throat went dry.

'This is Lara,' I said. 'Is something wrong?'

'Are you the owner of a silver Honda CR-V, licence plate . . .' He rattled off the numbers and letters.

I was utterly bewildered. How could he know that? It didn't make any sense.

A second later, the reality of what it all meant hit me like a punch in the stomach. The police. My car.

Jamie.

'Yes, that's my car.' My words came out in a rush. 'Has something happened? My housemate borrowed the car today. She left a few hours ago.'

'What's your housemate's name, ma'am?'

'Jamie Sheridan.'

'OK, ma'am.' His voice took on a new tone. 'I need to inform you that a silver Honda CR-V with that licence plate, registered in the name Lara Gibson, was involved in an accident this morning at approximately ten a.m. The vehicle left I-35 and collided with a safety wall.'

I could hear the ragged sound of my own breathing. Distantly, I noticed one of my hands had reached out and was gripping the cool granite countertop. I stared at the white knuckles as if they belonged to someone else.

'Jamie,' I said, my voice low. 'Is she alive?'

'Miss Sheridan is currently in surgery . . .'

She was alive.

'Which hospital?' I demanded.

'St David's—'

I didn't wait to hear more. 'On my way.'

'*Ma'am.*' The officer's raised voice stopped me in the act of hanging up. 'We need to speak with you as soon as possible. You should know that witnesses reported that the accident . . . well, it might not have been an accident. They told officers at the scene the Honda didn't lose control. They said it was forced off the road by another vehicle.' He paused. 'They said it was intentional. We're investigating this as a crime.'

NINETEEN

The next few minutes of that day are hazy. I remember the sergeant asking if anyone had threatened me and not knowing how to answer that question. In fact, I have no idea what I said. I think I told him I had to go to the hospital, and that I'd call him back. I remember very clearly that I was halfway to the door before I realised I didn't have a car any more.

What followed was the longest twelve minutes of my life as I stood on the little front porch, every muscle knotted, the escape bag at my feet, the heat turning my skin damp, while I waited for a taxi. I can picture it all: the pretty, empty street, the cicadas' shrill warning filling the air, the sweet summer smells of cut grass and sun-baked pavement, all of it lost to the ice-cold fear that had pervaded me. I could feel nothing. Smell nothing. I was nothing, an empty space, waiting.

When at last I saw the battery-powered black Toyota gliding down the street, I raced towards it, my rubber-soled shoes thudding.

The driver glanced up, startled, as I yanked the door open.

'Are you Lara—' he began.

I cut him off. 'Yes, I'm going to St David's Hospital, and I'll tip you fifty dollars in cash if you floor it. It's an emergency.'

One thing is for certain, that guy earned the fifty bucks. He drove like a demon. And for once, traffic was on my side. Less than fifteen minutes later, I was running into the cold, alcohol-scented entrance of the hospital and skidding to a stop at the front desk.

'I'm looking for Jamie Sheridan.' I spoke rapidly. 'She's been in an accident. The police said she was brought here.' Looking back, I'm surprised by how sane I sounded. How the words came out in a coherent and understandable order.

The receptionist at the front desk gave me one of the looks those workers have perfected – professional, cautious, polite, disinterested.

'Are you a family member?' she asked.

'I'm her sister.' I said it without hesitation. I had no intention of playing *that* game today.

The woman typed something into the computer and stared at it for far too long, as if that machine held all the knowledge and wonders of the universe. I noticed her name tag said 'Bells' and I thought it was a nice last name.

She lowered her voice. 'Miss Sheridan is in surgery now. You need to go to the Bastrop wing. It's in the red zone. They'll give you more information there.'

By the time she finished speaking, I was already running.

All hospitals are designed, I sincerely believe, by deranged architects wreaking revenge on the world for some past slight none of us can remember. The hallways tangle and twist into alternate universes that contain nothing except more hallways. I followed a stripe of red low on the wall as it bent and turned through what felt like a hundred miles of corridors.

I would learn later that it wasn't far at all – time and space stretch when you're frightened – but right then it felt like a marathon just to reach the right wing.

When I did finally arrive, another receptionist sent me to another desk, and when I got there, that person asked again if I was family and again I lied.

Jamie and I look nothing alike. She's dark and I'm fair, she's tall and I'm average, she's beautiful and I'm ordinary, but nobody notices that stuff in a hospital. We all look the same to them. We are a problem they have to solve.

Someone pointed me to a waiting room and said a doctor would talk to me when she got the chance.

And then I was in that odd two-speed medical world, where the workers run fast and talk fast and push mysterious machines down hallways at tremendous speed, and everyone else just . . . waits.

There were a dozen people sitting on rows of blue vinyl chairs, all of them probably just as worried as me, but I took no comfort from that.

You are always alone in a hospital. It's the loneliest place on the planet.

I stood by a window and took out my phone. Riley had been very specific that I shouldn't call him again, but frankly, fuck that.

As I dialled his number, a sudden, overwhelming rage fired through me. His familiar voice said tersely, 'Leave a message here.' Last night, I'd found that voice so comforting I'd almost cried. Today it made me angry, and my own voice quivered when I spoke.

'I did what you said. I stayed home. My housemate borrowed my car and those bastards tried to kill her. She's in the hospital now and I don't know if she'll live . . .' My voice broke and I fought for control. 'I hate this, Riley. I hate these people. I hate you. I'm not leaving. I'm staying right here with her. They can kill me if they want. I don't care. I've had enough.'

I don't know how long I was in that waiting room. People came and went. A TV blasted a game show from one corner, the audience laughter as jarring in this environment as vodka shots in a mausoleum.

At last, after an endless amount of time, someone called, 'Lara Gibson?'

A woman in a white coat, her brown hair unruly, her face blurred with exhaustion, stood near the desk. I hurried over to her.

'How is Jamie?' I said, no longer hiding my fear and desperation. The telling pause before she replied shattered me.

'Let's go over here.' She took me around the corner, out of sight of the waiting room.

'I understand you're her sister?'

'Yes,' I said impatiently. 'Please. Is she alive?'

'She's alive, but she's in pretty bad shape. She has multiple injuries. Her left leg is broken in three places. She has a hairline skull fracture. But the most pressing injury is here.' She gestured at her chest. 'She's broken four ribs, one of which perforated her lung. Between the depressed oxygen levels and blood loss, we thought we might lose her, but she's a fighter.'

I listened intently, my hands tightening into fists at my sides. I wanted to scream, but I made myself speak calmly.

'Can I see her?'

The doctor shook her head. 'She's going to be in surgery for a while yet. My part is done – I'm a pulmonary surgeon. Now they're working on her leg. It'll be another hour at least. All I can tell you is that she's young, and her heart is strong. I think she'll pull through this.' She rested a hand on my arm gently. 'But it wouldn't hurt to pray.'

She asked about our parents, and I realised I had to call Jamie's mother. I told her she could leave it with me.

When she walked away, I leaned back against the wall, covering my face with my hand. I'm not sure I'd ever felt so lost.

That was *my* car. They'd done this because they thought it was *me* behind the wheel. I'd loaned it to Jamie without thinking it through. I might as well have handed them a gun to shoot her with.

This rage at myself paled, however, in comparison with my fury at the men who'd run her off the road. I knew only one thing for certain: I would kill whoever did this to her.

When I'd calmed down enough to steady my voice, I called Jamie's mother. The second I heard her voice, I burst into tears, and through sobs, I told her what had happened.

Mrs Sheridan was a senior attorney at one of the biggest banks in Houston and not the type to become hysterical, but I heard the tremor in her words as she calmed me down and asked for the name of the hospital.

'The doctor says she's strong,' I told her, wiping my eyes. 'But you should be here. It's bad.'

'I'm leaving now. Tell her I love her.' Only on that last sentence did Haley Sheridan's voice break. But she hung up so quickly, it could have been my imagination.

Oh, my friends, hospitals are awful places.

Time lost its meaning. I paced and waited for who knows how long. When they finally brought Jamie out, she was unconscious. Her head was bandaged, her face swollen and unrecognisable. She looked as if those men had beaten her with baseball bats. Every part of her seemed to be connected to miles of tubes and cables.

I sat beside her, holding her one undamaged hand, telling her in a soft, steady whisper that I was there and her mother was on the way.

The guilt was killing me. Looking at her like that, the bruises and bandages and wires, I found myself sobbing again. When a nurse came in, I stood quickly and slipped out of the room into the corridor.

Leaning back against the wall, I took deep breaths, trying to steady myself. I had to be calm for Jamie. I owed her that.

It was so quiet, I heard the official voices when they were still far away. Glancing up, I saw two police officers in dark uniforms at the far end of the corridor. They were walking towards me with the female doctor I'd met earlier. None of them had noticed me yet.

I couldn't stay here. If they did their work at all thoroughly, the police would figure out that there was no Lara

Gibson, and that was a complication I didn't need right at this moment.

Turning, I lowered my head and walked swiftly in the opposite direction until I reached a stairwell and dived into it. Just as I reached the ground floor, the phone in my pocket buzzed.

I pulled it out to see a call from an unknown number.

I answered. 'This is Lara.'

A familiar husky voice said, 'Hello, Lara. It's been a while.'

I stopped, mid-stride, astonished.

'Amber?'

'Riley tells me you've got yourself in a pickle. Tell me where you are. I'm coming to get you.'

TWENTY

It took Amber less than twenty minutes to pick me up. The silver SUV I remembered from Houston had been replaced by a newer, darker version, but Amber looked exactly the same, her light brown skin smooth, her wavy hair neat.

'Hello, again,' she said when I opened the passenger door and dropped my bag on the floor before climbing in after it. 'Déjà vu.'

I couldn't seem to speak, but she was right: this was just like the last time she'd come to my rescue. Me, confused and frightened. Her at the wheel.

I'd have given anything not to be doing this again.

As we pulled onto the freeway, heading west, she glanced at my tear-stained face and the hands clenched in my lap.

'What happened?'

It took all my strength to compress the last twenty-four hours into a few exquisitely painful sentences. Amber listened attentively, her eyes on the road.

When I finished, she said, 'Well, son of a bitch. I'm sorry it played out like this.'

She sounded genuinely regretful, and this uncharacteristic show of sympathy touched my heart. I blinked hard, turning away from her.

'These guys Riley's been undercover with, they're clinical, obsessive,' Amber continued. 'Everything they do is focused on not being caught, not ever leaving anything unfinished – it's why it's been so hard to bring them down. They get rid of anyone who could incriminate them. I hoped if you went dark, eventually they'd feel safe enough to let this go, but . . .' she paused, her brow creasing, '. . . apparently not.'

Through the shadow of my pain it occurred to me that she seemed to know a lot about the crime syndicate Riley'd been investigating. More than she'd let on the last time we'd met. She spoke about them almost personally. But I couldn't seem to think about what that might mean. After all, I knew less than nothing about Amber.

'I'm being hunted,' I told her. 'I did nothing wrong and now Jamie might . . .'

'How is she?' Amber asked when my voice faded.

'Alive. Barely.'

I thought of Jamie's swollen face, and couldn't continue. Instead, I stared out of the window. It was early evening by then, and the sun had faded from glaring white to lemon yellow, bathing the city in a warm wash of gold. If I turned my head, I could see the office skyscrapers downtown, and in the other direction the low-slung houses and verdant landscape that make the city so green and lush. All of it made my heart ache. I didn't want to leave.

I had to leave.

For a while we drove in silence, and Amber seemed willing to leave me in peace. At some point, we turned off the freeway and headed west. I had no idea where we were going and I didn't think it mattered. Wherever I went, I'd be found.

After a while, Amber turned onto a narrow road. We were at the edge of Austin, where the suburbs bled into wilder, rougher land marked by boulders and scrub-covered hills. It occurred to me that this landscape was all that had been here a hundred and fifty years ago – hardscrabble, untameable, unbearable. Too hot, too rocky, too populated by tarantulas and poisonous snakes to make it comprehensible why anyone would have wanted to live here. Droughts destroyed crops and killed livestock, and the hard life killed the people who tried to own the land.

I'd seen their pictures in local museums and office buildings. The thin women with their bonnets and bony hands. The men with tangled beards and hundred-mile stares. The native people with fiercely determined expressions. They were all fighting a losing battle and they knew it.

And yet they kept trying.

I should fight harder, I thought. Like them.

But then, I reminded myself, they all died young.

'Are you hungry?' Amber's voice made me start.

'No,' I told her shortly.

'Well.' She signalled and turned left. 'I'm famished.'

I didn't know this part of the city at all. Austin's affluence hadn't reached this far. The small houses with sagging eaves and faded paint were evidence of poverty, as were the large, unkempt yards fenced with rusted chicken wire. Even with the windows closed I could hear music blasting from somewhere.

Amber turned left and then right, navigating a tangle of streets with ease, her hands loose on the wheel. She seemed to know this area well.

I tried to remember what she'd told me the night I'd met her. That she and Riley had been rookie cops together in Houston seventeen years ago — eighteen now. That made her at least thirty-eight years old by my count, although she looked younger.

I studied her curiously. She was an odd person. Smart, clearly. And capable. There was a distance to her, but she wasn't cold. She was just impossible to read. Sort of like Riley, but also . . . different. Like no one I'd ever met.

She glanced over and caught me watching her. Her brow creased. 'What?'

'You never did tell me who you work for,' I said.

'No,' she said. 'I didn't.'

She turned her attention back to the road. But that wasn't going to work with me. Not after today.

'Are you a spy?' I asked flatly.

She laughed, a pleasant, throaty chuckle. 'In Texas? If I am, I must be lost.'

'That's not an answer.'

'Oh, you're serious.' She sounded disappointed. I was starting not to trust the way she treated all conversations like a game.

When I said nothing, she gave a small sigh. 'Well, I can't tell you who I work for, that's a secret I can't divulge. But you can call me a spy if you want. I'm afraid I don't have a business card or I'd give you one.'

At that moment, a dog dashed out from behind a wrecked car at the side of the road and threw itself in front of us.

'Shit.' Amber hit the brakes hard, and we were both thrown forward. I braced my hands against the dashboard. The car stalled. The dog, so thin and ragged its breed was impossible to identify, skittered away into an alley.

Amber sat still for a second, holding the wheel. A long, low vehicle passing in the other direction slowed and the three young men inside all swivelled to look at us. Two of them had gang tattoos on their faces.

'What the hell are we doing here?' I demanded, turning to Amber. 'Are you trying to get us killed?'

She gave me a cool look. 'We're just getting some supper.'

She put the car in gear. Before I could launch into more questions, she turned into the parking lot of a small restaurant in a breeze-block building painted the colours of the Mexican flag. A faded sign out front said 'La Hacienda'.

'Here we go,' Amber announced, switching off the engine.

I stared at the place doubtfully. 'You want to go here?'

'Definitely,' she said, and opened her door. A wave of hot, dry air swirled in. 'It's my favourite.'

I didn't move. Whatever game she was playing, I didn't have it in me today.

'Maybe I should just go back to the hospital,' I said. 'Jamie might be waking up. I can call a cab.'

Tilting her head, Amber gave me a measured look. 'Well, you could do that. But there were four police cars parked in front of that hospital, and I'm guessing you don't want to talk to them and have them look into your background. Also, bear in mind that it won't take long for whoever ran Jamie off the road to figure out they tried to kill the wrong woman, and then they'll come looking for the right one.' She paused. 'Now do you still want to call a taxi?'

Defeated, I opened my door and climbed out to join her.

'You're always taking me to weird restaurants,' I grumbled as we walked through the evening heat to the glass doors.

'Just because you're in trouble that's no reason not to eat,' Amber said.

A brightly painted wooden sign facing us read '*¡Hola!*' When Amber opened the door, I saw that on the other side the same sign read '*¡Vaya con Dios!*'

Go with God.

Yeah? Well, where is he when you need him?

It was around five o'clock, too early for supper for most people, and the place was largely empty. A small woman with chubby cheeks and a bright smile hurried over towards us. Amber seemed to know her.

'*Hola*, Zoraida,' she said, and held out her arms.

The two women hugged, speaking in rapid Spanish. Then Zoraida gestured at the back of the room and said something.

'*Ah, sí. Gracias*,' Amber said.

I looked at the table Zoraida had indicated. A man in a pale blue button-down shirt sat alone, his head angled down. As if sensing my gaze, he suddenly glanced up.

My heart jumped. I recognised the sharp jawline, those piercing blue eyes.

'Riley.' The word came out in a whisper.

He stood, and I flew across the room into his arms, sobbing before I reached him.

'I can't do it,' I said, over and over again. 'I can't do this, Riley.'

'I know.' I felt his breath against my hair, warm and soft. 'I'm sorry.'

If he was surprised by my emotion, he said nothing. He just held me and let me cry.

I didn't have the energy to think about what Amber would make of it all; I was just so relieved to see him.

When I was calmer, we all sat at the table.

Amber was next to me, looking at Riley speculatively, although he didn't seem to notice.

Zoraida had discretely disappeared but soon returned with glasses of ice water and menus.

'I'll give you a moment.' Her eyes rested on me with sympathetic curiosity. 'Coffee?'

Riley, who already had a cup in front of him, nodded. 'For everyone,' he said.

I couldn't stop looking at him. His face looked as I remembered, all angles and planes. But he was thinner. He looked as tired as I felt.

'When did you get here?' I asked.

'An hour ago, give or take.' He glanced at his watch. 'Maybe two. I flew down as soon as I got your message. How is your friend?'

'She was alive when I left the hospital,' I said. 'She has a chance. The police came to interview her.'

His eyes sharpened. 'Did they see you?'

'No.'

'Good.'

'What about Chicago?' I asked. 'Shouldn't you be there?'

'Well, I'm sort of taking a leave of absence.' As he said it, he glanced at Amber. Her eyebrows rose.

'Does anybody know about this leave?' she asked.

Riley gave a slight shrug. 'They'll figure it out.'

Amber's lips tightened, but just then Zoraida returned with three coffees and a bowl of sugar and we all fell silent.

'Thank you, Zoraida.' Riley drew the fresh cup over and slid the old one out of the way.

'Well,' he studied me with a faint smile, 'I like what you've done with all of this.' He gestured at his face. 'Very different from the Maya I knew.'

'Yeah, I really worked on it,' I told him. I felt steadier now, and a little ashamed of my outburst when I'd first seen him. 'I don't think it was easy for those guys to be certain I was who they thought I was.'

'No, I can imagine they must have had doubts.'

'How do you think they found her?' Amber directed the question at Riley.

He told her about the divorce, and she grimaced. 'Yeah, that'd do it. Especially with Anthony Cleary in charge. He'll have half the lawyers in the Midwest working for him.'

'True.' Riley gave a bitter laugh. 'He doesn't skimp on lawyers.'

I looked from one to the other. 'Who's Anthony Cleary?'

For a second, nobody replied. Something unspoken passed between Amber and Riley.

'Are we doing this?' Amber asked him.

He nodded. 'I think it's time.'

She held his gaze for a second, and then picked up a menu. 'Well, if it's confession hour, I'm going to need nachos.'

She motioned Zoraida over. Amber and Riley both ordered in Spanish. I chose something at random and ordered in English. As she took my menu, Zoraida gave me a kind smile, and I wondered who she was. Nobody had explained how they knew her.

When she'd disappeared into the kitchen, Riley turned to me.

'I think you deserve the whole story. I didn't want to tell you before because I didn't want you to do anything stupid, like go look for the people involved to plea your case or . . . something worse. But now there's no point in that. I think you understand where you are.' He paused. 'Anthony Cleary is a criminal. He runs a sophisticated operation out of Chicago – the one I've been undercover with for far too long. Cleary's a murderer and a con artist and a drug dealer, but he's also got a degree in law from Loyola University, an undergraduate degree from Yale, and contacts in Washington. Unfortunately for us, he is brilliant.'

It seemed to me there was admiration in his voice, as well as loathing.

'I was sent in by the FBI to bring him down. But up against someone like him, so far the law has failed. The local cops didn't stand a chance, and I haven't, I'm sorry to admit, done much better. He prepares better than we do, has a better staff and corrupts good people into doing very bad things. He surrounds himself with the best. And no one can get through that.'

'Was he the one who killed . . . ?' I made a gesture.

'Not him.' Riley's voice was taut. 'It's never him. He gets people to do it for him. He doesn't get his hands dirty. Plausible deniability – Tony's the master of it. The people who work for him sometimes get caught, but they never take him down with them. He takes care of their families, gets them the best lawyers. So far, nobody's ever talked. No matter what we offer them. They're all either too scared or too loyal.'

'But you were there when Castleton was killed,' I said. 'Surely that's something we can use.'

Amber's head jerked up; Riley didn't look at her.

'I wasn't there,' he reminded me. 'I was outside. All I can testify to is that I saw Castleton go into that house, and then you arrived and I was ordered to leave the area and go find you. That's not enough for a court.'

There was a strange brittleness to his voice that I couldn't identify.

'You were literally there, though,' I insisted. I was so frustrated by all of this. 'How is that not enough to bring the killers down?'

Riley glanced at Amber, but her face had closed. 'This is your show,' she said.

At that moment, the kitchen door swung open and Zoraida arrived with a tray holding tortilla chips and Amber's nachos. Riley waited until she'd gone, and then picked up right where he'd left off.

'It just isn't enough,' he said. 'We know when we have

enough to bring a case, and we don't have enough on Tony Cleary.'

Amber ate a nacho, chewing thoughtfully, a slight frown creasing her forehead.

'You know where Castleton was when they killed him,' I pressed.

'Listen.' Riley's voice was even but his body had tensed. 'If the FBI had, theoretically, told a court or even the local police what we knew about the senator, they'd want to know how we knew it. That would mean revealing an ongoing undercover operation. Trust me when I tell you that information would have made it back to Tony Cleary. It would have put my life at extreme risk. So the FBI decided not to do it.'

For the first time, Amber spoke. 'Is that really what they decided? That doesn't sound right to me.'

Her voice was measured, but I thought I saw a dangerous glint in her brown eyes.

'Oh, great. Now you too?' Riley gave a humourless laugh and reached for his glass of water. 'I can't fight both of you.'

'It still doesn't make sense,' I objected. 'Hundreds of people spent weeks looking for a missing senator, and the FBI knew he was dead but didn't tell anyone? And now the killers have come looking for me, as if they know the FBI won't do anything and that makes me their only problem—'

'We did tell people,' Riley cut me off curtly. 'We told the senator's family we believed he was dead.'

'But not that you knew who killed him,' I fired back.

'No,' Riley said, after a long pause. 'Not that.'

Amber picked up another nacho. 'I think I can summarise where we are right now.' She tilted the chip at Riley. 'Anthony Cleary knows what Maya or Lara here saw, and he wants her dead to cover things up. Your bosses won't protect her, because they can't admit that they know what happened to Senator Castleton. In particular, they can't admit that a federal agent was present when whatever happened to him happened.' She set the chip down again. 'Jesus Christ, Riley. This is a class A clusterfuck.'

'Why do you think I'm here?' His tone grew angry. 'None of this has been handled right. Everyone knows it was messed up, and everyone is covering their asses. The thuds you've been hearing are the lids on the velvet coffins of FBI senior staff slamming shut. They won't let anyone disturb their plans.' He pointed at me. 'Including Maya.'

A chill ran through me. 'The FBI blames me?'

'You shouldn't have been there that day,' Riley said simply. 'As far as they're concerned, that's both of our faults. Mine for saying you wouldn't be there. Yours for showing up. And you were working for Gina Kushman, who's in it with Tony Cleary's gang up to her neck. As far as they're concerned, you must have been in on it, too.'

I was stunned to speechlessness. The FBI was meant to protect me and instead it was *blaming* me for witnessing the aftermath of a murder? I'd had no idea Gina was involved with anything illegal.

Before I could say anything, Zoraida arrived, carrying more food. Seeing the dark faces arrayed around the table, she hesitated, the tray wavering. 'Is this a bad time?'

'No, Zoraida.' Amber reached for her water and leaned back in her chair, smoothing her expression. 'It's perfect.'

On any other occasion, the food would have looked irresistible. The plates were heaped with rice and beans, sending steam twisting up to the light above the table. But even Amber seemed to have lost her appetite. When Zoraida had gone, we sat in silence.

'What happens now?' I asked, hardly daring to look at either of them. 'If you can't help, I should really go home. At least then I'd be with Jamie.'

For a second, nobody replied. A battered pickup truck drove by on the street outside, music blaring through its open windows. When it had gone, Riley spoke.

'Wherever you go, they'll find you. And we can't hide you again because now that he knows you're out here, Tony will be relentless. I can try and convince the FBI to help you, but you are the kind of problem they don't like to have. So right now, it's down to us.' He glanced at Amber. 'You can say this is impossible, but we have to try. You know I'm right.'

For a moment, Amber just stared at him. Finally, she gave a slow, unhappy nod.

'OK, then,' she said, picking up her fork. 'I guess we better come up with a plan.'

TWENTY-ONE

We stayed at the restaurant until the dinner crowd began pouring in. Riley and Amber insisted on paying when Zoraida tried to decline their money.

Riley offered to pay cash, but Amber shooed him away.

'I've got this.' She pulled out a credit card. 'If this goes the way I think it will, you might need to stretch that money.'

The colour rose in Riley's face, but he put his wallet away.

I could see a new dynamic developing between the two of them. Amber was more in charge now. And Riley more worried.

They hurried out, talking, but when I followed them towards the door, Zoraida rested a hand on my arm, holding me back.

'Good luck,' she said, with a gentle smile. 'I wish you well.' Unexpectedly, she leaned forward to hug me. As she did, she whispered very quietly in my ear, 'Be careful with them.'

I looked up in surprise, and saw a cool intelligence behind her brown eyes. Before I could think of anything to say in response, she turned towards Riley and Amber, who had paused to look back.

'Drive safe,' she said.

'It's so good to see Zoraida again,' Amber remarked to Riley as we stepped outside into the warm summer evening. 'I didn't know you'd stayed in touch with her.'

'Yes,' he said. 'I thought she might come in handy.'

'Who is she?' I asked, Zoraida's warning still ringing in my head.

Amber unlocked the car. 'Former Mexican intelligence. She works with the DEA these days, I think.'

'You don't *think*,' Riley scoffed, opening the back door. 'You know.'

Amber gave him a steady look across the top of the car. 'Fine. I know.'

A motorcycle drove by, the rider revving its engine, his head turned towards the three of us.

'Anyway,' Amber said, 'we better get moving.'

When we climbed into Amber's SUV, Riley took the back seat.

Over dinner, they'd decided the safest short-term plan was to head to Houston. It was, they agreed, the best place to hide. But the thing that unnerved me was how little plan we had beyond 'hide'.

I kept thinking about Zoraida's warning. What had she meant? She was a spy who knew them well and yet she didn't trust them.

On the other hand, they'd always looked out for me. If it were not for Riley and Amber, I'd be dead already.

Maybe there was no safety. Not for me, anyway.

The sun was sinking towards the hills in the west, sending rays of gold and magenta streaking across that huge Texas sky. As Amber drove onto the freeway and turned south, the atmosphere in the car seemed to darken along with the horizon.

In the back seat, Riley was silent and morose, while Amber's face had settled back into an enigmatic mask.

'Tell me about Anthony Cleary.' I turned in my seat to look at Riley behind me. 'You say he's smart, and I get that. But I still can't understand why the FBI doesn't bring him in. They must have ways. What about wire taps?'

'Cleary has twenty burner phones on a table in his living room. He changes them out every few days.' Riley made a small gesture with his hands. 'We could bug his home – we've done it in the past – but he has most of his conversations in one of his cars, or outside. He knows how we work. He's studied us for years. He's hired retired agents to teach him.'

I stared at him. 'Former FBI agents actually work for him?'

'FBI agents, cops, lawyers . . . That's what we're up against.' Riley looked out the window at the houses below the freeway. 'It's why they decided to send me in undercover. But even then the risks were very high. At any point, I could have run into someone I knew at Quantico. Someone who trained me or partnered with me on an early operation. The only reason it hasn't happened is because I was mostly based down here in the past and I didn't meet a lot of agents in the Houston office.' He gave a bitter chuckle. 'I thought they chose me for the job because I was good. In reality, they were looking for someone nobody knew. Somebody young enough and dumb enough to believe going undercover was his big break. Somebody they could let fail. And I ran straight in.'

In the rear-view mirror, Amber met his eyes. 'Anyone would have done the same.'

But Riley didn't seem convinced. 'I was particularly willing to be their fool. Served myself up on a platter.'

'I don't understand,' I said. 'Why would the FBI want you to fail?'

'Because the FBI doesn't really want to bring Tony Cleary down,' Riley said. 'The FBI is too deep in his pocket to want that.'

I was so shocked by this, for a moment I couldn't think of anything to say, but it wasn't me he'd directed the comment to. When he'd said it, Riley had been looking at Amber.

If she was shocked, though, it didn't show.

'Now you just sound self-pitying,' she told him.

'Do I?' Riley looked at her in the mirror. 'Or am I just saying what you already suspected? Surely your people have some idea of what's been going on? They must have known Senator Castleton was on the take, the same as we did. They knew the FBI declined to run multiple investigations into Tony's operations. And they must know that when the pressure got too much and Tony went too far, the FBI chose to place a junior operative undercover and *bury* him there.'

His spat out the last words, fury in his tone.

'My people know you're good,' Amber said.

'*Bullshit.*' Riley said it angrily. 'Don't do that, Amber. I rely on you to tell me the truth. We've known each other too long for anything else.'

There was a brief pause. Amber glanced at me and then back at Riley. 'Let's talk about this later.'

'Maya can handle it,' he said. 'She's not a child.'

But Amber refused to take the bait, and they fell into a taut silence – Amber with her eyes on the road, and Riley staring out the window to where the hills in the distance were disappearing in the twilight.

I tried to understand everything he had just said. Did he really believe the FBI was corrupt? If that was the case, who would protect me?

Despair washed over me. This was hopeless. They should have just left me with Jamie.

After that, none of us talked much. The hills were soon replaced by miles of flat farmland, most of it lost in the darkness. One knife-straight freeway merged into another until Houston announced itself with endless unlovely strip malls, garishly lit gas stations, car dealerships the size of casinos, and gun shops. It was like Austin and completely different at the same time. And much, much bigger.

The actual city of Houston is relatively small – it's home to just over two million people. But the suburbs sprawl for miles and hold an additional five million residents. Add in the surrounding communities, many of them now virtually consumed by the city's endless, voracious growth, and you have a total of nearly ten million people living across a gigantic landscape. I supposed it was a good place to be right now. I would be the needle in Houston's haystack.

By the time we finally pulled up in the driveway of a

low-slung brick house half hidden from the road behind a row of shaggy pine trees, the stress and the lack of sleep were catching up with me.

'Is this your house?' I asked Amber.

'It's a safe house I've used before. You can't stay here for more than a few days, but . . .' she glanced at Riley '. . . I have a feeling you won't need it for long.'

It was hard to make out much in the darkness, but the house looked small and neat, with a wide driveway and garage. The front lawn was well maintained. It was nothing you would even look at twice. The number mounted in chrome on the dark painted door read '3291'.

Amber unlocked the door and switched on the lights, illuminating a plainly furnished suburban entrance hall. The air was warm and smelled slightly stale, as if no one had been here in a while. She paused in the hallway to turn on the air conditioning while Riley and I walked past her. The floors were a forgettable taupe ceramic tile; the walls were all white. A wide hallway led into a large living room, where cheap sofas were arranged in a neat rectangle. There was no television.

Beyond that was a kitchen with wood cabinets and a round table with four chairs.

'Make yourselves at home.' Amber glanced at her phone quickly before sliding it into her pocket. 'You're going to need supplies, so I'll run to the supermarket and get some basics. Is there anything you particularly want?'

'Coffee,' Riley said.

Amber glanced at me, but I shook my head.

I couldn't think right now, so many questions were swirling in my mind.

Amber paused and held out her hand. 'I need to take your phone, Maya. I'll get you a new burner while I'm out.'

There wasn't any point in arguing. Besides, I had a list of all the phone numbers I wanted to keep inside my escape bag. This wasn't my first rodeo.

I handed it to her, and she slipped it into her pocket and headed for the door.

Riley stood in the middle of the living room. In the glare of the ceiling light, I could see that his fine-boned face needed a shave. His skin looked grey from exhaustion. His shirt was rumpled, his hair was tangled.

But to me, he looked wonderful.

For a year, I'd wondered about Riley Maguire. Dreamed of seeing him again. Longed just to talk to him. And I believed he'd missed me, too. I'd known it the moment I'd run to him in the restaurant. The way his arms had closed around me without hesitation.

Surely I could trust him? Even if nobody else on this planet was trustworthy, he must be.

For a moment, I thought about telling him what Zoraida had said, but I couldn't make myself do it. The look in her eyes stayed with me — a knowing, cautioning look. And I thought of Riley saying carelessly, 'I thought she might come in useful.' As if Zoraida were a used car or a spare hammer.

Of course, Zoraida herself was a spy, and spies used disinformation to get what they wanted.

Be careful with them. Even that sentence was a trap. It had made me doubt everything, and I couldn't discuss it with the only people who might be able to tell me what it meant. And Zoraida would have known that.

Sensing my gaze, Riley glanced up at me.

'Not what you expected?' He gestured at the plain space around us. 'It's not exactly the Ritz.'

'It's fine.' I cleared my throat. 'I'd like to call the hospital and check on Jamie.'

He gave a slight headshake. 'It's getting late. Why don't you leave it until tomorrow?' He hoisted the bag that he'd brought from Chicago onto his shoulder. 'I need a shower. Do you want to choose a room before I choose mine?'

I wondered what it would feel like to care which room in a strange house in a strange city I would sleep in while killers searched for me.

'Any room is fine. Take whichever one you want,' I said.

He smiled, a flash of even, white teeth. 'See you in a minute.'

When he'd gone, I stood still, listening to his footsteps as he walked down the hall, the faint squeak of doors opening. Then the sounds of water running and Riley whistling tunelessly.

My own bag still lay on the floor in the entrance hall.

I kept thinking of the house on Dove Lane, the familiar smells and sounds of it, and suddenly I was lonelier than I'd ever been in my life. Everything had been stripped away from me in a matter of hours. My home, my friends, my job, my plans. Riley was right that it was too late to call, but what if Jamie was dead? I wouldn't know. And what about Elaine?

She'd phoned while we were driving here, and Amber had told me not to answer. What would she think?

Tears ran down my cheeks and I fought to make myself stop. But my exhausted, shocked body wouldn't listen, and I realised I was shaking, unable to control the reaction.

Riley called from somewhere. 'The beds aren't made, but I found sheets and towels in the hall closet.'

I sank onto the sofa and lowered my head onto my knees, wrapping my arms around myself. I didn't want him to see me cry. I was stronger now than I'd been last time. I really was.

'Hey.'

Riley's concerned voice came from right beside me, but I didn't look up.

'Hey,' he said again.

The sofa cushions shifted as he sat beside me. I felt the warmth of him as he put his arm across my shoulder.

'Maya . . .' he began, but I shook my head.

He placed both hands on my arms and lifted me up. Again, I shook my head, my eyes squeezed shut, but he pulled me close, pressing my head against his shoulder.

His chest was hard against mine, and I could feel his damp hair against my cheek, smell his clean soap and toothpaste, the sandpaper-rough whiskers against my skin.

'You are going to be fine,' he told me, softly. 'You have come through things that have destroyed trained officers. You've lost it all and come back. This will not defeat you.'

'What if Jamie's dead?' I whispered, voicing the fear that threatened to crush me.

His hold on me didn't loosen.

'You have no reason to believe she is. She was doing fine when you left. Hang on to that.'

His voice was so reasonable, and the feel of his arms around me so comforting, some of the cold loneliness began to ebb.

'You won't leave me?' I heard myself ask.

He shook his head, his cheek moving against mine. 'Not this time.'

At last, I lifted my head, and our eyes met.

He'd changed out of the rumpled shirt into a black T-shirt and jeans. His dark hair was wet and tousled. He looked rugged and clean.

I'd dreamed about those blue eyes so many times, and now they were looking into mine. A surge of electricity passed between us.

His hands slid down from my shoulders to my waist. They felt hot against my skin.

'I'm sorry you're going through this. It's the last thing I wanted for you.' He hesitated. 'I can't tell you how often I've thought about picking up the phone to call you. To make sure you were safe. I kept thinking something would happen and you'd call me, but you never did. Not until yesterday.'

'You told me not to,' I reminded him.

His lips curved up, and I found myself watching the movement with a kind of fascination.

'You really listen to instructions.' He said it softly, and the way he looked at me made something tighten inside me.

In the quiet that followed, we both very clearly heard the key enter the lock.

Instantly, Riley dropped his hands. I turned away, my face flaming.

'I'm back.' Amber walked in, her arms filled with bags. She flicked a glance from Riley to me. We were about six feet apart by then, but there was a pause before she said, 'There's more in the car.'

'I'll get it.' Riley walked out the door, not even stopping to put on shoes.

Still holding the bags, Amber turned to watch him go.

I stood for a moment, trying to process what had just happened. Nothing he'd said had been anything other than kind, and yet the skin on my back still burned from his touch.

Nobody had looked at me like Riley just had in a very long time. And I would give anything – any amount of money – for him to look at me like that again.

'Everything OK?' Amber asked, and I realised she had turned her focus to me – tear-stained, heat high in my cheeks. Every emotion written there for her to read.

'It's fine,' I said. But nothing was fine. Nothing at all.

TWENTY-TWO

'I'm sorry it took so long, I didn't know where anything was,' Amber explained as I helped unpack the grocery bags in the kitchen a few minutes later. 'I had to go down every row and I'm not great at shopping at the best of times.'

The safe house kitchen was straight out of the twentieth century, with faux-oak cabinets and cheap countertops, but it was very clean. When I opened a cabinet, I saw it was completely empty, save for a small stuffed dog, a little dirty, with one loose ear.

I found myself lifting it out and smoothing the soft fabric. Poor little dog. Left behind.

'Oh, look at that.' Amber leaned over to see the toy. 'Someone who stayed here must have forgotten it.'

This was a child's toy, and obviously much loved. I wondered what kind of situation would have meant a family with children needed the protection of a safe house.

The realisation put my own situation into perspective, and I set the little dog down on the counter and went back to unpacking bags, glancing occasionally at its small, open face.

Amber opened the refrigerator and said without glancing at me, 'I don't mean to pry, but it looks like you've been crying.'

I set a loaf of bread on the counter.

'I'm fine, I promise. I'm just really tired, I think.' I thought of Riley's hands on my waist, his breath against my cheek, and felt my cheeks go warm. 'A bit of a meltdown.'

Amber turned to face me.

'Look, it's been a hell of a day. I'm surprised it didn't happen earlier.' She searched my eyes. 'Did anything happen? Anything you want to tell me?'

There was real sympathy in her expression, but behind it I sensed a sharpening of her attention. I was aware already of the intensity always half hidden behind that deceptively smooth expression. It seemed to me Amber was constantly assessing, judging and considering every slight movement. I'd observed it often – a quick flash of cool in her eyes that disappeared as suddenly as it arrived. It unnerved me.

I leaned casually against the counter, my hands behind me. 'To be honest, Riley and I had a bit of a disagreement. I wanted to call the hospital and check on Jamie, but he said to wait until tomorrow.' I paused. 'I'm so worried about her.'

Amber pulled her phone from her pocket and held it out to me.

'Call. Use this phone. Hospitals are always open.'

In an instant, I forgot all about that moment in the living room and snatched the phone from her eagerly.

'Thank you, Amber.' My voice shook a little. I felt intensely grateful – grateful to be trusted, and aware that maybe I didn't deserve to be.

'Go on,' she said, tilting her head at the door to the living room. 'Make the call. I can handle the rest of this.'

As I walked out, I passed Riley coming the other way carrying two more bags of groceries. His bare feet made no sound on the tiles, and I found myself wondering if he'd been outside the kitchen while Amber and I were talking.

But when he spoke, his voice was light. 'How much did you buy? There's enough here for weeks.'

'You never know what you'll need,' Amber said.

My back was to them, so I couldn't see their faces, but Riley must have made some gesture at me because Amber said, 'She's calling the hospital.'

I stepped out into the living room and closed the door behind me as I searched for the hospital's number. It struck me that the phone felt warm, as if Amber had been talking on it recently. I wondered if that was the real reason she'd been out so long.

After I found the right number, I was on hold for a few minutes before the hospital receptionist picked up and put me through to Jamie's room. The phone rang four times before Jamie's mother answered.

'Hello? Jamie's room.'

'Mrs Sheridan? It's . . . Lara.' After a year of it feeling real to me, the name felt false again. An invention. A lie. 'I just wanted to check on Jamie.'

'Lara, sweetheart. Thank God. We've been trying to reach you, but your phone just rings and rings.'

Her words turned my heart to ice. But before I could find the breath to ask what had happened, she continued.

'Jamie's doing better, honey. Her breathing's getting stronger, and the doctors think they'll be able to take her off the oxygen tomorrow. She's responding to the treatment better than they'd hoped. No infection, and that was the big fear.'

My body sagged. It took a moment for me to find my voice again.

'I'm so glad,' I said. 'I've been scared to death, Mrs Sheridan. She looked so hurt.'

'I'll bet you have. She frightened the daylights out of all of us, but her doctors are really hopeful.' She paused. 'She's out of it right now, honey, but earlier she was asking for you. Are you going to come see her tomorrow?'

I bit my lip hard, trying to find the right words. 'I can't. I had a family emergency and I had to leave town this afternoon. I feel terrible about this. I'm so sorry not to be there for her.'

'My Lord, Lara. What happened?' Jamie's mother sounded puzzled and worried, and I couldn't blame her. My story sounded absurd even to me.

'It's my dad. He had a heart attack. I found out while I was at the hospital today and I just had to run. I'm in Florida now.'

'Oh, you poor thing. Don't worry, I'll tell Jamie. I know she'll understand.'

'I hated leaving her,' I said. 'It's the last thing I want to do, but my dad's really bad. These things all happening at once . . .'

I ran out of lies, and my voice faded.

'She'll understand. You have to be with your family.'

Her kindness was a kick in the stomach. I didn't deserve her sympathy. I wanted to tell her, 'Jamie is my family, and

I'm the reason she nearly died. It's all my fault.' But I could never say those words to anyone. It would be my life's shame.

Instead, I dug my fingernails into my palms to steady myself, and said, 'I'll call to check on her tomorrow. If she wakes up, tell her I love her so much. And that I'm . . . I'm just sorry.'

'You have nothing to be sorry for, sweetheart,' she told me firmly. 'Go be with your family. I'll be here with Jamie. Oh, by the way, your boss was in here. She was asking if I'd seen you. Did you tell her about your father? She sounded worried.'

I covered my eyes with one hand and let out a shaky breath.

'I'll call her,' I promised.

After I hung up, I stared at the unfamiliar white walls, and thought about Jamie lying in a hospital bed, wired to half a dozen beeping machines. Her life on hold.

All because of me.

TWENTY-THREE

A short while later, I went upstairs, pleading exhaustion. Riley and Amber were still in the kitchen, but I didn't want to talk any more. My head throbbed. I was heartbroken about Jamie and confused about what had happened with Riley. I needed to think.

On the upper floor, I found four bedrooms. Riley had taken the one closest to the stairs – he'd left the door open and the light on, and I could see his leather shoulder bag on the bed, and a damp yellow towel slung over the back of a plain wooden chair. The scent of his cologne still hung in the air. The cool, green fragrance was so familiar to me – as if I'd known him for years rather than two days, one year apart. I breathed in, half closing my eyes.

I'd spent a year building Riley up into an almost mythical figure – a hero who came to my rescue when I needed him. Now that he was in my life again, I was increasingly confused about what I felt. He'd changed since last summer. He seemed distracted, unhappy. I was certain he was hiding something from me. And yet every time he touched me, my body reacted. I could still feel his arms around me, his hands against my skin.

I felt a little out of control and it scared me. I'd spent

a year getting myself together. I didn't want to fall apart now.

I chose the bedroom furthest from his, at the far end of the hallway, and closed the door behind me. It was simple and spacious, sparsely furnished with a double bed and a white-pine dresser. There were no pictures on the walls or ornamentation of any kind; it was as plain as a convent cell. When I opened the closet door, I found the big walk-in space eerily empty. Bare hangers clattered like dry bones.

I crossed to the sole window and peered through the blinds. The backyard was mostly lost in darkness, save for a bright rectangle of light from the kitchen window.

I wondered what Riley and Amber were talking about. When I'd walked in to tell them about Jamie, they'd fallen silent as soon as they heard my footsteps. We all had secrets to keep. Each of us, in our own way, was lying.

I got the sense that, despite their long history, Amber didn't entirely trust Riley. And that he was cautious of her.

They both knew more than they were telling me. And as I looked at that long stretch of reflected light, it occurred to me they'd been talking for a long time, and they could be saying things I needed to know.

I crossed to the bedroom door and cracked it open. I could hear nothing. The hallway light was off and the stairs were lost in shadow. Carefully, I crept down the corridor to the staircase. From the landing, I could hear the murmur of voices but couldn't make out any words. I slipped down the stairs, pausing three steps from the bottom to listen.

Riley was mid-sentence: '. . . go and see him. He says he'll help if he can.'

'Great.' Amber didn't sound happy. 'God, I can't believe you're dealing with him again, Ri. He's a drug dealer.'

'Does that matter?' he asked.

There was a pause before Amber spoke again. 'You know, I honestly don't understand how you got yourself in the middle of this. How did you not stop this from happening?'

'Maya wasn't supposed to be there that day.' Riley's voice was tight. 'We paid off the guard, and he told us she wouldn't be there. We believed him. And that idiot manager, Gina. She was supposed to make sure Maya avoided that house, but she had some meeting and she forgot, or at least that's what she told us later.'

My chest tightened, and I sank down onto the step.

'Why would she lie?' Amber asked. 'Did Gina know what was supposed to happen that day?'

'Gina does whatever Tony Cleary tells her,' Riley said. 'She's getting a percentage from the sale of that house, so she knows better than to ask questions. He's one of the owners of the development, you see. One of the original investors. It was a good place to hide money.'

The pieces fell into place. Anthony Cleary owned The Gateway. Gina and Ed – along with everyone there – were part of his operation. The moment I'd taken that job, I had been working for criminals. Those houses with their extraordinary views were how Cleary laundered his money, and I was right in the middle of it.

I lowered my head until it rested on my wrists. I'd been

doomed from day one. The job I'd thought I was so lucky to have had been a trap. What a fool I'd been, over and over.

I felt hopeless. Everywhere I turned, trouble sat waiting.

The voices from the kitchen rumbled on, but for a while I was too lost in my own thoughts to listen. And then Amber's voice rose, catching my attention.

'This is your fucking life, Riley. It'll be the end of your career. And for what? Cleary will get Maya in the end and you know it. If we moved her to Bali, he'd find her there. You know he's obsessive.'

Riley replied with a hint of anger. 'Yes, I know that. I also know him far better than you do – I've spent years watching that psychopath. But it doesn't matter. I couldn't just leave her there in the middle of that mess. She wouldn't last one day.'

'Get your people to put her in witness protection,' Amber said. 'It's her only chance.'

'Oh sure, I'll just run and do that.' Riley's tone was sarcastic. 'I'll add Maya to the top-secret government list. And then I'll give myself a million dollars and a long vacation.'

'Don't be a child. You can't do it, but Will can.'

Amber's words seemed to leave Riley speechless.

I frowned. Who was Will? Someone they both knew. Someone important.

Amber continued, her tone less angry. 'Does Will even know you're here, Ri? Does he know you've got Maya? Have you told him anything at all?'

A long, telling silence followed.

Finally, Riley said, 'I haven't told Will because I know

it's pointless. I've asked him repeatedly to step in for Maya, and to get me out of this operation in Chicago, and he won't listen. He's caught up in this somehow.'

'Caught up with Cleary?' Amber sounded sceptical.

'I think so,' Riley said. 'This Castleton murder – it's career ruining, for him as much as me. He had the chance to stop it, and he didn't. The agency is right in the middle of it. But he's halfway up the golden ladder at Quantico, so he has much more to lose than I do.' He paused. 'I think he's looking for a way to throw me under a bus.'

'And you think what you did today *helps*?' Amber asked. 'Riley, you're AWOL in the middle of an operation the FBI considers critical. They will figure out where you are and what you're doing, and then there'll be hell to pay. Will doesn't have to throw you anywhere. You've climbed under the bus yourself.'

'Maybe I have,' Riley said shortly. 'But Tony Cleary was coming for Maya. She was going to die. I'm sorry if there wasn't time to file my paperwork.'

He said it with contempt, and Amber let out a long sigh. 'Look, I don't understand what's going on with you right now. You're good at what you do. You've worked on the Cleary case for so long, why would you sacrifice everything for someone you hardly know? I don't want anything bad to happen to Maya, but I wouldn't throw my career away for her.'

'Well, there we differ.' Riley's tone was clipped.

A long silence fell. I could imagine them looking at their cups of coffee, thinking about what to say next.

'Is this some sort of hero syndrome, Ri?' Amber asked suddenly. 'Don't make that face. I've seen the way Maya looks at you, like you're the greatest rock star and she's the only groupie in town. That stuff's pretty irresistible—'

'Stop it, Amber.' Riley sounded genuinely angry. 'Don't patronise me. I simply didn't want an innocent woman to die. Is that so unusual? In a way, you might say I'm doing my job for the first time in three years. I'm finally helping someone escape a murderer. Isn't that why we got into all of this in the first place? To help people?'

There was a plaintive note to his voice. But when she spoke again, Amber still sounded unconvinced. 'I get that you want to help her, but if you throw away your career for her, you won't be much help to anyone.'

Riley gave an explosive sigh. 'If you won't accept my explanation, what can I do? I've spent years watching people suffer and be victimised and killed by a criminal gang, and I've done nothing but record their suffering for posterity. Not one thing has changed because of all I've seen. People just keep getting hurt. I told Will that Senator Castleton's murder was the end of it, so he won't be surprised to find out I've had enough. I'm going to keep Maya safe, and you can either help me or you can walk out that door. No one's going to blame you if you go. I've known you too long for that.'

There was another tense silence.

Amber broke it first, her voice even. 'I'm not going anywhere. But listen to me. I've seen the way you look at her, and I've seen the way she looks at you. So be careful. Some lines shouldn't be crossed.'

I held my breath, my fingers gripping the cold banister, waiting for his answer.

'Like you've never crossed a line,' was all he said.

His voice sounded closer and, without warning, the living-room door flew open, sending light flooding into the hallway and spilling towards the stairs.

I jumped to my feet and ran back to the bedroom, closing the door quietly behind me.

Alone in my room, I heard Amber's voice in my head. *'I've seen the way you look at her . . .'*

And despite everything, warmth spread through my body.

The next morning, I walked down to the kitchen a little after nine o'clock, my hair damp from the shower, my feet bare.

I'd awoken an hour earlier, bewildered to find myself in an unfamiliar room where everything was white. For a second, I'd wondered if I was in a hospital.

When I passed Riley's room, the door again stood open. His bed was empty, the covers neatly in place, but the towel was no longer on the chair.

Downstairs, the curtains were drawn back and sunlight poured through the windows, settling on the ceramic tile floors in warm, bright pools. There was no sign of Riley. Instead, Amber sat at the breakfast table, a mug of coffee and an open laptop in front of her.

'Good morning,' she said, glancing up. 'There's coffee on the counter and food . . .' she waved one hand expressively '. . . everywhere.'

I found a white mug with bright pink flowers in the cupboard. It looked to me as if the place had been furnished from garage sales. Nothing matched, but everything was serviceable. The coffee was rich and dark and the air was instantly perfumed with it.

When I turned back, Amber's attention was focused on her computer, so I could study her with impunity. She and Riley must have been up late – I'd been awake for an hour after I'd run upstairs, and no one else had come up – but she didn't appear tired. Her dark hair was as neatly styled as it had been yesterday, and her make-up was perfect. She'd changed clothes and was wearing a snug navy-blue top with skinny black trousers and black leather tennis shoes.

'Did you spend the night here?' I asked, sliding into the chair across from her.

'No, but I don't live far away. I've been here about half an hour.' She closed the laptop and pushed it aside. In the sunlight, her brown eyes were liquid, her eyelashes a soft, dark fringe. 'Riley asked me to come early – he had to go meet someone.'

'He's not here?' This realisation jolted me, in the wake of their argument last night. 'Is he coming back?'

Amber cocked her head as if I'd said something strange.

'Of course. It's only a meeting.'

'Oh good.' I took a sip of coffee to disguise my nerves. 'It's just all the things you guys were saying about Anthony Cleary made me think it's not safe for him out there.'

To her credit, Amber took this comment seriously. 'I think it's fair to assume Cleary doesn't know yet what's going on.

He hasn't had time to put it together. We have a window of opportunity with him. The FBI is a different story.'

'What are they going to do to Riley?' I asked. 'How much trouble is he in?'

Instead of replying, Amber considered me, her eyes taking in the face I'd seen in the mirror that morning – tired, worried, puffy-eyed.

'I feel like we've somehow skipped important questions like "How did you sleep?" and "Are you hungry?" and jumped straight to "Is Riley going to get fired?"' Her tone was pointed.

'I slept well, and I'm going to make some toast in a minute,' I said. 'Is Riley going to get fired?'

Amber sighed. 'I'd fire him, if I were his boss. He's being a real pain in the ass right now.' Picking up her cup, she walked over to the coffee maker. 'Why he couldn't call and tell them he needed some personal leave, I simply don't understand. He does shit like this sometimes and it drives me crazy. It's irresponsible.'

For a second, she sounded like an exasperated sibling dealing with her difficult younger brother.

I had a lot of questions, but I'd overheard so much last night, I had to be careful not to reveal that I knew things I shouldn't.

Taking another casual sip, I said, 'I think you told me once that you two have known each other a long time. When did you meet?'

'Years ago.' She poured coffee into her cup, steam rising. 'I was twenty-two. We were both straight out of college, working for HPD. Drinking too much, taking too many risks. We were wild back then. Bulletproof.' She lingered at the counter, a hint of a smile softening her face. 'We made detective in the same month, our careers were on the same track. It was a kind of competition — who could outrank the other. I usually won.'

I studied her with interest. 'I've got to say, I can't really imagine the two of you as normal cops.'

Amber's eyebrows rose. 'Why not?'

'You don't act like you enjoy rules.'

Amber gave a quick, surprised laugh. 'Well, that's true enough.' Still holding her cup, she walked to the window and looked out. From where I sat, the backyard was almost blindingly green. A low wooden fence surrounded the lawn, while two mature trees blocked views from surrounding houses. 'I think it's fair to say we pushed everything to the limit. The rules, the hours, ourselves.' She sat down and regarded me frankly. 'We were good at our jobs, and we knew it. But you're right, that cocky attitude doesn't go down well, and eventually they put us in separate units, working different parts of the city. Then the FBI came calling for Riley. And I left at about the same time.'

I paused, building the courage to ask the next question.

'Amber, who exactly do you work for?'

During the pause that followed, I could hear the ticking of the coffee maker on the counter and the faint rumble of a car driving by outside. Amber looked at me, unblinking.

'I can't—' she began, but I cut her off.

'Oh, come on, who am I going to tell?' I held up my

hands. 'You know, it's kind of hard to trust you if you don't trust me.'

She gave me a quick, condemning look, but seemed to give in. 'I can't tell you the name of the agency. You'll never have heard of it anyway. All I can say is that we work closely with the CIA, the FBI and the DEA on major criminal operations, like Anthony Cleary's. I can't say more than that, but that's enough, isn't it?'

'Were you working with the FBI on the Cleary case?' I asked.

She shot me a flat look. 'You know I'm not going to answer that, right?'

It didn't matter. It all made more sense now, anyway. Riley had sent me to Texas because Amber was here. He knew she'd work outside of the rules, and because of their long friendship, he'd counted on her to help. And she'd come through.

'Why do you think Riley's helping me?' I was fishing now, hoping she'd tell me some of the things they'd said to each other.

Amber set down her coffee and gave me a direct look. 'You know, you ask a lot of questions about Riley Maguire. Is there any particular reason for that?'

Telltale heat rose to my face. 'Just making conversation,' I mumbled, looking down into the dark heart of my coffee cup.

'Look, Maya.' Amber angled forward, almost forcing me to look up. 'I've known Riley a long time. But I can't recommend falling in love with him.'

'I'm *not*,' I insisted, my flush deepening.

'Of course you're not,' she said steadily. 'All I'm saying is, he's a good-looking guy, and he's done this swooping in and saving thing. And that can get confusing.'

'I'm not confused,' I insisted, although that was the least honest thing I'd said so far that day. 'Besides, didn't you date him? Isn't that what those cops said?'

'For about two seconds a hundred years ago.' Amber sounded exasperated. 'Don't misread me, Maya. This isn't jealousy. This is good, sound advice. And you should take it.'

I squirmed in the glare of her unwavering gaze. 'I don't know why you're saying this to me. You and Riley are the only people I know in this city, and I'm talking about the two of you to each other, as I'd imagine you're talking about me.' I gave her a defiant look. 'I'm not in love with him any more than I'm in love with you.'

'Well, good.' She drew back, picking up her coffee. 'Because I'm not interested.' When I didn't smile, she grew serious. 'Just don't let yourself get caught up in this thing. Be careful.'

There it was again. The same warning Zoraida had given me.

Everybody wanted me to be careful of everyone else.

'Careful is all I know how to be.' I stood with all the dignity I could muster. 'I'm going to make breakfast now.'

We talked about other things after that – safe things. Who owned the house – the government, but through a shell corporation. And where in the city of Houston we were – on the west side somewhere. A suburb called Westchester.

When Riley returned an hour later, we were still at the table.

'There you are.' Amber looked up at him. 'How'd it go? Did you meet Danny?'

'Yeah, he's fine. He's going to get us a car. He said he hadn't seen anyone new in town that might be one of Tony's guys, but he'll keep an eye out.' He was carrying a bag, which he set down by the table. 'Is the coffee fresh?'

Amber nodded.

'It's already hot out there,' Riley said over his shoulder as he walked across to pour a cup. 'I'm sweating.'

He hadn't so much as glanced at me, and I was avoiding looking at him.

'I checked with my people while you were out,' Amber said. 'Nobody's flown in from Cleary's crew.'

'Tomorrow could be different, though,' Riley said. 'We can't stay here.'

He leaned back against the counter, holding his cup.

'Where can we go?' I asked.

Riley and Amber exchanged quick looks.

'That's what we need to decide,' Riley said. 'I'm working on it.' He walked back to the table. When he pulled out a chair, the bag fell over with a thud.

'Oh, yes.' Picking it up, he held it out to me. 'I got you a new burner phone.'

For the first time, our eyes met, and he smiled at me. I felt that smile on my skin.

When I took the bag, his fingers brushed mine and my heart jumped, and everything Amber had said five minutes earlier evaporated from my mind.

I pulled out a clear plastic case holding a black phone. 'Thank you so much.' I glanced at Amber. 'I'm going to call Jamie again, if no one objects.'

'Go ahead. Don't tell anyone where you are,' Amber warned.

I gave her a withering look. 'Oh, really? Because I was going to ask everyone to come visit.'

She had the grace to smile. 'Fine, fine, you know the drill.'

I took the phone upstairs to the bedroom and turned it on. It had one bar of battery. Enough, I thought, for one call.

Out of habit, I tried Jamie's cell first, but it went straight to voicemail, so I called the hospital again and was put through to her room.

On the third ring, someone answered. 'Hello?'

The voice was weak and airless, but it was Jamie's.

'Oh my God, it's you,' I said, my heart jumping. 'You're awake.'

'Lara?' Her voice was so faded, it was like talking to a ghost. 'Where are you?'

In the background, I could hear the unmistakable sounds of a hospital – the beeping and whirr of machines connected to her by yards of tubing.

'Did your mom tell you? My dad had a heart attack. I had to go to Florida.'

Every word hurt me. She'd nearly died and here I was, lying and lying.

'She did . . . Lara . . . Is he . . . OK?'

She sounded so weak. The long pauses while she fought for breath were like knives plunging into me.

'He's hanging in there.' I swallowed hard. 'But tell me about you? Are you feeling better?'

'I have to have . . . an operation.' She paused to breathe. 'Tomorrow. My leg. Some pins.'

'Another one?' I pressed my fingertips against my eyes. 'I'm so sorry this happened, Jamie, and I'm not there to help you.'

'You have to be . . . with your . . . dad,' she whispered.

'But I hate my father. You know that,' I reminded her.

She gave a slight laugh. Barely there, but very her. 'We have to . . . accept . . . our families.'

'You're my family,' I told her simply. 'I'm going to come back and be with you very soon.'

The second I said it, I knew with cold clarity that it was true. I would go with Riley for a while to do whatever we had to do, but I wouldn't start a new life somewhere else. Not again. If I had to kill Anthony Cleary to get my life back, I'd do it.

Unaware of my inner turmoil, Jamie said, 'That's good because . . . I'm going to need help . . . with the dishes . . .'

'I'll do everything,' I promised. 'You'll just sit on cushions like a queen.'

'That will . . . be . . . a change.'

I laughed. 'You're definitely getting better.'

'I am.' She drew a breath. 'I forgot . . . The police . . .

were here . . . looking for you . . . They said . . . your . . . name . . . isn't Lara . . .'

My smile froze and then faded as Jamie struggled to find the air to continue.

'They said . . . they're looking for . . . someone named . . . Maya . . .' She paused to wheeze and catch her breath before adding the final nails in my coffin. 'And . . . something . . . about . . . Montana'

TWENTY-FOUR

Everything went quiet. I couldn't find the words to tell Jamie a lie. I couldn't seem to think at all. How could the police know my real identity? How could they have figured that out so quickly?

'I d-don't understand,' I stammered. 'That must be a mistake.'

'That's what . . . I said . . .' she agreed.

Her breathing was more laboured now, and I hated hearing her struggle. I didn't matter. What the police thought didn't matter. She mattered.

'I think we've talked enough. You need to rest,' I told her. 'I love you so much, Jamie. You keep getting stronger. I'll call you later.'

When she replied, it was with sudden, firm strength. 'I love you.'

And then the noise of that hospital room with its beeping machines disappeared, and my room seemed so quiet. Despite the heat of the day, I felt cold to my fingertips.

I ran down to the kitchen. When the door swung open, Amber looked up and saw my expression.

'What's wrong?'

'The police know who I am. They told Jamie.'

The words were barely out of my mouth before Amber was on her feet, her face set, her phone in her hand. She stormed out of the room.

Riley stepped closer and took my arm, turning me to face him. 'Tell me what she said again. Every word you can remember.'

I went back through the conversation. As he listened, Riley's brow furrowed.

'This doesn't make sense. The police might figure out Lara Gibson isn't real, but that wouldn't lead them to Maya. There are no strings tying Lara to you. And for them to figure that out in hours . . . That's virtually impossible.'

'What does it mean?' I asked.

Turning, he met my gaze directly. In the sunlight, his eyes were almost turquoise.

'Someone told them.'

I drew in a shocked breath. 'Who would do that?'

'I don't know.' Riley's lips tightened. 'But I have an idea.'

We both heard the sound of footsteps before the kitchen door swung open. Amber stood in the doorway, her expression dark.

'It's worse than we thought.' She held up her phone. 'They're not just looking for Maya, they're looking for you, too, Riley. The FBI has listed you as a missing person and asked law enforcement to find you.'

She turned to me, and I knew it was bad before she spoke, the way gunshot victims say they sensed the bullet before it hit. 'And there's a warrant out for Maya's arrest. For murder.'

I was speechless.

'*Murder?*' Riley stared at her. 'Who is she supposed to have—' He stopped himself as Amber gave him an expressive look. 'Castleton? They're charging her with killing Senator Castleton?'

Riley wasn't easy to shock, but he looked stunned.

I'd gone numb. I'd never hurt anyone. I was a gentle person. I didn't even kill spiders. I just sort of ushered them outside. How could this be happening?

'I don't understand,' I whispered.

But neither of them looked at me.

'Who's behind it?' Riley asked Amber.

'Could be Cleary,' she said. 'Could be your guys settling scores.'

Riley swore, loudly and viciously, shoving a chair against a wall so hard it sent chips of paint showering to the floor.

'There's no reason for this,' he growled. 'This is ludicrous.'

'This is a *distraction*.' Amber emphasised the last word. 'It's very smart. If it was the FBI, then they've figured out you're with Maya, and now they're smoking you out.' She sounded almost impressed.

'It could be Tony Cleary behind it all, pulling strings,' Riley said. 'He could have Will working with him without Will even knowing he's being manipulated.' He was calmer now, intensely focused. 'I need to talk to someone in the Chicago office.'

'Is that a good idea?' Amber asked. 'Let me talk to my team again first.'

But I had finally found my voice.

'Who's Will?'

They both turned to look at me with nearly identical expressions of surprise. I think they'd momentarily forgotten I was there. I remembered overhearing the two of them talking about Will last night, but this was the first time either of them had mentioned him openly in front of me.

It was Riley who answered. 'Will Fulton. He's my supervisor.'

'And you think he might be behind this?'

'It's complicated.' Riley looked at Amber, who made an impatient gesture.

'Just tell her.' She turned to me. 'You know Riley believes the FBI has been messing around with Anthony Cleary?'

'Yes, I've heard you say that, but what do you mean?' I asked. 'Messing around how?'

'In a lot of ways. Usually, Cleary gives the FBI a little useful information and in exchange they back off his people. It's a common tactic, but we think he might have taken it too far, and that might have left some people compromised. If Will took too much from or gave too much to Cleary, he could get in a great deal of trouble, and that makes him vulnerable to more pressure from Cleary. He can be blackmailed, basically. Riley thinks this is affecting Will's judgement.'

'But I don't understand.' I turned to Riley. 'If the FBI is cooperating with Cleary, why put you in there to investigate him at all?'

'I was told the FBI wanted to bring Cleary down once and for all. But I'm not sure that was ever the plan.' Riley's voice was flat.

Amber regarded him thoughtfully. 'I've been wondering about that. You think they put you in there as a spy? Just to find out what Cleary was doing?'

'Maybe to find out how much money he had. Or to make sure he wasn't going to expose the FBI's duplicity.' Riley rubbed his jaw. 'It felt like I was babysitting him rather than stopping him. If I'm right about that, then they just used me to protect themselves.'

Amber stood looking at him, her mind working. 'Shit,' she said, after a second. 'That really could be it, you know.'

'But why are they saying I killed Castleton?' I demanded.

'Cleary may have told them you did,' Riley said.

'Or,' Amber interjected quickly, 'the FBI knows you're with Riley and you're on the run. And they want to find you.'

'But they can't say I killed him. They know it's not true. Riley was *there*.' My voice grew heated as I turned to him, suddenly desperate for one person to tell the truth. 'Castleton was dead when I walked in the house. You know that. You told them.'

'Yes, but now Riley's disappeared.' Amber glanced at him. 'And I've got to say, it does look bad. They only have Riley's word that one of Anthony Cleary's men did the murder. And if Cleary's telling them that Riley lied to them about it, and has now run off with the real killer . . .'

Riley nodded, his jaw tight.

I pressed my hands against my head. 'How can this be happening?'

Avoiding my gaze, Riley turned to look out of the kitchen window, his face bleak.

Amber wasn't about to let him walk away. 'You have to fix this,' she told him.

He gave a terse nod but didn't reply, and she took a step towards him.

'I mean it, Riley. I'll do what I can, but only you can fix it.'

'Give me a break,' he snapped. 'I'm figuring it out.' He paused to think, his brow creased with worry. 'I've got to talk to people in person – the phone's no good if they're hunting me. I need to get to Chicago, but how the hell do I get there?'

'Good point. You can't fly,' Amber said. 'You'll be on the list.'

'Yeah,' Riley agreed. 'I'll have to drive. If the car Danny's getting me is any good, I can use that.'

'You should go tonight,' Amber said. 'Can he get it here that soon?'

Riley shook his head. 'He can't get it until tomorrow.'

'I can get you one—' Amber began, but Riley cut her off.

'The car has to come from Danny. You have to be completely disconnected from this, Amber. I'm not taking you down with me.'

I watched the two of them, guessing at all of the unspoken words. They were like chess players moving the pieces on the board.

'You should go after dark,' Amber said.

'Tomorrow night, sunset,' Riley agreed.

'What about Maya?' Amber asked.

They both turned to look at me.

'I'll take her with me,' Riley said.

Amber's eyes shuttered, but her voice remained measured. 'Is that safe? She could stay here. It might be better for her.'

'I don't want to leave her alone,' Riley said. 'They're using her to get to me, and they know you and I go back. They'll be watching you.'

'Maybe.' Amber flicked me a look and I saw the doubt on her face, but there was no point in arguing and she knew it. 'I still think you should go tonight.'

'The car comes tomorrow.' Riley's voice was clipped, final. 'It has to be Danny's car. It can't be in either of our names, and it can't be hot.' He gave her a piercing look. 'What's the matter? Why are you nervous?'

She shook her head, fingers drumming against the top of her thigh. 'I've got a bad feeling, Ri.'

'I've got a swarm of bad feelings,' he said tersely. 'All of this is bad. There's not one good thing about it.'

Amber drew a breath. 'Fine. Danny will get you a car. You leave tomorrow at sunset.' She looked at the window again. 'I should go soon. Work is wondering where I am. But I'm going to do a search of the neighbourhood first, make sure it's quiet.'

Riley gave a crisp nod. 'When you're gone, I'll do some surveillance of my own.'

As they walked to the door, talking, I was still trying to make sense of it all. Anthony Cleary was too close to the FBI, and that meant the FBI could be in trouble if the connection was uncovered – I got that much. But why that would make them go after me for murder? That part I didn't understand. To get to Riley? To cover up their own mistakes?

I was in the middle of some cat-and-mouse game between Riley, his bosses and Anthony Cleary. And things were moving so fast that if we stood still, one of them might hit us.

It felt as though everything had changed in the last ten minutes. Amber and Riley weren't relaxed old friends any more, they were two spies, figuring out how to outsmart the FBI and a criminal who genuinely frightened them. And I had no choice but to trust that they knew what they were doing. My life depended on it.

TWENTY-FIVE

After Amber left, Riley kept his distance, disappearing outside periodically, wearing a baseball hat and sunglasses. Through the windows, I saw him standing in the heat of the sun, making phone calls I couldn't quite overhear.

I was left alone to deal with the fact that the police thought I was a murderer. Using the burner he'd given me, I searched for the name 'Maya Landry' on news websites, but nothing came up. Whatever the FBI were doing, they hadn't gone public with it, and that, at least, was something.

It felt odd to know the police were searching for me. I couldn't let myself think about it for long or I'd sink into despair. But there was nothing much I could do to distract myself. The house was very quiet, and I was completely alone. After a while, I must have fallen asleep on the couch, because when I woke up it was dark, and Riley was standing in the kitchen doorway, watching me.

'What time is it?' I asked groggily, sitting up.

'It's nearly eight. You haven't eaten in hours. Come on.' He gestured at me. 'I'm cooking. And don't say you're not hungry. If you don't eat, you won't be any use.'

Slowly, I stood up. When I rubbed my hands across

my face I could feel the lines of the sofa cushion indented there.

In the kitchen, Riley was already putting pots on the stove, setting water to boil, whistling under his breath. His mood seemed to have changed completely.

'Is everything OK?' I asked hesitantly. 'No news?'

'Dead silence,' he said. 'And that's a good thing. You like pasta?' He began digging through the cupboard for supplies. 'You're not gluten intolerant, or whatever they call it?'

'No, I'm fine. I love pasta.'

'It'll be basic,' he warned. 'Bottled sauce. Not my usual cordon bleu quality.' He opened the refrigerator and disappeared inside for a moment. 'I will not be earning a Michelin star. However . . .' He emerged, holding a bottle. 'I have found wine.'

The change in his mood threw me. He'd been anxious all day, but now he seemed very different. Like he'd figured out something that had been bothering him.

'Did anything happen while I was asleep?' I asked. 'You seem different.'

He put a pot on the stove to boil and turned to look at me. 'In what way?'

'I don't know.' I hesitated. 'It's like you're kind of . . . cheerful.'

Riley slit open a bag of pasta with a quick, professional slice of a knife. 'Well, I'm confident nobody's watching this house. Amber is sure nobody in her office knows we're using this place. It's off the books because they're planning to renovate it. Nobody's going to come here for any reason, so we have twenty-two hours before we need to panic again. By then, we'll be on the road to Chicago. And I, for one, am taking advantage of a brief night of peace.'

'But they still want to arrest us,' I reminded him.

'Wanting isn't doing.' He gave me a mock-stern look.

Humming to himself, he opened the cupboard and found two juice glasses, which he set on the counter.

'The fine crystal,' he announced.

The wine opener was the old-fashioned kind. I watched the fluid movements of his body as he wound the corkscrew in and then, tucking the bottle under his arm, forced the cork out, his biceps bulging from the effort.

I stood across the kitchen from him, my back pressed against the cool metal of the refrigerator door, as he poured the wine and handed me a cold glass. As I took it, I decided to share his good mood.

I held up my drink. 'To freedom.'

When he smiled — really smiled — Riley looked ten years younger. He stepped closer and clinked his glass against mine.

It's hard to explain, but in that moment, it was like we were soldiers under a ceasefire, exhilarated by the sudden belief that nobody was targeting us for just a little while and it was safe to let our guard down. I had no reason to feel that way, except for Riley's behaviour. He seemed certain that we were fine.

The wine was ice-cold and tasted of flowers and sunshine. I closed my eyes, savouring it.

When I glanced up again, Riley was watching me.

'Maya,' he began, but at that moment the pot on the stove hissed and the water boiled over.

'Damn.' He hurried over to turn down the heat. 'Better get cooking.'

Whatever he'd been about to say, he let it go, busying himself with the mundane work of making supper.

As the kitchen filled with steam and the scent of tomato and basil, we talked for the first time about things that were not my situation or his job. Over dinner, I told him about my father and his family in Florida, and how distanced I felt from my mother. He told me about his younger brother, who'd died in a boating accident at camp when Riley was eleven, and how that death had changed his life.

'My parents never got over it,' he said, pouring more wine and moving our empty plates aside. 'The house was so quiet. I can still remember the clock in the hallway – that steady, hollow ticking. Tick-tock. Tick-tock. I've hated quiet houses ever since. This house.' He gestured at the building around us. 'It's too quiet.'

The emotion in his voice was real. Before I realised what I was doing, I started to reach across the table for his hand, but then thought better of it and quickly withdrew.

Riley stared at the space on the table where my fingers had just been.

'You're allowed to touch me,' he said, unexpectedly. 'Amber doesn't get to decide everything.'

Our eyes met, and he looked at me with such intensity it sent heat spreading through my body.

The moment seemed to hold too much and stretch too

long. Riley gave an uncomfortable laugh and stood up, gathering the dishes.

'Well, that got serious suddenly. I'm sorry about that.' He clattered everything into the sink and turned on the water. 'It's just been a very strange day.'

'Don't apologise. It's nice to talk about real life.' I gathered the pots and pans and carried them over. Once they were in the sink, I dug around in the cupboard for a towel.

'Real life.' Riley gave a dark laugh. 'I suppose that's one way to look at it.'

'I can't think of what's happening to me as real,' I explained. 'You do realise we're fugitives now, you and I, don't you? How can I accept that as real?'

His eyes searched my face. 'Don't accept it. Don't believe it's real. It will immobilise you. And we have things to do.'

For a second, I thought he might kiss me and my breath caught. But then he turned back and began washing dishes and whistling.

After the plates had been put away, we retreated to the living room. I didn't like it there – the bare walls and stained carpet made it feel abandoned and cold – but the only other option was a bedroom, and we couldn't go there.

There were no lamps, only a brutal overhead light that must have had four hundred-watt bulbs in it. I switched it on, but Riley reached past me and flipped it off again.

'Too bright,' he said. 'We don't need it. Do you want another drink? I've got some whisky.'

We'd left the lights on in the kitchen and the door open so we weren't in total darkness. I sat on the sofa while Riley produced the bottle and poured us each a sturdy drink before sitting in the armchair. There his body was in the light, but his face was lost to the shadows.

Now that there was no food to make or dishes to wash, I grew more aware of how alone we were in this house. Last night, Amber had been here. Now though, it was just the two of us.

It was my chance to say something that I'd always wanted to tell him.

'I never thanked you,' I said, and he tilted his head enquiringly. 'For the money. You put all that money in my bag. I still have some of it upstairs.'

'You didn't spend it all?' I could hear a smile in his voice.

'I spent most of it, but I was careful. I couldn't have got through those first months without it.' I paused, remembering those early days in Austin and the green stack of hope in the freezer. 'You changed my life, Riley.'

'I ruined your life, you mean,' he said. 'I'm the one who told you it was over.'

'You're the one who took me to safety and gave me money to survive.'

'That's not how I would have seen it, if I were you.' In the shadows, he shook his head slowly. 'You are something else, Maya.'

The blood rushed to my face, and I changed the subject.

I held up my glass, pretending to examine the liquid inside. 'Where did all this booze come from, anyway?'

'Amber knows me well enough not to put me in a house with nothing to drink,' he said. He must have seen my expression, because he added, 'I'm not an alcoholic – don't look at me like that. I just go stir-crazy in a situation when I have nothing to do.'

'It's pretty horrible,' I said, glancing around the bare room. 'There are no books. No internet. It's surprisingly boring being in hiding.'

Riley nodded. 'Ask any agent who's worked in a safe house and they'll tell you they end up longing for something terrible to happen.'

'You're so bored you want a shoot-out?' I laughed.

'Sometimes.' He leaned back, crossing his right ankle on his knee. He was wearing a white shirt, open at the throat, and his skin gleamed golden against the fabric. I wondered what it would feel like to touch him there. Was his skin soft or rough? Did he have hair on his chest or was it perfectly smooth?

When I glanced up, Riley was watching me and I realised he must have some idea what I was thinking. I took a hasty gulp of the whisky, and it sent fire threading through me.

But all he said was, 'It's weird for me, ending up back here again. We're not far from where I grew up.' He gestured at the window to my right. 'I went to high school fifteen minutes' drive that way.'

I thought of the city I'd seen from the car on the journey here, miles of perfectly flat land covered in concrete, lush trees, neon signs, and low buildings.

'I can't imagine you growing up here,' I confessed.

'Why not?'

'I don't know.' I paused to think. 'It's a blank-canvas town.'

Riley shook his head. 'No, no, you're getting it wrong. This neighbourhood's a bit blah, but Houston isn't one place. It has no real centre. It's actually dozens of small towns, each loosely connected to the others.' He knitted his fingers together, holding them up. 'My small town was friendly, a bit wild on Friday nights, and not unsophisticated.' He sounded almost wistful. 'It was a good place to grow up. I guess that's why I stayed around so long.'

He reached for the bottle and topped up his glass.

We grew quiet for a while. From outside, I could hear the low, omnipresent rumble of the air conditioning compressor.

'Are we really going to Chicago tomorrow?' I asked.

'That's the plan.'

'And you know what you're going to do when we get there?'

I regretted it instantly. There was a pause, and I could see his muscles tense.

'I can't talk about that tonight, Maya. I don't want to. I just want to be here with you and think about other things. Better things.'

He drained his glass and set it down carefully on the battered coffee table. Then he stood up and stepped closer to me, reaching down for my hand.

I put mine in his, and he pulled me to my feet. His face was so close, I could smell the whisky on his breath and that maddeningly cool scent of his cologne. If I'd leaned forward just a little, I could have kissed his neck.

'Maya.' He said my name softly, almost breathing it, one hand reaching up to smooth back my hair, his touch impossibly gentle. 'I have thought about you every single day for a year. Worrying that you might be in trouble.' His hand slipped to the side of my face and lifted my chin until I looked into his eyes. 'Wondering if you thought about me.'

'All the time,' I whispered. 'I thought about you all the time.'

Even before I'd finished saying it, he'd crushed me in his arms and his lips were on mine.

His kiss tasted sweet, of honey and whisky. His tongue flickered at my lips until I opened to him, leaning in, at last knowing how it felt to be close to Riley Maguire. Feeling the hard planes of his chest against the softness of mine. His hands pressed against my back, pulling me closer.

Reaching up, I twined my arms around his neck, bending him to me, tasting his lips, his tongue, the salt and sugar of him.

'I was so glad when you came to the restaurant,' I whispered against his mouth. 'So relieved you were alive.'

Then he pressed his mouth against mine, silencing my words.

My breath came in short gasps. I felt dizzy from it. I knew this was everything we shouldn't be doing, and I didn't care. I'd wanted him for so long, and I'd felt so alone, and now he was close and warm and real, and he wanted me as much as I wanted him.

His breath came fast, too, as his hands slid underneath my top, finding the sensitive skin of my lower back and sliding gently along it, sending flashes of fire through me until it was nearly impossible for me to stand still.

I pressed my lips against his ear and whispered, 'I want you so much.'

I felt him react, the jerk of his body, and then he was lifting my top, spinning me around to kiss the back of my neck as he unhooked my bra. I turned again and my fingers flew down the front of his shirt, unbuttoning it until, with a growl of impatience, he stepped back and pulled it over his head. His skin was smooth and I ran my hands down his chest, dizzy with the realisation that I could do that. He wanted me to. And then my hands were undoing his belt, unbuttoning his trousers, feeling the warmth of him.

He slipped an arm behind my back and another under my knees and lifted me gently onto the carpet.

'You're so beautiful,' Riley whispered, his lips hot against my neck.

And then he reached across to the kitchen door, and shut out the last of the light.

TWENTY-SIX

The next morning, I woke up in Riley's bed, alone. My mouth was dry as dust, and my head thudded.

When I reached out to touch the sheets beside me, I found that they were cool and smooth. The room still smelled of Riley, but he hadn't been there in a while.

The house was so silent, my own breathing sounded loud. I couldn't hear movement downstairs.

For a while, I stayed where I was, my mind replaying moments from the night before. The wine, the whisky, the living-room floor . . . And everything after.

I had a very clear memory of an interlude on the stairs which started well but grew uncomfortable until we moved on to his bedroom and began again.

We must have made love five times – an explosion of need and tension and desire.

I hadn't been with anyone since Brandon left me. Sex with Brandon had been fine, or at least I'd always thought it had. I'd had little experience when we got together – a boyfriend in college, and another a few years later. Really, everything I knew about sex, Brandon had taught me, and I'd thought I knew how it worked. But last night had been different. I hadn't known it could feel like that – freeing and dangerous and exhilarating. My whole body felt alive even now, as if it had awakened. But my emotions were a tangle of happiness and confusion and worry, and I kept returning to the same thought: why wasn't Riley here? Why hadn't he appeared in the doorway with a cup of coffee and that enigmatic smile?

His leather bag was open on the chair, a towel slung over the back of it. Raising myself up on my elbow, I saw that my clothes had been folded neatly and stacked on top of the desk – he must have brought them up this morning at some point while I was asleep.

Finally, I had to stop pretending that he was going to reappear. The realisation left me feeling curiously hurt. But I wasn't a child, so I got on with things – showering and dressing with more care than usual before heading downstairs.

The house was too quiet, my footsteps the only sound. The kitchen and living room were both empty, but the coffee maker was on and a cup in the sink told me that Riley had been here earlier. The plain grey curtains were open, letting in a flood of sunlight. It was after nine o'clock.

I was pouring myself a glass of water when I heard the sound of a key in the lock. I rushed to the kitchen door, nerves jangling, a hopeful smile fixed in place.

But it was Amber, her phone pressed to her ear.

'Yeah, I'll be there in an hour or so.' She glanced at me and nodded. 'I just have to take care of something.'

She ended the call and headed straight to the kitchen. 'Good, there's coffee.' She grabbed a clean cup. 'It's only nine and I've already had a hell of a morning.' She glanced at my glass of water. 'Aren't you having coffee?'

'I was about to,' I said. 'I just came downstairs.'

'You slept late.' She sounded approving. 'Finally getting some rest.'

I'd hardly slept at all, but I wasn't about to tell her that.

'Where's Riley?' she asked, glancing around.

'I don't know,' I confessed, reaching for a cup. 'He was gone when I came down.'

'I wonder if Danny called about the car,' she mused, pulling out a chair near the window. 'Did he say anything last night?'

He said he wanted me, and that I was beautiful, and that he'd thought about me every day for a year . . .

'Not really.' I poured milk into my cup. 'Nothing about Danny.'

Amber sighed. 'He's so pointlessly secretive.'

'That's a bit rich coming from you,' I observed.

'Touché.' She studied me over the rim of her mug. 'What'd you do last night?'

By then, we were standing in the doorway to the kitchen, where the light from the windows was too revealing, and I shot a quick glance around for evidence of the truth, but the house was spotless. Not even a whisky glass had been left out.

'We ate pasta, drank some wine and went to bed.'

This wasn't actually untrue, but Amber had the instincts of a hunting dog and she looked at me piercingly, as if sniffing out the deception behind my words. With effort, I made myself meet her gaze without blinking, until at last she took a sip of coffee.

'I bet you can't wait to get out of here.'

I exhaled with relief.

'Well, I wish I knew more about where we were going and what's going to happen there.'

'Me too. Damn it, where is he?' Amber checked her watch. 'I need to get to the office, but I have to tell him something first.'

'What is it? You could tell me and I could pass it on.'

'I better tell him myself,' she said. 'It's bad news, and I should be the one to give it to him.'

My stomach dropped.

'What happened? Did you find out something about Cleary?' I asked before I could stop myself.

'I'm not sure Anthony Cleary has anything left to surprise me,' Amber said dryly. 'I know him better than I know my own family at this point. No, it's something else.'

Again that little spark of warning in my mind. She knew him better than her family? Why would that be?

Before I could ask more, though, the front door opened and Riley walked in. He wore a dark shirt and jeans, and he'd shaved. His blue gaze skipped from Amber's face to mine, where it lingered for the merest hint of a second, and that was enough to send warmth through me. I'd looked into those eyes when his body was on top of mine, and when mine was on top of his. And seeing him now, I wanted to do all of that again.

'What's going on?' he asked.

'Just work. Where've you been? Meeting Danny?' Amber asked.

Riley held up a black key fob. 'I went out early to get the car.' A quick, apologetic glance at me. 'It's decent.'

'And he's sure it's clean?' Amber pressed.

'It's not stolen. It was seized from a drug dealer last year and has been in the car lot ever since, waiting to be sold at auction, but they're behind and they won't notice it's missing for months. I think it's where he gets most of his cars.'

'Fine,' she said, crisply. 'Look. My office had a call.'

All the pleasure drained from Riley's face. 'What's wrong?'

'Will Fulton is telling my people that he thinks you're compromised. He's saying you disappeared because you've turned, and he suspects you're working for Cleary's team now.' Amber's voice was dispassionate, but there was real worry in her face. 'He's going to get you arrested, Ri.'

Riley threw the key fob across the room, sending it clattering off the wall.

'Goddamn it,' he swore. 'What's wrong with him?'

'You know what's wrong with him,' Amber retorted. 'He's worried. He thinks your disappearance is going to come back on him. You're a liability now.'

'That bastard. I'm going to kill him.' Riley growled the words.

I flinched, but Amber just watched him steadily.

'As long as you're missing, he's going to stir up trouble,' she said. 'You have to call him. Reassure him. Tell him you have a family crisis and you forgot to get leave, or even that you thought you wouldn't get it and you just went. Admit to insubordination if it avoids something worse.'

Riley's face darkened. A muscle flickered in the tight line of his jaw.

'I mean it.' Amber's voice grew cold. 'Call him. Buy yourself some time.'

For a second, the two of them glared at each other. Then Riley spun on his heel and walked to the kitchen. I started to follow him, but Amber touched my arm, holding me back.

'He doesn't need help,' she said.

There was something knowing in her eyes, and I realised that she understood exactly what had happened last night. I don't know how she'd figured it out, but she had. I couldn't hold her gaze; I'd done everything she told me not to.

I walked over to the coffee maker and busied myself refilling my cup, but Riley didn't close the kitchen door and we could both hear him pacing on the patio and, after a while, the sound of dialling and a phone ringing somewhere. For the first time I could think of, he'd put his phone on speaker.

'Hello?' A man's brusque voice, New York accented.

'Will. It's Riley.'

'Riley . . . ?' Will sounded genuinely shocked. 'What the hell. Where've you been? You've got everyone here concerned.'

'Yeah, I'm sorry about that,' said Riley. 'I had a family emergency. My mother fell down a few days ago. She's in the hospital, and it's not looking good.'

There was a pause before Will replied.

'Riley, I'm sorry.' But he didn't sound sorry. He sounded angry. 'Why didn't you tell me about this? You didn't use our signal. I heard nothing until I got word you were gone.'

Amber touched my arm and said very quietly, 'Got word where?'

I knew she was thinking Anthony Cleary must have told him.

'Well, I have to be honest with you,' Riley replied, 'the last few times we've spoken, you haven't been open to my leaving the operation for any reason. I couldn't take the risk that you'd refuse me now. So I just left. Family comes first, you know? You're always saying that.'

Amber, who was listening intently, gave a humourless smile, but my stomach tensed. Will didn't sound stupid to me, or like someone who would have missed the underlying irony in Riley's tone.

'Family does come first, but so does protocol,' Will snapped. 'You've wasted a lot of people's time and government money while we searched for you. For all we knew, you could have been dead. Some people here thought you were. I've had to explain right up the food chain why I don't know where my own operatives are. I've been fighting your corner for months around here, but you look flaky, Riley. And I can't have that on my team.'

There was a pause before Riley replied.

'So, how do you want to handle it?' His voice was cold. 'Do you want my resignation? I can give that to you if that's the way you want to play this.'

Amber closed her eyes.

'Of course I don't want your resignation.' Will's temper snapped. 'But it's not up to me. As I've said, this goes over my head. I need you in this office tomorrow to explain to my superiors exactly what happened that caused you to walk out of a multimillion-dollar operation right as we were about to bring in our target.'

Amber's eyes flew open and she stared through the window at Riley.

'Fine. I'll be there tomorrow,' he said. 'Should I tell your superiors that I believe someone in our office is in Cleary's pocket? That someone has sold us out? Would that be a good time?'

I heard Will take in a breath. 'What are you talking about?' His tone had changed. He sounded confused, even worried. 'I know you've had a difficult year and I think it's taken a toll, but this isn't like you.'

Riley lifted a hand to his forehead.

'Let's deal with this in person,' he said. 'I'll see you tomorrow.'

I watched as he put the phone back in his pocket and stared out across the green grass.

With visible effort, Amber lowered her shoulders and turned towards the back door as Riley walked in, riding a wave of heat. His jaw was set and his eyes were furious.

'I thought that went well,' Amber said acidly.

'That *son of a bitch*.' Riley kicked the door frame three times, with enough force to make the wall shake. 'That thieving, conniving, stealing, corrupt son of a bitch.'

I backed away, recoiling from his fury. I'd never seen him like that.

But Amber just waited until he'd finished.

'He's a douche. But at least now he has no reason to call in my office, and I can smooth that over for you. I just have one question. Why did he say he was about to bring Cleary in?'

Her voice was dangerously even.

'I have no idea,' Riley told her shortly. 'I know nothing about it. Maybe someone else was listening to the call and he said it for their benefit.'

Amber studied him for a long moment. 'Well,' she said, at last. 'You bought yourself time to get to Chicago and sort this out. You'll probably be fired, but you knew that from the moment you got on a plane to come to Austin to meet Maya.'

Calmer now, Riley smoothed his chaotic hair and nodded. But there was a dangerous ice in Amber's expression.

'So, now you go and handle this,' she continued. 'I'll do what I can at my end. I'll let my people know about your suspicions about Will. See what I can find out.'

'Great,' Riley said. 'Thanks.'

I couldn't take my eyes off him. His rage had been unbearable. What I'd liked about him was how cool he was under pressure. The way he'd been at Cooper's in Montana and then later that night – nervous and high-strung, but never angry.

It was clear that Amber had seen that anger in him before. She'd handled him like a zookeeper with a panther – she knew just which gates to lock, and when to throw raw meat to keep everything safe. What would I do when she wasn't around? I'd just spent a night having sex with Riley, but I didn't really know him. I didn't know what made him happy or what to say when everything went wrong. Amber was the one who could do that.

'Now,' Amber glanced from me to Riley, 'you should leave the house in rush hour. Even if someone suspects you're in Houston, it won't matter. Nobody could find anyone in that mess.'

'Understood,' Riley said. 'We'll be ready.'

He was calm now, as if the earlier outburst had never happened.

'Keep an eye out,' Amber told him. 'If you're right about Will, you could have trouble on the way. And if you do, you're on your own.'

The two of them exchanged long looks, and my heart stuttered.

That was the first time I realised with absolute clarity that it wasn't Anthony Cleary who frightened them the most. It was the FBI.

TWENTY-SEVEN

After Amber had gone, Riley's unease was palpable. He paced from one window to another, liked a caged animal. When he finally disappeared through the front door, I was relieved. I didn't know how this was going to work. I couldn't imagine spending hours in a car with him.

Last night was starting to feel like a dream. Or a mistake.

I longed for a friendly voice, so I tried to call Jamie, but the nurse who answered the phone told me she had been taken down for surgery, adding cheerfully, 'She's doing better, though.'

That was something at least.

I still had a headache – a legacy of too much whisky and too little sleep. After I'd packed my things into my battered bag, I found a painkiller in the kitchen that knocked the edges off my hangover as I sat watching my coffee go cold and thinking about last night. Riley had been completely present. Warm and eager and kind. But all day today he'd been far away, even when he was in the room with me.

Once again, I remembered Zoraida and her whispered warning: 'Be careful with them.'

'I think I understand what you meant now,' I said softly.

'What who meant?'

I jumped. Riley stood in the kitchen doorway, watching me.

'Oh, nothing.' I pressed my fingertips against my temples. 'Just thinking aloud.'

I expected him to walk away again, but instead he said, 'Have you got a headache?'

He crossed to stand behind me and, gently moving my hands away from my forehead, began to massage my scalp with firm, circular movements that chased the pain away.

'Is it bad?' he asked.

'I've had worse,' I said.

He lowered his hands and sat down at the table across from me.

'Listen. I'm sorry.'

I watched him cautiously. 'About what?'

'About today.' He raised my left hand off the table and gently turned it, angling forward to kiss my palm. I watched him warily even as the warmth of his breath made my spine liquid. 'I've been caught up in trying to think of everything that could go wrong and I haven't been here for you. I'm always focused like this when I'm on an operation. I know it must seem strange and alienating, but I don't want you to think last night was a mistake. It wasn't. At least, not for me.'

It was unnerving how well he saw me. It was as if he'd been reading my thoughts.

I could not figure Riley out. He'd been emotionally absent all day, and yet here he was again – the same Riley from last night. Affectionate. Sympathetic. Charmingly apologetic. But I felt like he was reading me, and just giving me what I wanted.

For the first time, it occurred to me that Riley was a professional liar. His job was to convince criminals that he was one of them – to make them believe he was something he wasn't. How hard would it be for him to convince a woman that he had feelings for her?

Not hard at all.

His eyes were steady and warm, his thumb pressed lightly into the soft part of my palm, he breathed heat into my fingertips. He was beautiful – everything I'd ever wanted in a man. He made me feel safe and protected. And last night he'd made me feel more alive than I had in years.

The things we'd done together – had that all been an act? Would I ever be able to tell?

'I'm sorry about the timing,' he continued in that same confessional tone. 'I didn't mean for it to happen last night. I thought maybe when this was all over, we might . . .' He gave me an expressive look. 'But I'm not sorry it happened.'

With his cheeks flushed, he looked boyish and embarrassed. And I didn't know if I could trust him. But I desperately wanted to.

'Are we going to be OK?' I asked. 'Riley, why would Will want to harm you? Aren't you on the same side?'

Riley's smile faded. Casually, he dropped my hand and leaned back in the chair.

'I don't really want to get into that now – we'd be here all day.' He gave me another of those piercing looks. 'We can do this, right? Go to Chicago, deal with everything. You're going to be fine with it, aren't you?'

'Of course,' I said. 'It's not our first all-night drive.'

The approval in his eyes made my heart jump, and I had to steel myself against that. Amber and Zoraida knew something about him that I didn't. I had to be careful.

'Why do you need me in Chicago?' I asked. 'Amber thought I should stay here.'

His expression didn't flicker. 'I want you to be safe and I don't think it's safe for you here.' He stood, pushing the chair away. 'I'm just going to go look around outside. Back in a few.'

I got up, too, watching as he paused to check the street through the front window before opening the door.

When he'd gone, I stayed right where I was, my fingers tugging nervously at the hem of my top. He didn't think I was safe here, and Amber didn't think I was safe going with him.

I had a bad feeling about all of this. But I was in it now. I had to see it through.

In the end, when everything went to hell, it happened very quickly.

It was an hour before we were due to leave. We were ready to go, just counting the minutes. The streets around the safe house had been empty all day. Riley had been keeping an eye out, so it was ironic, in a way, that I was the one who spotted them.

Two men in a black SUV, parked a few houses down. Not moving. Not getting out. Just sitting.

I had only looked out the living-room window at all because I'd heard a car pull up and hoped it was Amber.

I missed her sarcasm and her calming effect on Riley. He'd grown more manic as the day went on, constantly going in and out, walking through the neighbourhood like a security guard on patrol. But at that particular moment, he was in the kitchen getting a glass of water.

'There's someone out there,' I called over my shoulder.

I heard the clatter of him dropping something and then he was at my side.

'Where?'

'In front of the brick house, near the corner,' I said. 'An SUV.'

The curtain had been left slightly askew so we could see out but no one could see in.

Riley looked where I'd directed. There was a long silence. And then he stepped back and turned to me. For the first time that day, he seemed absolutely calm.

'We have to go,' he said. 'Get your bag.'

'Go?' I stared. 'How? They're watching.'

'Don't argue. We don't have time. Get your bag.'

Bewildered and frightened, I picked up the black bag I'd put near the door. By the time I turned back, he'd collected his leather shoulder bag and was heading for the kitchen.

'We can't go together,' he announced over his shoulder. 'You have to go on your own and meet me at the car.'

I didn't like this at all.

'Why can't we go together?'

'It'd be too obvious – they'll be looking for two people. You go first. I'll hang back. If I see them notice you, I can distract them. Now, pay attention. The car you need to find is a black Mustang, Texas licence plate beginning NDK.' As Riley spoke, he picked up his blue baseball cap, placing it on my head. 'It's parked three blocks away on Sapphire Street. Tuck your hair inside the cap.' Numbly, I did as he ordered, pushing the short blonde strands up. 'You go out the back door and into the yard of the house behind us. Walk across that garden and out the side gate, turn left, then right at the corner. Two blocks from there, you'll see the car. I'll meet you in ten minutes.' Taking me by the shoulders, he turned me to look at him. 'Are you ready?'

I nodded.

'What car are you looking for?'

'A . . . black Mustang. NDK plate.'

'That's right.' He gave me a faint smile. His eyes were bright.

He thrives on this, I realised.

He opened the back door. 'Go fast. Don't get caught. I'll meet you there.'

There were so many questions I wanted to ask, but by then I was outside, the soft summer heat wrapping around me as Riley closed the door.

It all happened so fast. One minute we were inside, waiting, and the next I was on the patio alone. It took a moment to get my bearings. The houses around seemed empty, but this was a commuter neighbourhood – most people would be at work for another couple of hours. Some, though, worked from home. There would be no way of hiding from them.

Hefting my bag onto my shoulder, I strode quickly across the cropped grass towards the low wooden fence that separated the safe house property from the red-brick house behind it. The humidity was a hot wave breaking over me. In the distance, I could hear the rumble of cars on the freeway. Closer, cicadas sent out their rhythmic call. Sweat trickled from beneath the baseball cap. Tiny, vicious mosquitos, attracted by salty perspiration, feasted on my arms and ankles, and I swatted at them futilely.

As I hurried my pace, stumbling across the uneven ground, I kept thinking about that SUV. The two shadowy shapes inside, both heads turned at the same angle, neither moving.

Riley had expected them all day long. Staring out of the window, ducking outside to look for trouble. He'd looked for trouble because he'd been certain it was coming.

And Amber must have known as well. Or had she told someone where we were? I'd seen her expression earlier when Riley was on the phone with Will — the sudden suspicion she couldn't disguise.

When I reached the fence, I stopped. I could see the windows on three houses, so they could all see me. I'm not sure there's a single act that looks more suspicious than climbing over someone's fence, but there was no other way. Best to do it fast.

I hurled my bag over first, before grasping the sun-warmed fence post and pulling myself up. It wasn't hard — the fence was only four feet tall — and I swung myself over, dropping down on the other side. The lawn, dry from weeks of no rain, provided no cushioning. It was like landing on concrete.

It was not lost on me that this was almost exactly Montana all over again. Except it was light now, and very warm, and I hadn't hurt myself.

'I have *got* to stop ending up in this situation,' I muttered through my teeth as I hoisted my bag and stomped across a stranger's yard. The windows on the brick house mirrored the sun, giving me no indication whether anyone inside might be looking out. I kept waiting for the back door to swing open and someone to bellow, 'What are you doing on my property?'

But the voice didn't come.

With increasing confidence, I headed to the right, where I could see through to the cars parked on the street. There wasn't actually a gate there at all — the side of the house was open to the front — and in under a minute I was on the street, heading left to the corner and then right, as Riley had directed.

The air had that unique smell of sun-baked road and ozone that I will always associate with south Texas in the summertime.

At a different time of year, those streets would have been full of kids heading home from school, but it was July and everyone was at the pool or the beach, so the sidewalks were empty.

About a block ahead, I spotted a black sports car parked at the side of the road — that had to be the one. There was no sign of Riley.

My steps slowed. Now that I was here, I really didn't want to get into that car. I didn't want to go to another safe house in another city. I didn't truly trust Riley or Amber. I didn't want to be part of any of this. What I wanted was to go home to Austin.

And I could do it. At the cross street ahead, I could turn right and keep going. Lie low for a while. Call an Uber, catch a bus . . . I could be in Austin by dinner time.

The realisation made my heart sing.

I knew it was denial – Anthony Cleary wanted me dead. But I longed to do it all the same.

When I reached the corner, I paused, trying to make up my mind. Stay or run?

Before I could choose, I heard footsteps approaching, steady and quick.

It was Riley, wearing a black jacket and baseball cap. When I met his eyes, he smiled. And my doubts faded.

'Let's do this,' he said, and unlocked the car.

PART THREE

Chicago

TWENTY-EIGHT

Amber hadn't been exaggerating about the traffic. We were stuck in it — miles of cars on an interstate six lanes wide in each direction, elevated thirty feet above the ground — for nearly two hours. It was a sea of cars. A tsunami of SUVs.

As we crawled above the city, I got to see the Houston I'd missed while locked in the safe house, and I marvelled at its odd juxtaposition of endless strip malls and forests of trees. Its beautiful, compact downtown held skyscrapers with crenellated stone peaks and trapezoidal angles, all rising from a verdant green bayou like a hallucination.

If Austin was pure practicality, Houston was openly eccentric.

Finally, though, the city was behind us and the streams of cars began turning off into tributaries flowing to the northern suburbs, and we were able to pick up speed. By then, we weren't worried about being followed. Nobody could have found us here.

For a while, we drove in silence, each of us lost in our thoughts. When Riley gave a sudden laugh, I glanced at him in surprise.

'What?'

'We're doing it again,' he said, gesturing at me, him and the car.

Despite everything, I smiled. 'I guess we never learn.'

Riley was relaxed in the driver's seat. We'd both thrown our baseball caps into the back with our bags, and he'd stripped off his jacket. The windows were cracked, and the hot evening breeze teased my skin. With each mile that passed, I found it harder to believe that I'd thought about running away.

Riley's sleeves were rolled up and the late sun turned the soft hairs on his forearms gold. His eyes were hidden behind sunglasses, but his long, angular face was so beautiful I could hardly bear to look at him.

Behind the wheel, with night ahead of him and danger on his heels, he was *electric*. Utterly focused. Completely present. And in those hours, he was mine.

Getting out of Texas wasn't quick. It is eight hundred and fifty-seven miles from the eastern border of Texas to the western edge, and it's not much smaller north to south. No matter which way you travel, it takes a hell of a long time to get out of that state. We didn't know whether the FBI had notified the police about Riley with some trumped-up charge, but we did know the police had my name and image on their system as a murder suspect, so we couldn't speed – getting stopped by the highway patrol would be a fatal error.

I understood now why he had told Amber the car had to be clean and legal.

Riley deliberately followed every traffic law, signalling to change lanes even when there was nobody behind him, and never going over seventy miles per hour.

All the same, every time we passed a patrol car, I shrank down in my seat.

'Relax,' Riley would say, keeping his eyes on the road. 'We're good.'

And each time, we were. But every encounter was a reminder of what we were up against. This journey would buy me some time, but that was all. Unless we could think of a way to prove I hadn't killed Senator Castleton, I would go to prison.

And how on earth would I convince anyone I was innocent if I didn't know who was guilty?

'Riley,' I said abruptly, 'who killed Castleton?'

He glanced at me, his eyes shielded by dark lenses. 'You know the answer.'

'No. I mean, I know Anthony Cleary ordered the murder, but who killed him? Who was the killer?'

Riley looked at the road, his hands steady on the wheel. A long time seemed to pass before he spoke.

'Two men went into the house – Jace LaRoss and a guy named Serge Destino. Jace is young, no more than twenty-three, I don't think it was him. Serge is Anthony Cleary's closest advisor, I guess you could say. His confidant. He's been around a long time. He's someone Tony trusts to handle cleaning up messes.' He shot me a look. 'You met him. He came into the Speakeasy. He's tall and thin, missing part of one finger.'

I drew in a sharp breath, remembering the two men

who'd sat in my section that last day. The older man who'd tried to appear fatherly, but whose cold eyes had shot fear through me.

'Serge is ruthless, soulless,' Riley continued. 'I think he was the one who did the killing, but I don't know. Like I told you, they left me outside.'

His voice was hollow. There was always a melancholy note when he talked about that day. I believed he saw it as the worst day of his life. The day he decided he didn't want to be with the FBI any more. The day he lost faith in himself.

Outside the windows of the Mustang, the road ran on and on. It was late when flat, green north Texas at last merged into hilly, leafy Arkansas. As the hours ticked by, the road grew steadily quieter, but if anything, Riley grew more tense, his focus fixed on the dark road behind us and the cars that remained.

We stopped only when we needed gas. It was the same method he'd used on the previous journey, choosing busy truck stops and using the pumps furthest from the door.

As midnight came and went, I found myself looking for ways to distract him, and myself.

'How do you think they found us at the safe house?' I asked.

'It was Will.' His tone was conclusive. 'Those were local federal agents, sent to bring us in. Following protocol – watching the house, waiting for backup. Standard procedure, just a little badly done, or we wouldn't have spotted them.'

I was puzzled. 'Why would they be so obvious? And why

would Will do that? You told him you were coming to him. Didn't he believe you?'

'If I'm right about Will making some deal with Tony Cleary, then Will sold his soul long ago, but now he's realising how hot hell is and he's covering his ass.' He glanced at the rear-view mirror. 'Anyway, it's my fault. I gave him the ammunition when I left without notice. Now he's just firing it at me.'

He sounded sad.

'I'm sorry this is happening,' I said. 'You were only trying to help me. It shouldn't cost you your job.'

His face softened, and he reached for my hand. 'Don't say you're sorry. I've had it with Will and the entire operation for some time. It's ruined. They ruined it. And I don't want to be on that plane when it crashes.'

I tightened my fingers on his.

'Do you think it will?' I asked. 'Crash, I mean.'

There was a pause before Riley responded. When he did, he didn't answer the question.

'You know, when I joined the FBI, I thought I'd really made it. From street cop to detective to FBI agent in twelve years. Straight to the top. It took me three years undercover to understand why they chose me. I was smart, but not smart enough. A little loose with the rules, careless with my life. No family connections at high levels. Someone they could use and discard.' There was no self-pity in his voice. If anything, there was self-contempt. 'Will was on the committee that hired me. He'd met me at Quantico when I was training, and he remembered me a few years later when he was looking for someone to investigate Cleary. He told me they wanted just the right person – someone who could go undercover straight away and embed inside a criminal operation. I told him I could do it. I told him I was ready. So, I own this, Maya.' He glanced at me. 'I was a detective, trained in observation. If anyone should have seen a set-up, it was me. But I was ambitious and arrogant. I believed I was *that* good. So good that the Chicago office had noticed and wanted me on this team. When, in fact, I think Will Fulton saw me for what I was – a useful idiot – and threw me to the wolves.'

I gripped his hand.

'Amber said you were a good cop, and I believe her,' I told him. 'You got used. Well. I know what that's like.' I lifted his hand to my mouth and kissed it lightly.

Riley's body relaxed and the look he gave me made my muscles liquify.

The car swerved and he straightened it hurriedly, withdrawing his hand from mine.

'Stop that,' he said, with a grin. 'We'll get in trouble.'

We drove in silence for a while, but I kept thinking about what he'd said.

Will threw me to the wolves.

'How do you think Anthony Cleary got to Will?'

'I don't know for certain. Will had been investigating Tony Cleary for years. He'd met with Tony more than once when he was a special agent. I think Tony flattered Will, told him he was a big man, that he wanted to work with him, make him a star in the FBI. He must have given Will something to convince him he was on his side. And whatever that something was — probably some low-level drug dealers that Will arrested so he could claim a victory in the drug war — whatever it was, it didn't stop there.'

'How do you know that?' I asked.

'Because of the way Will's acting now,' he said. 'He's panicking, and he's trying to pin everything on me.' Riley glanced at me. 'I think Tony holds some evidence about Will Fulton that could destroy him.'

I noticed that he always referred to Cleary as Tony, like a friend.

'What do you think about Cleary?' I asked casually.

There was a slight hesitation before Riley replied.

'Tony's intelligent, I've told you that. He's charming, and he knows how to make people like him, to manipulate them.' He paused. 'It's hard to describe.'

I studied his profile, the tightening of his jaw, the way he didn't glance at me.

'Did he charm you?'

'Of course he did. I mean, when I went undercover, I was ready for him to be difficult — he doesn't like strangers. But he liked me. I had a great backstory — a former Texas cop who'd got kicked out of law enforcement for breaking the rules one too many times. That was the history we decided to use when I went in. Tony's too smart to buy a completely fabricated history — he does his homework. He ran my credit history before we ever met. There's no way to completely lie to him. All you can do is move around pieces of the truth. So that's what I did. I played the bitter ex-cop, and he loved it. He took me under his wing, decided to make me his project.

He took me to his country house for Christmas.' Riley gave a dark smile. 'He loved to hear stories about cops busting the bad guys. He got a kick out of it. "Idiots," he'd say. "I'd never get caught like that." And it was true. A cop's biggest problem is a truly intelligent criminal. Luckily, there aren't many of them. But there's a reason nobody's ever brought Tony down.'

'But you fooled him,' I said. 'He never suspected you.'

'Yeah, but I think that changed after Montana,' Riley said. 'I started getting left out of meetings, told not to handle things I'd always handled.'

'He figured it out?' I asked.

'Or someone tipped him off. Someone on the inside.'

But that didn't make sense to me.

'If he suspected you, why wouldn't he just have you killed, like Castleton?'

There was a long silence.

'I have asked myself that question five hundred times,' Riley confessed. 'Why didn't he kill me? Why'd he let me keep working for him? I simply don't know. Maybe he simply didn't want to believe it.' He lifted his fingers off the wheel and then dropped them again. 'We were friends, in his mind. He didn't want to believe his friend was a liar.'

There was real regret in his voice.

'You like him, don't you?' I said, watching his face. 'Despite everything you know about Anthony Cleary, you like him.'

A slow-moving Greyhound bus lumbered in front of us,

and Riley signalled and moved into the fast lane. He didn't speak until the bus was behind us.

'Sometimes cops like criminals,' he said at last. 'Nobody talks about it, but everyone knows it's true. The people we target can be interesting. Lines blur.' He glanced at me, as if appealing for understanding. 'I was there three years and Tony was *kind* to me. I know it's hard for you to believe, given what he's done, but he's funny and he can be thoughtful. Life isn't black and white, and Tony was right in the middle of the grey.'

I could see the conflicted emotions in his expression even after he'd turned back to watch the road. It was dark now; his sunglasses had long ago been put away, and his eyes were lost in some memories I could only imagine.

'I worked by his side, and I saw the best and the worst of him. I know he's done awful things, but I watched him do wonderful things as well. He runs a charity for poor children that brings food to their houses weekly and takes them to school if their parents can't or won't do that. He thinks about this stuff. He changes lives. So, yes. At times, I did like him. But that wouldn't stop me from arresting him.'

His voice grew defiant. 'I always did my job. I was there to bring him down, and I did my best. I nearly had him. When Tony ordered Castleton's murder, I was there. He was so angry, he threw a chair across the room. He wanted to kill the man himself.'

That puzzled me. I could have sworn he'd told me long ago that he didn't know the plans for Castleton's murder, but

I couldn't remember the precise details. Maybe I was getting confused.

Anyway, I wanted Riley to keep talking. He was telling me things he'd never shared before.

'What had Castleton done to make him so angry?' I asked.

'He blackmailed him,' Riley said simply. 'He tried to take Tony's power away, and nothing could have been more guaranteed to set him off than that.'

'And you told Will.'

Riley flung up one hand in disgust. 'All we had to do was show up and catch the killers in the act. The setting was ideal for us to take them all down. And it was *Tony's own house* where the murder happened. He had no deniability at all.'

He kept talking, but I wasn't listening any more. I spoke over him.

'White Pine Lodge? Cleary owns it?'

Riley glanced at me. 'He did back then. He sold it six months ago to some tech billionaire. For eleven million dollars.'

The pieces fell into place. I could see it all.

'So, that was how you got in,' I said. 'Cleary had a gate pass, like all the owners.'

And Gina and Ed would have known they were there. Everything was tracked.

Thinking about White Pine Lodge made my stomach curdle. I gripped the door handle hard to steady myself.

Oblivious to this, Riley nodded. 'Yep. It was so easy — the place is dead in the summer. I told Will about Tony's plans, and that he should have a local team in place. He said he'd try. And then . . .' He held up his hands. 'Everything went down, and there was nobody there to stop it.'

I looked at him. 'You couldn't stop it by yourself?'

'I tried,' Riley said. 'But it was too dangerous. Serge never trusted me. If I'd lifted one finger to help Castleton, I'd be dead now too.'

I thought of the man in the Speakeasy with cold eyes and a missing fingertip. The garish house down that long, isolating forested drive. The dead body on the floor.

Suddenly, in a rush, that day came back to me. I closed my eyes and I could see it all again in sharp detail. The wind through the branches. The senator dead on the white tile floor. His pale eyes staring sightlessly at the ceiling. The acrid smell of fresh death.

My ribs closed around my lungs, cutting off my air. I clung to the door handle.

'Pull over,' I said thickly. 'I have to get out. I can't . . .'

Riley gave me a quick, puzzled look. When he saw my face, he said, 'Hold on.'

There was a rest stop just ahead and he drove in at speed, the tyres screeching as we came to a hard stop.

I unsnapped my seatbelt, vaulted out and stood at the edge of a flower bed, my body shaking.

You are safe, I promised myself as I struggled to breathe. You are safe. You are safe.

I heard Riley's door open and the sound of his footsteps as he followed me. He put his hands on my shoulders.

'Just breathe,' he said quietly. 'You can breathe.'

He held my gaze, and I felt his hands holding me. Giving me strength.

I drew in a breath.

'I'm sorry,' I said, gasping.

Riley shook his head. 'It won't always be this bad. Some day you'll be able to think about that afternoon without your insides ripping out.'

'That would be nice.' I managed a wan smile. I was breathing better now. The panic attack was fading.

The car stood a few feet away, both its front doors open, the interior light glowing. The thought of getting back into it made my chest tighten again, and I said, 'I think I need a second.'

Riley didn't seem surprised. 'Let's stretch our legs. I could use a break, anyway.'

We began to walk together. The rest area was surprisingly nice – one street lamp and beyond that, a scattering of picnic tables, well-landscaped walking paths, and trees.

It must have been one in the morning. Aside from us, the parking lot was empty. It was warm but not hot. More a soft, velvety warmth.

'Where are we?' I asked.

'Somewhere in Arkansas.' Riley glanced around as if expecting a map to materialise. 'It's a shame it's so dark. It's a much prettier state than people give it credit for.'

I was starting to feel steadier. It took a few minutes to walk to the end of the neat gravel path under the long-limbed trees. If it hadn't been for the occasional trucks roaring past on the interstate, we might have been in a park.

With his hands stuffed in his pockets and his head down, Riley seemed lost in thought.

'What's going to happen in Chicago?' I asked. 'You said you had a plan.'

'I'm still working on it. I'm more concerned about you right now.' He linked his arm through mine, pulling me close. 'Are you OK?'

'Oh, I'm hunky-dory,' I said, adding ruefully, 'What a day, huh?'

He gave a faint smile. 'Could have been better.'

'It would be nice to see you when my life isn't falling apart.'

He chuckled. 'I'll try and arrange that.'

We turned and headed back down the crescent-shaped path, through the trees.

In the shadow of the branches, Riley said suddenly, 'You liked Austin, didn't you?'

I replied without hesitation. 'I love it. I don't want to leave.'

'We'll figure something out,' he said. 'I promise.'

He threaded his fingers through mine. His hand was warm, and his touch made my breath hitch.

'Hey.' Riley turned to face me, pulling me closer until the length of his body was pressed against mine, and I had to tilt my head up to see his blue eyes. 'You're going to get through this. You're a fighter. And more than that – you are a genuinely good person.'

I thought of Jamie, lying in that hospital bed.

'No, I'm not,' I said firmly.

'You are, but I like that you don't realise it.'

He lifted his hand to touch my chin, and his fingers brushed against my breast. It felt as if he'd scalded me. Every nerve in my body was instantly alive.

Riley's breathing quickened and he slid his arms around my waist. He lowered his head until his lips were so close to mine the warmth of his breath made me shiver.

'Maya,' he whispered. 'What do you want? I'll give you anything.'

Each word was a maddening flutter against my skin.

I should have told him that I wanted to go home. That I wanted my life back. And my freedom. But I didn't. No, I very much did not tell him that.

'You,' I said, twining my arms around his neck, pulling his lips to mine. 'I want you.'

With a groan, he tightened his arms around me. This time, his kiss was demanding; he was taking what he wanted. And I wanted him to have everything. Because I wanted all of him.

With my mouth against his, I pulled his shirt out of his waistband and felt his shudder as my hands slid up the skin of his back, nails scratching lightly at his flesh. His reaction sent a thrill through me.

I kissed his face, his cheek, down his neck to the warm skin in the open V of his shirt. He tasted of sunlight and the natural salty sweetness I'd discovered the night before.

'Maya,' he whispered when my mouth returned to his.

Grabbing my hand, he pulled me back to the car. We'd parked far away from the lone street lamp, and the darkness formed a protective curtain around us as he climbed into the passenger seat. Without a word, I got on top of him and closed the door.

This time, I was in control, kissing him, touching him. Ripping off my top and then bending to kiss him again as I fumbled with the buttons on his shirt until he shoved my fingers out of the way and unbuttoned it for me.

We were both feverish with the need for each other. We didn't even remove all our clothes, impatiently pushing fabric aside until we could touch skin.

Our lovemaking that night was urgent and breathless, Riley's hands hard against my thighs, moving me to where the need was greatest. And I wanted him to do it. I wanted all of it. I cried out from the need and my own longing for him.

Afterwards, he held me in his arms as our breathing steadied. I could feel the beat of his heart, even and strong. I'd have done anything for him in that moment.

With our bodies still nestled together in a simulacrum of safety, he whispered into my hair, 'I won't let anything happen to you, Maya. I'm going to find a way to fix this.'

And I believed him.

TWENTY-NINE

It was after noon the next day when we finally reached the outskirts of Chicago.

We'd driven more than seventeen hours, seeing the country through a haze of exhaustion and caffeine until one farm town blurred into the next, all with the same big store chains, long rows of parking lots, and brightly lit gas stations. Like people lost in a forest, if we'd been going in circles, I'm not sure we would have noticed.

After we'd left the rest stop in Arkansas, I'd slept for a few hours, curled up in the passenger seat while Riley drove.

When I woke, my arms were cold and my neck felt stiff and painful. The clock on the dashboard read 4:53.

'Hey,' I said, stretching my arms above my head. 'Where are we?'

'Missouri.'

His voice sounded hoarse, and I turned to look at him. In the glow of the dashboard lights, he seemed utterly finished. His eyes were so bloodshot it looked like he'd been in a fight.

'Why don't I take over driving for a while?' I suggested. 'I'm rested, and you look done in.'

I was a little surprised when he agreed readily.

Riley pulled over so I could move to the driver's seat. As

he handed me the keys, he said, 'Keep the car pointed north. Don't get pulled over.'

His tone was friendly enough, but it was as if the intense emotion of our encounter had been a figment of my imagination. He was all business again. By now, I guess I should have been used to this; it had been the same in Houston. But I found it a little hurtful, and I watched in silence as he stretched out in the passenger seat, pulling his jacket over him and closing his eyes.

I settled behind the wheel and started the engine. The Mustang purred into life, the dashboard glowing with insane cheer.

In the rear-view mirror, the road stretched behind us, long and empty. Riley had stopped at the edge of the highway where tall trees blocked my view of what lay on the other side. It was so isolated we might have been the only people in the universe.

If that was the case, I thought grimly, then I was going to be a very lonely woman.

I pushed the accelerator hard and the car leapt forward, catching me off guard.

Swearing under my breath, I lifted my foot.

'Careful there,' Riley murmured, his voice already thick with sleep.

I stared at the darkness ahead of us, and said nothing.

It bothered me that I couldn't figure him out. When we made love, he was entirely present. But as soon as it was over, he withdrew into his own mind, where it was impossible to reach him.

I was very different. To me, Arkansas had *mattered*. I didn't do things like that. Sex in a car? I'd never done that in my life. But with Riley, everything was possible. It was scary and exhilarating how I was someone else when he touched me. Someone wilder. Someone braver. But it didn't seem to mean that much to him.

He must have been great working undercover. Nobody would ever know what he really felt about anything. He was an illusion.

The only problem was, right now, he was all I had.

Riley was still asleep when the sun rose and the skies transmuted from black to grey and then a washed-out pale blue. Alone, I watched with a kind of wonder as the fields around me transformed from black and white to Technicolor green.

I'd never driven through the centre of the country before. The Midwestern plains seemed endless – thousands of miles of flatland. Hours passed when I didn't see a single hill.

The emptiness lulled my mind into an almost meditative state. I thought about my mother, and wondered why we couldn't seem to connect. What had gone wrong between us that I could live miles from where she thought I was, having a life she knew nothing about, and she didn't even notice? Her incuriosity sometimes hurt me deeply. Other times, I accepted it. After all, families are a crapshoot. Every birth the turn of a card. One baby gets a family that coo and cuddle and adore. The baby in the cot next to her gets a family that fights with fists. The next child along gets a family who doesn't know how to love. A baccarat table in Vegas offers more guarantees than a family.

Anyway, I knew I shouldn't complain. My family had kept me safe until I was old enough to drive. But I longed for parents like Jamie's, and for a while back in Austin, I'd pretended they could be mine. Now that was all over. They'd never forgive me for what had happened to their daughter, and I wouldn't blame them if they hated me.

This thought caused a stab of pain that made my eyes burn.

I wished so much that I could tell them the truth. But even the note I'd left for Jamie said only: *I have to go. Use this to cover my rent. I love you.*

If I could undo everything, I would. Jamie was the family I'd chosen and I had lost her, just like I'd lost Brandon and everyone I'd ever loved.

I simply couldn't seem to hold on to people. No matter how hard I tried.

'Hey.' Riley sat up. 'Where are we?' He rubbed a hand across his face, squinting in the sunlight.

I blinked hard, forcing my thoughts back into the shadows. When I spoke, my voice was steady.

'Indiana. I think.'

He glanced at a map on his phone. 'We're only a couple of hours from Chicago. I slept longer than I meant to. You OK? I can take over if you want?'

'It's fine,' I said. 'I like driving.'

I drove until the gas tank ran low and we pulled into a

busy truck stop to fill up. I hadn't realised how long I'd been behind the wheel until I climbed out and my legs felt unsteady.

'I think I need a real break,' I told Riley as we walked to the front door.

'Yeah, me too. Let's get some food.' He yawned. 'I'm starving. I need a shower, too. Let's meet in fifteen minutes in the café.'

It was one of those truck stops that had everything. The showers in the women's room were basic, but the water was hot, and it felt good scrubbing the night off my skin. I brought my bag in with me and changed into clean clothes. Everything was a bit wrinkled, but it would have to do.

When I saw myself in the mirror, I stared for a moment. My skin was flushed from the heat, and there was a new caution in my eyes. I looked older than I had a few days ago.

As I stood in that truck stop, brushing my teeth, I promised myself that, whatever happened in Chicago, I wasn't going back to being Maya – a weak, fearful, shattered woman. I was going to be Lara forever – resilient, capable and strong.

The café was busy and it took a moment to locate Riley, who was sitting at a table filled with plates of food. He'd ordered both eggs and pancakes for me.

'I didn't know what you wanted, so I got you everything,' he explained when I slid into the chair across from him.

'That works,' I said. 'I'm famished.'

As I poured cream from a thick-handled jug into my coffee, I could sense Riley's gaze on me.

'It's funny. You look different,' he said.

I never stopped marvelling at how much he and Amber saw. They noticed tiny changes in human behaviour the way you or I might spot a car crash. But I didn't want him to see my thoughts like that, and I smoothed my expression.

'Different how?' I asked, picking up my fork.

He studied me again, and then shrugged. 'I don't know. Just different.'

'Well, I washed off about three inches of dirt.' I took a giant bite of the pancakes, adding with my mouth full, 'I look better clean.'

'It's not that,' he said, but he let it go.

He looked better, too. The five o'clock shadow was gone, and his hair was damp and combed. He wore a long-sleeved shirt, neatly buttoned.

Around us, waves of conversation flowed from other tables. Waitresses in plain blue aprons swept past with platters of food, raising their voices to be heard above the noise.

'You want bacon with that? Hash browns? OK, honey. I'll be right back with your coffee.'

Both Riley and I ate voraciously. Truck-stop pancakes are the best pancakes, and we devoured ours.

The waitress had brought a fresh carafe of coffee to the table and Riley reached for it to top up our cups. I was relieved that he didn't want to rush back out to the car. I was enjoying being here, surrounded by normal people.

The family at the table next to ours finished their food and rose, heading for the door. I waited until they'd gone before leaning forward and saying quietly, 'Can you tell me the plan? I'd like to know what's going to happen.'

Riley pushed back his plate.

'First, I need to meet Will in person,' he said. 'And I don't want to do that at the FBI building. I don't trust him enough for that. I need to get him to meet me somewhere neutral.'

As he spoke, his fingers tapped the edge of the table. An uncharacteristic betrayal of nerves.

'What are you going to say to him?' I asked.

'I'm going to make him think I want us to work together to bring Tony in. I'll tell him I saw Serge Destino kill Senator Castleton, but that he threatened to kill me if I reported it. With that information, we can move forward and stop wasting time.' He made an impatient gesture. 'We have to focus on bringing Serge in. That's what matters. He's the killer.'

'But that's not true,' I said. 'You didn't see Destino do it.'

Riley held up his hands. 'I know it's what happened.'

I studied him worriedly. It didn't sound like much of a plan to me. If Will Fulton really was the person who'd sent federal agents to the safe house, then he was no fool. And if he had been bought off by Anthony Cleary, then Riley wasn't going to convince him of anything. It sounded desperate.

Riley must have seen the doubt in my eyes, because his face darkened.

'You don't agree.' His voice was flat.

'I'm afraid,' I said, choosing my words carefully, 'if you say that to Will, he'll want to know why you didn't tell him earlier. And he simply won't believe you.'

'That's why I wanted you to be in the meeting.' He held my eyes. 'You were there. You can back me up.'

'But, Riley, I didn't see anything except a dead body,' I reminded him. 'I didn't see who killed Robert Castleton.'

He stared at me, his eyes suddenly blank.

A waitress hustled up to our table. 'Can I get you folks anything else?'

'Nothing, thank you,' I said automatically, still watching Riley. He waited until the waitress had gone before speaking.

'I have to talk to Will, Maya,' he said, with stubborn determination. 'I have to make him believe me. I don't have any other choice.'

I straightened in my seat. I was tired of being at the mercy of other people's plans. I'd had hours during the night to think about this. Plenty of time to contemplate criminals and law enforcement, and who really wielded power in some cities.

I was ready to take some control over my own fate.

'Look, I've had an idea that could work,' I told him. 'And if I'm right, it just might get us out of this altogether.'

THIRTY

Seen from a distance, the city of Chicago is stunning. Its glass-and-steel towers rise up at the edge of Lake Michigan like the Emerald City. Up close, of course, it's different. I was overwhelmed by the noise, the traffic, the crowds. Austin is a big city, but it spreads over so much land you almost don't notice it. In Chicago, everything is condensed and people come at you from everywhere.

But Riley knew the place, so he handled the driving while I made the phone calls.

We'd talked at the truck-stop diner for an hour and continued the conversation in the car. At first, he'd argued, searching out all the tiny holes in my idea. But gradually he'd started considering it seriously, turning it around in his mind until he could see a way to make it work.

By the time we'd reached the city, we had a plan. It was risky, and we both knew it. But it felt like we had two choices. We could turn ourselves in and trust the system. Or we could fight.

The first place I called was a restaurant in Chicago, where I booked a table for three. Riley chose the place, and I found the number. My second call was to Will Fulton. That one was harder.

He answered on the third ring.

'Hello?' The voice was gruff and impatient.

'Will Fulton?' I used my most professional voice. 'I'm calling on behalf of Riley Maguire. He's just arrived in Chicago and he'd like to meet you for lunch.'

'Who the hell is this?' Fulton demanded.

'I work for Mr Maguire,' I repeated politely. 'Can you do two o'clock at The Gage?'

'This is ridiculous. Tell *Mr* Maguire to come to my office.'

'Mr Maguire has information for you, and he'd rather discuss it with you somewhere more . . . public.'

Will swore viciously. 'Fine. I'll be there at two. But it won't make any difference. This is over. And you can tell him I said that.'

He hung up before I could reply.

'He sounds wonderful,' I said, setting the phone down.

'Oh, he's a delight when he's angry.' Riley drove in silence for a while, his eyes fixed on the road. When he spoke again, he said, 'You know the sad thing is, Will used to be a really good investigator. But it's as if something broke inside him and now there's nothing left of that guy. Nothing at all.'

We abandoned the Mustang in a crowded downtown parking garage and struck out on foot into the humid afternoon, carrying our shoulder bags. We wouldn't come back to the car again.

Chicago moved fast and talked fast. Everyone was in a rush. It's one of those cities that make you feel small, surrounded at all times by towering skyscrapers. But that served our purpose, and we let the crowd propel us through the grid of office buildings.

Everyone around us was dressed in suits, and I grew increasingly aware of my wrinkled linen trousers and ageing sandals. Riley had a blazer to wear with his button-down shirt, so he could fit in. But I stood out.

I mentioned this quietly to Riley, who thought for a second, then pointed at a shop ahead of us and said, 'Let's go there.'

It was the kind of clothing boutique where the window held a row of slim, headless mannequins wearing pencil skirts.

The racks inside were draped with delicate pieces of clothing in neutral colours. There seemed to be only three sizes of anything. I'd never felt more rumpled and out of place.

The glossy blonde woman behind the counter looked up at us eagerly, but before she could say a word, Riley swept a dove-grey jacket off one rack and a white blouse off another.

Turning to the young woman, he held them up and said, 'Which slacks would go with these?'

As thoughtfully as if he'd asked her to explain the Pythagorean theorem, she studied me from my face down to my feet and then – there is no other way to describe it – she *shot* across the room and plucked a pair of black cigarette trousers from a rack and held them up.

'These.'

Riley handed them all to me and the two of them propelled me to the changing room. As he navigated me inside, he said, 'If they fit, take off the tags and give them to her. If they don't, tell us so we can get another size.'

The last thing I heard before I shut the door was the saleswoman saying confidently, 'They'll fit.'

She was right. The clothes fit beautifully. I am always amazed by how expensive clothes change your appearance. In the trousers, my legs looked longer and my ankles thinner. The white blouse made the lines of my body appear lean.

But when I looked at the price of the jacket, my breath hissed between my teeth.

Six hundred dollars?

The other tags were just as bad. Worse, actually. The outfit was going to cost more than fifteen hundred dollars. That was all the money I had left in the world. Everything that was left of the freezer money and the tips I'd saved over the year. My entire life's savings.

I wanted to warn Riley, but in the quiet shop, and with the saleswoman hovering, it wasn't possible. Slowly, reluctantly, I tore off the tags and opened the cubicle door.

Riley and the blonde saleswoman watched me step out.

For a second, I saw something in Riley's expression. Something bittersweet. But it was gone as quickly as it appeared.

'I knew they'd fit,' said the saleswoman, with satisfaction.

'The shoes look worse now,' Riley observed.

'We can fix that,' the woman said, and the two of them walked across to a small collection of high heels displayed on a glass shelf. At the last second, I caught Riley's wrist and held on until he turned to give me a questioning glance.

'It's expensive,' I whispered.

He shrugged and said, 'It needs to be.' Then he returned to the row of shoes.

They chose a pair of glossy black high heels and handed them to me. While I tried them on, Riley told the saleswoman, 'We're in a hurry. Can you ring this up for me?' And handed her a card.

I was astounded. I'd never seen him use a card to pay for anything. I didn't see how much it all cost in total because I was busy stuffing my old shoes into my bag and getting used to the high heels. But it must have been a lot.

While he paid, I smoothed my hair, put on lipstick and powdered the shine off my nose. I felt I had to live up to the expensive outfit somehow.

The whole experience was unexpected and bizarre. But when we walked out of that shop a few minutes later, I looked like the other women on the street. And the second I saw The Gage, I understood why Riley believed the new clothes were necessary. Everything, from the wide windows and the leather chairs visible inside to the landscaping out front, said: 'Money'.

The restaurant was on the ground floor of an elegant office building, in a row of other office and apartment towers on the lakefront. American flags angling out from the stone walls fluttered and snapped in the breeze, and below the banners, crowds hustled towards the subway or the park.

At the door, Riley paused to straighten his blazer and smooth his hair.

'Why are we meeting him here?' I whispered.

Riley kept his eyes straight ahead, as if he could see everything that was about to happen.

'This is his favourite restaurant,' he said. 'I needed him to show up.'

Inside, The Gage looked like the kind of place where the martinis would be perfectly chilled. It was clearly popular – even at two o'clock, every table was taken by a high-end business-lunch crowd. The atmosphere was lively.

The long row of windows at the front, the clubby leather chairs and the jazz trumpet floating from hidden speakers made me instantly homesick for the Speakeasy. For a fleeting instant, I wondered if I would ever see it again. Or would Chicago be the end?

But this wasn't the time for regrets, and I focused my attention on the meeting ahead.

At the front desk, Riley gave his name to a man in a dark suit who nodded and said quietly, 'The other member of your party has already arrived. This way, please.'

The host led us to a table on the far side of the room near the bar, where a stocky, muscular man with thick brown hair and quick, intelligent eyes sat alone. When he saw Riley approaching, he started to say something, but then he noticed me and the words died in his throat.

'Enjoy your meal,' the host told us politely.

That seemed unlikely.

Riley took one of the leather chairs, and I took the other.

For a long time, nobody spoke. Will tried not to stare at me, but his gaze kept flicking back in my direction.

I stared at him openly. He didn't look like I'd expected an FBI special agent to look. He wasn't as handsome as Riley, or as controlled.

So, this is the man who ruined my life, I thought. He seems so ordinary.

'Will Fulton,' Riley said pleasantly, 'this is Maya Landry.'

'Yes, I know who she is.' Will snapped the words out. 'What the hell is she doing here?'

I answered that one myself.

'I'm here because I don't want to die. And I'm asking you not to let me be killed.' My voice was cool and steady, although my guts felt like jelly.

'What the hell are you talking about?' Will's voice rose. 'Why would I let you be killed? This is crazy.'

'Keep your voice down.' Riley spoke sharply. 'We're here to have a conversation. The waiter will be back in a minute. Let's decide what we're going to order. I intend to keep this as civilised as possible.'

'This is absurd,' Will muttered, but he picked up his menu. Riley and I did the same. The words swam in front of my eyes, a meaningless sea of letters.

When the waiter appeared seconds later, I made myself order a steak sandwich. Riley suggested a bottle of Pinot Noir for the table and Will agreed impatiently.

As soon as the waiter disappeared into the kitchen, Will leaned forward, thrusting his finger at me. 'I'll not be accused of crimes. If it happens again, I'm leaving.'

'No one's accusing you of crimes,' Riley said evenly. 'You're being accused of failing to report what you knew to the agency, and of letting an innocent person be charged with a crime she didn't commit, when you have known for a year what happened that day.'

'Do I know what happened?' Will shot him a cold look. 'I know what you said happened. And I didn't believe it. I couldn't send through a report I knew to be false. And then we got evidence that Maya here was the killer, and that you were protecting her. Is that true?'

'Who gave you this evidence?' Riley asked, his eyes fixed on Will's face.

'People who would know,' Will said, with slow deliberation.

The air between them crackled with resentment.

'Why?' My voice broke the tension, and they both turned to look at me. 'Why would I kill Senator Castleton? I didn't even know who he was.'

Will turned to look at me.

'That's what I'd like to know,' he said. 'It's why we were looking for you. We need to interview you.'

'I've never hurt anyone in my life.' I fought to keep the emotion from my voice. 'I found Senator Castleton's body when I was cleaning the house. I called the police.'

It felt so good to tell him that. I'd longed to tell someone in authority the truth for more than a year. It was like weight leaving my shoulders. But Will's reaction brought the weight back instantly.

'There's no record of anyone reporting a body.' His eyes were filled with suspicion.

'There was no body when the police and I got back,'

I explained. 'It was gone. The police accused me of making it all up.'

'There's no record of that either, Miss Landry. I've checked all the police records for the county and the state, personally.' Will turned away, dismissing me.

'They wouldn't make a record. They threatened to arrest me for wasting their time.' My voice was small.

'You have no proof of that—' Will began, but Riley cut him off.

'And you have no proof that she killed anyone, and yet here we are.' He held Will's eyes. 'Who told you Maya was the killer? Was it your good friend Tony Cleary?'

Will looked nonplussed. 'My friend . . . ?' His brow creased. 'Cleary's not my friend, Riley.'

'Isn't he?' Riley was fighting to control his anger; I could see it in his clenched hands, the short, angry breaths. 'Isn't it true that you got too close to him, and that's why you wouldn't let me out? Why you kept me undercover year after year? Is that why you wouldn't protect me that day? Or did Tony have something on you all along – some evidence of money changing hands?'

I'm no expert in honesty, but in that moment, Will appeared genuinely baffled. If Riley had suddenly started speaking gibberish, Will could not have been more confused.

'Riley, I don't know what you're talking about right now. Is this what you've been telling yourself? Is this why you went AWOL?'

Riley shook his head, as if trying to avoid a buzzing fly. 'Don't lie, Will. It's time to tell the truth.'

'You want the truth?' Will leaned towards him. 'Has it never once occurred to you that I was protecting you? And that was why I didn't take your story up the chain?'

'Now you're being ridiculous,' Riley said. 'I told you the day before it happened that Tony was going to kill Castleton. Surely you remember that?'

'Of course I remember it,' Will replied evenly. 'And I sent you to prevent that from happening. And yet Senator Castleton ended up dead.'

'What are you talking about?' Riley snapped. 'I asked you to send backup. You sent no one. I could have died that day.'

'We don't send backup to undercover investigations.' Will looked genuinely puzzled. 'You know that. Why would you think—'

He fell silent as the waiter returned with three glasses and a sleek bottle. There was a pause as he held the bottle for Riley to approve. Riley waved one impatient hand, and the waiter removed the cork with excruciating slowness.

I kept studying Will, trying to find signs that he was as duplicitous as Riley had told me, but he seemed genuinely confused, as if none of this had been what he'd expected.

'Would anyone like to taste the wine?' the waiter asked.

'Just pour it,' Riley snapped.

We all sat, unmoving, as the waiter filled our glasses. When he'd finally gone, Will continued as if there'd been no interruption at all.

'Why would you think I'd break protocol on this? It was your job to keep Castleton safe. I counted on you.'

'I did everything we agreed, and Castleton was killed all

the same,' Riley said angrily. 'It was Serge Destino who killed him. You know what he's capable of. He threatened to kill me if I ever told anyone what happened that day, but I told you.'

As I watched him tell this story, I didn't believe him. He was talking too fast, pulling words from anywhere. Will seemed to feel the same, his expression doubtful.'

'At that point, I absolutely should have been pulled from the investigation,' Riley continued. 'My role was compromised. But you left me there for a year. Why did you do that?'

'Because I didn't believe you.' Will said it flatly. 'You told me Castleton was dead, but you didn't know where the body was, and you said you hadn't seen the crime committed. You saw Castleton go into the house, and you never saw him come out. That didn't make sense to me. And you . . .' he pointed at me '. . . are the most likely suspect. There's proof you were there that day. We were told by The Gateway manager that you went into the house twice, each time staying only a few minutes. You reported no crime, and yet according to Riley, Castleton was killed there on that day, at that time. And then the two of you went on the run together.' He moved his hand back and forth between us, creating a connection. 'You can see how that looks, right?'

'The Gateway manager' – Gina had told him about my visits. Made it sound suspicious. She was setting me up.

I couldn't hide my frustration. 'But I had no reason to kill Robert Castleton. No reason at all.'

Will fired back immediately. 'You worked at The Gateway, and The Gateway is owned by Anthony Cleary. That's reason enough, right there. Cleary wanted Castleton dead.'

'I didn't *know* Anthony Cleary owned it.' My voice rose, but Will just waved my words away.

'Oh, come on. Everyone who works there is connected to his organisation. Why would Gina Kushman hire someone who wasn't in on it? Kushman's been with Cleary for twenty years. They don't come more loyal than her.'

I stared at him, my mouth slightly open. How could I argue with that? I'd been in a trap from the moment I'd accepted the job at The Gateway. I was found guilty as soon as that gate opened for the first time.

'I didn't know that,' I said, and even to my own ears it sounded unbelievable.

I thought of the moment in that interview on the snowy day in Montana when Gina had held up her empty left hand and said, 'I get it.' Had all of that been an act? And if it was an act, why? Why choose me?

I tried to quell the panic rising in my chest.

'I'd never heard of Anthony Cleary until this week. Even when he tried to have me killed, I didn't know who he was.' My voice broke. 'I swear to you, I'm not a criminal. I didn't kill anyone. I was just a witness.'

Will said, 'At a minimum, you knew Castleton was dead and failed to report it.'

'I *did* report it!' I insisted. 'I called the police, but the body had disappeared. They thought I was crazy.'

Will gave me a sceptical look.

'What would you think if the cleaner called and said there was a murder and not only was there no body, there was no forced entry? No sign of any crime at all?' My voice trembled, and my hands had begun to shake again, but I balled them up tightly. I would not be afraid. Not now.

I noticed that Riley had said nothing through all of this. He seemed to be absorbing Will's words, thinking them through with a slight frown, as if he didn't understand them.

Will took a long drink of the wine. 'Well, all I know is your fingerprints were found at the scene, and immediately after that you disappeared, and an FBI agent who was also present at the scene of the crime hid you away.' Turning to Riley, he said, 'Bringing her here today was a huge violation of protocol, and if you weren't fired already—'

'Oh, give it a rest, Will,' Riley cut him off. 'This goes well beyond my future employment. You don't have to fire me. I want out. That isn't the problem. The real problem is that you are too close to Tony Cleary and that impacted how you managed the investigation and the amount of risk you forced me to take on.'

Will stared at him for a long second and then, unexpectedly, he laughed. 'Me? *I* was too close to Cleary? Have you lost your mind? I've only met the man once or twice in my life. What are you talking about?'

Riley sat stony-faced, twisting the stem of his wine glass between his fingers until I feared he'd break it.

At that moment, the waiter arrived bearing a tray of food, and we all fell silent. Nobody spoke as he set plates in front of each of us. If he noticed the icy atmosphere at the table, his expression gave nothing away.

After he'd gone, nobody touched the food.

'Can I tell you, Will,' I began, and his head jerked as he turned to look at me, 'what happened that day in Montana?'

'There's no point,' he said dismissively.

But I wasn't about to back down. 'Humour me.'

Talking quietly, I told him everything I could remember. How I'd sensed the danger before I found the body. How I'd had to drive down the mountain to get a phone signal, and then race the police back up to The Gateway. I gave him the deputies' names, and described them – I remembered them so clearly.

'You can look them up when you're in your office. Call them. They'll remember me,' I said. 'They nearly arrested me. But they didn't want the paperwork.'

Will started to look away, but I reached across the table, touching his wrist.

'That is all I had to do with the death of Robert Castleton. I found his body. He'd been strangled with fishing wire. I reported it to the police. *They* did nothing.' I drew a breath. 'You need to understand that I've never killed anything or anyone in my life.'

Will gave me a cool glance. 'Look, I hear you. If your story pans out when I've made some calls, I'll remove the arrest warrant from our system. But you should know that living under a false name is fraud.'

The small flame of hope that had kindled inside me died.

'Leave her alone, Will,' Riley snapped. 'You'd only go after her to get to me, and I'm sitting right here. I'm the one who told her to use a false identity. I set her up in Texas.'

'And why did you do something stupid like that?' Will demanded.

'Because I knew she was innocent and I wanted her to live until you and I could figure out what to do about Tony Cleary. But you didn't want to do anything about him.'

The two glowered at each other across the white linen tablecloth.

Will made a dismissive gesture and picked up his knife and fork. 'I'm not letting a good steak go to waste while you talk bullshit.'

Riley and I watched as he cut a bite and chewed with little evident pleasure.

'All we're asking is that you bring in Tony and Serge on the back of what you've been told by me and by Maya,' Riley said. 'Bring them in and question them.'

Will set down his fork with a clatter. 'I can't do that, and you *know* I can't.'

'Why not?' Riley asked. 'You've got hours of evidence from me. You have tapes. You have reams of testimony.'

'I can't do it because your testimony is compromised,' Will said. 'None of it is usable.'

'Compromised how?' Riley demanded.

Will fixed Riley with a piercing stare. 'If I brought Cleary in, I know what he'd say, and it would destroy all of our work. I've spent a year trying to avoid that situation. A year of moving papers around, trying to explain to my superiors why we haven't got what we need. A year of covering up your mistakes. All while you pretended none of it was happening.' He jutted his knife at Riley. 'It's been a nightmare, but I've reached the point where I have no choice. I'm going to have to tell them what I believe to be true. Especially after what I've heard from Maya today.'

Will turned to me. 'You see, I believe you. I don't think you killed anyone.'

I looked from Will to Riley, waiting for Riley to ask what he was talking about, but Riley sat frozen, the colour draining from his face. His eyes were fixed on his former boss, and he had the strangest expression. A kind of horrible understanding.

A growing sense of dread filled my heart.

I swallowed hard and made myself ask Will the question. 'What *do* you believe?'

Will looked at me. 'I believe I know who really killed Robert Castleton.'

'Who?' I asked, my voice quivering.

Will pointed at Riley. 'He did.'

THIRTY-ONE

In the seconds that followed, Will's words hung in the air. Unbearable. Impossible.

It was so ridiculous, I couldn't seem to get my brain around it.

I heard myself speak before I knew I was going to do it, surprised outrage in my voice.

'That's not true! Riley was outside.'

After all, I knew the story well. Riley had described what had happened that day so completely, I could see it in my mind – Anthony Cleary's two thugs ordering him out, telling him to watch for trouble. The cold fear he'd felt in that moment, knowing they were going to do something terrible but unable to stop them without revealing the truth about who he worked for. And later, Riley hiding in the trees, seeing me arrive, helpless to stop me.

I turned to Riley, waiting for him to explain that Will was wrong, but he seemed pinned to his chair, staring at Will with a kind of mute horror.

Will kept his focus on Riley. 'It's true, isn't it? Because I've read your notes and it doesn't add up. The explanation of your whereabouts makes no sense. It seems to me you lied in your report and you've been lying ever since. That's why

I haven't been able to issue a warrant for Anthony Cleary's arrest, because I suspect he'd say, "Oh no, I didn't kill that nice senator. An FBI agent did."'

Will's face was as hard as a blade, his eyes locked on Riley's.

I kept waiting for Riley to tell him he was wrong, but he didn't speak. Didn't defend himself. His hands gripped the edge of the table as if he were keeping it from spinning up to the ceiling.

And suddenly, horribly, I realised Will was right. And that, on some level, I'd known it all along.

'Here's what I think you left out of your report,' Will continued. 'I believe your friend Anthony Cleary set you up. You were supposed to go scare Castleton into backing down from his demands for more money, but Cleary sent his chief thug Serge Destino with you that day. I think Destino ordered you to kill Castleton.' He watched Riley intently as he continued. 'I believe you had no choice – Destino is fucking terrifying. It was Castleton or you, and you wanted to live. So you talked yourself into it. What the hell, Castleton was a crook anyway, right? So, you wrapped that fishing wire around his neck and pulled it tight—'

Riley stood so abruptly it sent his chair tumbling over with a bang that silenced the room.

Everyone turned to look, but Will and Riley saw only each other. Riley's face seemed suddenly haggard and drained. Still he said nothing. It was as if he'd lost the ability to speak.

Will kept talking, his voice low, every word a knife in my heart.

'And then Maya walked in, and you realised what you'd done. You'd put her life in danger. And ever since then you've been trying to fix it.' He held out his hands, pain clear in his face. 'Tell me I'm wrong, Riley. I'm begging you. I want to be wrong.'

But Riley didn't tell him he was wrong. Instead, with an anguished look at me, he turned on his heel and strode out of the restaurant.

A cluster of black-clad waiters rushed over to our table, picked up the chair and returned it to its place.

Gradually, conversation in the long room returned to normal.

I stared at the glass door as it closed. Riley was gone, and I never once considered going after him. Because I'd seen the truth in his eyes.

Riley had killed Robert Castleton. Riley was the one who'd turned a living human into that contorted corpse that haunted my nightmares.

'He didn't . . .' I began, but I couldn't bring myself to finish the sentence.

I'd meant to say, 'He didn't deny it,' but Will misunderstood me.

'He did do it.' He looked at me gravely. 'I'm very sorry to say that, but I'm sure it's true.' He picked up the napkin from his lap and threw it onto the table. 'Goddamn it.'

I couldn't hide my bewilderment. 'He's not a criminal. He's . . .'

Instead of answering, Will motioned for a waiter. Half a dozen of them hovered within reach, watching us worriedly, as if we might damage something other than a chair.

'Clear these things, won't you?' Will gestured at the cooling plates of food. 'And bring two glasses of brandy, neat.'

The waiter gathered the plates hurriedly, his expression betraying none of his thoughts. Only when he'd gone did Will speak again.

'I've known Riley Maguire for years. I helped train him when he first joined the agency.' He gave me a direct look and added with disarming honesty, 'I'm good at what I do, Miss Landry. And I do know you didn't kill Castleton – I'm sorry if I frightened you. I needed Riley to understand what was at stake before I told him what I knew.' He exhaled heavily. 'You see, it's my job to figure out when I'm being lied to. And I've known Riley's been lying to me since Robert Castleton disappeared. I knew it, but I couldn't figure out why. I thought he was protecting Cleary. I kept trying to pull him out of that investigation, but he fought to stay in. He told me he was close to having the proof we needed, but that was all a lie. He's the one who kept us from bringing Cleary in, year after year. He'd got too close to Cleary, and I should have seen it coming.'

He paused to rub his eyes. All of the anger had gone from him now, and he just looked sorry.

'Anthony Cleary read him like a book from the start. He treated Riley like a son, and Riley needed a father more than I realised. I think I simply didn't want to see what was happening. Now I have to go back and tell my division head everything. And that will be the end of Riley, and possibly the end of me.'

Even in the fog of shock, I admired his honesty.

I thought of the things Riley had said about Will – that he was weak, that he wasn't trustworthy, that he'd been seduced by Anthony Cleary – and realised with sickening clarity that Riley had actually been describing himself.

'Oh God,' I whispered, covering my face with my hand. 'I trusted him.'

I felt a hand touch my arm and looked up. Will was watching me.

'So did I,' he said.

At that moment, the waiter returned with two heavy glasses of amber liquid.

Will picked his up and motioned for me to do the same. 'Drink. It'll help.'

The brandy set smooth fire to my stomach. My hand was steadier when I set the glass down again, but calm nerves didn't make any of this easier to handle. And when I spoke, my voice was hollow.

'If Riley had told you the truth, I would never have had to run away. I lost an entire *year*. A friend of mine nearly died this week because Riley lied.' I paused as the full enormity hit me. 'My God. Anthony Cleary didn't want to kill me to protect himself. He wanted to kill me to protect *Riley*.'

Will's lips tightened. 'I'm sorry for what you went through. I'll put it right for you, somehow. What Riley did – you have to know that's not how my agency works. We enforce the law; we don't break it.'

But his words felt hollow. How could anyone put things right? Will couldn't give me a year back. He couldn't heal Jamie. What Riley had done was irreversible.

Betrayal is destructive. It takes away all of your power and leaves you exposed. I think, in that moment, I hated Riley Maguire.

'What will happen now?' I asked.

Will turned the empty glass in a circle on the table. 'I'll file a report when I get back to the office. A warrant will be issued for Riley's arrest, and he'll be brought in for questioning.'

'What about Anthony Cleary?' I pressed. 'This was all his fault. He ordered the murder.'

Will made a helpless gesture. 'The problem is, we have no proof of that. Riley's word isn't worth a thing. Because of his actions, we have no evidence of any crimes committed by Cleary. We know he's a killer and a drug dealer, but the court will want proof. And our proof goes down with Riley.' He waved one hand as if to stave off an objection I hadn't made. 'Don't get me wrong, we'll start over, but Cleary will know we're coming. And to be perfectly frank, Miss Landry, I'd say we haven't got a snowball's chance in hell of bringing him down.'

The idea of Cleary getting away horrified me. Everything I'd been through had been for nothing.

Suddenly I didn't want to be in this restaurant any more. I wanted to be far away. But I had nowhere to go.

'As for you, we will need to ask you some questions,' Will continued. 'Just to fill in the blanks – where you've been for the last year, and what part Riley played in that. I'll arrange an interview in the next day or so. But I understand that you're a victim here, so please don't worry — you're not a suspect.'

There was no reason left for me to doubt him on this. I gave him my number and he handed me his card, making me promise to call him if I 'needed anything', whatever that meant.

Finally, he paid the bill and we left the restaurant, pausing in the sunshine on the sidewalk to say goodbye. Will shook my hand. 'I feel I should apologise again for all you went through, although I doubt my words do much to help.'

'I'm grateful to you for your honesty,' I told him. 'But I have one more question for you. If Anthony Cleary stays free, will he still want to kill me?'

In the sun, Will's eyes were such a pale grey they were almost clear as he said, 'Do you want the truth or a lie?'

A few minutes later, he climbed into his car, and I was alone. He'd offered me a lift, but I wasn't sure where I was going. Barely an hour had passed since Riley and I had walked into that restaurant. Michigan Avenue still gleamed in the summer sun and people rushed by in the same hurried way. But everything had changed.

I was alone in a city I didn't know at all. I was scared, and I needed help. Despite the warmth of the day, my fingers felt frozen as I fumbled for my phone and turned off the voice recorder that had run throughout the lunch. I saved the recording and emailed it to myself.

If I'd learned nothing else from Riley, I'd learned that you should always have a backup plan.

Riley. The thought of everything we'd done together — the

trust I'd placed in him and his betrayal – burned. He'd known how vulnerable I was. He'd known everything I'd been through, and instead of being honest with me, he'd used it to manipulate me.

Had he cared about me at all? Maybe. I'm not sure even he knew how he felt. Riley Maguire was a chameleon – he could display whatever emotion he needed, and even feel it for a while, if it suited him.

But I was certain he'd used me. Certain that he'd hidden me away in Texas solely to protect himself and Anthony Cleary. And I think he'd made love to me because he knew it would make me more loyal to him. Nothing more.

I'd wanted a hero to rescue me. When I should have just had the guts to save myself. I was never going to make that mistake again.

Someone bumped my shoulder and I jumped, swinging my fists up.

A sturdy man in a charcoal-grey suit stared at me, his heavy brow creasing, and grumbled in a thick Chicago accent, 'Jesus. Could you move?'

Only then did I realise I'd been standing, lost in thought, in the middle of the busy sidewalk, blocking the way.

Muttering an apology, I made myself turn and walk towards the park on the other side of the street. The heels Riley had bought me that morning clicked with every step, a staccato record of my progress as I headed along the well-tended paths with no particular destination in mind until the ice-blue waters of Lake Michigan appeared in front of me and took my breath away.

As big as a sea, Lake Michigan is beautiful and deadly; so huge and unpredictable, it has rip currents that drag people down to their death. And yet it looked benignly lovely, its waves dancing in flashes of glittering gold.

As I stood at the edge, barely noticing the joggers on the paths behind me or the tourists taking pictures, my mind kept returning to the last thing Will had told me: no matter what happened, as long as Anthony Cleary was free, my life wasn't worth much at all.

It was absurd, the power a man I'd never met held over my life and death. Ridiculous that the police couldn't figure out how to stop a single wealthy criminal. It was lawlessness. And I was sick and tired of living in fear. I had to do something about it.

With every passing minute, I was starting to think more clearly.

This time, I wouldn't try to hide.

I was alone, but I wasn't helpless. I had a small amount of money. I still had a plan. And I wasn't about to go down without a fight.

THIRTY-TWO

Hours earlier, in the truck-stop café, over stacks of pancakes, Riley and I had concocted a plan to take down Anthony Cleary. The first part had been to confront Will Fulton and get him to back off. Clearly, that hadn't gone as intended. But the other part of it was still worth doing, and I was determined to try.

I didn't need Riley for this. But I did need some supplies.

After a quick search on my phone, and cursing my too-high heels, I walked five blocks to a pawnshop recommended online. It turned out to be a sort of department store of pawn – huge and brightly lit, with separate sections for weapons, televisions, jewellery and computers.

'I need a laptop,' I told the man at the counter. 'But I need it to work. Are these any good?'

The salesman was enormous, well over six feet. His black 'Citypawn' T-shirt was stretched tight across his bulging chest. Behind him, long metal shelves held rows of laptops and tablets, gleaming silver and black in the fluorescent lights.

Pointedly, the man took in the expensive outfit Riley had insisted on buying for me and folded his thick arms.

'I'm sorry, I didn't mean to insult you. It's just kind of an emergency,' I explained feebly. 'I need your help.'

'They're all good,' he said, taking pity on me. 'We get 'em all checked out. Some kid who knows computers comes in and tests them for us before we buy.'

This was less comforting than he seemed to think, but I had few options. It was already after three o'clock and I had work to do.

'Honestly, which one would you buy, if you were me?' I asked.

He considered the stacks of devices on the shelves seriously before picking one up, switching it on and setting it in front of me. The screen glowed in oceanic shades of blue.

'The kid said this one was a solid option. Only two years old, lots of memory.' He gave an apologetic shrug. 'I can't remember everything he said, but he liked it. It's got software loaded. You're not supposed to keep the software when you resell 'em because of licensing or something, but I figure who's gonna notice?'

I pulled the device towards me and slid my fingers across the trackpad. Icons for Word, Excel and familiar browsers popped up. He was right, it had everything I needed.

'How much?' I asked.

'Four fifty.' He said it without hesitation.

My heart sank. I could afford it, but I had so little money left.

'Would you take four hundred?' I asked.

He raised an eyebrow and said nothing.

I gestured at my clothes. 'Listen, I know how this looks. But I swear to you, I'd pawn these shoes if I could. I hate them.'

Leaning over the counter, he looked down at the black

leather high-heeled shoes and uttered the most unexpected phrase anyone had said to me all day: 'Are those Jimmy Choos?'

I stared down at my own feet and tried to remember the name I'd read on the insoles when I'd hastily tried them on in the boutique.

'I'm not sure,' I confessed.

He gave me a look that said, 'How can you not know this?'

Clearly, this man knew more about women's footwear than I did.

I'd never cared much about clothes, and designer shoes were just something I occasionally read about in a magazine while waiting to get my hair cut. Besides, when I'd put these shoes on, we'd been in a hurry. But I had a clear memory of Riley and the salesgirl huddled over a table where high-heeled shoes were arrayed like jewels. I'd never seen the price because Riley had paid for everything.

Holding on to the counter, I pulled off the left shoe and held it out for him to see. He took it from me carefully and tilted it into the light, peering inside.

'I bought them this morning,' I explained. 'They've been worn once.'

He glanced up at me, his eyes suddenly flat. 'If you throw in the shoes, I'll let you have the laptop for a hundred.'

I knew he must be making a profit on me; I could see the excitement he was trying to hide. But now wasn't the time to haggle.

'You've got a deal,' I said, and balancing on my bare foot, I removed the other shoe.

While he found the cables that went with the computer, I pulled my old leather sandals out of my bag and strapped them into place with relief.

I paid the hundred dollars in cash. The man gave me a carrying case for free. 'Because you seem to be havin' a bad day.'

He didn't know the half of it.

'Actually,' I said, 'you might be able to help me. I need to find a good, safe, cheap hotel. One that won't mind if I pay cash.'

As if he heard this request every day, he replied without missing a beat, 'You want the Renoir. It's on Federal Street. About six blocks from here. They don't ask questions, and the rooms are clean. Tell 'em Leo sent you.'

Leo was a saint. The Renoir, when I found it, was a small, neat budget hotel surrounded by much more expensive places. The woman at the front desk didn't blink when I told her I'd pay cash.

She did require ID, and I showed her Lara Gibson's fake driving licence – the one Amber had sent to me in those first weeks in Austin.

My room was surprisingly large, with basic pine furniture, a wall-mounted TV that I was willing to bet didn't work, and a window overlooking Federal Street, four floors below. The Wi-Fi was excellent. All for seventy bucks a night.

By then it was after four o'clock, and my anxiety was growing. I was running out of time.

I set myself up at the computer and started to type the

article Riley and I had discussed hours earlier in what felt like a different life.

BREAKING: FBI and Local Police Plan Arrests of Chicago Crime Bosses

By Mary Lewis

After a five-year investigation, undertaken with the cooperation of the business executive Anthony Cleary, sources say the FBI is finally ready to make arrests.

Cleary, who is known to have extensive connections in the underworld through his many businesses, has been working secretly with law authorities for years, introducing their undercover agents to the violent criminals who supply drug gangs, conduct people smuggling, and murder with impunity.

These men are not street-level criminals, we've been told, but are instead very senior figures in the crime world. They own office buildings through shell corporations, and hide their dark money in complex financial arrangements designed to fool investigators.

Their identities have been known for many years, but this is the first time evidence of their crimes has been gathered in a way that will allow police and the courts to act against them. And after years of exhaustive work, the FBI now says it's ready to start by bringing in three major crime figures.

The names of these men are being closely held, but we're told these arrests could mean peace on Chicago's streets. They could raise the prices of illegal drugs. These arrests could change lives.

    Senior FBI contacts tell me the arrests should happen this week.

I read the article through three times, wondering each time if I dared to go through with this. After all, it was libellous. Cleary had never cooperated with the FBI. But this wasn't about getting to the truth. It was about stirring up trouble.

This was my part of the plan. It was the one role I had to play in a game of lies.

Opening a web browser, I navigated to one of the less meticulous news blogs — the kind that allows you to publish pretty much anything for a small fee. There are dozens of them, but I'd decided on one that I knew legitimate journalists often preferred and where news stories sometimes broke.

Back in Lansing, I'd written my first news articles and reviews on that website. It was where I'd started my writing career, before any legitimate magazine or blog would give me a chance.

I hadn't used it in years, but I tried setting up an account under the name Mary Lewis, chosen at random. Once I'd filled in the information required, it greeted me with a cheerful 'Welcome, Mary!' as if we were old friends.

It was so easy. I didn't have to explain my experience or justify writing a news story out of nowhere. The automated system didn't ask for a résumé or background check.

They really shouldn't have fired all the human editors and replaced them with AI. But they had, and that makes everything simpler when your motive is pure disinformation.

I ticked two boxes, one saying I took personal responsibility for the content, and the other saying I was Mary Lewis. And that was all it required of me.

While I waited for the software to approve or reject it, I began compiling a list of social media contacts.

Fifteen minutes later, when my computer pinged a notification that the article had been approved and was live, I was ready.

I copied the web address of my article and sent it via social media to six Chicago news reporters, using anonymous accounts I'd quickly created. Along with the link, I wrote: *Have you seen this? What's happening with Anthony Cleary?*

By the time I'd finished, it was five o'clock. An hour before the six o'clock news.

Had I been too late? An hour wasn't long. But reporters are the most competitive people on the planet. Someone would follow up on it. The FBI would tell them no comment, because that's what the FBI did. The Chicago Police Department would say it didn't comment on FBI operations, which would make it sound as if there *was* an FBI operation. And if I was lucky, at least one reporter would cover it and kick off a feeding frenzy that would burn like the sun before anyone ever realised it wasn't true.

And that mattered. Because the idea I'd had on that long car journey wasn't to write an article that would get the FBI involved. The idea was to convince Anthony Cleary's many violent associates that he was planning to betray them.

This was what Riley and I had talked about for so long at the truck stop. The idea he'd resisted the most. He'd eventually given me the names of a few journalists who he knew had been trying to dig up dirt on Anthony Cleary for years.

'It won't work,' he'd assured me. 'But you're welcome to try.'

Maybe I should have felt guilty or scared. Either of those emotions would have made sense. But I had been kicked around for twelve months by Anthony Cleary and the FBI. And now, at last, it was my foot doing the kicking.

For an hour, I sat in that room, looking out at the slivers of blue sky I could see between the tall buildings outside my window. I tried not to think about Riley.

I kept refreshing news websites, looking for anything about Cleary, but nothing appeared.

Nerves made it hard to focus. I had no idea what I would do if it didn't work. Cleary had so many reasons to want to kill me now.

At six, I turned on the television and began switching between local stations, first one, then another. There was a story about a car crash, one about a shooting, and something on schools that had everyone worked up. But nothing about Anthony Cleary.

Back and forth I switched as they worked through the news stories, until finally one channel went to sporting news and I knew it was over. They hadn't gone for it.

There was still hope the newspapers might pick it up, but

they were more meticulous. I'd always considered TV news my best chance.

I went back to the first station. A young woman with symmetrical features and smooth, dark hair sat at a desk with an active-looking graphic behind her, a swoosh of maroon and white.

Beneath her face, a chyron read, 'Crime Reporter Alex Johnson'.

Hastily, I fumbled with the remote to turn up the volume – her name had been on Riley's list. I'd messaged her on social media.

'Before I go, one last note,' she said. 'We are looking into a news report published today about an FBI investigation into local crime bosses.'

I held my breath as she continued. 'The report says local business executive Anthony Cleary has been quietly cooperating with the FBI in their investigations into drug offences. We've been trying to reach Mr Cleary for comment this evening, but the story is just breaking and we haven't heard from him. But if it's true, this could change the landscape of crime in Chicago. My sources in law enforcement say they've been attempting to find evidence against Anthony Cleary for many years.' She turned to the anchor, who was listening with a small, interested frown on her forehead. 'The FBI declined to comment.'

'More to come on this one, I'd imagine,' said the news anchor seriously.

'You bet,' Alex replied.

With the news still playing, I turned back to the desk and

refreshed the page of the *Chicago Sun-Times*. It took twenty minutes before a new article appeared: 'FBI Investigates Crime Bosses'.

It was short and more dubious of the source than the TV report had been, but that didn't matter. It was there.

I'd started a fire. Now I had to wait and see who would burn.

THIRTY-THREE

To my surprise, I slept like a rock that night. I must have been exhausted. The next morning, I turned on the TV as soon as I woke up, but no one was talking about last night's story. When I went out to get breakfast, I bought a copy of the *Sun-Times* and found the article on page two. It was no more than two column inches, with the headline: 'FBI Won't Comment on Mob Crackdown'.

The journalist had also tried to reach Anthony Cleary, who had hung up the phone as soon as the reporter identified himself.

When I was walking back to the hotel, my phone rang. I snatched it from my pocket, thinking foolishly, ridiculously, that it might be Riley.

'Is this Mary Lewis?' a familiar husky voice drawled.

My heart jumped. 'Amber?'

'The one and only.' To my surprise, I realised I'd missed her dry, sardonic voice.

'That blog post about Anthony Cleary is you meddling, isn't it?'

'How could you possibly know that?' I asked, genuinely astonished.

'You're the only writer I know who is interested in this

particular topic, and Mary Lewis doesn't exist.' Amber gave a throaty laugh. 'That was an interesting piece – very well done. But I need you to stop messing around with this stuff. If I can figure out who Mary Lewis is, other people might.' She grew serious. 'In fact, Mary's little article has stirred up shit at high levels. Will Fulton was called in to explain himself late last night after it broke. His bosses think he's responsible. It seems Mary Lewis isn't the only one spreading stories. Someone at the FBI is leaking, and the FBI thinks it's Will.'

I stepped out of the flow of pedestrians into the shade of an office building. I thought of the FBI supervisor sitting across from me at the restaurant yesterday. Will Fulton was too careful to leak this stuff to the papers.

'I don't think Will would leak,' I said. 'He's not the type.'

'Yeah, I agree. So, I guess it has to be another disenchanted FBI insider with knowledge of the Cleary operation.' Her tone dripped with significance.

My breath caught.

'My God, *Riley*? He must be going ahead with the plan.'

'What plan?'

'We planned this together,' I said. 'Before . . . Wait, Amber, do you know what happened? Do you know that Riley killed Castleton?'

I heard her long, quiet exhale before she spoke. 'Yeah, I heard last night. It's what I was afraid of. I knew there had to be a reason he was so determined to protect you. The poor, stupid bastard.'

'Do you know where he is?' I asked.

'Not yet.' She said it with deliberate understatement. 'Listen, what matters right now is that everybody's shitting the bed, and they're all looking for someone to blame. Coincidentally, they are also suddenly very interested in questioning Anthony Cleary. He's agreed to come to speak to the Justice Department today with his lawyers — to sit down and discuss various allegations of impropriety in his business affairs. Among other things.'

Excitement thrummed in my veins.

'They're going to arrest him, aren't they?'

'Mmm, I'm not so sure. Cleary's slick, and they've got Riley's actions to worry about. It's a delicate situation.'

'At least they're bringing him in,' I said. 'That's a start.'

'Exactly. And I thought you might want to be there when it happens,' she said. 'After everything he's put you through.'

My chest went tight. Did I want to be that close to Anthony Cleary? Yes, I did. I wanted to see him in custody. I wanted to see that man in chains.

When Amber gave me the address, I typed it into my phone.

'If you want to watch without being noticed by Cleary, stand across the street in front of the bank building,' she advised. 'You'll be out of sight there. I think it's best if he doesn't see your face. Be there at noon for the show.'

After she'd hung up, I headed back to the hotel, walking fast. My pulse was racing. I was excited and anxious in equal measure. My plan had been to create so much attention, either the police had to arrest Cleary or his enemies would turn on him – I didn't much care which. And now it was happening.

I was a little sorry about Will, though. I hadn't intended for him to get into more trouble. Although a nagging voice in my mind wondered if Riley *had* wanted that to happen.

Everything Riley did seemed to have a sting in its tail.

I wondered where he was hiding. He knew this city well; he'd have a bolthole somewhere nobody knew about, I was certain of that. He'd also have cash squirrelled away for emergencies. He'd have been prepared for anything.

At first, Amber had seemed the more mysterious of the two of them, the one who wouldn't tell me anything about her job or her life. But she was nothing compared to Riley. He seemed so clear when you were with him, but the second you walked away, you realised none of it had been real. It was all smoke and mirrors.

I was so distracted by Riley even then that it didn't occur to me to wonder how Amber knew about internal FBI affairs, or who might have told her that Anthony Cleary was being brought in that day. Nor did I consider why she might have decided to tell me about it.

That's just how Amber is. She knows things. And she tells you what she wants. I accepted that as part of the world I'd stumbled into.

But I should have wondered. I wish I'd thought about it more.

Instead, when I reached the Renoir, I stopped at the front

desk to pay for another night and then went up to my room to get ready.

At eleven forty, I walked up out of the subway at Jackson station. The internet had told me this was the closest stop I could get to the address Amber had given. They weren't taking Cleary to the FBI offices, which I would later learn was a good thing. Those were in a particularly soulless and secure section of the city. That said, the dark, hulking federal building on South Dearborn Street wasn't much better.

I stopped long enough to buy a bottle of water from a kiosk. The sun was directly overhead, roasting the pavement, and there was precious little shade to be found, but I positioned myself as Amber had suggested, across the street, among a row of trees that provided some shelter from the relentless heat.

I wore the trousers from the day before with a white sleeveless top and my old sandals, and I fit in well with the office crowd, who ditched their jackets and rolled up their sleeves the second they stepped out into the sunshine.

It was lunch hour, and workers flowed out in an endless stream, alone or in clusters. Some sat on steps, eating their sandwiches or talking on their phones.

A busker half a block away began playing a jazzy but odd song on the trumpet, and it took me a while to figure out it was 'Stairway to Heaven'.

The mood on the street was lively. Cars and buses rumbled by; drivers honked and gestured. The shriek of a siren made me jump, and I turned to see an ambulance racing towards me, its siren echoing off the buildings deafeningly.

Someone stepped around the busker and for a second, I thought I recognised Riley's tall, lean figure and wavy dark hair. The man had his back to me, but his blue chambray shirt looked like one I'd seen Riley wear. His walk was different, though – he had a slight limp, as if he'd injured his leg. I stared at him as he turned the corner and disappeared.

I held my breath, poised to run after him, but in the end I didn't move. It couldn't be Riley. He would never come this close to the people who wanted to arrest him. Besides, the man's gait was entirely wrong. He had none of Riley's easy athleticism.

Still, the moment set my nerves on edge. I'd been almost relaxed in the sunshine until then, but now every muscle in my body was tense.

Shielded by the crowd of workers milling around me, I studied the blank face of the black building across from me. Nobody else seemed aware that something was about to happen. I alone stood waiting.

Down the street, the busker paused his playing, and the air suddenly went quiet, like the intake of oxygen before an explosion. But soon he'd started again, switching to 'Stormy Weather'.

He was in the middle of the second stanza when three dark Mercedes SUVs rounded the corner in a caravan. My eyes fixed on them instantly. There was something about the way they moved – slowly but with ominous intent.

I switched on my phone camera and started to film as they

stopped in front of the federal building and the doors of all three cars opened simultaneously. Eight people got out — six men and two women. All wore sunglasses and dark suits. At the nucleus of this gathering was a stocky man in an expensive suit. He wasn't an impressive figure — no more than five foot seven, by my reckoning — but he had an undeniable air of authority. His heavy face was not attractive, but he was a sharp dresser. His suit was perfectly cut, and his shoes were polished to a fine sheen. Dark sunglasses hid his eyes.

Around me, everything continued as normal while the group in front of the black building aligned themselves, preparing to go in as the busker played on.

I was watching the man who had ruined my life. A man who had ordered the murder of a US senator. Outsmarted the Federal Bureau of Investigation. Outsmarted everyone. A man who was, according to all accounts, unarrestable. A man who had no business being free.

I'd begun to shake with rage. I *hated* Anthony Cleary with a fervour that frightened me. I wanted him in jail. I wanted him dead. It was sickening to see him standing there, apparently without fear.

Cleary laughed at something one of his people said, and my hand clenched around the phone.

As I watched him, I became aware of the high mosquito whine of a motorcycle. The engine was being pushed hard, drowning out the trumpeter's song.

It was loud enough that I turned to look, shielding my eyes against the sun. A black Honda motorcycle, with a single rider wearing a jet-black helmet, sped down the road.

At that moment, Riley stepped out of the crowd near the trumpeter and into the street, holding up a hand to block traffic. He was wearing a blue chambray shirt.

It *had* been him I'd seen earlier.

'*Tony!*' he shouted.

Cars sped around him, honking angrily, but Riley didn't flinch.

Cleary turned and saw him. His face hardened and he moved away from his colleagues.

Over the sound of the engines and the trumpet, he shouted, 'What do you want?'

Riley continued to cross the wide street, ignoring the cars around him. A taxi slammed on its brakes to avoid him, and my hand rose to my chest.

'What is that guy doing?' I heard someone say behind me.

Cleary seemed to be wondering the same thing. He stepped to the edge of the sidewalk.

'What are you doing here?' he shouted.

Riley walked towards him, moving through the cars as if they weren't there. His eyes were fixed on Cleary.

Still, the motorcycle roared towards us, its engine drowning out their voices.

From across the street, I saw it all. The speeding motorcycle, the two men converging.

The motorcyclist pulling out a gun.

Everything seemed to slow, and I saw each moment clearly; *felt* each moment in my heart.

Anthony Cleary noticed the gun first. He shouted something and pointed. Riley turned to flick a puzzled glance where he indicated. His eyes widened and he flung out his hands.

'No!' he shouted, and lunged towards Cleary.

Later, some people said he tried to run away, but that wasn't true. I saw it perfectly. He hurled himself between the gun and Anthony Cleary.

The motorcyclist never slowed – he fired twice before tossing the gun carelessly aside, leaning low over the handlebars and speeding away.

It was over so quickly. The whole thing took two seconds. One intake of breath. Two beats of a heart.

And then two men lay on the pavement, inches from each other. Anthony Cleary. And Riley Maguire.

THIRTY-FOUR

Chaos followed. Cars screeched to a stop. People on the sidewalk scattered. The trumpeter stopped playing. With a strangled cry, I ran to where Riley lay face down at the edge of the street, one arm flung out towards the prone body of Anthony Cleary.

'No, no, no, Riley, no.'

I crouched beside him, reaching for his shoulder, feeling the warmth of his body through the fabric.

Warm. Still alive.

But I could smell the coppery scent of blood. And that distinctive, acrid smell I'd first encountered at The Gateway – the smell of death.

Around me, a low, urgent ripple of voices rose.

'Did you see that?'

'Where'd he go?'

'Did anyone call the cops?'

'I'm calling an ambulance.'

With traffic stopped, the once-busy street was oddly still. An almost respectful pause. Death was passing by.

I was aware vaguely that Cleary's team had gathered around him, but my focus was on Riley. He stared at me intently, his lips moving but no sound emerging. His breathing was shallow and rapid.

'I'm here, Riley,' I kept saying. 'I'm here.'

It was the first time I'd ever seen him helpless, and it felt so wrong. Riley was the fixer, constantly on the move, finding a way. But he couldn't fix this.

The hand I'd pressed to his ribs felt damp, and I lifted it up to find my palm covered in warm, red blood.

When I looked down, I could see it seeping beneath him, forming a dark stain on the street. A shard of ice entered my heart. That was too much blood.

'How bad is it?' A familiar female voice spoke at my shoulder.

Amber stood next to me. In her dark suit, with her hair pulled back into a tight ponytail and sunglasses hiding her face, she looked very different. That was why I hadn't recognised her when she'd stepped out of Anthony Cleary's Mercedes a few minutes ago and stood near him.

I stared up at her, stunned, a thousand questions begging to be asked. But now wasn't the time.

'He's bad,' I said, and showed her my bloodstained hand. Her face crumpled.

'Oh, Riley,' Amber said softly, kneeling next to him. 'Why did you get in the way?' Glancing up at me, she said, 'Help me get his jacket off.'

Working together carefully, we rolled him onto his side. Riley's blue shirt wasn't blue any more. It was soaked in red.

Until that moment, I had no idea the human body held so much blood.

I heard the faint sound of sirens in the distance.

'We have to stop the bleeding.' I struggled to unbutton Riley's shirt, but fear made my fingers numb and the buttons were suddenly impossible to work.

'Maya, don't.' Amber put a hand on my arm. When she took off her sunglasses, her dark eyes were unbearably sad. 'The paramedics are nearly here. Just talk to him.'

I looked back at Riley's face. He was paler now, and his lips no longer moved. All his effort was focused on breathing, and that had become a struggle.

'You're going to be fine,' I told him, tears spilling down my cheeks. 'Help is coming.'

I was holding his hand, and I felt his fingers tighten on mine. With visible effort, he took a breath and whispered, 'So . . . sorry . . .'

Maybe he was lying. Maybe it was the truth. Either way, it broke my heart.

With a sob, I buried my face in the warmth of his neck, and breathed in that scent of soap and sun that was so distinctly him.

I didn't hear the ambulance pull up, but I became aware that a team of paramedics in dark blue uniforms were gently moving us out of the way and surrounding Riley. I rose and stood next to Amber. We watched in silence as they worked with quick, practised movements, placing an oxygen mask over his face first, before they cut open his shirt and connected tubes to his arms.

'What's his name?' one of the paramedics called to us.

I couldn't speak, so it was Amber who answered. 'Riley Maguire.'

'Riley?' The paramedic spoke in a loud, calm voice. 'Can you hear me? We're looking after you. Just hang in there.'

I was sobbing, and Amber reached for my hand and gripped it tightly. She'd never done anything like that before.

The ambulance crew worked in controlled chaos, everyone moving fast. Bags were ripped open, a pressure bandage applied, a backboard slipped carefully beneath Riley.

A few feet away, a second group of medics were clustered around Cleary, but they moved with less urgency.

Seeing me watching them, Amber told me, 'Cleary's dead. Shot in the head.'

Hearing that, I felt nothing. Just a void where my emotions should be.

I'd wished Anthony Cleary dead, and now he was.

A woman's voice, urgent but passionless, caught my attention. 'He's crashing.'

The group around Riley worked even faster now, connecting wires and electrodes, running to the ambulance for more supplies. In the end, they jolted his body with electricity three times.

When I glanced at Amber, she wasn't watching. She was standing very still, looking into the distance.

At last, the group around Riley began moving more slowly. The paramedics gathered near the ambulance, talking in low voices.

'What's happening?' I turned to Amber.

She let out a long breath. 'He's gone,' she told me gently. 'Riley's dead.'

'*No.*' I don't know why I said it when the truth was right in front of me. I could see the medics ripping off their gloves, talking into their radios, packing up, deciding who was going to give us the bad news.

It couldn't be true. But it was.

Riley was gone. My beautiful liar.

I tried to say something but choked on the words. 'I don't . . .'

Wordlessly, Amber put her hand on my shoulder, and I reached up to cling to it.

I think from the moment she saw the blood on Riley's shirt, Amber knew he wouldn't make it. But her pain was real. You can't fake that.

I felt hollowed out, drained of every emotion. So it didn't really matter when four people in suits walked out of the federal building and headed straight to us.

The one in front – a tall, broad-shouldered man with thick dark hair – spoke in an authoritative voice that brooked no argument.

'Maya Landry? We're with the FBI. I need you to come with us.'

Amber took a step back, her hand slipping from mine.

Turning, I gave her a questioning look, and she nodded. 'Just tell them the truth.'

I wondered why they didn't want to question her, and why she had been in that SUV, but there was no time to ask as I was hustled past the two ambulances and the crowd around Anthony Cleary, then up the front steps and into the federal office building.

After the scene outside, the office lobby seemed preternaturally quiet. We passed a small group gathered at the front windows, watching the activity on the street, but everyone else appeared to be going about their work, as if double shootings happened on South Dearborn Street every sunny afternoon.

Making it clear that I had no choice, the agents – three men and one woman – walked me into an elevator, and I watched passively as one of them punched the button for floor five. Nobody spoke as the elevator rose silently; they all stared straight ahead, their faces blank.

On the fifth floor, we stepped out into an open-plan workspace, but they hurried me by the rows of desks to a meeting room with dark glass walls that revealed nothing and hustled me inside.

The room was big enough to hold thirty people but held only three – Will Fulton, a woman in a dark suit, and me.

The agents who'd brought me up did not come inside but left immediately, closing the door. Aside from that one line spoken on the street, no one had said a single word.

'Maya—' Will began, but I didn't let him speak.

'He's dead,' I said, my voice breaking. 'Riley's dead, Will.'

Two tears slipped free and fell on my cheeks.

Will's jaw tightened and he glanced at the woman. She tapped something in her ear and said quietly, 'Status update?' A moment later, she gave Will a sombre look and nodded.

Something seemed to give inside Will; his shoulders sagged and he turned his back to us, making a fist with one hand but punching nothing.

When he turned around again, his emotions were under control.

'I'm very sorry,' he said. 'I know you were close. I'd hoped he'd make it.'

'Who did this?' I demanded. 'Who was on that motorcycle?'

I didn't want to believe that the person who'd done this was me. I wrote that article. I'd stirred up forces I didn't understand in order to bring down Anthony Cleary.

The woman stepped forward. She was in her early forties, her straight blonde hair pulled back with a clip, her dark suit and white buttoned shirt a mirror of Will's clothing but without a tie.

'Miss Landry, my name is Jo Thomas. I work with Will.'

I couldn't have cared less about her; my shock had turned to fury and someone needed to pay.

I held up my bloodstained palm. 'This is Riley's blood. Now do me the favour of not wasting my time. Who murdered him? Was it you?'

'Maya . . .' Will began, but Jo shook her head at him and stepped towards me.

'We can't say for certain, but I'd bet this building it was one of Cleary's competitors. Probably Paul Orland. I'm sure he didn't do it himself, but he knows who to call when he wants someone taken out.' She gestured at the black chairs surrounding the table. 'Would you like to sit down? I can get you some water.'

Without waiting for my response, she walked to a corner table and filled a glass from a pitcher of ice water.

I watched warily as she set it in front of me. I didn't want to do anything she suggested, but suddenly I was exhausted and sitting down seemed like a good idea.

I lowered myself onto the nearest chair. Jo and Will sat across from me.

'Why would this Orland want to kill Riley?'

'He didn't,' Will said. 'Or at least, we think killing Riley was a mistake. He was aiming for Anthony Cleary.'

'I've reviewed the CCTV footage and it appears Riley stepped in front of the bullet,' Jo said. 'I don't know why – it looks almost like he was trying to protect Cleary.'

Will met my gaze, and I saw loss and resignation in his eyes. I remembered what he'd said at lunch, and what I'd come to believe myself.

'Riley was undercover too long,' I said tiredly. 'He knew Cleary was a criminal, but it all got confused in his mind. In his heart.'

'That's why we wanted to talk to you,' Jo said. 'You're not in any trouble, please believe that. But we think you know what's been going on in Riley's head better than we do, and that's something we'd like to understand. There will be an investigation into what happened outside, and we want to know everything.'

'Riley was . . .' I bit back tears. 'I think maybe he was a good man who made mistakes. I was one of his mistakes. And today . . . I think maybe he wanted that bullet to hit him.' I looked at Will, my lip shaking. 'She's right – he walked straight into it, Will. He walked straight at that gun.'

To my surprise, he reached across the table and put his hand on mine for just a second.

'He cared about you, he made that clear to me,' he said, holding my gaze.

I gave a humourless laugh. 'He didn't care enough to tell me the truth.' I looked at Jo. 'I don't know if I can help you, because I didn't really know Riley. But I can tell you what I think. I think he wanted to fix everything. Anthony Cleary, Robert Castleton, and me. He wanted Cleary arrested, but he didn't want to do it himself. He definitely didn't want him dead. To be honest, I think he kind of loved Cleary. Maybe more than he loved anyone else.'

I reached for my glass of water and concluded, 'I'll tell you everything I know.'

We talked for two hours. As Amber had directed, I told the truth. All of it. I don't think I told them much they didn't already know, but I cooperated as fully as I could. It's the only time I ever told anyone all I knew.

Only Jo and Will were in the room, and they took no notes.

I noticed it at the time but didn't think about it. Jo explained that the meeting was being recorded and I accepted that.

When we finished, and they'd asked all their questions, I was drained. Every part of me ached, as if I'd run a hundred miles. I kept thinking about Riley whispering 'Sorry'. Why did his last word have to be an apology?

It was wrong. It was all wrong.

Finally, Jo and Will spoke quietly, and Jo nodded and leaned over, taking a sheet of paper from the briefcase at her feet and a pen.

She slid the paper across to me, and said, 'Do you know what a non-disclosure agreement is?'

The paper was letterheaded 'US Department of Justice'. It was dated that day, and had my name at the top.

> I, Maya Landry, enter into this agreement for the purpose of preventing the unauthorised disclosure of Sensitive Information as defined below. Maya Landry agrees to never disclose certain sensitive, proprietary or protected information revealed today at the offices of the US Justice Department in Chicago, IL.

'You want me to sign this?' I stared at Jo.

'Yes, I do. What happened today is a legal matter, and should not be discussed with anyone outside of the legal system.' Her voice was steady and cool. 'This is non-negotiable, Maya. You and Riley broke numerous laws together, and you could be held accountable for crimes including fraud, failing to report a crime, evading arrest, and false identification. Most seriously, despite what you've said today, we have grounds to charge you as an accessory to murder. But if you sign this agreement, all of that goes away.'

It felt like a punch in the gut.

I shouldn't have been shocked, but I was. I'd honestly believed she wanted to get to the truth, but now I realised she wanted to know everything so she knew what to cover up.

Will was watching me, his face guarded, his hands still on

the table, but I could see the tension in his shoulders. This hadn't been his idea, I was sure of that. But he couldn't stop it. He was in trouble, too. If I didn't sign this, I had a feeling Jo Thomas would go for both of us.

Tightening my lips, I looked away from them at the dark, reflective glass walls.

'You're going to hide all this, aren't you? Everything you know. I'm going to sign this, and then you'll stop investigating Castleton's murder. You'll attribute everything to gang shootings.' I shook my head. '*This* is justice?'

'This is reality,' Jo said simply. 'It would be best for all of us if you signed.'

I guess if I were a hero, I'd have walked out of that room without touching that paper. But I'd had a year of lies, and death, and loss, and loneliness. I'd just held a man's hand and watched him die. A man I'd thought I loved. And anyway, I'm no hero.

I signed the paper.

Jo walked me to the front door herself. I looked back at that cool, dark office building where people's lives were played with like toys.

'I hope it was worth it for you,' I told her. 'That was your soul I was signing away, not my own.'

And then I turned and walked out into the sun. And I never once looked back.

PART FOUR

Present Day

Epilogue

I love Austin in the summer. The intense heat, and the lethargy it summons. The sun calls out for you to stop. Slow down. Sit by the pool and drink something cold. Watch the world go by.

I'm not rich enough to do that all the time, of course, but on my days off, that's where you'll find me – sitting in the sunshine, letting the warmth soak into my bones. Thinking about how lucky I've been to survive.

A lot has happened in the two years since Chicago. I changed my name, for one thing. Maya Landry is gone. I'm Lara Gibson now, officially. My driving licence is real. I have a credit card and a bank account – everything I need to be Lara for the rest of my life.

You might wonder why I would do that when I had every right to be Maya again, and it's hard to explain. It was an emotional decision, I guess. Lara felt real to me. And Maya? Well, Maya was too associated in my mind with pain, and loss, and loneliness. In the end, I just didn't want to be her.

When I came home from Chicago, I went straight from the airport to see Elaine at the Speakeasy, and I told her the truth. Or as much as I was allowed to tell, at least. She was shocked and a little hurt, I think, that I hadn't trusted her enough to tell her before.

'I always knew you were hiding secrets,' she said when I'd finished. We were sitting in her tiny office at the back of the restaurant, behind the staffroom. It was the middle of the afternoon – the quiet time in the service industry. The time when we unpack our bags, as it were. Elaine had taken off her glasses, and her beautiful brown eyes observed me with empathy and understanding. 'I knew something had happened to you, and I always assumed that one day you'd tell me. I just didn't think it would be this.'

I showed her the articles about the shooting from the Chicago papers. I even told her a bit about Riley and Amber.

That was two days after Riley's death, and already I was frustrated by my decision to sign that piece of paper. After a year of deception, I'd longed to be free of lies. But when it comes to crime and justice, the lies never end.

Still, I tried to put it all behind me. Elaine let me keep my job at the Speakeasy. And I returned to the little house on Dove Lane.

For the first six weeks, I lived alone there. Jamie was in the hospital for ten days, and then in a rehab centre in Houston, close to her parents.

I couldn't bear to upset her while she was healing, so I handled that all very badly. Mostly, I avoided her. It was made easier by the fact that I no longer had a car, and just getting to work was a complicated combination of begging rides from the other waiters and throwing myself on the mercy of the somewhat unpredictable Austin public transportation system.

So, it was only after Jamie came home, on crutches, with one leg still in a brace, that we sat down together and I told her everything that had happened. Aside from Amber and the FBI, Jamie is the only person who knows the whole truth. I told her every single moment of what had happened. To hell with the NDA. Jamie is my sister in all but blood, and I will never lie to her again.

We were in our cosy living room. She was on the sofa, wrapped in a blanket, a mug of coffee at her elbow. Thinner, weaker, but getting stronger every day. I sat on the old Eames chair we'd found at a garage sale and restored by hand. Jamie had sewn the covers for it from some fabric we bought at Goodwill.

She watched me closely, her eyes searching my face as I told her who I really was.

'My real name is Maya Landry.' My voice was steady, although I held the wooden arms of the chair in a death grip. 'I was born in Michigan, and I lived there until a little over a year ago, when my husband left me. That much of what I told you was true, at least. He really did leave me for a co-worker. I really was heartbroken. After that, I moved to Montana. I've never been to Kansas in my life.'

Jamie tilted her head at that, giving me a long, measured look that said everything I know she thought. *Why did you lie? Why didn't you trust me?*

'It will all make sense, I think, when you know the whole story.' I told her about my job up at The Gateway, what the lodge houses were like, the unfathomable luxury and complete isolation. And the body I found there one afternoon.

'Maya,' she breathed, horror in her face.

'The dead man's name, I would learn later,' I said, 'was Senator Robert Castleton.'

That was when Jamie knocked over her coffee and we had to have a break while I got a cloth to scrub the rug and poured her a new cup.

'I think I need a whisky instead,' she said, and I told her, 'Not with those painkillers you're on.'

This broke the tension and we were both calmer as I picked up the strands of my story.

Jamie was sitting up straight on the sofa; she listened with the same absolute focus she had when her law books were open in front of her and she was studying for the bar exam.

I told her about Riley and Amber. And I told her why it was my fault she'd never run another marathon. I was the one the killers had been after that day, and I'd never forgive myself for not knowing they might try something like that.

I told her about Chicago, and what had happened on the street and inside the FBI building.

When I'd finally finished, I held out my hands. 'That's everything. You know more than I'm legally allowed to tell anyone. I hope some day you can forgive me. But I will move out of this house tonight if you want me to. I wouldn't blame you at all. No one wants to live with a liar.'

'Don't you dare say that to me,' Jamie said, suddenly angry. 'I love you, Lara. You are my best friend. You were attacked and your trust was violated. What kind of monster would I be to blame you for that? You came to Austin trying to survive, and you did it. If I had to have this . . .' she patted the hard brace on her left leg '. . . in order for you to be safe? That's fine with me. It's just a leg. I have another one.' By then, though, I was sobbing, and she reached out and took my hand, pulling me onto the sofa with her. She was still so strong, despite everything she'd been through. 'You made it through, Lara. You did it. That's all that matters.'

She forgave me, but I never entirely forgave myself. Once Jamie was truly healed and the brace came off, I started looking for my own place. It felt like time.

I was forty years old by then. My work was steady, and Elaine was considering me for deputy manager. I'd received a settlement from Brandon after our house in Lansing sold, which was just enough for me to put down a deposit on a small house. I'd begun writing articles again for blogs and local magazines, but I didn't enjoy writing the same listicles and small pieces about culture. It didn't seem to matter in a world where the things I'd experienced could happen.

So I went back to that neighbourhood at the edge of town where Zoraida's restaurant was located and began researching the disparity between Austin's wealthy new enclaves and the people who were being left behind as the city changed. That article was bought by *Texas Monthly* magazine – the biggest news magazine in the state. After that, I started getting real assignments from bigger magazines and newspapers.

Based on that, I applied for a one-year fellowship to study journalism at the University of Texas, and I was accepted.

Six months ago, I finally quit my job at the Speakeasy. It wasn't an easy decision to make. After all, I owe Elaine everything. But she understood.

'You'll always have a place here,' she told me that day. And she will always have a place in my heart. I see her all the time – I often have lunch with her and her family on sunny weekends. Jamie sometimes comes too, and it feels like I finally have the family I longed for.

My parents know where I live now, but we never speak. I'm told Brandon and Hannah have a little girl. And that's enough said about that, I think.

Jamie passed the bar six months after her accident, and is now working for a criminal law firm in Austin. Her specialty is pro bono work, defending people who can't afford to pay for a lawyer. She's an avenging angel for them, and when I have an afternoon off, I like to go watch her in court.

I've been dating Gabe, from the Pecan Café. Remember him? The one who makes the most amazing iced coffee? He's far too young for me, but he doesn't care and I don't care, so I guess that means it doesn't matter. He's the kindest man I think I've ever met. It's a very different relationship from my marriage with Brandon and from my brief encounters with Riley. With Gabe, it's a partnership. We talk a lot. He makes me laugh. He knows my story, and he likes me anyway.

Who knows how things will work out? It's still early. But right now, it's kind of beautiful.

I think it's fair to say I've been happy. I have the life I wanted at last. Or I did, until the afternoon when Amber knocked on my door a few weeks ago.

How she knew where I lived, I'll never know. Actually, ignore that. Of course she knew where I lived. Amber's a spy, and what she doesn't know already, she can find out. Maybe

I shouldn't have been as surprised as I was, in that case, to open the door and see her standing there looking like no time had passed at all.

'Hi, there. Did you miss me?' she asked, and walked straight past me into the house.

'No,' I replied with feeble rebellion, and closed the door.

She gave that familiar throaty laugh. 'Well, I missed you.'

I hadn't seen Amber since that moment on the street in Chicago when she told me to tell the truth to the FBI. When I later emerged from the federal building, with its dark glass and twisted logic, she had gone. I'd tried calling her in the days that followed, but she hadn't answered, and she never returned my messages.

I wanted to talk to her back then because I had questions for her. Questions about Cleary and Riley, and about what happened that afternoon. Over the years, I'd spent a lot of time thinking about that day. About the gunman on the motorcycle and Riley's futile effort to protect Anthony Cleary. Most of all, I'd thought about what Amber said to Riley as he lay dying.

Why did you get in the way?

I'd wanted to know why she was in that car with Anthony Cleary, and why she'd told me to be at the federal building at the precise moment the gunman arrived.

Eventually, though, I'd given up on tracking her down and let go of my questions. If she didn't want to be found, I certainly wasn't going to locate her. And yet here she was, breezing into my life again like a bad dream.

'Christ, it's hot,' she announced, dropping her bag on the

hardwood floor that I'd sanded and polished myself when I'd bought the 1950s bungalow. 'Do you have any iced tea?'

I stood for a minute in the living-room doorway, balancing my desires. Part of me wanted to throw her out – Amber was a reminder of everything terrible that had happened in my life. But the rest of me wanted to know why she was here.

After prevaricating just a little too long, I stalked into the kitchen and filled two glasses with ice and tea, and brought them back. Amber took a long drink.

'Delicious,' she pronounced, and wiped the condensation from the bottom of the glass before setting it on the coaster on the coffee table.

She looked annoyingly great. Her dark hair was cut shorter, and it suited her. She always looked so much younger than she was. Her skin was still smooth and unblemished, and she wore the same dark, fitted clothes she'd always preferred.

Jamie had given me the Eames chair as a house-warming gift, and I sat in it then, as if it would somehow protect me from whatever Amber was bringing with her.

'OK, I give up. What's happened?' I asked. 'Why are you here?'

She met my gaze. 'They caught the guy who killed Riley,' she said. 'I thought you'd want to know.'

I sat frozen, the blood rising in my face as if she'd slapped me. All the things I'd saved up to ask her evaporated from my mind, replaced by the image of the black-clad man on the motorcycle, his face hidden by a helmet, a gun in his hand.

I've never been able to listen to 'Stormy Weather' since that day.

'Are they . . .' I fumbled my words. 'Are they sure it's him?'

'It's him.' Her voice was flat. 'His name is Dejean Fletcher. He's a gun for hire for Paul Orland. The FBI has been trying to get him on a murder charge for years, even before this.'

'How did they catch him?' I asked.

'Paul Orland gave him up for free.' Amber took another sip, and again swiped the bottom of the glass before setting it down. 'Orland's been arrested for money laundering, and he was offered a little discount on his time behind bars if he'd give up Riley's killer. He was very interested in taking that offer. His information led us to the motorcycle that was used that day, and Fletcher's DNA matches DNA collected off the gun discarded at the scene. Everything fits. It's him.'

I let out a long, shaky breath.

'So, it's over.'

Amber gave a faint, sad smile. 'It's over, Maya.'

'Lara,' I corrected her, automatically. 'I'm Lara now.'

'Of course. My mistake.'

Her tone was polite, but I had the strangest feeling that she'd got my name wrong intentionally. That sense of being wrong-footed – brought back to her world of snakes and ladders – cleared my head, and I sat up straighter.

'I'm glad they got him. I hope they throw the book at him,' I said. 'You know, I tried to reach you, after that day in Chicago, but you never answered.'

'Oh, you know me. I'm always changing phones.' Amber shrugged. 'Occupational hazard.'

'Yes,' I said coolly. 'There were some things I wanted to discuss with you. Some things that happened that day in—'

'This iced tea is so delicious,' Amber said loudly, as if I hadn't spoken. 'You must make it fresh.'

Before I could speak again, she shook her head slightly, a warning look in her eyes.

She didn't want to talk about that day. Not only that, she didn't want me to talk because someone else was listening.

My throat clenched and a sense of helplessness swept over me that I hadn't felt since Chicago.

Why had she come here? Why had she brought the fog of her world into the sunshine of mine?

Amber took another drink, letting me absorb the unspoken message, her gaze moving interestedly around the living room. 'I like your house, by the way.'

I replied stiffly, 'Thank you. I decorated it myself.'

I wished so much that I could trust her. She's one of the most fascinating women I have ever met. She's brave, and cool, and funny. But she is an absolute enigma.

In fact, here's a listicle (remember listicles?) of all the things I know for certain about Amber:

1.
2.
3.
4.
5.

I still don't know why she said what she said to Riley after he was shot, or what she was doing in Anthony Cleary's car, but here's the thing – on more than one occasion, she has been there when I needed her. And this appeared to be one of those times.

We talked for a while after that, about the house and my work. My own words rang awkwardly in my ears. When she left a short while later with another significant glance, I leaned back against the door and took a long breath. I wanted to feel relieved. But suddenly my house didn't seem safe any more. It felt watched.

I thought about the way she'd looked at me, that slow shake of her head. I could not have misunderstood that. And what had she been doing with her glass, every time she set it down? That odd movement of her hand.

I walked over to the coffee table and picked up the empty glass. When I turned it over, I discovered a small piece of paper beneath it, stuck to the bottom by condensation.

Carefully, I peeled it loose. It was no more than two inches by two inches, as thin as cigarette paper, and when I lifted it up, I saw that it held tiny letters written in some strange ink that was already starting to fade. I had to hold it to the light to make out the words. It read: *The FBI is watching you.* Under that was a phone number.

Even as I read it, the letters began to disappear, one by one, until all I could make out was *The* and *you.*

Running to the kitchen, I found a scrap of paper and a pen and scrawled the phone number down before it faded away. When I'd finished, I stared at those numbers until they started to swim.

How could this be happening again?

'Damn you.' I said it aloud. To the FBI. To the gods. To whoever was determined to ruin my life.

Then I grabbed my wallet and my keys, got into my car and drove to the store to buy a burner phone. I didn't call the number until I was in my backyard. I'd learned that from Amber and Riley – always the open air for phone calls.

Amber answered on the first ring.

'Good,' she said. 'You got my message.'

'What the hell's going on?' I demanded. 'Why are they after me again?'

'It's not you they want,' she said calmly. 'It's Gina. They want The Gateway.'

I hadn't thought of Gina in so long. Those expensive wool dresses, the gold bangles and perfect hair; driving me around The Gateway that summer in Montana with the ease and practicality of a cabbie.

I dropped my head into my hands. 'What do I have to do with Gina? I haven't been to Montana in *three years*.'

'They think The Gateway is being used by organised criminals as a base,' Amber explained. 'And it is, of course. With Cleary gone, the whole thing is now owned by a man from New York they've been trying to get for numerous crimes for years, with no success. They think Gina is their way in. She liked you, and they know that. They want to get you back inside, see what you can find out.'

'I won't do it.' I was furious. 'They can't make me.'

When she didn't reply, I added, 'Can they?'

'They're not nice people, Lara. They look for leverage

and they use it.' There was a hint of regret in her tone. 'Before you signed that NDA, you should have made them formally waive all other charges. But you didn't, so those charges can be filed whenever they choose. Fraud, failure to report.'

'They wouldn't do that . . .' I began, and then I shut up. Because of course they would.

'Look,' Amber said, 'I came today because I don't like the way they're using you. I don't like the FBI at all, to be honest. They irritate me. Those suits. They all look like funeral directors. I don't like what they did to Riley. And I don't want them to hurt you. You need to protect yourself from this.'

'How can I protect myself, Amber?' I demanded angrily. 'They're the *FBI*.'

'Think, Lara,' she urged me. 'You have to use the weapons you have. Information is a weapon.'

I was so angry and frustrated, I didn't get it at first.

'I still don't know what you mean.'

'You know a great deal,' Amber said. 'More than anyone. Rather secret information. Things they don't want people to know. Things that could ruin careers.'

And suddenly I understood perfectly.

We talked for only a few minutes longer as I stood on the little patio in the small, neat backyard where Jamie had helped me plant the roses and honeysuckle that filled the air with scent. By the time we hung up, I knew precisely what I had to do.

When I went back inside, I took out my laptop and wrote down everything Amber had said. She was right. I knew a great deal about Riley Maguire, Robert Castleton and Anthony Cleary. That knowledge was the only card I held in this game. If I played it right, I could get the FBI out of my life forever. If nothing else, I could at least make them regret ever dragging me into their world.

That's why you're reading this book now. I want every word to be out there in the open. Every single thing that happened. The truth the FBI didn't want anyone to know.

I still have the tape of Will Fulton and Riley in The Gage. And I have other recordings of conversations with Riley in the car on the way to Chicago, and in the truck-stop café. Conversations with Amber. In fact, I recorded far more than anyone ever knew, and I kept all of it safe. I have proof. And I won't hesitate to make it all public.

Here's the thing. Riley Maguire's name wasn't Riley Maguire. Amber isn't Amber. I am not Lara Gibson. Will Fulton is someone else entirely. Every name in this book is a lie. But I know every true name. And if the FBI ever knocks on my door, those names are all in an envelope in the hands of someone I trust, and they will be sent to every newspaper in the world.

So this is the deal. Leave me in peace and those names go up in flames. But if anything happens to me — if I am not left alone — they'll be published everywhere.

I want out. I was just a witness. I committed no crime. I never asked to be part of this world, and I'm done with it.

This is my card. One I held for far too long. And by God, I'm playing it now.

Acknowledgements

No book is possible without a wonderful team, and I owe huge thanks to everyone at Century in the UK and Ballantine in the US. I'm especially grateful to my wonderful editors Selina Walker and Alicia Clancy for their wisdom and kindness. There are so many people who contributed to this book, and I owe them all a debt, especially Mary Karayel, Caroline Johnson, Joanna Taylor, and Meredith Benson.

As always, huge thanks to Madeleine Milburn, Hannah Ladds, Meghan Capper and everyone at the Madeleine Milburn Literary Agency who make it possible for me to keep writing. And I'd also like to thank Anna DeRoy and Sanjana Seelam from William Morris Entertainment – I'm so lucky to have you on my team!

In addition, many thanks to the powerhouse publicist Tory Lyne-Pirkis, who personally puts my books into more hands than I can count. And I'm so lucky to work with Emma Waring, who is one of the first readers of all my books, and who makes sure I show up for things on the right days and remember to smile.

Finally, to Jack, my husband and best friend, without you this book would never have been written. This is for you. Always and forever.

Enjoyed *THE HIDING SEASON*?

Dive into the gripping Emma Makepeace series from bestselling author

AVA GLASS

OUT NOW